FIRE IN
THE STARS

FIRE IN THE STARS

An Amanda Doucette Mystery

Barbara **Fradkin**

DUNDURN

TORONTO

Editor: Shannon Whibbs
Design: Jennifer Gallinger
Cover design: Laura Boyle
Cover image: © Igor Zhuravlov/istock.com
Printer: Webcom

Library and Archives Canada Cataloguing in Publication

Fradkin, Barbara Fraser, 1947-, author
  Fire in the stars / Barbara Fradkin.

(An Amanda Doucette mystery)
Issued in print and electronic formats.
ISBN 978-1-4597-3239-1 (paperback).--ISBN 978-1-4597-3240-7 (pdf).--
ISBN 978-1-4597-3241-4 (epub)

    I. Title.

PS8561.R233F57 2016   C813'.6   C2015-906826-6
                                               C2015-906827-4

1 2 3 4 5   20 19 18 17 16

We acknowledge the support of the Canada Council for the Arts and the Ontario Arts Council for our publishing program. We also acknowledge the financial support of the Government of Canada through the Canada Book Fund and Livres Canada Books, and the Government of Ontario through the Ontario Book Publishing Tax Credit and the Ontario Media Development Corporation.

Care has been taken to trace the ownership of copyright material used in this book. The author and the publisher welcome any information enabling them to rectify any references or credits in subsequent editions.

— *J. Kirk Howard, President*

The publisher is not responsible for websites or their content unless they are owned by the publisher.

Printed and bound in Canada.

VISIT US AT
Dundurn.com | @dundurnpress | Facebook.com/dundurnpress | Pinterest.com/dundurnpress

Dundurn
3 Church Street, Suite 500
Toronto, Ontario, Canada
M5E 1M2

In memory of my father, Cecil Currie

CHAPTER ONE

Amanda didn't begin to worry in earnest until a hint of land shimmered through the early morning fog. Slowly, Newfoundland emerged in a ragged silhouette of rock and the blurred white spire of a lighthouse. The MV *Highlanders* had ten decks and she was on the top, her favourite place. The powerful engine of the ferry throbbed beneath her and the cold ocean foamed below. She leaned on the railing and sheltered her cellphone from the mist. It had finally registered a signal from the town of Port aux Basques.

No messages. Not one word from Phil. Normally this would be a minor frustration. Black holes could swallow him up for days on end, but he'd spring out of them ebullient and cleansed as if they had never happened. *Even my wife calls me Mr. Unreliable,* he'd once said with a twinkle in his eye.

But this time was different. For one thing, this camping trip had been his idea, and Amanda had sensed a manic edge to his excitement when he'd begged her to come. *You need this,* he'd said. *We need it. There's nothing like the wilds of nature to heal a broken soul.* She wasn't so sure, but it was the closest he'd come to admitting to a problem.

For another, he'd promised to do all the planning. Newfoundland was his adopted home now, and he wanted to show off its charms. All Amanda had to do was get herself, her motorcycle, and a sleeping bag over to the Rock and he'd find them the perfect getaway. Imagine miles of rugged coast, tangy surf, the wind in her face, and the call of ocean birds. After her long, bleak year spent clawing back from the terror of Africa, it had sounded like paradise.

The problem was, he'd never told her where this paradise was. Now that she was about to disembark on the southern tip of the island, she had no idea where to meet him. Newfoundland's coastline was ten thousand kilometres of switchback coves and ragged headlands, most of it wild. There were island bird sanctuaries and dark, unexplored inland forests. Its oceans teemed with whales, dolphins, seals, and polar bears, its forests with moose and bears. The perfect getaway was everywhere.

Amanda had always loved nature. As a child trapped in the tidy residential crescents of suburban Ottawa, she had escaped whenever possible to the lakes and forests of the surrounding countryside, much to the bemusement of her parents, who considered a wine tour of Tuscany to be the ideal holiday. During her postings in the hot, arid climates of developing countries, it had been the wilderness that she had missed most about her homeland. The lush green of the forest floor, the delicate birdsong, and the chatter of brooks tumbling over rocks.

The solitude.

There are not many people in Newfoundland in September, Phil had promised her. No machetes, masked marauders, or homemade bombs. Not even many tourists left. We'll have the campgrounds and coves to ourselves.

The ferry was churning through the narrow channel toward the dock, past the breakwaters and pastel cottages scattered along the barren shore. Passengers had begun to head toward the stairs leading to the car decks, clutching their pillows and bedrolls blearily. *Where are you?* she texted one last time before slipping her phone back into her jacket and heading to the pet kennels. The sound of barking was deafening as the dogs woke to the sight of their masters. For a moment, when she couldn't hear Kaylee's bark above the din, she felt a familiar surge of anxiety. *My dog's safe*, she assured herself. *You know she's safe. It's only a seven-hour crossing, and she's had plenty of water.*

Nonetheless, Amanda was surprised by the rush of relief that coursed through her when Kaylee's high-pitched scream joined the fray. She spotted the frenzy of red fur as she drew closer. Kaylee hurled herself against the door of the kennel, every inch of her wagging. Amanda opened the door and knelt down to press her face into the dog's long, silky fur.

"Sorry, pumpkin," she whispered. "No more, I promise."

Kaylee tugged at the end of her leash as they made their way down to Amanda's other prized possession, her brand-new motorcycle. Having spent almost all her adult life in the developing world, she was much more at ease on two wheels than on four. She loved the lightness, agility, and thrilling speed of motorcycles. In anticipation of this trip, she had traded her smaller bike and splurged on this latest-model Kawasaki, which could handle a trailer, but she had not yet found the perfect name for it. For now, she called it Shadow, which had an intimate, evocative ring. Not only did it have its own shadow of sorts — the small, custom-built trailer for Kaylee — but it felt like an extension of her soul. It gave her the freedom to roam the wide-open spaces, to race the wind, to follow any whim that beckoned her.

Kaylee leaped eagerly into her spot in the trailer, her tongue lolling and her eyes dancing in anticipation. As Amanda fastened the dog's seatbelt and undid the straps and cables that secured the bike, she smiled in response to the stares from the neighbouring cars. She suspected the red dog and the lime-green motorcycle made quite a spectacle.

She was almost thirty-five, but, dwarfed in her sheepskin jacket, leather boots, and red helmet, she looked barely fifteen. Hardship had aged her on the inside, but her fine freckles and long chestnut hair belied the decades. Noticing the little boy in the minivan beside her eying Kaylee solemnly, Amanda winked at him.

"She's looking forward to Newfoundland. Are you?"

He nodded. "What kind of dog is that?"

"She's a Nova Scotia Duck Tolling Retriever. Forty pounds of pure energy. Do you have a dog?"

He shot a quick glance at his father before shaking his head. "What's her name?"

"Kaylee. Since she's a Nova Scotia breed, I figured she deserved a good Gaelic name. Do you know what a *ceilidh* is?"

He shook his head again.

"It's a party. The lively, dancing-singing-making-music kind. And that's what she is, a party." Amanda leaned over to ruffle the dog's ears. "Do you want to pat her?"

The boy glanced at his father again. The two of them were alone in the minivan, father and son on a holiday. The man looked as if he hadn't slept or shaved in days, but he managed a bleary smile. But just as the boy was opening his door, car engines rumbled to life around them and the vehicles prepared to inch forward. The boy tugged his door shut and gave Kaylee a shy wave.

The long trail of vehicles wound through the ferry dock and out onto the open road, where the fog still hung thick. Amanda could see nothing but a blurry stream of red lights heading north along the only highway toward the interior of the island. Signs and landmarks leaped out of the fog too late to decipher.

She longed to lean into the wind and open up the throttle, but decided it was safer just to follow the tail lights directly in front of her.

She needed a decent breakfast and, more importantly, coffee, and just as she was beginning to despair of finding either, the lights of an Irving gas bar and diner caught her eye. She pulled in, fed Kaylee, and took her for a short stroll to a handy patch of grass before tying up the dog and heading inside the diner. The place was bright and bustling as if half the ferry passengers were inside, but Amanda found a small table by the window where she could keep an eye on Kaylee. The waitress was at her side instantly to fill her coffee cup. A woman of experience, Amanda thought with a smile of thanks. Once she'd taken her first sip, she pulled out her cellphone. No response to her text. Mr. Unreliable indeed.

While she looked up his home number in Grand Falls, she braced herself. Phil had confessed that things were rocky between himself and his wife, and Amanda wasn't sure how Sheri felt about this trip, nor about her. Phil had assured her that Sheri supported it, that in fact the trip had been her idea. Anything to get me out of her hair, he'd joked. She can't come because she's teaching, but she knows how much I need this escape.

Amanda hoped that was true. Despite their different temperaments, the two women had once been friends, but that was before Africa, and Amanda knew Sheri could be unforgiving. Did she still blame Amanda for Phil's decision to go?

It had been nearly two years since Amanda had last spoken to her, but time slipped away the moment the woman answered the phone. The same brisk, no-nonsense voice, with just a hint of Newfoundland.

"Hi, Sheri, it's Amanda Doucette. How are you?"

A pause, a drop in tone. As if the air had gone out of the room. "Amanda. It's been a long time. You're back in Canada for good now, I hear."

"I am. I just arrived in Port aux Basques." She paused, listening to the silence. Feeling the chill through the airwaves. Not forgiven, then. "Is Phil there?"

"How could he be? He's with you."

"No. I'm supposed to meet him, but I don't know where."

"Well, he's already gone. I imagine he'll call you, in his own sweet time."

Bewildered, Amanda plowed ahead. "When did he leave?"

"Two days ago. I'm surprised you haven't heard from him yet. Well, not exactly surprised, but …"

"Did he say where he was going?"

There was another long silence. Sheri's voice lost its chill, became uncertain. "He … we … I was out when they left. He didn't actually say goodbye."

"They? Who's with him?"

"Well, Tyler. Our son. He's going with you." She paused again. Amanda heard a small intake of breath. "Isn't he?"

Amanda felt her own small quiver of alarm. First, Phil's manic excitement about the trip, followed by the days of silence. What was he up to? "I'm sure it's just a misunderstanding," she forced herself to say. "You know Phil."

"Indeed I do."

Amanda rushed on. "He'll probably be in touch any minute. Meanwhile I'll head up toward your place."

"Why?"

Amanda floundered in the heavy silence. "In case he comes back. Or we can at least figure out where Mr. Unreliable has disappeared to." She hung up before Sheri could object and glanced outside to reassure herself that Kaylee was still there. The early morning fog was lifting, curling off the scoured coastal rock in pale, wraithlike swaths. At this rate, she could reach Grand Falls by afternoon. To what purpose or reception, she wasn't sure.

Her attempt at levity on the phone was fooling no one, least of all Sheri, who must know how close to the edge Phil could stumble. Indeed, she'd been the one to drag him back more than once over their twelve years together.

Amanda had heard it in her voice at the end. Sheri was angry and fed up, but she was also afraid.

CHAPTER TWO

As the bleak tundra of the southern tip gave way to the canyons of the Humber River valley, Amanda felt the tug of this extreme, unforgiving land. Over the centuries, countless explorers had been lured to the soaring cliffs and dark, secretive forests, but its storms were too fierce and its terrain too barren for all but the most intrepid to settle. The first nor'easter to come through blew most of them off the island, leaving only a few stubborn and contrary fishermen clinging to its sheltered coves.

But it was this primal challenge of nature that excited her. She was in search of a toehold in something pure and timeless, beyond the struggles and cruelties of man — a sense of awe and inspiration that would lift her above the quagmire of her life and help her see further down the road.

Because she knew she could not go back to Africa.

She leaned into the wind and felt the engine throb as she accelerated down the empty road. The bike chewed up the kilometres effortlessly, leaving her thoughts free to return to Phil. She hadn't seen him in nearly a year since they had both managed to reach the capital of Nigeria. Like her, he'd been a feral shadow of himself, scrawny with hunger and fear, his blue eyes hollow above his matted, black beard. It had taken her three hours in the hotel bath to soak the pain and filth from her body, but Phil had barely tried. He'd just wanted to go home.

Home at the moment was Grand Falls, Newfoundland, where Sheri had lived until her university years and where she and their son were waiting for him. Tyler had been born in happier times when they were all working together for Save the Children in Cambodia, but Sheri had wisely refused to bring him to unstable West Africa and had moved back home instead to live with her parents until Phil's return.

Nigeria was supposed to be a quick stint, four months at most to help the northern villages cope with the influx of refugees fleeing Boko Haram, but when the violence intensified and their replacements did not arrive, the posting had stretched to nine. Despite repeated entreaties from Sheri to come home, Phil had stayed on with Amanda. The makeshift refugee village in northern Nigeria had seemed so much more real and needy than the cozy Canadian town he barely knew.

Since their return to Canada, his emails to Amanda had been sporadic — crisp two- or three-liners about his latest joe job or his repair work on the little house they had bought on Sheri's teacher's salary. His determinedly upbeat emails skimmed the surface of his days, bouncing gaily over the pain of lost jobs, the empty hours, and the lingering wounds of Africa.

Just what was his state of mind? Amanda wondered now, as the afternoon shadows lengthened and the desolate expanse of black spruce continued to unfurl. Phil had never been a talker, unless it was to share a joke or a tall tale. Even now, he had couched this trip as a great adventure, not as the pilgrimage toward healing that she knew it to be. Not just for her, but for him. I can deal, he'd always say. Canadians have no right to complain. Unlike those we help, we have a warm, safe country to go home to.

But warmth and safety, she knew, was not a place. It was a state of mind.

The city of Grand Falls came up unexpectedly out of the rolling emptiness of interior Newfoundland. Unlike most of the rough-and-tumble fishing villages that had cropped up like barnacles along the rocky ocean coves, Grand Falls had been built as a pulp-and-paper company town, prosperous and orderly. But according to Phil, the closing of the mill after a hundred years had left it bruised and struggling for a new source of purpose and jobs. He'd been lucky to land seasonal work during the Christmas holidays and the mid-winter festival.

Amanda knew it wasn't about the money, for both of them had received modest compensation for their ordeal through the NGO's medical plan. It was about having a reason to get out of bed and a goal to aim for, preferably mindless and light. Amanda had spent her year focusing on her mind and body— yoga, meditation, and a rigorous fitness regime, all designed to make her feel in control again. Sometimes it even worked.

Phil and Sheri's house was a small bungalow in the older section of town down near the Exploits River. The clapboard siding was painted a vibrant yellow, and purple asters and miniature white roses spilled onto the slate path leading to the covered porch, complementing the large, hand-painted welcome sign on the door. The place had an optimism that belied the worn treads on the steps and the peeling paint on the siding. Like Phil, it was making the best of lean times.

She rumbled gratefully into the gravel lane that ran up beside the house. There was a white Cavalier parked against the house, and the door flew open just as she was easing her stiff body off the bike. Sheri appeared in the doorway, her lips a tight slash of red.

"Any word?" she asked before Amanda could even say hello, sending her hopes crashing. She studied Sheri cautiously. Neither woman had ever been a fashion plate; in the places they'd worked, comfort and availability in clothing trumped any thought of style. But the woman had obviously done herself over. She'd lost the residual mommy fat and clothed her now curvaceous body in skinny jeans and long red sweater. She had cut her long brown hair to a fashionable shoulder length and added auburn streaks. Oversized gold hoop earrings danced in the sunlight.

Amanda tugged off her helmet and ran a futile hand through the dusty tangle of her hair, feeling every inch of the long, sweaty, gas-fumed drive she had endured. She shook her head.

"Fucking Phil!" Sheri said. "What the hell is he up to?"

"Maybe it's just a mix-up. Cellphone reception over here seems to be pretty spotty."

Sheri seemed about to retort, but stopped herself. She shielded her eyes and squinted against the sun. Her restless gaze flitted the length of the street before it lit upon Amanda's motorcycle, where Kaylee was poking her nose eagerly through her mesh door. For the first time a smile broke Sheri's tense features.

"What in the name of God is that?"

"My dog."

"Oh, for the love of —" Sheri hopped off the porch, lithe as a cat, and strode over to release her. "Look at you!"

The dog bounded out to greet her as if she were a long-lost friend. "Dog in a trailer. This is a first even for you, Amanda Doucette," she said, laughing in spite of herself as she straightened up. "Oh, come on in then, I'll put the kettle on. Tea?" She paused on the steps. "Or something stronger?"

"Something stronger would be heaven!" Amanda's whole body ached. She reached into her saddlebag. "I picked up some wine."

Inside, the house was small and simply furnished in what looked like hand-me-downs, but the curtains and cushions were made of bright prints bought for pennies in Asian and African street markets. Late-afternoon sunshine spilled through the bay window, setting the reds and golds in the fabric aflame. Amanda followed Sheri into the kitchen and filled the dog's water bowl while Sheri opened the wine.

"This is a treat," Sheri said. "All I have in the fridge is half a bottle of blueberry wine. I don't keep much in the house because Phil —" She broke off and turned quickly to get the glasses.

Amanda hid her surprise. Phil had never been much of a drinker, despite the many opportunities afforded by the foreign aid circuit. Back in the living room, Amanda sagged into a rocking chair and took a grateful sip of wine. In the silence, Sheri paced to the window and stared outside. For the thousandth time, Amanda suspected.

She approached the issue carefully. "What's Phil doing, Sheri?"

Sheri swung around, tightening her jaw. "I thought he was going camping with you."

"Well, he was. He wanted to show me the whales and icebergs. He was very proud of your island. His adopted home."

Sheri blew out a small puff of air. Dismissive and impatient. "Where are you two supposed to be going?"

"That's the thing. He was looking into it, checking out the most spectacular places and what campsites were open where I could take the dog. He was going to tell me where to meet him."

Sheri's eyes narrowed, and Amanda could almost see her searching her thoughts. "Whales and icebergs. Now there'd be plenty of them in Newfoundland. Could be anywhere, from the Avalon Peninsula near St. John's to Gros Morne on the west. Even Twillingate, in Notre Dame Bay just up north there —" she pointed "— that would be the closest."

"I think he wanted something wild. Not a place full of B&Bs and tourists."

"Probably not the Avalon, then. But it's a big, empty island most of the year. Lots of rocks and ocean to choose from."

Amanda took another small sip of her wine, which was already going to her head after the long drive. Sheri, she noticed, had almost finished hers. "Did he drop any hints? Any place he really wanted to see?"

Instead of answering, Sheri turned away from the window. "You must be hungry after that ride. I've got some cookies in the cupboard."

Amanda followed her back into the kitchen. "Didn't he talk about the trip at all?"

Sheri's back was rigid as she rummaged through the shelves. "No, he didn't. That was between him and you. He knew I wasn't thrilled. He just said it was something he had to do. Something you and he had to do."

Amanda hid her surprise. "I'm sorry, I thought … he said it was your idea."

"Did he, now?"

Amanda cast about for a way out of the hole she'd dug. "He was doing it for me, Sheri. To help me get past the awful time in Nigeria. He thought your island — his island — would give me a lift. That's all. I would never —"

Sheri gave an odd, strangled grunt. "Since when have you needed help with that?"

"I've been kind of stuck back at home. I couldn't just go back to my old life on the front lines, but I didn't know what I wanted to do next."

"And you figured a few whales and icebergs with my husband would do the trick?"

So there it was. Tossed on the floor between them like a sack of stinking garbage. The rebuke and bitterness. The unspoken jealousy. Amanda wanted to say *Phil and I have been friends for a long time, since graduate school, and we've been through a lot together, but he chose you, remember? Without question, without doubt.* But that wouldn't be enough.

Sheri had piled almost the entire box of cookies onto a plate before Amanda reached out to stop her hand. "Sheri, Phil loves you. Always has. You were his rock during that terrifying time. But Nigeria wasn't like other posts. You just don't walk away from it. I needed a way to heal, and I know Phil needed that too."

Sheri managed a brusque nod, stared at the plate of cookies and eventually heaved a sigh. Her words tumbled out, as if they had been dammed up for months. "Yes, damn it. I know that. I've tried to be patient this past year. Tried to keep our home stable and happy, for Tyler's sake as well as Phil's. But he shut me out with this fucking, monstrous wall. Everything's hunky dory, he said. I just need a little time, a little space. Don't nag me. Goddamn! I'm not a needy wife, you know that, Amanda. He said I didn't understand, but I did. I haven't lived my whole life on this sheltered little island. We met in Senegal working with AIDS orphans, for God's sake!"

"Nigeria was different."

"He knew that going in! He chose to go there, even when I told him not to. He chose it —"

"Aid workers were pulling out in droves. He knew they needed him."

"And Tyler and I didn't? And now we're the ones paying the price!"

Not as much as the kidnapped school boys, Amanda thought. Anger was never far from the surface these days, and now she felt it bubbling through her, tugging at her thin, fraying reins of control. She tamped it down. "I know you are. So is Phil," was all she said.

Sheri snatched up the plate and stalked back into the living room. "Why do you think I've tried so hard? I know he's a good guy and if he's got a fault, it's that he cares too much. He can't turn his back on suffering." To Amanda's surprise, tears welled in Sheri's eyes. Sheri was seasoned and strong, and tears didn't come easily.

Amanda softened. "So what happened, Sheri? What's this about?"

The tears hovered on her lashes. For a long moment she said nothing. Took one breath. Two. "I turned my back," she whispered.

Amanda said nothing. Waited.

"I didn't mean to. I needed … a friend. At first it was just for Tyler. This friend. He was Tyler's hockey coach and kind of took Tyler under his wing while Phil was away. Later we'd all go out for pizza after the game, and he fixed a few things around the house here. Shovelled the drive during that awful winter last year." Sheri broke off. She picked up her wine with a trembling hand, brought the glass to her lips, and drained it. Once again, Amanda fought her own rising temper.

"Nothing happened. I mean, not then. When Phil came home, the guy backed off. But Tyler … Phil spent long hours out in the bush, fishing, riding his dirt bike, doing I never knew what."

"You don't have to tell me all this, Sheri. I get it."

Sheri must have heard the grit in her voice, for she shot her a glance. Flushed. "No, you don't! Because I didn't want it to happen! I know that sounds like a cliché, but I love Phil. He's Tyler's father. Tyler needs *him*, not some hockey coach! But the Phil who came home was a stranger. He pushed us both away. Tyler didn't understand why my friend no longer did things with him and why his own father ignored him. This cold, brooding, Mr. Unreliable was hurting my son."

Don't pretend you did this for Tyler, Amanda wanted to say, but she held her tongue. "Our work is brutal on relationships," she managed, strangling on her self-control.

"You can't imagine how helpless I felt," Sheri said. Then she paused, as if she heard herself. Flushed. "I'm sorry, I guess you can."

"Yes."

"And I know my problems sound trivial compared to Phil's and yours. They are trivial! But ... but ..." She raised her hands in futile defeat.

"Okay, so what happened? You started seeing the guy and Phil found out?"

Sheri thrust her chin out. She had always been a fighter and hated to be cornered. Amanda's challenge was enough to energize her. "No. I finally realized I couldn't help Phil if he wouldn't let me, but I could help my son. So I told Phil I was leaving him."

"When?"

"A week ago. I told him I'd met someone. I thought maybe it would be the jolt he needed. He wanted to know who, but I wouldn't tell him."

"And how did he ...?" Amanda let the silence hang, too upset to trust herself with more words. The image of Phil in Nigeria, haunted and hollow, rose before her.

"He took off into the bush for four days, and when he came back, he said I was right. He'd been a bastard and he was glad I'd found someone who treated me better. But he still wanted to be a good father to Tyler, so he hoped the father-son camping trip was still on."

Amanda felt a sliver of fear slip through her gut. Tyler had never been part of the plan. She and Phil couldn't predict what demons would be dredged up, what drunken rages and howling tears, what cathartic challenges the wind and the cliffs and the surf would hurl at them. It was not an adventure for a child.

But now Phil had cut her out and had taken off with his son, after feeding Sheri a pile of lies about forgiveness, understanding, and fatherly concern. Amanda knew Phil. He had always loved Sheri, but during the deepest darkness of Nigeria, he had clung to her memory like a drowning man. Afterward, he had ignored the advice of counsellors and debriefers in his headlong rush to get back to her.

Five days to put all that behind him, to master his rage and despair, and to reach a state of calm forgiveness?

Not a chance.

Instinctively she snapped her fingers to call her dog to her, so that she could sink her fingers into her soft, warm fur. Reading her distress, Kaylee nuzzled her and licked her hand. Amanda took a deep breath, stepped back from her fear, and rallied her common sense.

"What gear did he pack?"

"Camping stuff — tent, sleeping bags, cooking gear, life jackets."

"Boat? Kayaks?"

Sheri shook her head. "Those are still out back. He said you guys would rent what you need."

"Navigational gear? Sat phone, personal-locator beacons, GPS?"

"You know Phil. He likes the old-fashioned way."

"Didn't he at least take his cellphone? I've been texting him and he's not answering."

Sheri shrugged. "I haven't seen it. He may have it on him, but it could be turned off. He does that when he doesn't want to talk to people."

Amanda pulled out her own phone. "We should check in the house. If it's turned on, we'll hear it. We might find some clues too." She punched in Phil's number. She listened for ringing as she walked through the kitchen and dining area into the small den. The house was neat and full of local art from their travels, but no maps or guidebooks had been left on the tables to provide clues. When Phil's cheerful voicemail message came on, she dialled again.

"Do you mind if I check upstairs in your bedroom? It's ringing, so it's turned on. He may have left it there."

Sheri waved her hand in permission. "Since you called this morning, I've pretty much torn the place apart, but be my guest. Phil's been staying in the spare room since he came back from Nigeria. He has trouble sleeping so he's often up reading or watching TV. He says he feels better not disturbing me."

Amanda nodded. The depths of night were always the worst, when the wakeful mind filled the darkness with fiery images, screams, and the incessant yammer of self-doubt. She mounted the stairs, listening for a phone. Kaylee bounded ahead of her as Amanda had taught her, providing comforting reassurance that no danger lay ahead. Phil's little room was a mess; bedding was flung back, drawers opened, and clothing strewn about. Papers were spilled all over the desk, and Phil's laptop was open.

Sheri came up behind her. "I tried it," she said. "But he must have changed his password. It used to be 'password.'"

They both shared a spontaneous grin. How like impatient, cavalier Phil.

"Do you mind if I take it?" Amanda asked. "I'll try to figure it out later."

When Sheri shrugged her acceptance, Amanda closed the laptop and picked it up. She scanned the room, but there were no telltale maps or brochures, and the only books in the bookcase were dog-eared thrillers and university texts from his global development studies.

No sound of a cellphone ringing, either.

Tucking the laptop under her arm, she went back downstairs, with Sheri at her heels. "Let's check the shed."

Like their house, their backyard was neatly kept. The grass was lush and mowed, the perennials trimmed and mulched. Gladioli were swollen with buds, and purple asters and nasturtiums spilled over their beds. Phil's kayaks and small aluminum fishing boat were stacked on racks beside the shed.

As unreliable as Phil was with people, he had always taken excellent care of his physical space, as if it at least was under his control. Amanda opened the shed door. Inside, garden tools and bicycles hung on walls, and supplies and equipment were stored on shelves. Hockey and ski equipment was suspended on the beams overhead for next winter. A mower and snow blower took up one corner, a stack of winter tires another.

All the usual equipment of a middle-class homeowner. Nothing unusual struck her. He had an entire cabinet of fishing paraphernalia, but no guns or hunting gear. Phil had grown up in rural Manitoba with an annual family tradition of duck and deer hunting, but since his first encounter with tribal violence overseas, he had rejected all guns.

But that was before Nigeria.

Amanda turned to Sheri, who was examining his supply of fishing rods. "Did he have a gun?"

Sheri whipped her head back and forth. "He hates them now more than ever. My ... my friend wanted to take Tyler moose-hunting last fall — that's almost a Newfoundland rite of passage — but Phil blew a fuse." She paused, fingering the long, slim rods. "He's taken two of his salmon rods and his wading gear. That's not much help, since salmon brooks and rivers are everywhere."

"That's good, though," Amanda said. "It shows he's still following a plan."

Her cellphone had gone to Phil's voicemail again so Amanda dialled a third time. From deep in the farthest corner of the shed came the muted sounds of a trumpet call. Both women rushed over. The sound was coming from somewhere in a pile of equipment beside the fishing cabinet. They tossed aside a folded tarp, dug out a bag of fertilizer, and began to shove aside the stack of tires. The trumpet trill grew louder. Finally, half hidden beneath the tires, Amanda found the phone.

The front screen was completely filled with notifications, most of them text and phone messages from Sheri and Amanda, none of them even opened, let alone answered.

Sheri craned her neck over Amanda's shoulder to catch a glimpse. Seeing the unread messages, she swore.

"Oh, spectacular! So now he doesn't even have a phone!"

Still squatting in the corner, Amanda glanced around the shed. How had the phone ended up buried under the tires? Someone had to move a tarp, a bag of fertilizer, and four heavy tires in order to hide it there. That made no sense. If Phil had simply put his phone down while collecting his fishing gear, or if it had fallen out of his pocket, it should have been sitting in plain sight, on top of the tarp, not underneath.

It was almost as if he had hidden it on purpose. But why go to all that trouble? If Phil wanted to get rid of the phone, so that no one could reach him or track him, why not just throw it in a Dumpster on his way out of town?

She tried to imagine the twisted path of Phil's reasoning. He had discarded his phone, but rather than throwing it away, he'd left it within easy earshot of the house. Had that been deliberate? Had he known that a little ingenuity and detective work would discover it? Was he counting on that? Was he counting on the confusion and worry that discovery would provoke?

Amanda held the phone in suddenly nerveless fingers. Did he want Sheri to find it, she wondered? And to know that he had chosen to cut all ties? Did he want her to know that he was beyond reach? Beyond salvation?

The ultimate revenge.

She stood up, bumping into Sheri in her haste to turn around. "I think you better call the police."

CHAPTER THREE

To Amanda's surprise, Sheri balked. She leaned over to peer at the spot where the phone had been found. "He could have just dropped it and it slid down there."

"But he would have looked for it."

"Maybe it fell out of his pocket while he was getting his fishing gear, and he didn't even notice until after he left. Phil's like that, you know. Mr. Unreliable, remember?"

"But he'd have a checklist. All those years of training —"

Sheri set her jaw and headed out of the shed. "He would hate it if I called the cops on him. Even if he did leave the phone behind on purpose, so what? He just needs his space and time. This is a small town, and people have sharp tongues and long memories. He's having a hard enough time fitting in without having this written on his forehead. He'll come back when he's had time to sort himself out."

Amanda hesitated. She didn't want to scare Sheri by pushing the panic button prematurely, but Sheri's denial of the darker possibilities seemed odd. "I'm not so sure. He's been walking the edge a long time, and I don't think he's thinking clearly. God knows what he'll do if he's desperate."

They were crossing the grass toward the house, and Sheri turned to search Amanda's face. "He would never hurt Tyler."

Despite her words, there was uncertainty in her eyes. Amanda didn't respond. Desperate people hurt their children all the time, sometimes from the depths of a depression so black they believed they were saving their children from an impossible world and other times from a vengeful wish to hurt their partner by taking away the thing they loved most. "But what about hurting himself? Has he ever talked about ending it all?"

Sheri gulped a sharp breath. She strode inside, checked the house phone and the street yet again. Her jaw worked. "There was a time, this winter, when he asked me to hide all the axes and knives. I wasn't sure if it was to protect me, or him."

"Did he go for help?"

"Ask for help? Phil? Besides, here in Grand Falls, what kind of help is there? Trauma counsellors falling out of the sky, are they?"

Amanda came to her side and put a gentle hand on her arm. "I know this is scary, but we have to consider it. Because I think maybe it's what this is all about. He said he forgives you and he hid his cellphone where we would eventually find it, but only once he was too far away for us to stop him. I bet if we search it, or decipher the password on his laptop, we'll find a note."

Sheri's chin quivered. She snatched the cellphone from Amanda's hand and tried to thumb through links. Once again a password stymied her. Frustrated, she shook her head. "Goddamn Nigeria! It made him so paranoid! It swallowed a wonderful, caring, trusting man and spat him back, destroyed. But Phil is a strong man. He's a fighter. Even if he's on the edge, he's not going to quit on Tyler. He's seen too many children suffer ..."

"But would he quit on you?"

Sheri flinched.

"Please call the cops, Sheri."

Sheri averted her eyes and walked to the window as if to put distance between herself and Amanda's pressure. "I need to think. Let me call his family to see if they've heard from him. Maybe he felt a need to visit home. There are a lot of possibilities to explore before we press the panic button."

Amanda forced herself to back off. Every ounce of her screamed *danger*, but maybe she was overreacting. She could no longer trust her own alarm system; it had failed her one crucial time, and now its sirens shrieked at even the smallest hint of danger.

"Okay, good idea. I'll take Kaylee for a walk before she mutinies, and when I get back, we'll take stock again."

The walk through the quiet, leafy residential streets was peaceful, giving Amanda time to sort through her fears. She was surprised Sheri had not already contacted Phil's family in Manitoba, which seemed an obvious first step for a worried wife to take, but perhaps the family ties were tenuous. When you spend most of your adult life in tumultuous, faraway lands, a placid, prosperous home can feel like a very distant place.

As always, Kaylee's boundless enthusiasm for each new person or patch of grass made her smile, and by the time they rounded the final corner half an hour later, Amanda felt almost relaxed. She hoped there might be a police cruiser in Sheri's drive, but instead, parked behind her own motorcycle was a dusty red pickup.

As she mounted the front steps, she heard a low murmuring from inside, which stopped the moment the front door screeched open. She found Sheri in the kitchen, busying herself with a pot of tea. Lounging against the counter was a tall, lean man in jeans and a black T-shirt. His grey buzz cut and square shoulders screamed *drill sergeant*, but before Sheri could say a word, he eased away from the counter and extended a confident hand.

"You must be Amanda. I'm Jason Maloney, Grand Falls RCMP."

His hand enveloped hers in a warm, comforting grip. The skin was rough and weathered, like his face. "Nice-looking little Kawie you've got out there."

His smile was teasing and Amanda found herself blushing in spite of herself. Before she could ask about Phil, Kaylee rushed in to tangle herself in Jason's long legs.

"Hey, boy!" He stooped to ruffle her fur, lost in the moment. His manner was casual. At home. Not at all like a cop on a missing-persons call. Amanda's sixth sense prickled.

"He's a she. Kaylee. What's the plan about Phil?"

Maloney straightened as if called to attention.

"Corporal Maloney thinks we should keep it low-key —" Sheri began.

Maloney interrupted her. "Unofficial. For now. Phil's a friend of mine and he's having some rough times. No point in siccing the dogs on him."

Amanda shot Sheri a dismayed glance. The woman was still in denial. What the hell had she told this guy? "But —"

"We can still accomplish a lot without putting it on the books. This may be a big island, but it's a small place. People know each other and watch out for each other. They notice things. A word in the ear of a few friends in other detachments —"

Sheri was watching him as if mesmerized. When the kettle whistled, she blinked her eyes as if he had snapped his fingers. She returned to earth, flustered, and turned her attention to the tea.

"Phil has a friend who's a corporal in the Deer Lake detachment," she said. "They've both been through some difficult times in the past. If anyone can understand Phil, it will be Chris."

"Have you called him?" Amanda asked.

Sheri slipped Jason a hesitant look before shaking her head. "Jason thinks he should handle it. One cop to another."

One man to another, he means, thought Amanda. But he was probably right. If this Chris guy knew about the marital trouble between Phil and Sheri, he'd be much more likely to talk openly with Jason than with her.

Jason moved toward the door, brushing Sheri's hand with his fingertips as he passed by. Sheri edged away. "I'll make the call from my truck. You can fill Amanda in on the rest of our plans while I'm gone."

Sheri's hand shook slightly as she poured tea into two mugs and dumped more cookies onto a plate. Amanda had taken a few coffee breaks along her journey to ease her muscles and let Kaylee out, but her last real meal had been breakfast at the roadside diner more than eight hours earlier. Her stomach roiled in protest at the sight of the cookies, but she suspected Sheri was too distracted to even think about anything more substantial.

Kaylee, however, was watching Sheri's every move with eagle eyes, reminding Amanda it was well past her dinnertime too. When Amanda went outside to fetch her food, she spotted Jason on his phone, head bent. His voice was raised as if in argument although Amanda couldn't make out the words.

Back inside, she fed Kaylee before returning to the living room. Sheri was gazing out the window at Jason's truck, frowning. At her own private thoughts or at Jason's behaviour, Amanda wondered.

"Are you hungry? We could go out to eat, my treat."

Sheri flinched. Shook her head. "I don't want to leave, in case …"

"Of course. Order in pizza?"

Sheri shrugged in disinterest. "Maybe when Jason's gone."

"Okay. So … what's the plan Jason mentioned?"

Sheri wrenched her gaze away from Jason's truck. "That's it, mainly. Jason is going to phone around to his colleagues and send them a photo of Phil and Tyler. Phil's family hasn't heard from him, not that I thought they would." She pulled a wry face. "Nice enough people, but to them even a trip from the farm to Winnipeg is a trip to foreign lands. They don't understand what he's been doing all these years, mixing in other people's troubles."

Amanda smiled in rueful understanding, even though her own parents were university professors. Cloistered in their academic ivory tower, they had mouthed all the right words of admiration for her as they wrote out cheques for the latest world disaster, but Amanda suspected they felt much the same.

Sheri sighed. "I phoned as many of Phil's friends as I can think of, which wasn't many. He hasn't made many connections here yet. He's picked up odd jobs to help fill the hours, but there's not much work on offer in this town, especially for a development teacher who speaks four languages but none of them Newfoundlandese. That was getting him down too, I know that. It gave him too much time with his thoughts and memories."

She sat down and picked up her neglected tea, her hand steady now as she focused her thoughts. "It's even possible he's off looking for work. There is more to be had in the major centres like Corner Brook and St. John's."

"But what about Tyler? He's taken him out of school, hasn't he?"

Sheri smiled, a fond, maternal smile that lit up her face and gave a brief flash of the old Sheri. "Tyler was delighted, believe me. The school year is just beginning, and not much new work is being done yet anyway. And Tyler is very smart. Missing a couple of weeks won't hurt him at all."

Amanda wasn't surprised. She'd last seen the boy two years ago in Senegal, and even back then, home-schooled and left to his own entertainment in the village, his intelligence and curiosity had shone through. At the age of eight, Phil had put him to work tutoring the village children in basic reading. She remembered Phil's face, shining with pride and love.

"Phil and he always were close," she said.

Sheri's smile faded. "That was before. But Phil knew he's been neglecting Tyler this past year, and he felt bad about that. Tyler's been hurt and angry. That's why Phil was taking him along on this trip with you. Hoping to rebuild."

Amanda was saved from further comment by the opening of the front door. Jason's face gave away nothing about the argument or its resolution. *How like a cop*, Amanda thought. But Sheri's face was a different story. Hope, apprehension, and guilt collided in one flushed glance. Before she could ask, he shook his head.

"Chris Tymko's heard nothing. Knows nothing. Last he heard from Phil was a few weeks ago."

"What does he think —?"

"Like I said, nothing. He's as surprised as we are."

"I'm not surprised, Jason," Sheri snapped back. Her colour was rising and her jaw was set. Amanda had seen that look before, when militia diverted some supplies needed for the local villagers. Sheri had berated them like an outraged schoolmarm. "I've seen this coming. I just didn't …" Her voice shook. "Well, you know."

"This isn't your fault, Sheri." He walked over and stood by her. Close and protective, yet dominant as well. Sensing a mixed message of support and warning, Amanda's intuition stirred.

Sheri stepped away from him. "What is Chris planning to do?"

Jason shrugged. "Tymko marches to his own drum. If he has any ideas, he didn't tell me, but I wouldn't be surprised if he had a hunch. He might head off on his own private search."

"Then he's taking this seriously?"

Jason smiled. "Well, I guess there's not much action out his way. We'll find them, Sheri. One way or another, the whole island has their eyes peeled."

"Thank you, Jason. Corporal Maloney." Sheri headed for the front door, her face rigidly polite. For a moment Jason hovered on the threshold, his gaze lingering on hers, before with a quick nod, he was gone. Sheri stood in the open doorway, gazing out into the violet dusk.

"So," Amanda said, "does Phil know?"

Sheri pressed her lips tight. Every ounce of her quivered for calm. Amanda had expected surprise, bewilderment, or denial, but after a long minute of tense silence, Sheri shook her head. "Not about Jason. Just that there was someone."

"One of his friends. That would be a blow."

Sheri slammed the front door. "That's why I didn't tell him! How cruel do you think I am?"

"I don't think you're cruel, Sheri. But husbands can sense these things. Even I sensed it after less than half an hour!"

"I lied. I told him it was someone I met at a teacher's conference in St. John's."

"But does Tyler know? Did he ever witness anything?"

"Around him, we were always just friends — Jason and his son, and me and Tyler. The boys brought us together, in fact. There was never anything for anyone to see."

I wouldn't count on it, Amanda thought. Small town, handsome local cop, vulnerable mother ... denial would be no match for such a luscious brew. She suspected this Chris Tymko might be way ahead of any of them.

Two hours later, pink and languid from a hot bath, Amanda curled up beneath the handmade country quilt and stuffed a couple of pink ruffled pillows behind her back. The outrageous extravagance of the Victorian B&B was well beyond her camping budget, but after three days straddling Shadow, and facing the prospect of sleeping on a two-inch strip of foam in a tent, she decided to toss her budget out the window.

After Jason left, Amanda had picked up fish and chips for them from the local diner, and although Sheri had extended an offer of lodgings for the night, Amanda sensed her reluctance and declined. She had her own plans for the night. Tucked into her backpack were Phil's laptop and cellphone, neither of which Jason Maloney, as the cop on the case, had asked to see. All through the desultory dinner, during which Sheri kept one eye on the phone and the other on Tyler's empty kitchen chair, the devices had beckoned to her. Now, propped on the bed with Kaylee happily stretched out on the crocheted throw at her feet, she was finally free to open Phil's computer.

As the computer came to life, the cursor blinked stubbornly in the password box. Amanda tried the usual suspects — *Password*, his son's name, his wife's name, even her own — before typing in Nigeria. Nothing. Passwords were supposed to be memorable and unique. What could be more so than Nigeria? She cast about, mystified. Typed in the name of the village, and finally *Alaji*, the name of the boy who had died in his arms that last night.

Bingo. An array of icons opened up before her. She clicked on his email account and watched the messages flash across the screen as they downloaded. Dozens of emails from charities and businesses, Facebook and Twitter updates, the usual clutter of banal correspondence from cyberspace. She scrolled through the trivia in search of gems. There were emails from herself, of course, and from the RCMP cop Chris Tymko, whom Jason had spoken to. None of the messages in the past two days had been answered, or even opened.

Among the emails were replies from several campgrounds and one boat tour, but these were over a week old. She spread out her map on the quilt beside her to check locations. Phil had apparently been exploring options as far away as the Avalon

Peninsula to the east and the Great Northern Peninsula to the west. No bookings had been yet made, but at least as of a week ago, Phil had still been planning their camping trip.

Frustrated, she checked his Internet search history and was surprised to discover it had been cleared. She knew people who cleared their search history every hour, but they were paranoid people living in dangerous places, exploring information that could get them killed. Had Phil brought his paranoia home with him, which was entirely possible, or had he wanted to erase his trail for a reason?

She knew that cyber detectives could still find the footprints he was trying to erase, but she had no such skill. Her vision blurred with fatigue and her eyelids threatened to close. Pouring herself another glass of wine, she set aside the laptop in favour of Phil's cellphone.

This time the password was easy to crack — the same boy, who even after a year obviously loomed larger in Phil's thoughts than his own family. Phil had never talked about him. He had simply thrust his body aside and raced to the children who were still waiting. Cowering. Hoping. It had been a long night.

The cellphone was synced to the laptop, so she ignored the emails and went directly to the history of his phone calls. Besides the calls and texts from herself and from Sheri, three texts stood out. Two received, one sent. All dated three days ago, just before she'd stopped hearing from him.

All to or from Jason Maloney.

She read the first, which was an invitation from Jason to get together for a beer. The next was from Phil asking when and where. The third named the place, a bar that Amanda remembered passing on the way into Grand Falls. Seven o'clock in the evening, three days ago.

Funny that Jason never mentioned a word of this.

She was tempted to drop by the bar to find out whether the two had actually met and whether any of their conversation had been overheard. But the pillows and the silky duvet drew her down into them, and she found she couldn't budge. Not a single muscle obeyed her. So she slipped naked between the cool cotton sheets and fell asleep.

CHAPTER FOUR

Tuesday dawned blustery and cold, reminding Newfoundland that summer was an elusive and fickle partner in the yearly dance of seasons. On the western coast, a deluge battered the seaside coves, but inland in Deer Lake, it was reduced to a chilly drizzle.

The kind of weather Corporal Chris Tymko hated. As a boy from the prairies, he was used to endless summer days of wide-open blue sky punctuated by fierce thunderstorms that rolled across the flat lands like a freight train. In his previous posting up north, he'd learned to cope with violent, changeable storms and long months of darkness and snow, but Newfoundland seemed on the collision course between massive celestial forces. Humid warmth from the south and gales from the Arctic swirled over the knobby outcrop of rock, dumping snow, rain, and sleet, sometimes all at once.

Roads could turn slick in an instant, hurling cars into ditches and knocking power out for miles. Chris arrived at the Deer Lake detachment early for his morning shift, hoping to use the extra minutes to check for news on Phil Cousins before the duties of the day began. Thoughts of Phil had intruded on his sleep several times during the night, and although there had been no reassuring phone call from Jason Maloney that morning, Chris hoped for some information in the routine police chatter. Not knowing Jason very well, he didn't know whether the man would afford him the courtesy of a phone call, especially after the argument they'd had. Jason was a local Newfoundlander from Corner Brook, and he'd been known to use his connections and credibility to hog the upper hand in an investigation. But Chris figured that on his own home turf of Saskatchewan, he would act the same. Canada was a big and disparate place, full of regional suspicions and loyalties.

As he made a dash through the puddles to the station, he steeled himself for half a dozen reports of traffic accidents that would send him and his team out on the road again. Fortunately the dispatch centre was quiet, giving him time to power up his computer and finish his coffee while he perused the daily updates and alerts for news on Phil.

Nothing, nothing, nothing.

He looked up at the rivulets of rain trickling down the window, matching his bleak mood. Phil was one of the few true friends he'd made since being transferred here from Fort Simpson last spring. Not a work buddy, but a friend in spirit. Not only did they share an outsider Prairie farm-boy identity, but they also shared a love of salmon fishing and country music. And in the languid hours spent together with rod and reel, they'd discovered a deeper tie — wounds of self-doubt and loss that would take a lifetime to heal. Rarely talked about, but understood through a glance or a small, sad smile.

Chris knew that Phil's wound was much deeper and his self-doubt threatened to overpower him some days. He also knew the danger of trying to soldier on while keeping the truth hidden. Until abruptly a line is crossed and brains are blown all over the wall of the house.

If that happened, there would be no warning, no words of goodbye or regret. The most Phil might do is to go far away where those brains would not be found by the woman who had already endured more from him than she should.

If so, why had he taken his son with him?

Chris poured himself a second cup of coffee. His hand hovered over the phone as he debated whether or not to phone Jason. The man was a straight, linear thinker who took people at face value. Phil had told him he wanted to bond with his son, so as far as Jason was concerned, that's what he was doing. Unlike himself, Jason rarely had any self-doubts.

Even when he should.

Chris withdrew his hand as a surge of anger took hold. Jason was the last person who would admit to worrying about Phil. As Chris sipped his coffee, the outer station door opened and his colleague Ralph from the night shift swept through in a swirl of cold and rain. He shook off his mackintosh and hung it by the door before coming through to the interior. Chris looked up, relieved to be rescued from his thoughts.

"Anything going on out there?" Chris asked.

"Fender-benders. One accident on the 430 near Norris Point, but no major injuries. I sent Hollis up to handle it. Otherwise —" he grinned "— nothing on your watch so far but paperwork and highway patrol." He nodded his head toward Chris's computer screen. "Did you read about the poor bastards spotted in a dinghy off the coast below Goose Cove?"

"Jesus! Wouldn't want to be caught out in that storm, especially in a dinghy. Kids? A fisherman in trouble?"

Ralph drained the dregs of coffee from the carafe, scowling at the sludge in his cup. "No self-respecting Newfoundlander would be out there in a dinghy. Half-brained tourists, more likely. Come up from Florida or over from Europe and think what's a little wind and waves? They won't last half an hour in that cold if they swamp."

Chris scrolled through the alerts again. The one about the dinghy had come in at 7:00 a.m., barely past dawn, but to his surprise it had originated not from the detachment in St. Anthony closest to Goose Cove, but from RCMP headquarters in St. John's. He unfolded his long body and walked over to study the map on the wall. Goose Cove was near the very northernmost tip of the Great Northern Peninsula, where it jutted into the fierce and unpredictable currents of the North Atlantic, and where the warmer currents coming up the Strait of Belle Isle collided with the frigid water coming down the coast of Labrador from the Arctic Ocean. The strait served as one pathway for the St. Lawrence River on its race to the open ocean, and even he knew that the clash of temperatures, tides, and currents could create a wild sea.

For a moment he felt a twinge of fear. Phil was not a Newfoundlander born to read the language of the sea, but he'd gone in search of wild surf and whales. Would he be fool enough to venture out in a dinghy?

"Why is HQ involved?" he asked.

Ralph was fiddling with the coffee, measuring and pouring a new pot. He shrugged. "Some border-security issue. The fisherman who called it in thought the occupants might be smugglers."

"Smugglers? What the hell would they be smuggling off the northern tip of Newfoundland?" Chris looked outside. The rain was slamming against the windows now, rattling like buckshot on a tin roof. "How could the fisherman see anything in this, anyway?"

"Well, that's the thing. Acted suspicious, he said. He says he went out in his boat to help but when they saw him, they took off out to sea."

"They? How many?"

"Four or five. Way too many for the size of the boat."

Chris felt a wash of relief. Not Phil! "That could mean anything. Maybe they had illegal fish in the boat. Or maybe they thought he was up to no good. They could have been tourists who never set foot out of the city. We used to get that up north too. People from Japan or Europe eager to see the wilderness, but with no idea how wild and empty it really is. Probably thought they could just dial 911 on their cellphones."

"Except when help was offered, these guys headed the other way. That's what's got HQ in a knot. So the coastal detachments are on alert to keep their eyes and ears open. It's gone out on the Internet, TV, and radio too, so the locals will be keeping an eye out." Ralph poured his fresh coffee, pried his wet boots off, and propped his stocking feet on his desk. "Let's hope those poor buggers aren't at the bottom of the ocean by now."

Amanda was chilled to the bone by the time she reached the RCMP detachment in Deer Lake just before noon. Because it was located in an obscure corner of town off the main Trans-Canada Highway, it took her some time to find it, but her first glimpse of the sleek, modern brick building filled her with relief. It was not the remote backwater she'd feared, so maybe someone would have heat and a pot of hot coffee on the go.

She had left Sheri the night before on polite but tepid terms, with promises to keep in touch. Amanda knew her concern and love for Phil were genuine, but distrust and blame had wedged its blade between them. There was little to be gained by staying in Grand Falls. Phil was no longer there, and if she was going to help him, she had to figure out where he'd gone.

Over a sumptuous breakfast at the B&B, Amanda had scrutinized the map. She knew Deer Lake was the gateway to the Great Northern Peninsula, which jutted like a gnarled thumb up into the North Atlantic. A long spine of mountains ran down its centre and its ragged coastline was carved into rocky points and cozy coves. At its southern base, Gros Morne National Park attracted thousands of visitors to its ancient, glacier-scoured mountains and silent green forests. At its remote northern tip, the discovery of a thousand-year-old Viking settlement drew scientists, tourists, and history lovers from all around the world.

Deer Lake, and RCMP Corporal Chris Tymko, seemed like a promising place to start her search.

On her way out of Grand Falls, she'd dropped by the bar where Jason and Phil had arranged to meet. It was closed but, in response to her hammering, the door was eventually opened by a red-eyed man carrying a mop. He squinted at her doubtfully, but didn't invite her in out of the rain. They might have been here, he said, but it was a busy night and the music was loud. What's it to you? he wanted to know. She thanked him and left.

The rain had eased to a drizzle by the time she nosed her motorcycle into the Deer Lake RCMP parking lot. She had not called ahead to alert Corporal Tymko that she was coming. She had sensed antipathy between Jason and him, and she wasn't sure whether it would extend to her as well. She wanted his first impression to be one of friend, not foe. If she were linked to Jason, or possibly worse, to Sheri, she might never earn his co-operation.

As she clambered off the bike and pulled off her helmet, a tall, rangy Mountie emerged from the building and headed toward a cruiser. He moved like a marionette, all angles and planes. Feet that flailed, elbows and knees that knocked against each other, and a nose like a ski jump beneath his visor cap. He reminded her of an overgrown teenager who hadn't yet figured out how his various parts worked together.

The effect was both comic and endearing. She suppressed a smile. Spotting Kaylee, he veered over toward her. As he drew closer, a beautiful smile crinkled his eyes. *Even better*, she thought with a self-conscious twinge. After hours on the road in the wind and rain, she suspected she looked like something spat out by the washing machine.

"Now that's a sight!" he exclaimed with no hint of the east coast lilt she'd come to expect. "Hey there, buddy!"

As usual Kaylee reacted as if she hadn't been patted in a million years. As he scratched her ears, he glanced up, first at the motorcycle licence plate and then at Amanda.

"All the way from Quebec? *Vous voyagez ...* ah *... très loin du Quebec.*"

She laughed and rescued him from his attempt at French. "Chelsea, just across the river from Ottawa. As Anglo as they come. And I was going camping by the ocean."

Her emphasis on *was* provoked a raised eyebrow. "Can I help you?" he asked.

"I'm looking for Corporal Tymko."

Now both eyebrows shot up. "I'm Tymko."

Beneath his curiosity, his blue eyes were warm. She felt some tension ease from her back. Over the years she'd become adept at sizing up friend or foe, for a split-second misjudgment could cost a life. She sensed she'd made the right choice in coming here.

"Amanda Doucette. I'm the friend who was supposed to go camping with Phil Cousins. I'm really worried about him and I'm hoping you have some idea where he's gone."

Thirty seconds later she and Kaylee were ensconced in his small but cheery office. Mist fogged the windows and lit the room in a pale wash. While Amanda peeled off her wet rain gear, Chris poured her a cup of hot coffee and Kaylee some water. As the first sip coursed through her, she decided she'd never tasted anything so delicious.

"I'm very glad you came," Chris said, swinging his desk chair sideways and jackknifing his gangly body into the small space facing her. "I've been thinking about him ever since Jason Maloney called yesterday. We were planning to go cod fishing up the peninsula later this month, but he hasn't been returning my calls." He grinned. "We're both Prairie farm boys, never seen an ocean surf in our lives until here, except to fly over. So it's the blind leading the blind. But Phil says he feels most at peace when he's on the ocean. Maybe because he's not hemmed in." He broke off, his eyes narrowing. "Amanda Doucette. Are you the one …?"

She nodded. "Nigeria? Yes."

He leaned over to yank open his bottom drawer and pulled out a computer printout from a newspaper. Amanda recognized the *Ottawa Citizen*. From the large photo, she knew exactly what it was — a close-up of herself surrounded by children as she demonstrated the construction of a pyramid garden. Nigeria, in happier times. The village, flooded with refugees, had pitched in together to build new gardens, wells, schools, and clinics, as well as extra security. For all the good that had done.

The headline read HEROES AGAINST ALL ODDS, and under the photo was a smaller caption. CANADIAN AID WORKERS FIGHT TO SAVE VILLAGE.

The journalist, Matthew Goderich, had become a friend over the course of their ordeal and its aftermath. A stringer for the Canadian Press, he'd been ordered to return to Lagos by his employer when the Islamist insurgency worsened, but instead he'd insisted on staying on in the north as a freelancer. These stories need to be told, he'd said. No matter how many people back home don't want to hear them.

Despite the passage of time and the warm safety of the RCMP office, Amanda felt that familiar vice pressing her chest. Sensing it, Kaylee nuzzled her fingers.

"I dug this up when I first met Phil," Tymko said. "What you two did was incredibly brave."

She pasted a blank expression on her face. "Foolhardy. You don't have time to think."

"Not everyone reacts like you did. Lots of people would have run for their own lives."

"Those children were like family." She paused, loath to revisit the memories. To perpetuate the great lie of her heroism. "You never know how you'll react until the threat is right there. The guns, the smoke, the blood ... It's all instinct. Fight or flight."

Or freeze.

"I know." He spoke as if he did know. As if he too had faced the devil head on. Well, he was a cop after all.

"I guess it's not all speeding tickets in your line of work, either," she said gaily to change the mood.

He obliged her with a smile but it was fleeting. "Afterward, though, when you've had time to think ..."

"About how you almost died? Yeah."

"And about who you didn't save."

No doubt he was speaking about himself, but her heart hammered. The coffee cup shook in her hand. Seeing that, he looked stricken. "I'm sorry, I shouldn't have said that. I know the memories must still be very raw. They are for Phil. He was really looking forward to your trip."

Grateful for the opening, she steered back to safer ground. To the reason she had come. "But something went wrong. Corporal Tymko —"

"Chris."

"Chris. He's taken his son with him. That wasn't part of the plan. And his wife had just told him there is someone else. She thinks he's just taking time to sort things out, but I'm scared it's more. He's been betrayed —"

"In more ways that you know."

Amanda hesitated. Chris's lips were a grim line, his eyes hooded.

"You mean Jason Maloney?"

He nodded.

"Sheri says she didn't tell him."

Chris shifted. His bony knee jiggled. "Jason did."

She sucked in her breath. *Even worse!*

"Jason said he had a right to know, said he didn't feel right sneaking around behind his back."

"Oh right! So why not spit in his face instead?" Amanda thought back to the exchange of cryptic text messages on Phil's phone, setting up a meeting. Was that when Jason had told him? Was that the last anyone saw of Phil before he packed up his son and took off?

She revisited Jason's behaviour from the night before, including his determination to handle things quietly, ostensibly to spare Phil the public humiliation of a full-fledged police hunt. She felt her blood pressure rise. Like hell. More to spare himself the censure. Or Sheri's wrath should she find out.

"Sheri doesn't know that Phil knows," she said. But even as she spoke, she remembered Sheri avoiding Jason's touch the night before. Was that just guilt, or did she have an inkling of what he'd done?

"No," Chris said, "and I told Jason he should tell her."

So that was the argument she had witnessed between Jason and Chris in the truck. Amanda stood up. "This makes it even worse, Chris. Everything Phil believed in, everything he hung on to, has been turned upside down."

She walked over to the large map of Newfoundland tacked to the office wall. "I've got to find him. Where would he go?"

No sooner had the question left her lips than her eyes settled on the remote, northern section of the island. A desolate finger where villages were few and far between, and where the North Atlantic, the Arctic, and the inner Strait of Belle Isle collided. The end of the earth. She tapped the peninsula with her finger.

He followed her finger. "Yes. I think you may be right."

CHAPTER FIVE

Amanda wanted to set off right away, for it was a huge area to cover, encompassing the twin UNESCO world heritage sites of Gros Morne and L'Anse aux Meadows where the Vikings had settled, as well as numerous fishing villages in between. From the map she could identify at least six government campsites, but there were surely smaller local ones tucked near the coastal villages. Phil had already had far too great a head start.

But Chris Tymko's pragmatism prevailed. "It's a big place," he said. "And much of the interior mountain range has no road access. If Phil is looking to get away from it all, he could be on foot in the mountains or in a boat on the ocean."

"He's not much good on the ocean. Prairie boy like you said."

He didn't smile. "In his mood, that might not stop him. If he's looking for freedom, or oblivion ..."

Sobering, she studied the map. There was only one road running north up the coast, dipping in and out of the fishing villages along the way. In each village, there might be boats available to rent. If Phil were trying to disappear, he would not choose an obvious path.

"Are there little roads leading up into these mountains?"

Chris was at his computer, fiddling with the keys. He glanced over briefly. "Just a few old logging trails. There's not much up there but moose and trees. Oh, some salmon rivers and logging camps, mostly abandoned." He swore softly at the computer. "Jason hasn't even put out an alert on Phil's licence plate."

She grimaced. "Part of his low-key approach. To spare himself."

"Right. I'm going to give it to the local detachments up there. The more eyes we have on this, the better."

She thanked him and headed toward the door. "I've got all my gear. All I need are some groceries and a good map —"

"Forestry maps. Much more detailed. I'll print them out for you here." He was already tapping on his computer again. "You've got a good smart phone and a GPS?"

She nodded. "My cellphone has a GPS. I'm not going into the real wilderness, am I? There are people around? Villages, fishing boats?"

"The people will help you, yes. But you'll need a satellite GPS. Cellphones can be useless, and one fishing village looks pretty much like another, at least to this Prairie boy. Nothing but boats, pickup trucks, and lobster traps."

She laughed. As he typed and the printer hummed, she studied the wall map. Newfoundland had essentially one highway, the Trans-Canada, running across it from Port aux Basques in the west to St. John's in the east, with local and community roads branching off like ribs from its long, curved spine. Deer Lake not only served as the gateway to Gros Morne National Park, but also as the juncture where the main road heading north up the peninsula forked off from the Trans-Canada. The first major campgrounds in the park itself were near the town of Rocky Harbour.

Chris saw her tracing the route with her finger. "Rocky Harbour's the main tourist hub for the park," he said. "That and St. Anthony's at the northern tip. They're full of motels and RVs and kids. Phil's not going to find his wilderness and solitude there."

"No, but it might be a good place to start asking questions. I should be able to get to Rocky Harbour tonight."

He glanced uneasily out the rain-streaked windows. "Anything goes in this weather. It's a twisty-turny highway, and fog and rain can make it deadly. And make sure you don't drive after sunset. At dusk, the moose take over the roads."

She nodded. "The countryside where I live in West Quebec is full of deer. You have to watch out for them too."

"You have a hope of surviving a collision with a deer," he said. "But a moose will win every time. Especially against your lightweight rocket out there."

"Rocket!" She returned his smile. "I like that. I've been looking for a name for her, and Rocket has much more attitude than Shadow."

He gave a mock salute. "Glad to be of service, ma'am. We've got an estimated twenty thousand moose on the northern peninsula alone, more per square kilometre than anywhere else in the world. And it's coming into mating season, and you don't want to catch their eye. If you by chance avoid the amorous moose, there are always the bears. The momma bears will be out foraging with their cubs, collecting food for the winter."

She looked down at Kaylee, who lay patiently by her chair with her head on her paws, as if human talk was an utter bore. "Oh, Kaylee, are you going to protect me from the big bad bears?"

Kaylee thumped her feathery tail on the floor, looking anything but fierce.

"Yeah, you might want to make a lot of noise and keep her on a short leash," Chris said. "Dogs have a bad habit of chasing them and then rushing back with an angry bear on their tail."

Kaylee raised her head, alert now that her name had been mentioned. Amanda scratched her ears. "I'm not worried. If it's not a ball or a stick, she won't give it a second glance."

The printer had stopped humming, so Chris reached inside

and flourished a sheaf of papers. With long, deft fingers, he rolled them up and slipped them into a plastic tube.

"Waterproof," he said. "You'll be really glad I did that when you hit your first big coastal rain storm. It will just about blow the Rocket off the island."

She winced as she thanked him. The drive from Grand Falls had been bitter enough. She'd been caught in a few rainstorms in Quebec, and of course in monsoons in the Far East, but even the heaviest tropical deluge would not compare to the icy needles of northern Newfoundland.

As September edged toward the fall equinox, daylight began to fade by seven thirty, so Amanda reached Gros Morne National Park just ahead of moose hour. The geography was breathtaking; the road twisted along the edge of deep bays and through soaring hills laced with jagged spruce. Roadside ditches were awash in goldenrod and fireweed.

Beneath her, the Rocket roared as she leaned into the turns and hugged the bends. She was stiff and aching by the time she stopped at the Visitor's Centre near the entrance to pick up a park map and information about campgrounds. Thankfully the rain had stopped, but the low, dark clouds blended sky with sea, and a wash of gilded pewter obscured the setting sun.

The town of Rocky Harbour was the commercial hub of Gros Morne, but by mid-September it already had a windswept, semi-abandoned look, with some of the businesses winding down and cottages empty. She had transferred some photos of Phil and Tyler from his laptop to her phone, and she showed these at gas stations and restaurants, as well as I's De B'y Boat Tours near town, but everywhere she went, she was met with the same worried stares and shakes of the head.

Not one sighting of Phil.

When she finally found the campground at Green Point that Phil had inquired about, the sun had already dipped below the ocean. Through a veil of dark trees, she could see the bruised lavender of twilight. *There will be other sunsets*, she told herself, as she nosed her bike into one of the private, grassy sites and peeled herself off the seat. She was bone-weary, and now that she had begun her odyssey, she realized just how vast the land was.

The campground itself was tucked into the woods between the highway and the ocean. Each private site was set into a circle of trees that protected it from the ocean gales, but the grass was soggy from the rain and the spruce trees dripped on her head as she set up camp. She was the only soul stupid enough to be camping that night, and because of the honour system of self-registration, she had no way of knowing whether Phil and Tyler had passed through. The day felt like an abysmal failure.

Thrilled to be free and undeterred by the chill wind that tore through the trees, Kaylee ranged around the camp snuffling the rich, loamy smells. Amanda watched her with envy. She was too stiff and exhausted to enjoy the rugged beauty of the camp. Every muscle screamed. Phil had promised to bring the cooking gear and supplies for their expedition, so she did not even have a simple camping stove, an oversight she would have to remedy in the morning.

The campsite was equipped with a metal barbeque box filled with soggy ash. Grimly, she collected sticks and coaxed them into a sputtering fire to heat the tea and the can of beans she'd bought at the grocery store. Then as chilly darkness settled in, she crawled into her tent, wrapped herself and Kaylee in her sleeping bag, and tried to sleep.

Long into the night, she listened to the wind moaning through the trees and the surf crashing against the shore below, remembering the nights in Nigeria when she had lain in her cabin beneath her mosquito netting, bathed in sweat and praying for a single breath of cool air. Listening to the whine of insects and the blend of voices and laughter from the village square.

Kaylee's growl woke her with a start. She flung back the sleeping bag and groped for the hatchet she'd stashed beneath her pillow. Her heart pounded. Kaylee was standing at the tent door, her growl escalating to a bark.

"Shh-hh!" Amanda clamped her hand over her muzzle and dragged her back, desperate to quiet her. As wakefulness took full hold, she shook her head sheepishly. *Don't be ridiculous*, she told herself. *You're in Newfoundland, in the middle of goddamn nowhere. There's no marauding militia for thousands of miles. Indeed, no one at all.*

Footsteps squelched on the grass outside. She tightened her grip on the hatchet. Then incongruously, the smell of coffee tickled her nose and Kaylee's tail began to wag. Amanda unzipped the bottom corner of her tent flap and peeked outside. Warm sunlight slanted through the campsite, sparkling like sequins on the dewy spruce. Directly in front of her was a pair of steel-toed boots attached to very long legs. She looked up.

Chris Tymko stood in the entrance holding two mugs of coffee. His smile, initially uncertain, broadened at the sight of her.

"I thought two pairs of eyes looking would be better than one," he said. "I got my buddy to cover some extra shifts, and I applied for some vacation days."

She yanked at the tent flap, relief and warmth rushing through her. "How long?"

"As long as it takes."

CHAPTER SIX

Norm Parsons squinted out across the water, which shimmered like fireworks in the dawn. His boat pitched in the ocean swell, its engine growling as it struggled to push through the chop. The wind lashed and the tow ropes to the net quivered taut.

They'd been working flat out for four days and nights, hauling the net in every three or four hours to empty it. His two sons were catching a bit of sleep, but he'd been up at the wheel since the big swells started. This was his tenth trip of the season, and he felt it in every bone in his body. *Getting too old for this*, he thought, ducking out of the wheelhouse to the top of the ladder.

"Time to haul 'er in, Lizzie," he shouted over the engine. "Get the boys up. We got a twelve-hour steam ahead of us back to port."

His daughter had climbed up by the winch to check the brake and tow cables, fighting with gloves so big they damn near swallowed her arms to the elbows. She was a small thing like her mother, but strong as a mink. Good thing too, because with the cutbacks in season shrimp quotas and single-trip limits this summer, he hadn't wanted to pay a proper crew this time out. She and her two brothers were all he had.

She swung around to look across at him. Beneath the black toque, her cheeks were peeling from the sun and her nose was red from the cold, but she wore the same stubborn scowl all the Parsonses had. Eighteen years old, already full of spit and fire.

"It's just dawn," she said. "Plenty of time to steam back."

"Not in this blow. I wants to get 'er all unloaded and weighed and the boat cleaned before dark, Lizzie."

She stepped down onto the deck and peered through the trap door into the hold. "But we don't have our trip limit yet, Dad."

He knew that. It was nearing the end of the season, and the ocean floor had been pretty well depleted. He blamed the huge factory freezer trawlers that were out fishing the grounds all year round, while the small local boats were trapped in the harbour by pack ice. The freezer trawlers could stay out on the grounds for weeks, while he and the other locals had to steam 250 kilometres back and forth from the shrimp area to port every few days with their haul.

He knew in his heart it was a dying industry for the small fishing boats. A few years ago he'd made very good money in shrimp and snow crab, but on the last net haul, they had picked up only a half load of shrimp in their allotted time.

"I'm burning more money in gas than I'll make doing one more haul," he replied. "And the dock monitor is expecting us by eight."

Lizzie still wore her stubborn face, but she banged on the wall of the cabin, where her brothers were already tossing back the blankets and pulling on their gloves and boots. Norm slowed the engine, and within minutes his sons had the winch going. The frame shuddered and the huge cable began to creak and groan. Lizzie leaned over the stern of the boat, peering into the churning wake for the first glimpse of the net. Norm felt the familiar quiver of anticipation. Even after years of trawling — first cod, and now snow crab and shrimp — that small, peculiar rush of fear and excitement had never gone away. That moment when the net came into view and he could see how big the catch was, or whether some unexpected rock or shelf had shredded his net. One time a discarded kitchen stove had ripped a hole so big that he had lost half his take.

The beam of the net broke the surface, followed by the floats, skimming along like a string of children's balloons. His sons ran to each side to guide the ends of the net. So far so good. Norm strained to see the cod end of the net. Plowing through the wake, fighting the tow ropes with a whoosh of foam, the net broke through the surface briefly before sinking back below. In spite of his caution, his heart leaped. Shrimp! Maybe as much as a thousand pounds!

Lizzie leaned way out over the stern. She didn't look afraid. That was Lizzie, too stubborn to know fear even when she should. Or maybe just too green. She'd been out in boats since near the day she was born, but the ocean had never treated her bad.

"Look at that ball, Dad! We hit the mother lode! Finally!"

He tried not to let himself get excited. He didn't hold much hope that the big ball was full of shrimp. More than likely they had picked up a whole lot of bottom junk. Lizzie could wish all she liked, but he knew there were not many shrimp to be had. Whole beds were near empty now where ten years ago, when he'd first switched from fish to shrimp, the ocean floor had been teeming with the little buggers. All you had to do was dip your net and haul them up.

No more. The smaller guys like him were lucky to pay for their boat loan, their gas, and the shrimp licence. Screwed once again by the pencil-pushers up in Ottawa, who always gave the big boys first rights. "Careful now!" he shouted back. A stiff wind was coming up, blowing clouds over the rising sun and dropping the temperature five degrees. Waves were beginning to slap the boat around. The net could spin away from her, knocking her clear off the boat into the frigid sea.

When the ball of the net was almost clear of the water, the boys slowed the winch to check the net. Something looked odd. The boat pitched and fought through the chop, and the ball swirled. Not smooth and symmetrical, but bulging out on one side. Setting the rudder, Norm left the engine and came aft for a closer look. Strange colours peeked through the bulge in the green netting. Not the shiny pink of shrimp nor the silver sheen of fish, but rather a chequered pattern of blue and red.

"Pull 'er in slowly, Lizzie," he said. "Let's see what we gots here."

Together they all guided the load in, bracing themselves against the pitch and toss of the boat. Soon the net was fully in view, the water, sand, and ocean muck streaming from it as it was winched up over the deck. He stopped the winches briefly to study the huge ball of wriggling pink shrimp suspended in the air. Saw the occasional flash of silver fish in the morning light. But something else too, buried in the squirm of shrimp. He peered closer. Cloth? A jacket blown overboard? A boot tossed by a careless sightseer?

He guided the ball lower toward the deck, turning it slowly for a better look. Spotted a red-and-blue jacket, black pants, and a running shoe.

Just as he made sense of the whole, Lizzie screamed.

Chris and Amanda loaded her bike into the back of his truck and were working their way slowly up the northern peninsula, asking questions and showing Phil's photo in every coastal village along the way. Chris was out of uniform and he'd learned the fine Newfoundland art of banter, but even so, people took his questions seriously. Legends of people lost at sea loomed large in village lore. By the end of the day, Amanda was even more grateful he'd come along.

It was nearly sundown before they had their first confirmed sighting at the Seaview Motel, a plain white clapboard bungalow on the side of the highway near Black Duck Cove. Phil and Tyler had stayed there two nights earlier. The poor buggers had planned to camp on the beach, the motel keeper said, but the rain was blowing sideways and your man took pity on his boy.

Amanda nearly jumped for joy. They were on the right track, albeit two days behind. More importantly, Phil hadn't done anything crazy. He was working his way up the peninsula, still apparently following his plan.

"Did they say where they were going after they checked in?" she asked.

"Well, we didn't stand dere in the rain chatting, but 'e did ask where they could get a bite of supper. I sent them to Nancy's Restaurant up the road."

"Did he use your phone or computer?"

"Nudding like dat, darlin'. No computer 'ere anyways. He was after a clean bed and a hot shower, das all." The motel keeper was laying the accent on a bit thick, Amanda thought, but perhaps in the tourism trade, he figured it was part of his charm. She and Chris had found him changing the sheets in one of his motel rooms and she eyed the accommodations longingly. They were certainly basic, as he'd said, but they looked like paradise after her night in the tent. Chris flashed her a sympathetic grin as he turned to go.

The man straightened as if a thought had just occurred to him. "I did hear somet'ing of their conversation, if you're interested."

Chris swung around. "Please."

"They was going out to their truck, and de boy was talking about going fishing the next day. He were jumping up and down, you know how kids are. Like they gots springs in dere feet."

"What did the father say?"

"Nudding, b'y. Just got in the truck."

Amanda didn't like the sound of that. "What kind of mood was he in?"

"Mood?" The motel keeper looked incredulous. "Fifty dollars a night gets dem a bed and a bathroom, my dear, not a palm reading."

Chris laughed. "I thought palm reading was a Newfoundland specialty."

"Well, he be wet and cold, I figures. Probably hungry too. And after listening to that kid yammering all day, even the Lord himself would be cranky." He snapped a pillow case and turned his attention back to the bed. Chris thanked him and they headed back across the patch of gravel that passed for a parking lot. The sun hung low over the ocean, a blurry orange smudge behind the gathering clouds. Chris gestured to it.

"Looks like there might be a storm blowing in. We should probably find ourselves a campground soon."

She cast one longing look back at the simple little motel. "We could take a page from Phil's book."

"Let's check out Nancy's place first. I tell you what. Will a nice, hot, sit-down meal of fish and chips do the trick?"

She opened the truck door and shooed Kaylee over to make room. "On real chairs? With a real server, and a pint of local ale?"

"Follow me, ma'am. I'll even spring for a bottle of wine!"

They found Nancy's Restaurant a couple of kilometres farther up the road. Splashy roadside billboards advertised it as having the best fish and chips on the northern peninsula, as well as sumptuous lobster in season, but when the restaurant came into view, Amanda laughed aloud. It was a little square saltbox house in the middle of a weedy field. The sign on the front door, painted pink with an inexpert hand, urged them to please come in. A single room greeted them, filled with a half-dozen tables covered in faded, mismatched plastic cloths like the leftovers from a church rummage sale. It was the dinner hour, but all the tables were empty except for one at the back, where a woman wearing a frilly apron was flipping through a magazine. Like many of the women Amanda had seen in Newfoundland, she had a round, cherub face and a short, plump body. Her hair was orange; whether by mistake or design, Amanda wasn't sure.

She looked up in astonishment at their arrival. "You wanting to eat?"

Chris was about to launch into his "Aw, shucks, yes please" routine, but Amanda stopped him. She'd been in many dubious restaurants in her years overseas, and the décor didn't deter her. The lack of customers, and the lack of cooking aromas or sounds from the kitchen, did.

She remained in the doorway. "We're actually looking for a friend of ours. I understand he and his son ate dinner here a couple of nights ago." She fished in her pocket for her cellphone, while the woman's eyebrows nearly disappeared into her hair. Only their dark brown colour saved them.

"Here?" she asked in disbelief.

Amanda crossed the room to show her the photos. The woman gave them a cursory glance. "Oh yeah, Mr. Personality. He came in here like he had his own permanent thundercloud over his head. Wanted a Quidi Vidi Premium to go with his fish and chips and when I said we had no liquor licence, he didn't want to stay. The boy was hungry, you could tell, and he begged his father to stay, but they left in a big, huge fight. He told the kid to shut up and slammed the truck door. I told them the only place still open now was a café near Anchor Point, so I'm guessing that's where they headed."

"How far is that?"

"Eight, nine kilometres?"

Amanda's heart sank. Night was stealing in from the east, cloaked in cloud and wind. She was hungry and tired herself by now, torn between the promise of a hot meal and the fresh sheets of the Seaview Motel. Chris thanked the girl and headed outside, cocking his head as they descended the wooden steps.

"Holding out for that bottle of wine, eh?"

"Trust me," she said. "I've seen more promising establishments in the villages of Cambodia."

"Looks can be deceiving. Sometimes these simple places have the best food."

"Right."

He laughed. "Got it. Well then, on to this café!"

Just as they were approaching the truck, his cellphone rang. He pulled it out as if it were an alien thing. "A signal!" he exclaimed. But as he studied the call display, his delight faded, and he wrinkled up his nose. "Uh-oh, the boss. Hang on. He's probably forgotten some password." He turned away and lowered his voice to answer the call. Amanda watched from the corner of her eye as she let Kaylee out for a quick run. Chris's expression grew sober, and he stiffened to attention. It was a quick call, but by the end of it he was nodding in agreement. Afterward, he turned to her, all hint of teasing gone from his face.

"A body's been pulled ashore in one of the harbours north of here. Quite the stir. The local detachment has only four officers and one's away on training, so my boss says since I'm in the neighbourhood, can I go help? At least with the preliminaries, until reinforcements arrive."

She went cold. "A body?" she whispered. "Whose?"

"The sergeant had no details, so let's not jump to conclusions. I'll go up there and keep you posted."

"I'm coming with you."

"No. It's too early to tell anything. You'd be better off going to that café and then getting a good night's sleep."

"Oh for God's sake, Chris. You think I'm going to sleep a wink? I can identify him."

"So can I." He pulled down the tailgate of his truck and turned to her, all cop now. "Bodies can wash up from anywhere, sometimes months after a drowning. It may be hours before we know anything. You'd just be hanging around behind the perimeter with the rest of the village, waiting for news. Let's get your bike off the truck and stick to our plan. The best thing you can do for us right now is to go talk to the people at the café."

Watching him roll the Rocket down the ramp, she struggled with fear and impotence. She wanted to plead further, but she sensed he wouldn't budge. She would be a third wheel at the scene anyway, feeling useless and hating it. "Okay, but please call me if —"

"I will." He gave a quick crinkly smile that softened him. A chill wind whipped across the open meadow, bringing with it the tang of salt and the smell of rain. It blew his soft, floppy hair into his eyes. "You'll be sick of hearing from me."

Then, with a screech of rubber, he was gone.

CHAPTER SEVEN

During Amanda's short ride up the highway to the café, the clouds unexpectedly began to shred and roll out toward the east. The ocean quieted, and the lingering dusk painted the sea and sky in muted swirls of lavender and rose. Amanda's fatigue and hunger evaporated under the spell.

The Fisherman's Dory Café was situated on a bay in an old saltbox house painted flamboyant turquoise with yellow trim. Surrounded by practical but humourless houses sporting white siding, pickup trucks, and piles of firewood and tires in the front yard, it looked like a dancer at a plowman's match. She parked by the front window, fed Kaylee, and ran her around the parking lot before shoehorning her back into the trailer with a promise of better walks tomorrow. The dog gazed out at her, sad-eyed and unimpressed.

A blast of steamy air redolent with fish, garlic, and beer greeted Amanda when she pushed open the barnwood door. A stout woman in her fifties glanced up from behind a counter at the back, and a smile lit up her wind-weathered face.

Amanda felt as if she'd walked into a nautical-themed Disney set. Netting was draped in swoops along the walls, with various shells and fish woven through it. Lobster traps and stuffed fish hung everywhere. The place was empty except for three men clustered around a television at the back, watching football. Celtic music from speakers clashed with the breathless play-by-play voiceover, and every now and then the men erupted in shouts of excitement or disgust. The woman looked delighted for the interruption, and within seconds she'd introduced herself as Jill and settled Amanda at a table by the window as far from the shouting as possible. As Amanda was placing an order for a draught, seafood chowder, and grilled turbot, Jill spotted Kaylee outside.

"Oh for the love of God, that's no place for a dog! Bring 'im in, bring 'im in, darlin'! Dere's nobody here but us, and the boys will take good care of 'im while you eat. I gots just the piece of turbot for 'im."

Amanda didn't raise the question of regulations, having learned that Newfoundlanders loved to ignore them anyway, and Kaylee wasted no time gobbling up the fish and charming her way into the middle of the men, who slipped her the occasional bite from the food in front of them. Relieved and happy, Amanda devoted herself to the bowl of steaming chowder Jill placed before her.

After the long day on the road, the chowder was divine, full of juicy chunks of cod, scallops, and shrimp. She waited until she'd savoured it all and Jill had returned with her plate of turbot before she picked up the thread of her search. Jill herself supplied the opening.

"You going up to the Viking settlement?"

Amanda shook her head. "I'm trying to find a friend and his son. The woman at Nancy's place said he came through here a couple of days ago. Did you see him?"

"A man and his boy?"

Amanda dug out her cellphone to show the photos. "Tyler's the kid's name and he's eleven."

The woman's face crinkled in delight. "Oh, Tyler! Yes, they come through here a couple of nights ago — Monday, was it?

— quite late. I was closing up the kitchen, but I fixed them some soup and burgers. The boy ate two full bowls of that chowder you had. Now that's a big bowl!"

Amanda could attest to that. She eyed the fish spread out before her, delicately breaded with a wedge of lemon on the side, and wondered whether she had room for any of it. No wonder there had been some left over for Kaylee.

Then Jill's smile faded. "The man hardly ate anything. Poked his food around his plate. Drank three pints of Quidi Vidi Premium, though."

"Did he say anything? Talk about his plans?"

She shrugged. "Just sat there staring into his beer, leaving the poor boy with nothing to do but watch the football game or talk to me. He followed me around, asking me questions about all the fish on the walls, and them paintings. He weren't much of a football fan and anyways it weren't the CFL, so I took pity on him. No one's asked me about this stuff in years, so I told him my husband — God rest his soul — caught them all and I still have all his boats and equipment in our stage down at the harbour. I still go out in the strait with my brother sometimes, but the money's better here. When Tyler asked if he could see our stage, I offered to take him down."

"His father let you do that?"

Jill must have heard the surprise in Amanda's voice. "This is Newfoundland, my dear. The father was happy for the babysitting and the boys here said they'd man the bar. So Tyler and I went down to the cove. It was dark by then, and all the boats were back in that was coming in, but a few fellers were still around, repairing their nets and the like."

She paused to pull a chair out from the adjacent table. In the silence, Amanda digested the implications. Phil was paranoid about safety, particularly regarding children. What kind of shape had he been in that he'd let his son go off with a stranger, no matter how motherly she seemed? Jill eased stiffly into the chair, hiding a grimace behind a wide smile. "What a lovely boy he was! Questions, questions, questions. Reminded me of my own boys, all gone now to Alberta and Ontario. Nothing for them here except a few weeks' work at the fish plant down in Port au Choix if they're lucky. He told me his own dad couldn't get work here either and that's why he's so sad. Well, he's not going to find work at the bottom of a beer bottle now, is he?"

"No. That's why I'm looking for him. I'm worried about him. Worried about the boy too."

"He's a clever one. Curious too," Jill said.

A chorus of cheers drowned her out for a moment. Someone had scored something.

Jill glanced over at the table and pulled her chair closer to be heard. "He seemed like a good dad, made sure the boy liked his food and such, and Tyler sure loved him, so he must be doing something right."

"Did Tyler mention any plans? Where they might go next?"

"Out in a boat," she said, laughing. "To an island where they could see puffins and whales. That's what the boy wanted. He was disappointed the deep-sea-fishing season wasn't open yet."

"Do you know where?"

"Well, there's boats all along the coast and plenty of fishermen eager to make an extra buck by taking them out."

"What about boat tours?"

"Couple of them up in St. Anthony. That's about an hour and a half up the coast. But St. Anthony's a busy place and Tyler said they were looking for wilderness."

She paused and swivelled to look at the men. "Hey Frank! Did that feller who was here a couple of nights ago — the one with the boy — did he say where he was going?"

Frank looked away from the game blearily. "The one sat over 'dere?"

"Yeah. Looked like he'd spent a week in the bush without a shower."

"He didn't talk to us," said another of the men.

"He talked to that other feller, though," said a third man, who sported a thick grey beard. Jill had all their attention now, lured away from a dreary game by the prospect of intrigue.

"What other guy?" Jill asked.

"The hitchhiker that hardly talked English. Greek or something," Grey Beard said. "You were gone by then."

"Oh right!" Frank said. "He came in late, some cold and wet and hungry, b'y. Must've walked in off the highway. Didn't have proper clothes for the Newfoundland coast, I can tell you. He was after free food, leftovers, scraps, anyt'ing. Turns out he only had a dollar in his pocket, just off a boat up at St. Anthony. Your friend bought him food and a couple of rounds of vodka too. That was before they started arguing."

Amanda grew alert. "What about?"

"Jobs. Fish. I dunno. We was watching the game."

"It was mostly the Greek arguing," said Grey Beard. "The drunker he got, the louder he got. 'Dey's all cheaters,' he said."

"Who?"

"Like I said, we was watching the game. Someone he was working for, I t'inks. Or supposed to work for. He said he just wanted to go home."

"What was Phil doing?" Amanda asked. "My friend, I mean."

"Trying to talk him down, weren't he?" Grey Beard said. "I couldn't hear what he said because he talked low and soft, but seemed like he were asking him questions. But each question just got the feller madder."

"Right," Frank said. "When the foreign feller started to cry, your friend said it was time to go. So he paid for everything and practically carried the feller out the door. Wasn't hard, guy couldn't have weighed more than a hundred and twenty pounds. Even soaking wet from the rain like he were."

"Wait a minute. They left together?"

Both men nodded.

"Did you see what happened outside?"

"No, it were raining and dark as pitch out that night. I heard a truck drive off, but I don't know whose."

Or who was in it, Amanda thought. She sat for a moment, contemplating the implications. How like Phil to take a cold and penniless stranger under his wing. But what had happened afterward? Had he given the stranger a few dollars and sent him on his way? Or had he shepherded him into his truck and taken him to the warmth and protection of their motel?

When Norm Parsons had radioed his frantic call to shore, he'd been directed by the Harbour Authority in St. Anthony to dock at the fish plant as usual, but to wait on board for instructions from the RCMP.

Driving along the coastal road and through the interior as fast he dared during the height of moose time, Chris reached the town of St. Anthony in slightly over an hour. He had never been there, but given that it was the major centre for the upper Great Northern Peninsula, he was expecting a bustling town with lots of commerce related to tourism and fishing.

As he topped the hill coming into town, lights twinkled in the valley below and glistened off the water in the narrow bay. Homes and businesses were strung along both sides of the bay and up the steep hills above. He followed the main road down past assorted heavy industry and turned off onto the eastern

shore road which twisted up and down the hilly side of the harbour. The streets were dark and quiet, but as he drew closer, he
caught glimpses of the main pier, ablaze in lights and bustling
with movement. Trucks and SUVs were parked helter-skelter
along the road and on the gravel verges, their occupants crowding against the cordon at the entrance to the concrete pier. Some
of the townsfolk had binoculars, Chris noticed, while others had
cellphone cameras, even in this remote nook of the island. St.
Anthony, he quickly learned, had an excellent cellphone signal.

An RCMP vehicle blocked access to the pier itself, splashing
the scene in eerie red and blue. For good measure, yellow tape
had also been strung across the entrance road. Stubby shrimp
boats bobbed in a line along the pier, and rigging clanked in the
stiff night wind.

Chris drew his own, very unofficial-looking GMC Silverado
right up behind the RCMP vehicle, prompting a warning shout
from the uniformed constable standing guard at the tape. Chris
fumbled in his jacket for his ID as he climbed out.

"Corporal Tymko from Deer Lake," he said. "Looking for
Corporal Biggs."

The constable snapped to attention. "He's up on the boat, sir.
The body's still in the net. We're waiting for the medical examiner."

Chris was amused. His corporal rank was brand-new; not so
long ago, he'd been standing at the bottom of the ladder himself,
gazing upwards in awe and hope. The constable pointed out the
small shrimp vessel rocking in the water at the end of the pier.
The edge of the pier was cluttered with storage boxes, netting,
and coils of rope, but the pavement next to the boat was clear. As
Chris strode along the pier, breathing in the sea air tanged with
fish and salt, he mentally braced himself. Bodies pulled out of the
sea could be bloated and chewed beyond recognition. *As long as
it isn't Phil*, he repeated to himself over and over, *I'll be fine.*

The detachment commander's vehicle was parked beside the boat with its engine running and three people huddled beneath blankets inside, obviously chilled by the wind that licked off the ocean. Part of the crew, he assumed, suffering as much from shock as cold.

Powerful floodlights had been set up on the pier to supplement the boat's lights, and, looking beyond the boat's high steel hull, Chris could clearly see two men inside the cabin. One was pacing, while the other projected a quiet, watchful attention. After showing his ID to the constable in the DC's cruiser, Chris clambered aboard and ducked into the cabin. The stench of fish nearly closed his nostrils and he suppressed a gag. He wondered, irrelevantly, whether the crew could ever wash themselves clean of the smell.

Corporal Biggs lived up to his name in breadth as well as height, and his florid face and bulbous nose suggested a fondness for Newfoundland screech. He reminded Chris of an oversized leprechaun, but there was no hint of mischief or merriment in his eyes tonight. A waft of booze floated around him as he shook Chris's hand and thanked him for coming.

Chris glanced out the cabin window. The boat deck was empty, but suspended above it by ropes was a huge net of shrimp "Where's the body, sir?"

"Still in the net as per the instructions we were given."

"May I see it?"

"Why?"

"I'd like to rule out a missing person."

Biggs grunted. "All in good time. Nothing to see yet but a hand, a foot, and some clothes. It's a waiting game until the doc pronounces."

"Any damn fool can see he's dead!" snapped the man who'd been pacing. He wore a seaman's cap and a heavy wool jacket.

Biggs hadn't bothered to introduce him, but Chris took him to be the skipper.

"Well, I know that, Norm," Biggs said, "but those are the rules."

"Meanwhile I'll have to throw all that catch away."

"Probably a wise move, anyway. Not too much call for shrimp that's been cozying up to a dead body for hours."

The skipper sank onto the stool by the wheel and yanked off his cap to rub his bald head. "Can't you at least let my kids go home? They been days on the boat and hours without food or rest."

"I'll arrange for some food. We have to take their statements before they go."

"What statements? We all saw the same t'ing! We pulled up the net, this foot near falls out, and we called to shore. You know the rest!"

Chris sympathized with the exasperated skipper. What the hell had Biggs and his detachment been doing since they got here? He'd seen shock take many forms in his career. As a seaman, Norm had probably experienced his share of drama and tragedy over his lifetime, but pulling a dead man up in his net was likely a first. Worrying about his children was a natural reaction.

"I can take their statements if that helps, sir," he said.

"Good idea. Take Constable Leger there with you. One by one, so they don't contaminate each other's stories."

Contaminate! Chris nearly laughed aloud as he descended onto the pier. Their stories had all been well contaminated during their wait in the car, if not on the twelve-hour trip back to port, but he held his tongue. More than once, a smart quip had landed him in trouble with his superiors, and if he ever wanted to make it up the career ladder in a police force with no sense of humour, he had to learn to behave.

It appeared the entire contingent of St. Anthony RCMP offi-cers was at the scene, but since it also appeared the entire town had turned out for the drama, Chris didn't suppose it mattered. He opened the cruiser door and peered at the expectant faces gazing back at him. Two men and a young woman. They all looked a pale shade of green, but perhaps that was the light.

He picked the woman and ushered her to a quiet corner of the pier. She hunched over against the wind. Her thin frame didn't begin to fill out the huge wool jacket that she hugged around her-self, but the dark eyes that appraised him were shrewd and sure.

"He's not a local, you know," she said before he could even record her name.

"You saw his face?"

"No, but not wit' 'dem clothes. Nudding on him but a plaid jacket, pants, and running shoes. You don't go out to sea like that."

"Maybe he was on the land."

"What? And swam 250 kilometres out to sea? Some trick, that!"

He laughed and asked her name. "Liz Parsons. My dad's the skipper. Me and my brothers crews for him when we're not in school. But we'll all tell you the same. This time of year, none of us locals would be wearing thin clothes like that. Don't keep the wind out at all. Most likely a tourist. You check whale-watching tours, I bet you'll find someone fell overboard."

Chris suspected those had already been checked, but he nodded appreciatively. "Good idea, Liz. What can you tell me about the area he was snagged?"

"It's prime shrimp waters, about 250 kilometres northeast of St. Anthony. Also has lots of other ground fish. It's about a hundred metres deep 'dere, but I can't tell you if we caught 'im on the bottom or in between. We didn't know he was 'dere until we hauled the net aboard."

Chris cast about for more questions. He knew nothing about the sea or the behaviour of bodies within it. The closest he'd come was Great Slave Lake in the Northwest Territories, where fishermen and unlucky tourists were occasionally caught out in a deadly storm. He knew that in fresh, warm water lakes, bodies sank to the bottom immediately and began to rise again after about a week as they bloated with gas. But the salt water and frigid temperatures of the North Atlantic could change all that.

"Is it possible to guess — say, from the prevailing winds or the current — what direction he likely came from?"

"Labrador current comes down the coast," she said, gesturing with her arms, "and the gulf current comes up the strait, so it can be tricky, but mostly easterly. So he could be from anywhere on the coast of Labrador to the open North Atlantic."

"Did you see any other boats around the area of your net?"

She snorted. "We was out there four days, towed miles with that net. That's prime fishing, so lots of boats going to and fro. But none of them hires on townies wearing running shoes and plaid jackets."

"Did you see any non-fishing boats?"

"You sees all kinds of t'ings. Trawlers, tankers, even cruise ships. And I don't spend all my days peering out to sea. I'm down in the hold sometimes too."

"Come on, Liz. You know what I mean. Anything odd? Suspicious? It would be a big help to our investigation."

The flattery worked. She shrugged in her nonchalant way, but narrowed her eyes as if thinking. While he waited, a vehicle turned off the road onto the pier to the murmur of the crowd, and the guard constable moved his cruiser to allow it access. Chris watched as it drove along the pier and pulled up beside the boat. A man climbed out, carrying a small suitcase. The medical examiner, Chris hoped. Liz watched him too, as he disappeared on board and then turned to Chris with a shrug.

"Maybe a couple of sailing yachts I was surprised to see out that far, some offshore trawlers."

Chris felt a quiver of interest. "Did they have names? Numbers?"

"Couldn't see."

"Would you recognize them if you saw them again?"

"Maybe." She pointed to the large ship moored in front of her father's boat. "Could be that one, but I couldn't make out the name. Lots of ships from places I never heard of. If it floats, that's all that matters."

The cabin door of the boat opened and Corporal Biggs stuck his head out. "Hey, Tymko!" he shouted. "You got a decent camera on you?"

Chris nodded. "In my truck."

"You any good with it? Low light and all?"

Chris was already moving, after a hasty thank you to Liz. Within two minutes he was up on the deck, fighting off the stench of fish as he stared at the seething ball of shrimp and netting that was still suspended from the frame above. Bits of foot and arms, and, incongruously, a vividly patterned jacket, were just visible amid the mass.

The doctor was already backing away, pressing his hand to his nose. "Put the biggest tarp you can find underneath, and we'll empty the net on it. That way, if there are parts of him ... ah ... loose, we'll get them all. Then use the hoist to move the whole thing off the boat. Once you get the tarp down on the pier, I'll have a better look."

Both the skipper and Biggs went in search of a tarp, leaving Chris alone with the body. He circled it, photographing it from all angles and scrutinizing it for hints as to its identity. He wracked his brains. Would Phil wear such a brightly coloured jacket? Possibly. Many of his clothes had been bought in Asia or Africa. The one visible running shoe was filthy and frayed, providing little protection or comfort.

Chris had just finished photographing when the men arrived back, hauling a large tarp, which they unfolded beneath the net. Chris watched in fascination as they worked the pulleys and tugged the net onto the centre.

"Try to release it slowly," the medical examiner said. "I don't want any fingers or toes going flying off the edge."

A complicated-looking knot held the ball in place. Once released, the bottom of the net burst open, spilling its contents of wriggling pink shrimp all over the tarp. Then came the body, jackknifing open from the ball onto the tarp, its limbs hitting the metal floor with a clunk. Chris had switched to video to capture the whole process, pausing only briefly when the head snapped back and long strands of coarse black hair fell back from the face. He raced forward for a close look at the perfectly preserved face, the Roman nose, high cheekbones, and sunken, nibbled eyes.

Not Phil! He nearly cheered aloud.

"That poor bastard's been down there no time at all," said the skipper. "The sea critters have barely started their dinner."

Corporal Biggs poked the foot gingerly. "Not much rigor mortis, either. Of course, the sea is damn cold. We'll let the boys in St. John's figure out —"

He stopped in surprise when a length of thick yellow rope came into view through the cascade of shrimp, one end of it peeking out from the waist of the coloured jacket. A second later the rest of the rope plunged through.

They all stared as a stone anchor crashed to the tarp with a thud.

CHAPTER EIGHT

Within seconds, Corporal Biggs was on the phone to the RCMP Major Crimes Unit in Corner Brook for advice on how to proceed. Judging from his tense, red face, Chris suspected Biggs had never faced a murder investigation in which the trail of blood did not lead straight to the perpetrator in the next room.

It was remotely possible that the deceased had not been murdered but had died instead from some misadventure or illness on the boat, and his companions had attempted a primitive burial at sea. If so, of course, they should have reported the death the moment they landed ashore. That was Biggs's first question to Corner Brook. No such deaths had been reported, Corner Brook replied, and advised him to sit tight until they could mobilize the Major Crimes Unit.

While Biggs was on the phone, Chris rummaged carefully through the man's pockets, finding nothing other than a sodden paper with some illegible printing scrawled on it. He knew the search went against protocol, but he doubted much forensic evidence would be left on the body after its watery travels. He stuffed the paper back and busied himself taking close-up shots of the body, particularly elements that might help with identification — the garish jacket, the dirty shoes, and, most importantly, the man's face.

He suspected they were in for a long night. Amanda had already texted him multiple times to ask whether the body was Phil. He was finally able to reassure her.

"Whew!" she replied. "Then who is it?"

"Don't know yet," he said.

He was just finishing up the photos when Biggs reappeared. The man seemed calmer now that he had sent the problem higher up. "They're sending the helicopter over from Moncton to evacuate the DOA to St. John's, and forensics and major crimes teams will drive up from Corner Brook in the morning to head up the investigation. Meanwhile, they instructed us to bring the body onto the pier so the medical examiner can do a preliminary examination, and to take witness statements from the crew and harbour staff so folks can go home. We're to keep the scene secured."

Chris stepped forward. "I can take statements, sir."

"Let's get the poor bugger off the boat first."

It was almost midnight by the time the officers managed to hoist the body, wrapped in the tarp, off the boat deck and onto the pier, where they laid it out under the bright RCMP spotlights. Chris took more photos while the medical examiner, who had been keeping warm in his car, re-emerged for a closer look. He lifted the clothing, moved the body carefully from side to side, and probed it for broken bones and lacerations. Then he took a temperature reading and used a powerful flashlight to look into the man's eyes, ears, and mouth. Finally he pressed hard on the victim's chest. Only a faint gurgle and a trickle of foam escaped his lips.

As he worked, he dictated into his iPhone and Chris bent close to catch every word. "Victim is an adult white male estimated age twenty-five to forty years, approximately six feet, thin build. There are no obvious broken bones or signs of trauma, only superficial lacerations on his exposed flesh that appear consistent with marine feeding. He appears malnourished and has had several teeth pulled. Health and dental care seem to have been poor."

"That goes along with the shoes and clothes," Chris said to Biggs, who was observing beside him. "This is not a rich guy."

"Not a tourist, either," said the skipper. "Look at his hands. Calloused, nails broken off. This feller did hard, dirty labour." He held out his own hands. "Just like my hands. You never get the dirt and slime out of them."

"A fisherman, then?" Chris asked.

"Not in them clothes."

The doctor cast them an annoyed glance before resuming his dictation in a louder voice. "Body temp is five degrees, probably about the same as the ambient water temperature where he was. Where was that?"

"We was 250 kilometres northeast. I gave Biggs here the coordinates."

"There's no visible mud or ocean silt in his mouth or ears, and rigor is minimal. At those temps, that's not unexpected, but those two facts taken together, I'd say he wasn't in the water too long."

"Can you tell how he died?" Biggs said.

The doctor sat back on his heels. "No water in his lungs. Now, cardiac arrest or laryngeal spasm could have killed him when he entered the cold water …"

"But he could have been dead before he hit the water?"

"That's one possibility of several." He straightened with a creak and a groan. "Well, I've done what I can. The autopsy in St. John's should tell us more, but meanwhile you can treat the death as suspicious."

Chris looked over at the ring of townspeople still pressed against the tape. A few had departed but most waited for news, worried about family and loved ones up and down the coast.

"How about I show the photos to the boat crew and the locals, sir. See if anyone recognizes him or has any relevant information. Then they can go home."

"Good idea." Biggs gestured to the constable on guard. "Send the photos to Leger too and we'll split up the interviews. It's going to be a long night."

People crowded around as Chris approached. Relief showed on their faces as one by one they shook their heads. They didn't know who the dead man was, but a few echoed Norm Parsons's belief that he was not a fisherman, indeed not likely even a native Newfoundlander.

"He don't look like one of us," said one elderly woman swathed in scarves and shawls. Chris knew that of all Canada, Newfoundland had the most homogeneous population. It was 95 percent white and Christian, comprised mostly of immigrants from southwestern England and southeastern Ireland. Many Newfoundlanders had the sturdy, compact frames, round faces, and blunt features of that gene pool, and Chris suspected the homogeneity, indeed, the shared bloodlines, was even greater in the remote fishing villages, some of which had been founded by a single family or two.

Like these Newfoundlanders, he had grown up in a fairly homogeneous community in rural Saskatchewan, settled by immigrants who had fled Europe at the same time and been granted land in the newly developing Prairies. In his case, however, they had been from the Ukraine. His mother could spot a kinsman at a single glance.

He studied the photo carefully, trying to see what the woman saw. The subtle differences that would set him apart from the locals. The dead man's features were sharper, his nose finer, and his skin, although grey and mottled from the sea water, looked darker. Not at all the British and Irish stock on which

Newfoundland had been built. Italian, perhaps? Or Middle Eastern?

Either way, he was a long way from home.

Amanda woke the next morning revelling in the soft mattress and the warm duvet. Outside, the surf ebbed and flowed against the rocks and sunlight slanted in through the motel window. Her languid stretch woke Kaylee, who crawled up to snuggle, her exuberant tail thumping the bed.

Amanda felt a warm thrill. She had slept without interruptions or dreams, without an all too familiar backdrop of formless dread. She sat up, wishing the feeling would never end, and headed into the shower. Only when she was sitting in the breakfast room with her first cup of coffee did she pull out her cellphone. To her surprise, she had a signal. One bar, but she would take it.

Chris had texted three more times during the night, first to tell her the man was likely not a local, second to say the death looked suspicious, and third to say a major crimes team would be arriving in the morning. "Sh-h!" he'd added. "Don't repeat that!" The last text had been at 3:00 a.m.

She smiled. How she wished he were here, with his teasing banter and crinkly grin, helping her figure out their next steps together. Poor Chris. It appeared as if he hadn't slept all night. In the hope he might finally be resting, she decided not to reply until later. She had nothing urgent to report yet anyway. Phil had had a drunken argument with a stranger, Tyler had explored a fishing stage, and they may or may not have gone off with the stranger at the end of the night.

The motel owner approached to refill her coffee and take her order of eggs and toast. "Where's your friend?" he asked with a twinkle in his eye. "His bed wasn't touched last night."

Amanda laughed. "No, he was called away. He's a cop."

The twinkle vanished. "Oh, that dead body down S'n Ant'ny?"

How news travels, Amanda thought. Of course, even here in this land where cell signals could evaporate in a strong wind, there were probably tweets and videos all over the Internet. "What are people saying about it?" she asked.

"From away. Off a boat, most likely. One of them big foreign freezer trawlers that's always sneaking into our waters. Some of them gots thirty, forty workers on 'em, paid next to nudding. Poor bugger probably fell overboard. Or jumped, hoping to swim ashore."

Mindful of Chris's admonition, Amanda said nothing about the major crimes unit. "Factory freezer trawler. That sounds ominous."

"It is. They's killing the local fishing industry all along the coast. Not just here, but in coastal communities all around the world. Big international corporations that can take in a haul of five hundred tons of fish at one go, freeze it on the boat, and ship it all over the place. Strips the fish right out of the water. First the cod, and now they're doing it to the shrimp. Most of it goes to Asia."

Amanda thought about the argument Phil had had with the stranger in the pub, who'd said he just wanted to go home. "What countries are these foreign ships from?"

"Oh, all over d' world, my dear. The United States, Norway, Korea, you name it. Mind you, the government's tried to put a few limits in place since all the cod disappeared. They tossed a bone to the Newfoundlanders here that were losing their livelihoods by extending Canadian waters to two hundred miles offshore and banning foreign-owned ships inside that — Jaysus b'y, dat was a helluva fight — but there's a lot of ocean for Fisheries and Oceans to patrol to keep the foreign boats out, and even the Canadian trawlers ship their catch to Asia. Still cuts the local fisherman out of the lion's share." He rolled his eyes and turned away. "Oh, don't get me started on Ottawa! Let me get them eggs on for you instead, darlin'."

Once he'd disappeared into the kitchen, Amanda browsed through news and Twitter updates. The official news reports made no mention of possible murder, and apparently the lighting had been poor enough that none of the spectators and cellphone addicts had seen anything suspicious. Speculation was along the same lines as the motel owner — a foreigner off a trawler. From the tone of most of the comments, little sympathy was being wasted on him.

Her phone buzzed, startling her. She glanced at the call display and her breath caught with hope.

"Hi, Sheri!"

"Any news?" Sheri sounded tense and focused.

Amanda wished she could be more reassuring. "Chris and I have picked up his trail on the northern peninsula," she said, avoiding mention of Phil's black moods and heavy drinking. "The good news is, he's still following a plan."

"He sent me a letter."

"When?"

"It arrived yesterday."

Who sends a letter? Amanda thought. *Not an email, but a letter!* "What did he say?"

"It was a thank-you letter. I know that sounds crazy, but that's what it was. Short and to the point. Thank you for giving me twelve great years and the joy of Tyler, thank you for taking a wreck of a man back and being so patient."

Amanda's breath caught. This was not a thank-you letter. While she was searching for the right words, Sheri supplied them. Her voice filled with tears. "He's saying goodbye, Amanda. He says he hopes I find a better life. Sweet Jesus! What about Tyler?"

Amanda pictured Phil with his son as she remembered them. Phil clowning, Tyler laughing — an intense, intellectual boy made playful by his father's infectious nature. *Phil, what the hell are you up to?*

"Sheri, it's time to report —"

"Jason's on it. He was so worried when he saw the letter that he's gone looking himself."

"What do you mean, gone looking?"

"I mean, he's booked off work, packed his truck, and gone looking. I wanted to go with him, but he said I had to stay here, in case Phil or Tyler got in touch."

"Sheri, you need to make an official report!"

"Jason did. The alerts are out. But one angry husband taking off on a bender? Jason says that'll be nothing but a little footnote on the police blotter."

Amanda scrambled for an answer. She thought of how quickly news had spread about the dead body. How Twitter and other social media had changed communication, even here.

"Get his picture out on Facebook, Sheri."

"I don't know how —"

"Then learn!"

A shocked silence fell. Anger, frustration, and fear roiled in the gulf between them. Amanda resisted the urge to apologize for her outburst. Sheri was a capable, resourceful woman, but she needed to be shocked into action. Finally Sheri drew a deep breath. "I will," she said. "And please! For the love of God, keep me in the loop, Amanda. I don't care what you think of me, that's my son out there."

Amanda felt a twinge of shame as she hung up. Sheri was right; she *had* been blaming her. But who was she, Amanda, to pass judgment? To hold herself above reproach? Who knew for sure how nobly they would react when desperation stared them down?

She was poring over the map with renewed urgency when the motel owner returned with her eggs still sizzling on the plate. His smile faded at the sight of her.

"Bad news?"

Amanda managed a wan smile of thanks as she took the plate from him. "I'm not sure. My friend is doing some worrying and puzzling things. He met another man at the pub where they went for dinner. Did he bring anyone back with him afterward?"

He gave her a quizzical look. "I was dead to the world, barely heard the truck. But the next morning, there was only him and the boy at breakfast."

"Did you overhear any of their plans?"

"Well, your friend wasn't much for talking. Mostly sat there staring at his food and looking at the map. The boy did the talking for two."

"What about?"

"Fishing nets, boats, birds. About a boat trip he wanted to take out to an island."

"Do you know where?"

"No, but the father didn't seem interested. Was looking at some places more remote."

"Where? Up at the northern tip?"

"Well now, that's a busy place what with the Viking stuff and St. Anthony being a big regional centre. But there's plenty to interest a young boy. Icebergs coming down from the Arctic, polar bears coming ashore on the floes, lots of moose, black bears, and birds. Beautiful country."

A family entered the restaurant and the owner gave her a quick wink before veering over to tend to them. Amanda's eggs grew cold as she bent over the map of the Great Northern Peninsula, looking for inspiration. Chris was up in St. Anthony, where the shrimp boat carrying the body was docked. The vast

North Atlantic opened up to the north and east of the town. The dead man could have been aboard a fishing trawler, or any other boat for that matter, and met his fate anywhere in the open sea before drifting into the shrimp boat's path.

As the motel owner said, the northern tip was dotted with settlements and tourist sites, but farther down the eastern side, the villages became separated by vast swaths of empty coastline, with a smattering of remote islands designated as ecological reserves. A third of the way down the peninsula, the road petered out all together.

As wild and untouched as it was possible to find.

CHAPTER NINE

"I'm on my way up there," Amanda texted Chris once she was packed and astride her motorcycle, ready to hit the road. "I may have a lead on Phil."

That was a considerable exaggeration, for it was more a theory than a lead, a theory held together mostly by spit and hope. But since it took her toward a reunion with Chris, it didn't really matter. She'd flesh out the theory as she rode.

On paper, the trip to St. Anthony looked like a simple ninety-minute ride, but she had forgotten the many little fishing villages she had to check out along the way. As she took the occasional stop to shake out her muscles and give Kaylee a break, she asked the local villagers whether they had seen Phil and Tyler pass through.

Only one person remembered seeing them. Amanda was detouring through a little village with the typically quirky Newfoundland name of Nameless Cove, when she spotted a fisherman painting the trim of his old lobster boat bright red. He seemed grateful for the chance to lay down his brush.

"Yes, I remember them. The boy was after having a trip on my boat. I can do that, I said, if you don't mind sinking to the bottom. She's a few holes in her yet."

"Did they have another man with them?"

"Not that I saw, but the truck windows were dark. I offered to take them in my brother's boat, but the father now, he were more interested in mine. How far out to sea could I take her and how many crew did she carry? She could go all the way to Labrador, I told him, and up north too, but her fishing days are over. I'm getting her ready to sell. She's too small to compete with the bigger shrimp boats, and since gas prices have gone up and the government cut back our shrimp quotas, I can't make enough to pay a loan on a sixty-five-footer." He picked up his brush again. "So some millionaire from New York will probably buy her and sail her around the Caribbean Islands. Not a bad life for the old girl, that."

"And what will you do?"

He shrugged. "Try to get hired on somewheres. Maybe a bigger boat, maybe even a trawler. Like your friend said, the bigger fish always eats the little ones. Way of the world, he said. He was some disgusted."

She'd wished the fisherman luck and continued on up the coast, mulling over the man's words. Phil's mood did not appear to have improved since that night in the bar, but at least he seemed to be continuing his quest to give his son an ocean adventure.

It was past one o'clock by the time she cruised down the hill into St. Anthony. All the fame and hype aside, it was still a modest town of boxy wooden buildings sprinkled higgledy-piggledy Newfoundland-style along the shores of the narrow harbour. A large, modern-looking pier and fish facility dominated the eastern waterfront and even from a distance one massive ship dwarfed the others at the wharf. She found the RCMP station on the main road without difficulty and walked in to find the room crowded with men, all peering intently at a computer screen. Chris's tall, lanky form towered above the rest. His brow was furrowed in intense concentration that broke at the sight of her. An easy smile lit up his face. He introduced her to the ring of curious men — a coast guard officer, the harbourmaster, and three RCMP officers, including a major crimes investigator from Corner Brook.

"Any idea who the dead man is?" she asked.

"No, but he looks —" Chris managed before the investigator cut him off.

"The investigation is ongoing."

Canned cop-speak, she thought, trying to steal a peek at the computer screen. It appeared to be an ocean chart, and an official-looking logbook lay open on the desk. The investigator moved to block her view.

"Corporal Tymko," he said, "your assistance has been invaluable, and thank you for responding to the emergency call-up. My team has the investigation well in hand now, so you may go back to your holiday." His Adam's apple bobbed as he leered at Amanda.

Chris flushed. "Not a holiday, sir. We're looking for our missing friend."

The investigator tipped his head in a small acknowledgement that revealed not the slightest interest or concern. "Then carry on, Corporal. We'll take it from here."

Only once Chris was outside the door and safely out of earshot did he call the man a poker-assed idiot.

Amanda laughed. "So why all the secrecy? Or is that just the way you guys operate."

"Yeah, we can all be poker-assed idiots when we have to be. But in this case I told them I thought the guy might be from the Middle East, so now the whole national security paranoia has kicked in. A few days ago, a boatload of unknown occupants was spotted off the coast not far south of here —"

Kaylee gave an outraged bark from the prison of her trailer, breaking Chris's mood. He headed over to say hello. "Come on,

I'm starving. Let's spring this young lady from her prison and find a nice seaside patio."

The sun was shining but a chilly wind raced down the harbour, slicing through her jacket and whipping red into her cheeks. When she cast him an incredulous look, she saw the twinkle in his eye. Within fifteen minutes, after giving Kaylee a quick walk, they had settled into the Lightkeeper's Restaurant at the tip of Fishing Point. They took a table by the window overlooking the ocean cliffs that formed the mouth of the harbour. Not quite a seaside patio, but spectacular nonetheless.

After they'd both ordered a large bowl of seafood chowder, Chris spread a map out on the table. In the soft afternoon light, he traced a finger over the coast and tapped a little village farther down the eastern shore of the peninsula. "Four or five men were spotted in a lifeboat by a local man here. They looked to be in distress, but when he went out to help, they sped away. The locals didn't recognize the boat or the men, and thought they might have been fugitives. Possibly foreign. Now we have a deceased individual picked up approximately here …" He moved his finger way out into the open sea northeast of the peninsula tip. "Prime fishing grounds, inside Canadian waters. But the dead man wasn't dressed like a fisherman, and odds are he's foreign."

"So you're thinking there may be a connection. He fell out of the lifeboat or something?"

Chris hesitated. He studied her soberly. "The man had an anchor tied around his waist."

Amanda's eyes widened. "They *threw* him overboard?"

"Possibly after he was already dead. We might know more after the autopsy. That is, Sergeant Poker-Ass might. I won't learn a thing. But they're thinking foreign national, possibly illegal, possibly murdered, so they're dragging in all the big guns — Coast Guard, Border Services, Fisheries and Oceans Canada.

When you arrived, they were looking at all the foreign vessels passing through that section of ocean, and looking at wind and ocean currents too, to see in what direction the body and the lifeboat would have drifted."

"And? Did they have any theories?"

"There are several foreign trawlers — Korean, American, and Russian — all supposedly fishing outside the two-hundred-mile limit, but that's a hell of a big area to patrol with a few over-worked DFO and Coast Guard vessels. If you knew their patrol schedule, you could sneak in. Sometimes it comes down to our fishermen sounding the alert."

"And have they?"

"We hadn't got to that report yet."

"I'm sorry I interrupted. You might have learned more."

He shrugged. "Poker-Ass would have kicked me out as soon as he remembered I was there."

The waitress brought their chowder, thick and garnished with shrimp. Chris paused to take a spoonful, closing his eyes to savour the moment. Exclaiming in ecstasy, he downed three more mouthfuls before returning to the task at hand. "It's an interesting mystery, but it's going to bog down in forensic and procedural minutiae. And we have our own case to pursue."

"Which has its own foreign connection!" she interjected, filling him in on the man Phil had met in the pub. "It may mean nothing — Phil's always talking to complete strangers about their lives — but it sure ruined his mood."

Pausing to sip her chowder, she let her gaze drift out the window. Houses and businesses were scattered in the hills as far as she could see. Far too settled for Phil's current state.

"There's more." She told Chris about the letter Phil had sent to Sheri. "I don't know exactly when he sent it, but at least a couple of days ago, so maybe after his argument with the foreign man in the café. I was hoping this trip with his son would gradually comfort him, but he seems more bitter than ever. Since Africa, his faith in humanity has taken quite a beating. That night might have been a tipping point. I don't know …" A vice closed on her chest. "I don't know what he's thinking. I can't believe he'd endanger his son …"

"Then let's not assume the worse." Chris leaned in, his fingers almost touching hers as he pointed to the map. "One of the locals told me there's a beautiful private campground down here that juts right into the ocean."

She followed his finger. "It's still pretty close to St. Anthony."

"Look at it," he said. "There's nothing around but wide-open spaces and ocean. It's a perfect retreat. And the nights are so cold right now only fools and hermits would stay there. I bet you a gourmet campfire dinner Phil the hermit is there."

Seeing the mischief in his eyes, she felt the vice ease. "You cooking?"

"Foil-roasted potatoes, salad, and barbequed steaks with a Prairie boy's killer homemade BBQ sauce."

She sat back, savouring the thought. "You're on. I might even throw in a bottle of wine."

The camp proprietor swung around in surprise when Amanda and Chris pulled into the empty parking lot. He was a massive bear of a man with a thick red beard and arms the size of tree trunks. He was tossing fire logs onto a pile as if they were matchsticks, but he dropped the task to hurry toward them as if he hadn't had human contact in a week. He was red-faced and sweating in a toque, wool jacket, and thick gloves.

"You're a brave pair! Welcome to the Arctic Circle. We had a polar bear come by for a visit almost right where you're standing."

Amanda blinked. Black bears were scary enough, but polar

bears had a reputation for being the most aggressive of all bears. The man laughed. "Don't worry. That was in the spring, and they're only after fish and seals, not us. Although that —" He pointed to Kaylee, who was shoving her nose out the truck window eagerly "— might be a tasty treat. Sam Pilgrim's the name. What can I do for you?"

"We're looking for a nice campsite near the ocean but out of the wind, and with room for two tents," Chris said.

"Two tents? Oh, one for the dog, you mean." Sam laughed at his own joke. "We've got all kinds of sites. Drive around and take your pick."

"Not too many campers?"

"We had some on the weekend and a few coming next weekend, but right now you've got the place to yourselves."

Amanda's heart sank. "A father and son aren't here?"

The man's florid face lit up. "Yeah! Phil and his boy. Yeah, they were here, going to stay a week, but I guess the wind scared them off. We had some blow that day."

"When was this?" Chris asked.

"Day before yesterday."

Amanda groaned. She and Chris were still two days behind! "Did they say where they were going?"

"Didn't see them go. They left in the morning to explore St. Anthony and never came back. Well, they came back, because their gear was packed up and gone, but I was out at one of the other sites. Big surf washed it out in the windstorm." He looked skyward, where the sun shimmered serenely in the blue sky. "But the wind's died down and it's looking pretty quiet for this evening, so pick as close to the ocean as you like, and I'll be along in a bit with some wood."

As Chris and Amanda walked back toward his truck, he turned to her. "I win."

"What are you talking about? He came, he saw, and he left. I win."

He stopped so abruptly she bumped into him. She jumped back instinctively, then blushed. His eyes crinkled as he gazed down at her.

"Okay, you're right. No one wins. Besides, we've got the wine and steaks in the cooler already. We can have a campfire feast and still live to bet another day."

The campground was beautiful. Each generous site was tucked away in a private nook surrounded by salt marshes, woodlands, and rocky points. They avoided the ones with the most spectacular ocean views and icy Arctic winds, opting instead for a sheltered clearing with a curtain of balsam fir and a bed of soft needles. Kaylee roamed in delight while they pitched their tents. Just as they were laying out cooking supplies, Kaylee's ferocious barking announced the arrival of the proprietor on his ATV, bearing a load of firewood.

"Well now," he said, eying Amanda's minuscule pup tent. "That's far too small for the dog. He'll get claustrophobic in that."

"Nick of time, Sam," said Chris. "I was about to chop down one of your trees."

"Don't you dare! They take more than a hundred years to grow to that height in this climate."

Amanda had a brief flash of the magnificent jungles of Africa, overflowing with lush greenery beneath a canopy of trees so tall you couldn't see their tips. Here on the coast of northern Newfoundland, not a single tree looked taller than thirty feet.

Sam settled himself comfortably on a rock by the fireside and eyed Chris's steaks wistfully. To Amanda's surprise, Chris spoke before she could.

"Would you like to join us, Sam?"

He accepted with alacrity and set about lighting the fire

while Chris prepared a foil packet of carrots and potatoes. Soon the aroma and sizzle of steak filled the air, and just as Amanda was rummaging in the supplies for the wine, Sam produced a bottle of Scotch.

"My contribution to the party."

Two hours later, with the steaks a distant memory and a soft darkness falling, they were nearing the bottom of the bottle. Amanda's eyes were beginning to close, and she was just wondering how to politely send Sam on his way when he suddenly switched the topic back to Phil. They had covered the state of the world, climate change, fishing, tourists, and even the meaning of life in a free-wheeling, increasingly incoherent conversation.

"Now your friend there," Sam said out of the blue, "he wasn't happy about the state of the world, either. Pretty much figured we were all going to hell on a freight train. I felt sorry for his boy, to be honest, because all he wanted was to see whales and icebergs, and Jesus, he was some excited about that polar bear. Travelled in on an ice floe, so the boy wanted to go out in a boat the very next day to look for ice floes."

Amanda's fatigue evaporated. "Maybe that's where they went. Are there boat tours around here they could have taken?"

"Are there boats?" Sam laughed. "You been down the harbour in St. Anthony yet? Nothing but boats, darlin'. But your friend didn't want a boat tour. He was interested in fishing. Deep-sea fishing. He wanted to know what fish were out there and what the regulations were, and if there were any trawlers in port that fished way out in the ocean. There's no recreational sea fishing for a couple of weeks yet, and it's late in the season for the commercial fishery. There's only one trawler in port at the moment, so maybe he was going down to talk to the captain. Maybe he persuaded the captain to take him and the boy aboard for a day or two."

"Is that allowed?"

The proprietor shrugged. "Who's gonna know? Lots of stuff happens out there on the high seas with no one around for miles to see. The captain calls the shots, and the crew's not going to care. They're just happy to have a job."

Half an hour later, with some trepidation, Chris and Amanda propped the camp proprietor back on his ATV and aimed him on his way. They stood in the flickering orange light of their campfire, watching his headlights waver down the path until the trees swallowed him up. Soon even the growl of the engine was lost in the murmur of surf.

"If I thought he was going to run into anything more than a moose," Chris said, "I'd never have let him drive off. He drank more than half that bottle of Scotch!"

She smiled. "We still have our bottle of wine." She breathed in the musky, salt-washed air of the woods and listened to the night chorus of insects and frogs. In the distance the surf whispered. "Let's take it to the ocean," she said.

Chris looked at the stack of dirty dishes by the fire, and then across at her. He shrugged. "We'll put another log on. No point inviting the bears along to the party, but the fire will keep them away."

Sparks shot high into the air and the fresh wood snapped as it caught fire. Amanda turned away to fight a sudden frisson of fear. Sometimes she wondered whether she would ever enjoy the warmth and smoky scent of a fire without that shiver of fear. Without the memory of unbearable heat and orange-lit smoke boiling into the night sky.

As if to ground herself, she touched Chris's arm gently while they walked the short distance to the shore by the glow of his wavering flashlight. The black press of trees opened up to a ground cover of sage and grasses, and the hiss of the ocean grew louder. Soon she could distinguish the white tips of waves dancing on molten silver. There was no moon but the sky was clear and the white rocks glowed in the starlight. All memory and fear slid away.

"Turn off the flashlight," she whispered. Together they stood on a tongue of scoured rock until shapes began to emerge from the darkness. Black shadows of land, pale strips of rock, a silver wisp of light across the western sky. And the ocean … dancing, undulating, like onyx glittering with stars.

Transfixed, Amanda walked to the water's edge, sat on the rock, and hugged her knees.

"He was here," she said. "Still alive. Still asking questions. That's a good sign, isn't it?"

"Yes."

"Do you suppose he's on a boat out there right now?"

"Maybe."

"Looking at the same stars, marvelling at the same infinity. Phil used to say the ocean was like the prairie. Home."

Chris eased himself down at her side and poured her a glass of wine. Together they stared out at the sea. Kaylee ranged over the rocks, entranced by smells. Amanda tilted her head to the sprinkle of stars overhead and breathed in the tangy air. Air free of smoke, sweat, and seared flesh. Free of gunpowder.

"Just think," she said. "Every one of those tiny pinpoints of light is a huge ball of fire more powerful than our sun. For over a thousand years, sailors have guided their ships by the stars when there were no other clues or guideposts in the endless wilderness of water." She found the Big Dipper and traced a line from its bowl to a single bright star in the northern sky. She smiled at it.

"Every Girl Guide learns to find her way by the North Star. You will never truly be lost if you can find the North Star." She sobered as reality stole into her joy. "I hope Phil remembers that."

She felt Chris's gaze upon her. Heard his hesitation. "Were you and Phil …?"

"No." She thought about Phil. His laughing, carefree face, the cowlick at his temple that gave him a rakish air, the stubby fingers that could bandage a child and wield an axe with equal skill. She thought of the way he could wiggle his nose to make the children laugh, pull candies out of their ears, and duck-walk across the room.

"It's hard to make close friends on the international aid circuit. Everyone is transitory, moving in and out. You share amazing experiences while you're together, but then you're on to the next post. Friendships don't have a chance to grow deep roots."

"Police postings are like that too. You always have to say goodbye."

And with each goodbye, the sense of loss and solitude builds, she thought. Had she forgotten how to love, how to imagine a future with anyone beyond the next few months? She thought of how Phil had held her on that fateful night, his heart pounding with terror and rage. She had loved him, certainly, with a love seared deep in that moment of terror. But was it more?

"Phil and I have been through a lot together, so there's a bond. But …" Her voice faded. Words were feeble vessels in which to capture the connection she and Phil shared. "But" was all she could muster.

Chris didn't touch her. He didn't even lean in. It was Kaylee who came to her side and nuzzled softly. Chris merely looked up at the stars and out to the ocean. Yet in his silence she sensed his understanding.

———

It was only the next morning, as she was getting ready to leave and tilting her red straw hat against the glorious sun, that he touched her arm.

"We'll find him, Amanda. He's too ornery a bugger to be snuffed out so easily."

CHAPTER TEN

Driving back into St. Anthony the next morning, Chris and Amanda encountered a traffic jam leading to the main turnoff. A small knot of union protesters was stopping cars to hand out flyers. SAVE LOCAL JOBS and FAIR QUOTAS, their signs said.

Once they had cleared the protest, Amanda and Chris wove down the narrow harbour road to the main pier. The large trawler Sam had mentioned was still there, a long, battered shark festooned with nets and cables. Amanda estimated it was nearly two hundred feet long and loomed thirty feet above the water, dwarfing the smaller local shrimp boats at either end. It looked as if it was undergoing maintenance; crew scurried over the wharf and up onto the decks, checking equipment.

The name ACADIA SEAFOOD COMPANY was stencilled on its hull and a Canadian flag flew above the top deck. When Amanda tuned her ear to the crew's conversations, she could hear nothing in a foreign tongue. Chris checked in with the harbourmaster and asked to be directed to the trawler's captain. While they waited, he squinted out toward the sea. "I wonder if I'll get further showing my badge, or not showing it."

"If he's got anything to hide, even if it's got nothing to do with Phil, he'll clam up at the sight of your badge." She grinned. "A lesson I learned on my travels."

He pulled a sad face. "And here I am, such a nice guy. I'd even rescue a fly from a spider's web."

Boots clomped purposefully along the concrete behind them, and they both turned to see a short, stubby man with sausage-like limbs and a barrel chest that strained the zipper of his jacket. He wore a grease-stained ball cap and mirrored sunglasses against the morning sun glancing off the bay. Behind the glasses, his face was inscrutable.

"Captain Boudrot is not here. I'm the chief mate, and I'm on a tight schedule," he said, "so make it quick. Those fucking picketers have thrown everything off."

He had addressed Chris, so Chris took the lead and explained that they were looking for a friend and his son, who had mixed up their rendezvous location.

"We were supposed to go out on a boat together and I understand he came to talk to your captain a couple of days ago."

The man's expression barely changed, but Amanda sensed a curtain falling, shutting them out. He shook his head. "This is a big harbour. Lots of boats come and go. But this is a shrimp trawler, not a pleasure boat. The boat tours run from over there." He flicked a disdainful hand toward a wharf across the bay.

"Thank you," Chris said, without even a glance in that direction. "But we were planning some deep-sea fishing, not a boat tour. I'm told he asked about that possibility."

"I doubt it. The captain's gone down the coast to pick up a new sonar."

When Amanda dug out her phone to show him the photos of Tyler and Phil, he barely gave them a cursory glance. "We don't do recreational fishing, either, even if it was in season, which it's not. You charter those boats from over there too."

"I understand that," she said, "but did you see them at all, sir? We're really at a loss here."

He sighed and tilted his head at the photo thoughtfully. Chris kept quiet, perhaps recognizing that her pleading approach might net better results. "No, I didn't see them. Well, maybe the kid, running down the wharf."

"Where were they heading? Over to the boat tours?"

"Could be. I had better things to do than watch."

The boat tour office was deserted, as was the wharf in front of it. A notice stuck to the window listed their hours as 8:30 to 9:00 a.m., when the boat tour departed, but also gave a phone number underneath for inquiries and reservations. Amanda phoned, but the woman who answered had no record of anyone named Phil Cousins having booked a tour. Just as Amanda was searching for her next question, a pickup truck pulled up outside the office, and a man climbed out. Handsome, confident, and in charge, he asked if he could help.

Amanda trotted out her usual explanation and showed him the photo. His eyes lit up. "I remember that kid. He really wanted a boat tour. We're still offering a half-day whale-watching and coastal tour every morning if the weather is good and we get enough people. But the dad was having none of it. He was going to go talk to the captain of that trawler across the harbour there. Left the kid on the wharf feeding the seagulls. A few minutes later he stormed back over here and said they were leaving. This is crap, I remember him saying. People are crap. That shut the kid up in a hurry."

"Did you notice where they went?" Chris asked. "Or did they mention it?"

"No, just away from here. Away from people, he said. He was in some black mood, that's certain."

Chris and Amanda walked back to their vehicles in silence. From his puckered expression, Amanda suspected he shared her worry. They now had more questions than ever.

Had the chief mate lied about the captain speaking to Phil, or had Phil in fact talked to someone else in the crew? What had put him into such a foul mood? Was he merely angry about being turned down or was there some deeper reason? After years in developing countries, Phil had learned to laugh at minor disappointments, but these days, who could predict what triggers would plunge him into despair?

And the most pressing question of all, where to now? "Away from people," Phil had said. That was their only clue.

The protest had heated up by the time they reached the main intersection again. The Fish, Food & Allied Workers union had formed a blockade across the road and were allowing traffic through only once they'd delivered their pamphlet and speech. Amanda glanced at the pamphlet before stuffing it into her pocket. LOCAL COMPANIES MEAN LOCAL JOBS, the headline proclaimed, with a photo of one of the stubby little shrimp boats she'd seen at wharves all along the coast.

The three officers from the local RCMP detachment, barely recovered from last night's discovery of the body, were struggling to calm the angry nerves of union members and local residents alike, as well as tourists caught in the middle.

Chris angled his cap low and slouched in his seat as they inched by. Afterwards he shot her a sheepish grin. "I'm damned if I'm going to give up more of my time off to police that hornet's nest. Time to get out of Dodge. Which way? North toward Cape Bauld, or south toward Roddickton?"

Amanda had been in charge of studying the map that morning while Chris, who was proving a much more adept campfire cook than her, served up their delicious breakfast of fried eggs and sausage. To the south, except for a few scattered fishing villages, vast swaths of coastline lay empty and untouched, even by road.

If Phil was trying to escape the toxic company of people, he might look no further. "South," she said.

Chris clambered down from his truck to stretch the kinks from his long legs and study the gravel side road that led to the remote coastal village of Croque. They could see the potholes on the road from here.

"How many kilometres of that?"

She snorted. "That's a fabulous road! You should see some of the roads in Africa. They take your tires out at least once a month."

Chris patted the hood of his truck ruefully. "Sorry, baby. I promise you a nice new wheel alignment when we get back home."

Amanda climbed down to join him, taking off her straw hat to shake her long hair loose. The sky was blue, the sun was deliciously warm, and the green hills beckoned. Perfect for an open-air ride.

"Let's leave it here and ride on the back of the Rocket! It's only twenty-five kilometres to Croque, and it might prove to be a complete waste of time and gas."

"No helmet."

"Live dangerously."

"Temptress." His eyes twinkled as he eyed her bike, but she could see the doubt and hesitation in his expression. "I just bought it," he mumbled sheepishly. "I haven't even paid for the logo on the hood. But there's not much room on the back there."

"Nonsense. Overseas, we rode two to a bike all the time. You should see what the locals fit on their bikes. Whole families and all their furniture! I won't even notice you."

As her words hung in the air, she felt her face grow warm. Embarrassed, she looked away. After a brief deliberation, he moved his truck onto a gravel patch off the road, parked it in the shade, and together they wrestled her motorcycle and trailer down the ramp. After a few final tender swipes at the dust on the truck's fender, he climbed aboard behind her. It was a snug fit. She felt the warmth of his body against hers, and the grip of his thighs. Heat rose within her and she was grateful that her helmet and sunglasses hid her blushing face. As she revved the engine, Chris hung his large hands awkwardly at his sides, but at the first pothole, he instinctively clutched her waist before jerking back.

She laughed. "It's safer to hang on," she yelled into the wind. "I promise to respect your virtue."

His arms slid around her again as cautiously as if he were grasping a gossamer web. They bounced and jolted down the road, leaning into the rollercoaster of twists and turns. A ridge of rounded coastal mountains loomed ahead, dense with spruce and fir. The road picked a path through it, climbing and twisting. After an apparent eternity, they began to spot small fenced gardens and stacks of firewood along the roadside, sure signs that they were approaching a village. A picturesque cemetery appeared on their right, well kept and surrounded by a low picket fence. Farther on, the first modest village houses were tucked into the hills.

Amanda had read up on Croque that morning while Chris made breakfast. She knew that it had begun as a French naval station in the mid-seventeenth century to supply and protect the French fishing vessels that fished the coastal waters of western Newfoundland. Three centuries later, the government of France still maintained the small cemetery where its officers had been buried.

The village itself was small, less than two dozen houses scattered like faded children's blocks over the hills. Despite the handful of trucks and cars parked outside, some of them and the washing hung on the lines, it had an abandoned air. As they rumbled through the village, Amanda's heart sank. The hills were gentle, and the ocean, when they finally caught a glimpse of it through the buildings, was a small inland fjord barely wider than a river. A few small fishing boats were tied up to a weather-beaten wharf. There were no wild and rugged cliffs here, no roaring surf.

And no sign of Phil's truck anywhere.

She parked the bike by a sign commemorating the French station, let Kaylee out, and they all waded down through the overgrown grass to the old wharf. All that was left of the grand French presence was a group of ageing wooden stages propping each other up like a row of drunken sailors. The little fjord sparkled serenely in the sun.

"Okay, that was a waste of time," Chris muttered, surreptitiously massaging his rear. "Hard to imagine this little place was once a bustling naval station."

She had to admit he was right. Driving in, she had seen a community centre of sorts, but no other sign of commerce or prosperity. But she heard the sound of hammering nearby and climbed the slope to find an old man repairing the front steps of his home. Quizzically, he watched her approach, as if strangers rarely ventured to this remote little relic of history.

Kaylee raced up to him and dropped a piece of old driftwood at his feet, breaking the awkward moment. The old man laughed as he threw it for her, and she was off, a flash of red through the tall fronds of grass.

"We're looking for our friend," Amanda said, producing her cellphone photos and repeating her story about the mix-up in meeting place. As she spoke, another old man emerged from his house and the two of them had a brief exchange. She couldn't understand a word of it, but could hear the doubt in their voices.

"Yeah, they come by," one of them said finally, "but there's not much here. No place for them to stay, no boats for rent, neither. Only fifteen families here now, and most of them old-timers. The young ones are gone away to work. We told your friend to try Grandois just up the coast."

Another gravel road, as it turned out, that branched off at Croque and led to the open ocean farther north. On the map, Grandois looked even smaller than Croque, so Amanda was delighted when they topped the hill by a little white church and saw a postcard-perfect fishing village spread out below them. Boats of all shapes and sizes lay on the pebble shore or bobbed against the wharf, and gaily painted houses were sprinkled in the meadow that curved around the cove. A few vehicles were parked in front of the houses, a woman was hanging out her laundry, and another played with her baby. Amanda spotted a man working on a fishing net on the wharf and headed down the hill toward him. This time Kaylee bounded gleefully after the sandpipers on the shore.

Chris repeated their story about searching for a friend. As he spoke, other men emerged from yards and houses. Soon a small crowd of men in blue jeans and windbreakers had gathered. Their faces were tanned and creviced by years on the open sea.

"Yes, we seen him," said one. "The man with the young fella. He wanted a boat for a few days to go out to the Grey Islands, but we didn't have none to spare."

"Well now, that's not quite right, Tom," said another, this one older and greyer. "He didn't seem like he knew how to skipper a boat and he had no gear, so no one wanted to rent him theirs."

"I offered to take them out in my boat," said a third. "Show them around the islands. Still a few whales in the bay, and lots of migrating birds. Gannets, terns, puffins. But he weren't interested in that."

"He has some temper on him, your friend," Tom said. "The young fella was tugging on his arm saying it's okay, Dad, we can go back to St. Anthony and take that boat tour. But the dad said he had something much more exciting in mind."

"Even tried to buy my old boat over there," said the older man, pointing to a small skiff lying in the grass. "I said she hadn't been in the water for five years and she'd sink like a stone before she got half a mile off shore."

Amanda shielded her eyes from the glare of the water and stared out to sea. The coastline curved and looped into points and peninsulas, with several small islands within easy view.

"Are those the islands he wanted to visit?" she asked.

"Oh no, m' dear. Some much bigger ones way out in the ocean. You can't see them from here."

She followed his finger but could see nothing but shimmering silver. "How far are they?"

"Oh … a good fifteen, twenty kilometres?"

She shivered. That was a long way to travel in a sinking boat. She fetched her binoculars from her side bag and trained them on the ocean. Even with the powerful magnification, she could see nothing beyond the low-lying points and islands that cluttered the waters in between.

"Nothing but birds there now. Used to be villages on them islands," said Tom. "Until the government shut them all down and moved everybody to the mainland back in the fifties. My father was born out there, so was Ted here. That was some rugged life, b'y."

Kaylee had been frolicking along the water's edge, trying to engage the sandpipers in play. One of the men hurled a stick of driftwood out into the water and she splashed out after it, diving headfirst into the surf and emerging with the stick clamped between her teeth. She raced back to the fisherman and flung it at his feet.

"Oh, now you're done for!" Chris laughed. "How many hours do you have to spare?"

Another stick, another gleeful dive. Amanda shifted her binoculars to the nearby islands and shoreline beyond the village, searching for signs of habitation. For Phil's truck. For any clue. The land stood empty and untouched as far as she could see. Nothing but scoured rock, grassy heath, and tangles of spruce, battered and misshapen by relentless time.

A twitch of movement shot across the lens. A moose browsing the shore? A bear? She focused harder. Rocks and scrub hid her view, but then the figure emerged again. Two, three, maybe four separate figures, leaping nimbly across the open rock before disappearing behind spruce again.

Human. Running full tilt toward the village. She waited with her binoculars trained until they came into view again. Closer now. A faint shout drifted in on the wind.

Kaylee perked up her ears and turned in the direction of the sound. Spotting the figures, she grabbed her stick and raced toward them. The fishermen turned to watch the figures approach. Running, leaping, flailing over the rocky shore.

"What in the love of …? What have those boys got on their tail?"

Amanda could see now that they were children, ganglylimbed and fearless on the treacherous rocks. She thought they looked more excited than afraid, but the fishermen were frowning in apprehension. When the boys finally splashed through a shallow tidal pool and came within earshot, Tom held up his hand.

"Where you to, Bobby?"

The lead boy reached them and bent over, panting to catch his breath. Before he could speak, a second one arrived and managed to blurt out, "'Dere be a boat!"

"A boat? Yes, b'y. Das an ocean out there."

"No!" exclaimed the first boy. "On the shore, washed up in the bush."

"Lots of stuff washes up on the shore over the years, son."

"No, Dad! This weren't there last week when we went clam-digging. And it's not a fishing boat. More like a lifeboat, with a big hole punched in its side."

Chris was instantly alert. "What kind of lifeboat?"

The boy shrugged. "Can't tell, but maybe it's that boat the cops are looking for."

Chris was already on the move. "Show me."

The boat was upside down under an old spruce whose spreading branches shielded it from view until the group was almost upon it. Chris tramped around it, fighting the spiky spruce branches as he looked for a registration number. Amanda could see that a section of the siding had been smashed and broken off where she figured the number should be. Deliberately or victim of the ruthless sea, she wondered?

Beneath her curiosity, dread needled into her gut. What if Phil, in his single-mindedness, had taken this boat, and foundered on the rocks? She wasn't even sure he had lifejackets, let alone other survival gear. Were he and Tyler lying on the bottom of the sea, or washed up on the shore somewhere farther down?

Chris raised his head to study the stony shore. It was low tide, but the wavering line of broken shells and seaweed clearly marked the high water mark, at least fifteen metres below the boat. His face was a mask of dispassion. "Could the waves wash it up here?"

Bobby's father shook his head. "There been some big storm surges this summer, but none strong enough to toss the boat that far."

"Looks like it's been hidden, then."

The boys were dancing around, excited now that Chris had identified himself as an RCMP officer, each eager to impress him with their detective skills.

"We never seen anybody," Bobby said, "but there are foot-prints in the sand."

Chris whirled around. "Where?"

"We'll show you!" The boys raced off.

"Stop!"

The boys froze in place until Chris reached them. "Stay on the rocks and don't go close. You point out where they are and I'll check." As if seeing their disappointment, he smiled. "We don't want to destroy evidence, do we?"

Amanda called Kaylee over and leashed her so that she wouldn't add excited dog prints to the scene as well. Together the small posse worked its way farther along the shore, careful to stay on the rocks. Chris bent his head to scrutinize each small patch of silt and mud in the crevices between the rocks. Amanda recognized bird tracks and small mammals, but no humans.

Farther along in a sheltered inlet, a swath of natural sand beach sparkled in the sunlight. Surf had washed seaweed, shells, and other ocean flotsam up to the high tide line. Below that line, the sand was washed smooth and clean, but above it footprints and other gouges were easy to make out. Some were the boot treads of small children, but at the far edge of the beach, larger prints had dug deep holes in the soft sand.

Amanda felt a rush of relief. Whoever this was, they had survived the wreck. Chris signalled for them all to stop while he walked cautiously forward, staying in the soft wet sand below high tide. Amanda watched with frustration and anxiety as he circled the patch of sand, clambered up on the nearby rocks, and took out his camera. He snapped a dozen shots, fiddling with the zoom and the angles, before disappearing over the ridge ahead. Kaylee strained at her leash, mirroring the impatience they all felt. Gulls wheeled overhead and sandpipers returned to cap-ture the minute creatures the waves lapped up. The wind rippled through the low-lying bushes, where bright coral berries nestled among glossy leaves. Amanda idly wondered if they were Newfoundland's famous partridge berries.

After an apparent eternity, Chris's tousled head bobbed into view above the ridge and a moment later he came back along the edge of the rocks to the safety of the beach. He signalled Amanda with a slight shake of his head before skirting the footprints and returning to the group.

"No more sign of them. I have to report this boat, but there's no signal here. The town of Roddickton has the closest RCMP detachment, so we'll go there and give them these photos. Meanwhile I need to rope off this section of the shore until the police arrive. We have to protect the evidence. It could be our friend and his son, or it could be those potential fugitives."

He sent two of the boys back to the village for a long length of rope. The other boys had a dozen questions. Will the police bring dogs? A helicopter? Trackers? Can Kaylee track? Chris teased them with bets that Kaylee could find every last ball in the village. Once they realized that he was not going to speculate further, the boys sensed the drama was over and began drifting away. Amanda and Chris were left to the silence of the surf and the gulls.

"What do you think?" she asked.

His brow furrowed unhappily. "I don't like it. That boat's not a regular fishing skiff. Possibly a lifeboat, although it's pretty small to be out on the open sea."

"Phil might have settled for any boat in the mood he was in."

He nodded. "But the fugitives were also in what looked like a lifeboat. And they were spotted in the sea only about thirty kilometres north of here."

"What about the footprints? Could you tell anything from them?"

He nodded. "Two people at least."

Her eyes widened.

"Both adults, I'd say."

"But Tyler is eleven. He might be at that age where his feet have outgrown the rest of him."

"I know." He gazed into the distance, chewing his lip.

"What? There's something else, isn't there."

"Two things. They could mean anything, but I have a cop's suspicious mind. First of all, the footprints were barefoot."

"So? Maybe their shoes were wet."

"I hope so, because those rocks will shred feet in no time."

"And second?"

"The village is barely a kilometre to the north, yet they headed south. Away from help. Into the wilderness."

CHAPTER ELEVEN

After another bone-jarring rollercoaster ride, they retrieved Chris's truck and drove on to Roddickton to talk to the detachment commander. Roddickton had only three RCMP officers who were responsible for a vast swath of remote wilderness, and one was on a training course, but the commander, Corporal Willington, seemed thrilled at the possibility of genuine intrigue. He was a chubby, jovial man with a loud, infectious laugh who plied them with tea and filled every spare moment with chatter while they awaited instructions from the investigator in St. Anthony about the seizure of the boat. It was nearly an hour before the order came for Chris to return to protect the scene until reinforcements arrived the next day to remove it.

"If Sergeant Poker-Ass thinks I'm camping out on those sharp rocks with the bugs and the bears, he can dream on," Chris muttered once they were safely out of the station. "We'll set up camp on the village heath; that's close enough."

By the time they returned to Grandois, the long shadows of the mountains had stolen over the village, and the salt air had chilled. They set up their tents in the meadow and were just about to cook dinner when Bobby arrived with an invitation to dinner from his parents.

Grabbing a bottle of wine, Chris and Amanda headed gratefully to the white bungalow perched on the slope above the cove. The kitchen was clearly the centre of their house. It was large, welcoming, and redolent with the smells of frying fish and cabbage. The wooden table, which bore the scars and burns of decades, easily fit ten people. Bobby's mother, a stout woman of boundless energy and talk, whirled around the kitchen tending the stove, fixing tea, and piling up platters of fish, potatoes, cabbage, and fried salt pork.

"This looks fabulous," Amanda said as she helped to set out plates. "Thank you so much."

"A real Newfoundland meal," the woman said. "Nudding fancy, mind, but it'll fill you up."

As they ate, it seemed as if the entire village drifted in, carrying cakes, berry pies, and bottles of blueberry wine, so that by the time the meal was finished, the room was packed. People laughed and traded quips so rapidly that Amanda struggled to understand every third word. She could tell from Chris's expression that he was equally befuddled.

Then someone produced a harmonica and a bottle of screech, Bobby's father dug out a guitar, and soon the whole house vibrated to the beat of Celtic rock. Kitchen spoons and pot lids became percussion instruments while the wood floor shook with the beat of dancing feet.

"It's a kitchen time!" Bobby's father shouted. "In the old days, before all this TV and Internet, there was nudding to do on the long, cold nights but play songs and tell stories."

Amanda's first shot of screech nearly tore her throat out, but by the third, she was tossing it back like a native. Chris was keeping up too. As one song finally came to an end, he reached over and took the guitar. Tucking it into the crook of his arm, he ran his long fingers across the strings in a rich, warm chord. Once, twice, and then with a grin, he broke into a rollicking rhythm and began to sing. Amanda recognized the melodies of Slavic folk music. The villagers hooted and began to stomp their feet. Before long they were joining in the chorus even though they didn't understand a word.

Amanda's mind flashed back to similar experiences in Africa, where the village gathered in the common, and drums and flutes were magically produced. *Music is a universal language of joy and community*, she thought. The melodies and instruments varied, but they all mimicked the beat of the heart.

It was past midnight by the time she and Chris staggered out of Bobby's kitchen. Their voices were hoarse and their heads spun. She stumbled in the darkness and linked her arm through his to keep her balance.

"You're quite the balladeer, you," she murmured.

"Country folk have to do something on those cold Saskatchewan winters," he laughed. "But I haven't sung those songs in a long time."

Swaying slightly, she gazed out across the rolling meadow, where pinpoints of light still glowed in some of the houses. A thousand replies sprang to her mind, but they were all too intimate. *I'm drunk*, she thought. *Really drunk. And in danger of doing something stupid.*

Instead, she hugged his arm briefly before drawing away. "Well, if you're ever fired from the RCMP, there's a job waiting for you on stage," she muttered before marching resolutely on ahead to her tent.

The police reinforcements weren't due until late the next morning, but even so, Amanda and Chris were barely coherent when a police cruiser towing a trailer pulled into the meadow. A single constable climbed out and greeted Chris with a curt nod.

"Protesters are still up on the highway at St. Anthony," he

said by way of explanation for his lateness. "Tempers are getting ugly because it's slowing down the shrimp trucks. The sergeant said he'd send out more help if I asked for it. Plus HQ in St. John's is interested in having a look."

As it turned out, more help wasn't needed. The constable interviewed the boys and took more photographs of the boat and the footprints before wrapping the boat into a huge plastic tarp with Chris and Amanda's help and dragging it by ATV back to his trailer. He was gone by mid-afternoon. He'd shared barely an extraneous word with either Chris or Amanda, except to thank Chris for his help and to tell him he was free to continue his holiday.

"Talkative guy, isn't he?" Amanda said as they watched the plume of dust from his cruiser trail up the hill. Even with her sunglasses and her hat pulled low over her eyes, the sun seemed too bright.

"Under orders from Poker-Ass, I'm sure," said Chris. "But this news will be all up and down the coast by nightfall, if it isn't already. A boatload of fugitives in this little village? That'll be a legend told for years. It'll be a whole ship and a heroic rescue by the time those boys are grown, with songs written about it too."

Amanda chuckled, the beat of the kitchen party still thrumming through her body. "I wonder what will happen to them," she said. "Especially if they're fugitives from one of those foreign boats. People in most parts of the world don't realize how vast and desolate the Canadian wilderness can be. There are no roads or villages for miles, no shelter or food unless you make your own."

"We know they didn't show up at Croque, but there are two more villages farther down the coast," Chris said, spreading the map out on the hood of his truck. "Two more places they might have passed through, if they stick to the coast. I think we should check with the locals at both places. Not just for the fugitives, but also for Phil. If it wasn't his boat we found, then he might still be looking for one."

And getting more and more bitter with every failure, she thought. She leaned over Chris's shoulder to pinpoint the next village down the coast. Conche. No road connected it directly to the one they were in, so they'd be forced to retrace their route inland to the main highway. More miles on that bone-jarring dirt road.

"Do you think we can make it to Conche this afternoon?" she asked. "We've lost a day with this lifeboat business, and we're falling farther behind him."

He folded the map and glanced at his watch. "Days are still pretty long, so yeah, I think so. Unless the road is even worse than this one."

The road was rough, the terrain even more rugged, and the hills steeper, but at the end of the trip, they were rewarded with a spectacular jewel of a village nestled in a bay between towering green mountains. The village of Conche was larger and more settled than Grandois, with a grocery store that doubled as a hardware store and a bustling harbour filled with boats. No sooner had they begun their inquiries at the local store than the villagers drifted in to offer help and to volunteer information. Word of their quest had already travelled from Grandois.

The villagers had seen no trace of barefoot men possibly speaking a foreign language, but Phil and his son had been through a couple of days earlier, wanting a boat. This time he had wanted to buy one outright, but he hadn't enough cash.

"Boats are our life out here," one man said to Chris. He was a burly, weatherbeaten man with a florid face and hands the size of hams, who introduced himself as Casey. "I offered him my wife instead, but it was no go."

Laughter ensued among the other men in the store.

"I might have liked my chances with him," one of the women shot back.

"The boy really wanted to go out on the sea, so Thaddeus took them out for a spin around the peninsula to the back harbour," said Casey, pointing out the window to a man unloading wood from his truck. "It was a short run, didn't even get to show them one whale before your friend wanted to go back in. Then he took off without even a thank-you."

"Your friend needs a good slap upside the head," added the wife with the caustic tongue.

"Where did he go?" Chris asked. "Back up the highway toward Roddickton?"

"No, he was after a hike along the shore —"

At that moment Amanda spotted what had escaped her notice in the sea of old pickups parked helter-skelter by the wharf. A rusty black Chevy like the one Phil owned was parked near the entrance to town. She broke away and jogged down the steps of the store and along the street for a closer look. Phil's licence plate! Her heart leaped. She shouted to Chris. As he made his way over, she cupped her hands to the glass to peer inside. Maps and chocolate-bar wrappers littered the floor. She peered into the truck bed, which was piled high with camping gear and clothes, along with several two-fours of empty beer cans and a pile of empty vodka bottles.

"Looks like Phil was doing some serious drinking," Chris muttered.

Casey came puffing up behind them, his face now nearly purple. "Yeah, I was getting to that. We never touched the beer. He already had a snootful when he arrived. Like I was telling your boyfriend here, he and the boy took off on foot across to the back harbour. Never came back. The kids went looking yesterday but didn't see hide nor hair."

"What's in the back harbour?" Amanda asked, visualizing the map. Nothing but cliffs and woods, she recalled. She didn't like the sound of this. Phil's behaviour sounded erratic and desperate — driving drunk on rough mountain roads with his son by his side and no clear idea where he was going. As if he were in full flight mode.

Casey shrugged. "Just Old Stink. Keeps to himself. Your friend won't get much help out of him. He hasn't hardly said a word in sixty years."

"Except to himself," the wife added. For all their apparent discord, they were clearly in sync, Amanda thought.

"Is he dangerous?" Chris cut in.

"Old Stink?" Casey snorted. "Might have been at one time if you got in his face, but he must be getting up toward ninety by now. Harmless as a fly."

"Well —" the wife began, but Chris was thinking like a cop. "Does he have a gun?"

"For hunting, yeah," Casey said. "An old Winchester 94. Shoots mostly ptarmigan and rabbits these days, and last time I saw him, his eyesight wasn't so good."

"How far away is he?"

"Oh, a couple of miles up the back harbour, on the cape across the way. You have to reach it by boat, but my brother's got mine out. Maybe in the morning —"

Amanda jumped in impatiently. "But if it's across the bay, our friend won't be able to reach it on foot, either. He'll still be on this side."

"There's an old boat," the wife said. She was getting in the spirit of the drama. "Part way up the harbour. You can walk to it, and there's a footpath that we use for berry-picking."

Amanda glanced at her watch. The sun had already slipped behind the mountains to the west, and within a couple of hours, darkness would settle in. Another day lost, another day farther behind. She called Kaylee, but before she could set out, Chris shook his head at her.

"We might make it there before dark," he said, "but we can't make it safely back. And Old Stink's doesn't sound like the ideal spot to spend the night."

"But every night is a night wasted! We have flashlights. Kaylee will keep us on the path."

Chris's eyes narrowed as he studied the distant cliffs and the steep forested mountains along the shore. "One wrong step, and we could be in serious trouble."

"Please, Chris. I don't like the sound of things. Phil sounds desperate!"

She knew he wasn't happy, that as a cop he should be the voice of caution. But damn it, you don't trek through the gun-toting jihadi hordes of northern Nigeria without learning how to survive.

She threw some power bars and emergency supplies into her day pack, tossed it over her shoulder, and set off. A short reconnaissance trip, that was all.

Either he'd follow, or he wouldn't.

He followed, as did Casey and an entourage of villagers, who picked their way single-file along the shore path. The tide was coming in, and tongues of foam licked over the rocks toward their feet. As the harbour widened, Amanda scrutinized the distant cape ahead. Had Phil been fool enough to try to swim across? Even if he could manage the distance, the waves and tides, not to mention the cold, would kill anyone who ventured out.

As she was crossing a small patch of stony beach, Casey suddenly called out from behind. She turned to him inquiringly. He was scanning the rocky hollows and scrubby bushes along the side. Finally he shook his head.

"Boat's gone."

"Whose boat?"

He shrugged. "Everybody's. We leaves it here for those that wants to get across the harbour. Good berry-picking up on Cape Rouge over the other side. Old Stink chases the kids off when he catches them."

She studied the pebbled sand. It was still damp and washed smooth by the last high tide, and all traces of the boat and footprints had been erased. The distance to the other shore looked nearly a mile, and the waves packed a punch as they rushed in. Phil was an inexperienced Prairie boy and Tyler was eleven years old. Moreover, they had left almost all their gear in the truck.

"What kind of boat is it? Big?"

The man laughed. "Little go-ashore, gets you from here to there. Someone put a 9 hp on 'er a while back that works sometimes."

Chris was studying the opposite shore through binoculars. "I don't see a boat over there."

"Well, nobody be fool enough to try to land on them rocks, not even your friend. You go up the cape half a mile or so, dere's a small beach. But Old Stink keeps his boat and stage dere, and his house is just up the hill, so your friend might have got a bit of an argument."

"We have to get over there," Amanda said.

Casey shook his head. "Not tonight you don't. I can take you over in the morning."

"But —"

"We have to go back to get my boat. Too late today."

Amanda chafed. She knew he was right, but she was staring out at the surly sea one last time, almost willing Phil and Tyler to appear, when a small piece of debris caught her eye. Bobbing up and down in the waves farther down the bay. She squinted. The area was now in deep shadow from the mountains to the west. Was the light playing tricks with her eyes? She took Chris's binoculars and focused them on the water. At first she saw nothing, but eventually a dark shape flashed briefly into view before being swallowed by the waves. Then again. Each glimpse so tantalizing yet too fleeting to be identified.

She pointed it out to Casey. "Is that the boat?"

He shielded his eyes. She could tell he was about to deliver one of his typical shrugs, so she held out the binoculars. "Please."

His blue eyes rested on her thoughtfully, deeply set in his weathered face. They softened a little. He took the binoculars.

"Too small for a boat," he said. "Could be part of a boat, but could be nudding. A fallen tree, a piece of old dock. Lots of debris washes up into that arm at high tide."

"We should check it out."

For the first time, he grinned at her, showing a classic Newfoundland sense of play. "In the morning, my dear. Time to go back before the bears start thinking about dinner." As if to reinforce his words, he turned to retrace his steps along the path. Chris turned to follow. Amanda cursed her own impotence. That piece of debris beckoned, so close and yet utterly beyond reach. The sun was sinking deep behind the hills, and they would be in jeopardy themselves if they went out on the water.

Moreover, she acknowledged with a sick feeling, if that was a piece of that boat out there, it might be too late anyway.

"First light?" she called.

Casey waved his arm. "Before first light, my dear."

True to his word, Casey was down at his wharf readying a little skiff when Amanda crawled out of her tent the next morning.

He had already loaded a tool kit, a pile of PFDs, and a tank of gas, and was tinkering with the motor. Mist was slowly wisping off the bay, shimmering pink against the pre-dawn sky. The ocean lay at half tide, and water glistened in pools along the rocky shore. Gulls and gannets swooped overhead.

"You don't need to do all this, Casey," she said. "You have work to do, so why don't we just rent your boat —"

"What, and miss the adventure? And the chance to get away from the wife for a bit?"

Amanda laughed. "Okay, but at least let me pay for the gas."

Even that offer was met with argument until she put her foot down. Dawn was a faint smudge of peach over the ocean when Casey, Chris, Amanda, and Kaylee piled into the little skiff and headed around the tip of the peninsula into the ocean swell. Amanda sat in the bow, which rose and fell as the boat slammed the waves and sent arcs of spray along the gunnels. Kaylee huddled against her on the narrow seat, her ears flattened and her eyes wide.

The swells softened once they'd rounded the northern tip of the peninsula and passed through the narrows into the back harbour. Casey slowed so they could search the shoreline. The mist had swirled away and visibility was good. Amanda searched with a mixture of hope and dread. Nothing. Nothing but endless rock and brush and spindly spruce struggling up the slopes. An inlet here and there, where gap-toothed shacks and broken wharves lay half-reclaimed by bush. They passed the beach where the boat should have been, but it was still empty. Farther up the bay, the dark shape they had seen in the water yesterday had disappeared. Likely carried out on the tide, Casey said.

Finally Casey steered the boat into a little cove on the opposite shore, where a sagging shed bleached almost white and missing half its roof sat on the edge of the pebbled shore.

A skinny wharf of equal vintage wobbled out over the water. Seagulls flapped in hopeful circles.

"Old Stink's wharf and stage," Casey shouted over the noise of the motor.

Amanda's heart sank. There was no sign of the little boat, nor any other boat. Casey guided them into the cove, cut the engine, and let the boat drift toward the wharf.

"Stink's boat's gone. Must be out fishing."

They had passed numerous craft out in the open ocean, and Casey had waved to most of them. "Was his one of the boats we saw?" Amanda asked.

Casey shook his head. "But Old Stink follows his own clock. Been known to go out in the middle of the night just so he don't have to say hello. He can navigate by the echo of the cliffs, knows every trough and shoal by heart."

The wharf was within reach, but Casey made no move to grab it. "Not sure there's much point us going ashore. Nothing here. Maybe your friend planned on walking all the way to Croque."

"How far is that?" Amanda asked.

"If you're a crow, twenty kilometres or so. If you're on foot, maybe two or three times that, through dense bush and bog."

Kaylee's growl stopped her mid-thought, seconds before the dog launched herself from the bow of the skiff onto the wharf and ran to shore. Calling to her proved useless. The dog stood on the shoreline, rigidly still and apparently deaf. Casey laughed.

"Don't think she liked the boat ride."

Amanda studied Kaylee carefully. The rigid stance and stiff tail suggested threat. "I don't think it's that. There's something on shore."

"Likely not something we want to meet, then. Let's get her back in the boat."

Casey secured the boat and they clambered onto the rickety wharf, which listed dangerously underfoot. Amanda took a deep breath and regretted it instantly. The stench of rot and old fish was suffocating. Casey grinned. "This ain't nudding compared to his cabin."

A thin path led from the shore up the slope. Kaylee stood at the entrance to it, her nose sifting the putrid air. Then her hair rose along her back and a low whine sounded in her throat. Before Amanda could reach her, she took off up the path and disappeared into the woods with her nose to the ground. Amanda yelled and scrambled over lichen-covered rocks to keep up.

"Don't!" Casey shouted.

"But the dog has detected something!" she called back, still running.

"Could be a bear or a moose. You don't want to go barging up there."

His protests faded as she plunged up the narrow path. She shouted for Kaylee, as much to alert any bear as to bring the dog back. She was furious, whether at Kaylee's disobedience or her own fear, she wasn't sure. Kaylee was nowhere in sight by now. Spruce branches tore at her clothes, and the dew-slicked moss shifted underfoot, forcing her to keep her head down. She didn't see the cabin until she was almost upon it.

She smelled it first, a fetid swamp of rotting fish and barnyard that wafted on the still air and choked her lungs. She slithered to a stop as the path opened into a clearing cluttered with human presence — an outhouse, a clothesline on which hung a single pair of work pants and a tattered towel, a chopping block surrounded by wood chips, and stacks of spindly firewood. Dominating the middle of the clearing was a hand-operated water pump of the sort she'd seen in developing countries and a wooden rack catching the best of the sun. *A drying rack for fish?* she wondered.

The cabin itself was little more than a shack that slumped to one side as if about to tumble over. Flakes of whitewash still clung to its bleached siding and its roof was a melange of broken slates and curling shingles. The single window was broken.

Kaylee was standing at the cabin door, her legs stiff and her hackles raised. She gave a low whine as Amanda approached and clipped on her leash. Amanda felt the clutch of familiar, formless dread. Her heart hammered as she stared at the doorknob, paralyzed.

"Don't be ridiculous, Doucette," she muttered. "This is a hermit's cabin in rural Newfoundland. Nothing to fear here." Nonetheless, her voice quavered when she called out. "Anyone here?"

Silence. An empty, dead silence. She tried the knob and pushed the door, which stuck and fought her as it creaked open a few inches. Kaylee shoved her nose through, whining.

Amanda peered through the gap. Saw the faded linoleum floor, a large table covered with peeling oilcloth, a woodstove, and an old rocking chair. The rocking chair was tipped on its side and it took her a moment to make sense of the mess on the floor — a thousand shards of glittering glass.

And in the middle of the glass, an axe with an old wooden handle and a filthy blade stained brownish red. Red glistened on the walls and on the shards of glass as well.

She recoiled and slammed the door. She'd seen that colour before. When a voice spoke behind her, she leaped a foot. Chris emerged into the clearing, his brows knitting with alarm.

"What is it?"

"Something's wrong," she managed, gesturing to the door. "There's blood in there."

He crossed the clearing in swift strides and shoved open the door. "Jesus!" he breathed, holding up his hand to keep her back. "Stay here!"

He disappeared into the cabin and she could hear him thumping around inside. Barely five seconds later he returned, looking grim.

"There's no one here, but there's clearly been a fight. Lots of blood inside, and furniture overturned." He studied the door frame and knelt to peer at the ground outside the front door. "There's blood on the door here, and some smears on the ground. Whoever it is, they came outside."

He stepped back into the clearing and headed across to the shed. A quick search of the ground revealed signs of trouble — scuff marks in the dirt, a broken latch on the shed, and trampled bushes.

Once again, it was Kaylee who made the discovery. She'd been straining against her tight leash, trying to pull Amanda up a trail into the bush. Finally Amanda followed, and a mere hundred feet into the bush, there was an old man, sprawled on his stomach with his gnarled hands stretched out in front as if he had been trying to claw his way up the hill. The back of his skull was a mass of blood.

"Jumpin' Jaysus!" said Casey, coming up behind her. "That's Old Stink."

CHAPTER TWELVE

Chris's first thought was for Amanda. From the horror on her face, he could tell it was bad. She had grown very pale and was propped against a tree trunk, clutching her dog. He suspected she was reliving every terrifying moment of that blood-filled night where, according to newspaper accounts, death had come not by neat bullets or explosions that obliterated everything to ash and dust, but by axes and machetes slashing and smashing limbs and heads in a lust of blood and rage.

Perhaps for a brief moment she was back there.

But there was something else in that expression of horror. A deep dread, for this had been a murder, and he could see her thoughts had taken the same dark path as his.

He went to her, took her hands, and gently turned her away. "Amanda, come. Move away from the scene, sit over there while I check this out."

She followed him, robot-like, and acknowledged her thanks with a small nod. He forced himself to step close to the body and leaned down to check the carotid pulse. The one visible eye was milky and flies were already crawling around his flaccid mouth, but checking for vitals was procedure. The skin was cold to the touch, rigor mortis already well established. Surreptitiously he nudged the foot, trying to recall the crime scene course he'd taken. Rigor began in the face and advanced down the body to the feet before dissipating in reverse order over forty-eight hours. Give or take.

The dead man's foot was rigid, which meant the man had probably been dead twelve to thirty-six hours.

"Poor old bugger," Casey said.

Chris backed away, holding up his hands to force Casey back. His thoughts were racing to form a plan. "Don't touch anything. I'll have to secure the scene." He turned to Casey. "You got any rope in the boat? I'll need at least …" He squinted down the path. Stink's cabin was about a hundred feet away and all points in between would have to be cordoned off. "Two or three hundred feet?"

Casey shook his head. "Nudding that long. But who's going to muck it up? There's nobody around."

Chris shook his head. "Procedure, that's all. If this ever goes to court, I have to be able to swear it wasn't contaminated." As the initial shock wore off, his training finally kicked in. He checked his cellphone. As he expected, they were in a dead zone. He walked over to Amanda, who was standing now, her eyes still bleak, but colour was returning to her cheeks.

"Amanda, you and Casey go back to the village and call the police. Poker-Ass again, I guess. Tell him I need a major crime team out here and a doctor to pronounce death." He swung on Casey. "You got a doctor in the village?"

"We can get one from Roddickton."

Chris did a quick calculation. That was just over half an hour's drive from the village, closer than many rural calls for service. "Get him out here as fast as you can. Have you got Internet in the village at least?"

"Yeah, no cellphone but we gots Internet."

"Good. I'll take some photos on my phone and Amanda, you email them to Poker-Ass so he has an idea what he's dealing with."

He could see her opening her mouth to protest, so he shook his head sharply. "It might take some time for the team to get here, so meanwhile, Casey, I want you to bring me a couple of tarps, some plastic bins, and … oh, I don't know, markers of some kind. Tent pegs or little flags. And tow a second boat over with you so I'll have some transportation."

Casey nodded. He was looking slightly green and seemed grateful for the chance to escape back down to his boat. Amanda, on the other hand, was standing in the path expectantly.

"What?" he said. "What are you waiting for?"

"The photos. And if I'm going to email them to Sergeant Poker-Ass, I'll need your phone."

His eyes met hers. *Such an idiot*, he thought, and forced a sheepish laugh. "I knew that."

A ghost of a smile curved her lips. "And I'd like Poker-Ass's real name and number. Calling him Poker-Ass, however tempting, probably won't get me very far."

"Sergeant Amis." He fished in his pocket for the man's card and entered the phone number in his phone. Then he circled the body and took a couple of dozen photos with the phone. Still photographing, he headed back down the path, searching the ground and underbrush for evidence. He knew the evidence had probably been trampled by the dog and the three of them, but he took photos of stains and gouges anyway. The forensics team could decide for themselves if they were of any use. Amanda watched him curiously but without comment.

At the cabin door, he signalled to her to stay outside while he inspected the interior once again. It looked as if the attack had taken place in the main room, where the attacker had dropped the axe. Had the killer simply left Stink to crawl for help with his last dying efforts? Or had Stink been trying to escape from him when he headed up the path into the bush? If he'd been crawling for help, he'd gone in the wrong direction.

Amanda poked her head through the open doorway, averting her eyes from the axe. "Can you tell where the killer went?"

"It's probably safe to assume he took Stink's boat. You should tell the police that too."

"I'd rather stay with you."

She looked determined, but the faint quaver in her voice betrayed her. He shook his head.

"I can help, Chris. Kaylee might be able to help too. Remember, if it weren't for her, we'd never have known there was anything wrong, and we'd never have found Stink."

"You can't stay. This is a crime scene."

"But we've already tromped all over it."

He straightened to confront her. "You know why."

Her gaze wavered and she looked away. "There were two boats, so two different people. Only one is the killer."

"Unless that debris we saw yesterday was the second boat. If he swamped that one ..."

"He didn't do this. I know him."

"When it comes to crimes, we can't assume a thing."

"I can. Phil would never, ever, swing an axe at another man's head."

He walked over to her. He wanted to touch her, to reassure her, but he merely looked down at her. "I'm as worried as you are. But Stink's boat is gone, and Phil was last seen coming this way."

Amanda tamped down her anger and forced herself to be charming. She knew her emotion had more to do with Stink's death and her own fears than with the prissy little Mountie on the other end of the phone. There is no bureaucracy more officious and obstructive than those in developing countries, and she had learned not to be deterred by the initial no. Or the second, or even the third. She could tell from the major crimes investigator's initial condescending comments that she was going to have to put all those skills to use again.

At first Sergeant Amis had instructed her to report the death through official channels, which meant the Roddickton detachment responsible for that location, so that they could initiate the proper procedure. If the death is deemed suspicious —

"Most of his head is missing!" she wanted to shout. "They'll be calling you soon enough!" But she held her tongue. She had reached Amis at the St. Anthony RCMP detachment, where he was presumably still working on the body recovered from the ocean. He sounded harried and tired, no doubt not thrilled with the prospect of rushing off to an even more remote death before the paperwork was even filed on the first.

"He was to be my next call, Sergeant," she replied breezily. "But Corporal Tymko took some photos which your investigators will need, and I thought it expeditious to forward them directly to you."

"Miss Doucette, without the proper chain of custody, any evidence —"

"Well, that's why I thought I should go straight to you, so the photos don't go bouncing around in cyberspace for hours — maybe even days — before they get to you."

"But they're of no use to us. Our investigators will take proper pictures."

"Of course. But the body is in a remote location accessible only by boat. Corporal Tymko is doing his best to follow procedure, but he's worried the evidence will disappear. There are wild animals, not to mention possible rain. At least these photos can show you how the body looked when we found it."

There was a pause. A sigh. Amanda looked out the window of Casey's house. The main wharf was buzzing with activity as the whole town pitched in to collect Chris's supplies. Tarps, food, and clothing, fishing and hunting gear, as if Chris would be out there for a month.

"Please forward the photos to me," Amis said finally, still sounding as if the whole exercise was an imposition that derailed his whole investigative strategy. "Advise Corporal Tymko not to disturb the scene and to expect a team's arrival by early tomorrow."

She was being dismissed with a flick of the hand. She was still smarting from Chris's refusal to let her stay, and the sergeant's pompous condescension, not only toward her, but also toward Chris, was almost the last straw. She forced herself to sound neutral, even through clenched teeth.

"I believe Corporal Tymko knows not to disturb the scene," she said. "What about the medical examiner?"

"Roddickton will take care of that."

In fact, the doctor in Roddickton had already been called and should be arriving within the hour, but Amanda chose not to mention that. Childish, probably, but the small exercise in power felt good.

The investigator seemed remarkably uninterested in any other information she had to offer, such as the bloody axe, so she hung up, stuck her tongue out at the phone, and dialled the next number on her list. She was not worried about this one; she knew cheerful, chatty Corporal Willington would be a breath of fresh air. Now she wished she'd phoned him in the first place.

He told her that Dr. Iannucci had already informed him and he was picking her up in ten minutes.

"I'm sorry," Amanda said. "I should have phoned you right away instead of phoning the major crimes guy. I thought it would speed things up, but …"

"Who did you speak to?"

"Sergeant Amis."

He laughed. "Oh, Amis. Yes. He's new from Ontario."

As if that explained everything.

"Donna — Doc Iannucci — says it's Old Stink?" he continued. "Bashed on the head?"

"Yes. Do you know anything about him?"

"Nobody knows much about Old Stink. Well, maybe the old-timers down there do, but he's been in the bush for fifty, sixty years. Went off his head, they say, but fifty years in the bush will do that. Used to live there with his mother, and when she died, he stayed on. Didn't know any other life, I guess."

"Was he paranoid? Would he attack someone who came on his land?"

Willington seemed to be thinking. "Maybe, but he's more likely to hide in the woods, from what folks say. Dr. Iannucci says she only met him once — the locals went to check on him after a hurricane ripped though a few years back — and found he had a busted leg. She said he wouldn't look her in the eye. Hardly remembered how to carry on a conversation."

Amanda digested the information. On the boat ride back to town, Casey had said Old Stink sometimes came into the village to collect his pension cheques and sell fish and game in exchange for supplies. Casey hadn't known of any disputes or altercations — in fact couldn't think of a single person who'd bother to kill him — but perhaps Willington knew more. The man loved to talk, but even he would eventually realize he'd said too much about an ongoing police investigation. She had to find a way to keep him talking.

"I'm worried," she said. "Chris Tymko is out there all alone. Do you have any idea who might have done this, and is Chris in danger?"

"Shouldn't think so," Willington said cheerfully. "Likely one of those arguments that got out of hand. Stink's been getting a bit ornery in his old age, sometimes stands on his wharf yelling at boats that get too close. The local folks know to stay out of his way, so I'd say the killer's not local. If Stink's been dead a couple of days, the killer's probably long gone by now."

Amanda could hear rustling in the background as if he was moving around. "I'm on my way," he said. "I'll get statements from all the townsfolk, ask about strangers in the area, and try to get as much done before the guy from Ontario shows up. With a bit of luck, by the end of the day we'll have an answer all tied up with a bow for him."

Amanda signed off with a heavy heart. She had not told Willington about Phil, but since the whole town knew about him and about where he was headed when last seen, she suspected by the end of the day, Phil would be the RCMP's prime suspect.

Chris sat on the end of the wharf and peered down the harbour, his ears tuned to the faintest sound of a boat engine. By now Amanda should have contacted the police and the doctor should be on his way. Chris had to admit he felt a little spooked. Stuck on a remote point of land surrounded by the ruthless sea, with a dead man rotting on the path behind him and an irrational fear of what lurked in the dark, empty woods.

He wouldn't admit it to a soul, especially not to his fellow officers. Just as he never admitted to the nights when he bolted awake awash in panic and sweat, with the sound of gunshots still ringing in his ears and the sight of a loved one spurting blood all over the walls. Sometimes it was his mother, or his sister, or even a daughter he'd never had. Just as he never admitted that, even two years after the horrific shootout that changed his life, the sight of blood still made him queasy.

He was a cop. No matter what he'd been through, he had a job to do.

After Casey and Amanda left, with Kaylee standing like a sentinel in the bow of the boat, he'd done a more systematic search, starting at the shore where the killer had presumably made his escape. He'd explored the wharf for bloody footprints. He'd crept cautiously over the sand and bent over to examine every mark and scuff in the damp sand. He'd found nothing useful. The sand was etched with bird tracks and Kaylee's paw prints, but the tide had washed out even Stink's old prints.

When boats putted into the bay occasionally, he studied their occupants through his binoculars. Most looked like regular fishermen or locals out on an errand. But how would he know? The killer would hardly be waving a banner saying KILLER. He cursed his own stupidity. He should have asked Casey for a description of Old Stink's boat. He assumed it was small, since Stink operated it by himself, and it was probably decrepit, but so were most of the boats that passed by. Wealth was a scarce commodity in these fishing communities.

After his futile examination of the shore, he had moved inland to search the path for signs of disturbance. The three of them had all trekked up and down it, of course, as had the dog, so he wasn't surprised to find nothing useful.

He worked his way past the cabin and up the hill to Stink's body. As the sun heated the day, more flies gathered. He felt an urge to cover the body but knew he had to wait for the tarp. He forced himself to look closely at the corpse again, at the mass of tangled hair and blood. The poor man had been hit from behind, and, judging from the amount of damage, more than once. The rest of his body, although smeared with blood, seemed unharmed. Chris noticed that his feet were bare and he was wearing stained yellow clothes that had probably once been white. Long johns. Had Stink been in bed when the killer surprised him? Something to check on when he returned to the cabin.

Stink's feet were filthy, but there were dirt streaks on the top as well as on his knees and palms. Stink had not been dragged here, but rather had crawled, mortally wounded, until he collapsed. There was no sign of a scuffle in the vicinity of the body, so if his attacker had followed him, he had not bothered to strike him again.

Stink's fingernails were chipped and so encrusted with dirt that Chris doubted forensics would be able to extract much usable evidence even if Stink had managed to scratch his attacker.

Looking beyond the signs of violent death, Chris studied the old man. His skin was like a parched prairie plain, with dirt embedded in every crevice. His hair and beard blended together in a long, stringy tangle of white. Chris could not bring himself to check, but imagined he had few teeth left.

The long johns hung on his body, draping loosely over the contours of his body. He was a tall man, probably once a big man possessing a strength to be reckoned with, but now his collar-bones and ribs stuck out. Either sick or starving, he would not have presented much of a fight. Chris felt a twinge of pity as he pictured the poor man, living by choice in the familiar isolation of his homestead, awakened abruptly in the night by a terrifying axe. Fighting for his life. Crawling, still fighting, up the path to what he hoped was safety. Only to have his life ebb out of him little by little.

Chris returned to the cabin to see what tales it could tell. He stood just inside the room, careful to stay clear of the blood, and studied it. An ancient mattress lay on the floor in the corner, but it was stripped bare. No one faced a Newfoundland winter without several quilts or blankets, but there were none in sight. Perhaps Stink had dragged them outside with him. Chris made a note to check around.

A pot-bellied stove occupied the middle of the room, with a single blackened pot on top. He felt the stove. Stone cold. He peered inside but could see nothing unusual in the thin layer of ash. Beyond this, the room looked stripped. No clothes on hooks, no boots. In what appeared to be the kitchen area, there was a single chair, a small table, and rows of shelving. One shelf held a few dishes, three bags of salt, and four jars of pickles, but the rest were empty. Had the man run out of food?

The room was surprisingly tidy. The axe and the blood were a violent intrusion, smearing the floor and speckling the walls. As part of his police training, Chris had taken a lecture on blood-spatter analysis, which he tried to remember now. If Stink had been struck more than once, there would be transfer blood from the axe to the walls and ceiling. Chris studied the spatter. It did indeed run in a single streak up one wall and across the ceiling, as if the killer had raised the axe over his head for a second blow. On closer examination, he found another streak near the door, where there was also a large pool of congealed blood.

Chris tried to picture the sequence. He was no expert, but it appeared that Stink had been struck at least three times as he moved toward the door. He had not been in bed, at least when the second blow had struck, but rather in the middle of the room, and the killer had been standing with the axe in the kitchen area. Stink had been nearer the door when the third blow struck. This one had felled him and he'd bled for quite awhile before getting up and escaping outside.

There were a lot of smears, but only one recognizable bloody footprint near the door. Likely Stink's, but given the quantity of blood on the floor, maybe the killer had stepped in it.

That would be one lucky break for forensics.

Outside, there were scuffs and footprints criss-crossing the clearing, but Chris could make little sense of them. He checked the shed, which contained very little. A shovel, a winch, some cable, lots of broken old tools, a bag of seed, a few gardening tools, and pots stacked away on shelves. No rifle.

He headed back down to the shore to check the fishing stage, holding his nose as he stepped inside. In the gloom, he saw piles of rotted old netting, rusty tackle gear, several broken fishing rods, and paddles. A stack of lobster traps and crab pots, a couple of functional fishing rods, but still no Winchester.

Chris sat down on the dock to think. Sometimes the clue to a crime lay not in what was there, but what was not. The boat and gun were both gone. But also missing were blankets and clothes. Stink must have had a winter jacket, hat, and mitts, but there was no sign of them.

There was also no food. Stink could have been running out, which explained why he was so thin, but it was unlikely he had nothing, not even the usual staples like canned beans, dried capelin, or hard tack. Nor, Chris realized now, had he seen any matches. Without matches, a homesteader would be doomed.

Chris didn't like the conclusion that he was staring at — that the killer had taken it all. Quite a lot to haul unless you have a boat to put it in. And why? It was sure to be worthless old junk, useful only if you needed those things — blankets, clothes, food — to survive. If you were on the run and had left most of your gear behind.

Don't even think it, he told himself. *Just listen for Casey's boat.*

CHAPTER THIRTEEN

After her phone call to Corporal Willington, Amanda lingered awhile inside Casey's house studying her topographical map and trying to imagine where Phil might have gone. Conche was tucked into the protected inner nook of a gourd-shaped peninsula, with a long, thin neck connecting it to the mainland. On the other side of the thin neck was the back harbour and another, larger, cape jutting out into the ocean. Stink's homestead was on that cape, but the map showed a few other homesteads as well, before the vast emptiness of rugged, barren wilderness to the north. Only three roads ran through the wilderness, the middle one to Conche, an upper one to the coastal settlements of Croque and Grandois, and a lower to the town of Englee farther south. Below Englee, there were no roads into the interior at all.

If Phil were on foot, rather than in a boat as the others believed, he could wander the wilderness for days without seeing or being seen by a soul.

But what if he'd taken Stink's boat? Far out in the ocean were the two large islands that the villagers in Grandois had mentioned. They were deserted now except for birds and the occasional adventurer. Phil had expressed an interest, but to get out there, he would have to cross twenty or thirty kilometres of open ocean swells. Surely too daunting a prospect for a Prairie boy.

Galvanized, she rolled up her maps and strode back down the harbour to Casey's wharf, where the man was readying the engine on his spare boat for Chris. Endlessly patient, fingers black with grease.

"I'm sorry," she said. "This is turning out to be much more adventure than you were looking for."

He still looked a little green, but he managed a shrug. "Least I can do for poor Old Stink. Did Willie say how long before he gets here?"

Willie, she guessed, was Corporal Willington. "He left about twenty minutes ago. Said he'd be an hour, tops."

Casey nodded. "Good. Might be she needs a new motor."

Amanda eyed the little skiff. Compared to the assortment of semi-buoyant junk heaps she'd used in developing countries, this one looked impeccable, although perhaps it dated from the First World War. She pictured Phil and Tyler all alone out on the ocean, piloting an unfamiliar boat in a cold, alien sea. Where would he go? Back up the coast toward the safety of the small coastal villages? Or down the coast into the wilderness farther south?

"What kind of boat did Old Stink have?" she asked.

Casey rolled his eyes. "He's had dat boat going on sixty years. Sixteen-foot dory, used to row 'er until he put a fifteen-horsepower outboard on 'er."

"Does it have a cabin on it?"

"Oh no, my dear, it's just a dory. Like dat one." He pointed to a boat lying on the grass, its hull gouged and its white paint scraped off. "Stink never went far out to sea with 'er. Mostly in the bay and around the head."

"Is it seaworthy, though?"

He shrugged. "Depends. Water's calm, you couldn't ask for a better boat. They'll all swamp in a good blow. But Stink's boat, now, the motor has a mind of her own. She'll cut out on you if you look at her wrong, especially in a headwind. Doesn't like the waves."

Amanda could see that the wind was picking up, rippling over the ocean and through the long shore grass. Would Phil know enough to keep the boat going? Overseas, they had both learned how to keep the most cantankerous of generators and trucks running and the most precarious of boats afloat. Phil could read river patterns and monsoon skies, but he knew nothing about the oceans, the tides, or the bruised black clouds of an incoming Atlantic storm.

Casey had been watching her, his expression softening. "Your friend likely won't get far. If he pushes 'er over ten knots, she'll quit on him. Mind you, if he heads south to Englee, he could go up Canada Bay to Roddickton. He could go by road from there."

"How long would that take?"

"No more than three to four hours, even in Stink's boat. And he'd be out of the ocean swell."

Too many options! Amanda thought with dismay. Phil's truck was still stranded here in the village, of course, but in his desperate state, that wouldn't stop him. He knew how to hot-wire just about any vehicle, and most of the locals left their keys in their trucks anyway.

"Speak of the devil," Casey said, jerking his thumb toward the road. Amanda turned to see an official RCMP vehicle from Roddickton crest the hill and began to curve down toward the centre of the village. Amanda and Casey watched as it slowed to a stop in front of the pier. Willington and a young woman piled out, along with an impossibly young-looking constable.

Willington gave Amanda a quick nod before turning to Casey. "Anything new to report, Case?"

"Body's not gone anywhere, Willie," Casey replied. "I'll take you all straight over."

"Constable Bradley will stay here to conduct interviews. Saves time, and details are forgotten so quickly."

"We already got a pretty good suspect," Casey began, gesturing to Amanda. "This lady's friend —"

"We don't know anything for sure," Amanda interjected before he could say more.

"Still, the feller's truck is back there —" Casey pointed toward the entrance to town. "He was after buying one of our boats a couple of days ago. Now he's gone missing, and Stink's boat's missing too."

Willington hesitated. Amanda could see him eyeing the truck and then the boat, debating how to proceed. The medical examiner, a vibrant young woman with olive skin and cropped black hair, laid a hand on his arm.

"Let's have a look at the body first, okay, Willie?"

Willington gestured to Phil's truck. "Check that out, Bradley," he said to his constable. "Get the man's ID and find out what people saw. I'll be back in an hour or two."

After they left, the village hummed with that peculiar mixture of excitement and horror that always surrounded a major disaster. Some of the houses were vacant, their owners away at jobs in Labrador or Alberta, but a handful of children, their mothers, and grizzled old-timers were visible, the children running happily in the September sunshine and the adults doing house repairs or laying in firewood for the coming winter. They all stopped their work to watch the police drama unfold.

As Bradley questioned them, Amanda edged close in an effort to eavesdrop. Several villagers gestured down toward the back harbour and Amanda caught the words "truck" and "boy." After a few interviews, Bradley climbed in the RCMP cruiser and drove down the road to Phil's truck. Amanda watched as he circled the truck and rifled through its interior before pulling out his radio.

She drifted closer. "Right, sir," she heard him say before signing off and placing another radio call. This time he turned his back on her so that she couldn't hear, but she could clearly see him reading the numbers off Phil's licence plate. Her heart sank. Soon the police would know there was a missing-persons report out on him, with concern expressed about his mental health.

After Bradley had signed off and was heading back toward the harbour, Amanda walked up the hill leading into the village, hoping to snag a wayward cellphone signal from somewhere. After a few minutes of searching, she climbed on top of a picnic table and got lucky.

Sheri snatched up the phone on the second ring. "Any word?" she asked.

"Not directly." Amanda chose her words carefully, opting not to mention Old Stink or his murder, for Sheri sounded tense enough. "We found his truck in the village of Conche, but we're still a couple of days behind and we're not sure what direction he took. The police may contact you with questions about his …" she groped for neutral words "… his state of mind."

Sheri didn't seem to be listening. "Jason thinks he's got a lead on him."

"What?"

"He said a fisherman spotted a man and a boy in a small boat near a place called Nameless Cove. I've looked it up on the map. It's near the tip, just north of Flower's Cove."

And Deadman's Cove, Amanda recalled with a shudder. She'd spoken to a fisherman there a few days earlier, on her way up the western shore. If Jason was correct, she and Chris were way off track. Yet Phil's truck was here. That made no sense!

"When was this?" she asked.

"I don't know exactly. But he called this morning, so it was probably in the past day or so. Jason's going to rent a boat and check out the coast. That's good news, right? Phil and Tyler are still safe, doing what they'd planned."

Amanda forced a cheerful agreement. "Keep me posted, and I promise to do the same. The minute you hear from Jason, call me. And leave a voice message if I don't answer. Cell service is pretty iffy where I am."

Sheri laughed. "Welcome to Newfoundland, my dear."

Amanda hung up, glad that at least one of them was able to laugh. She wasn't nearly as optimistic about this latest news from Jason. Phil's truck was sitting in plain view at the bottom of the hill, probably 150 kilometres across the northern peninsula from Nameless Cove, and according to the locals it had not moved in several days. There were only two ways he could have shown up in Nameless Cove; either he had succeeded in piloting Stink's dilapidated old boat all the way up and around the northern tip of the peninsula and down the western side, or he had stolen a vehicle in Roddickton, and had made his escape across the peninsula. Toward airports, ferries, and places far away.

More likely, Jason's witness was mistaken. How could anyone clearly identify two people in a boat on the ocean, probably wearing hats and lifejackets, caught in the glare of the sun off the ocean?

She was just turning to head back down the hill when her cellphone chirped. She glanced at the text message. From Matthew Goderich, succinct and pointed.

WTF???

She sucked in her breath. She knew Matthew was back in Canada, having abandoned Nigeria at the same time she and Phil had, and she knew he was trolling for worthy stories that could rebuild his connections to the major papers. He checked in on her and Phil periodically, out of what she hoped was sympathy and concern rather than a thirst for juicy follow-up material. He'd known she was going to meet Phil in Newfoundland, but those three letters *WTF???* suggested something more ominous than idle curiosity.

She stayed on the picnic table and punched in his contact number, hoping the cellphone signal remained strong enough for a proper conversation. The smallest cloud or puff of wind seemed to defeat it.

The line crackled to life almost immediately. "Amanda, thank god! What's going on?"

Matthew's voice sounded even more ragged than usual. Decades of smoking and bad air had left his lungs starved and his throat lacerated, but she wondered whether he was taking enough care of himself. Like herself, he was a global wanderer with no place to call home and no one to nag him. She pictured his short, fireplug body and the perpetual five-o'clock shadow that lent him a seedy air, and she felt a rush of affection. How like Matthew to forget everything, even hello, in his headlong pursuit of a story.

"Hello to you too, Matthew. What do you mean — 'going on'?"

"Are you with Phil?"

"No, why? What's up?"

"I just got it off the police scanner! There's a province-wide alert out on him. What the fuck has he done?"

"I don't think he's done anything, Matt. What does the alert say? Wanted for questioning? Suspect?"

"Wanted in connection with a suspicious death. They say he may be armed and dangerous."

She drew a sharp breath. "That's ridiculous! Armed with what? A Swiss Army knife?"

"It didn't say. You know how these things are — cop baffle-speak. The alert covers all of Newfoundland and Labrador, land and sea. What happened, Amanda?"

Amanda hesitated. Matthew was a friend, bonded by their shared horror, but he was also a reporter hungry for a story. In the silence, she heard his whispered curse.

"I'm not looking for a story! Trust me, I've been worried about him for months. What the hell has he got himself into?"

She took a deep breath. She had few friends and allies in this part of the world, and none, except Chris Tymko, who would understand Phil's struggles and his lines in the sand. But Chris was also a cop.

"An old fisherman was found murdered. He lived alone out on a remote cape and Phil was last seen heading in his direction."

"Murdered how?"

"Axe to the head. But that's not public knowledge, Matt, so keep it zipped."

"Oh god," Matthew breathed.

"It makes no sense. Even as desperate and screwed up as Phil was, you know how much he hated violence."

"Did he and this man have an argument? Could he have gotten angry?"

"They didn't even know each other."

"Then why was Phil going to see him?"

"I think to borrow a boat."

Matthew was silent a moment and when he spoke again, his voice was tentative, as if he was loath to venture further. "What if the man refused?"

"What are you getting at, Matt?"

"Has Phil been having any weird PTSD symptoms recently? Beyond the usual mood swings?"

"He gets anxious, yes. He gets short-tempered. So do I."

"No, I mean worse than that. Flashbacks, hallucinations."

It took a moment for the implication to catch up with her. She had vivid memories that flooded in due to the most unexpected triggers. Darkness could make her mortally afraid. Fires still made her tense. Running footsteps, the smell of meat … all those triggers could throw her right back into that awful time. But she recognized them as such. She wasn't reliving the nightmare, just remembering it. Sometimes she heard screaming that she thought she might have imagined. But true flashbacks? Not in a few months. And hallucinations, never. But she had sought professional help and, although she knew she would always be haunted by them, she'd insisted on confronting and trying to conquer those dark days.

Phil had not.

She scrambled to formulate an answer. "Honestly? I don't know. I haven't seen him since we got back. But I can't imagine … No matter how upset he was, no matter what bad memories were triggered … an axe to the head? Never."

Silence crackled for so long she wondered whether she'd lost the connection. "Matt?"

"I was never going to reveal this," he said, so softly she had to cover her other ear. "But last fall in Nigeria, Phil told me he killed a man."

It was Amanda's turn to be speechless. Literally robbed of breath to force out words. "Who?" she managed eventually.

"One of the Boko Haram fighters he encountered in the desert."

"Oh! But … but in self-defence, then."

"No. In a rage."

"How? Why?"

"Fog of war, Amanda? He wasn't sure. It was dark, he was trying to sneak through the grasslands, keeping to the shelter of a wadi. He smelled smoke and heard sounds of a group somewhere in the night but he didn't know whether it was a village or a fighter's camp. Creeping forward, he came upon a sentry beside a fire. He recognized him — a kid from the security force you'd hired to protect the village. Now with an AK-47, bandana, camo, the whole Boko Haram shit. Ahead, Phil could hear screams and see fires burning. In a split second, Phil was on him."

The image was as vivid as if she were still there. The betrayal of those they'd paid to protect them. The howls, the shooting flames, the thunder of fire consuming the flimsy wood huts. The mingled cries of pain and protest and triumph. The staccato of gunfire. *Save them*, had been her only thought. *Whatever it takes.*

And yet …

Fighting back the memory, she forced herself to focus. "But the sentry would have killed him."

"He didn't even turn around."

"Still … how did Phil kill him? We never even had weapons."

"An axe he found lying at the fireside. Still bloody from killing people," he said.

As she absorbed this final shock, she spotted Bradley down below by Phil's truck, on his radio again, nodding and taking notes.

"Matt, I gotta go."

"I'm coming there. I'm looking up flights to Deer Lake as we speak."

"Okay, but cellphone coverage is bad here. If you can't reach me —"

"Don't do anything until I get there."

She had no time to lose. The police search was kicking into high gear. Phil would be a fugitive once again, fleeing through unknown territory, driven by a single goal. Escape. Safety.

Would he even know where he was, and what he was fleeing? "I can't promise that, Matt."

———

Amanda raced back down the hill and through town, keeping a sharp eye out for Constable Bradley, who was no longer in sight. She had left Kaylee playing ball with the children, and now the dog came bounding up in delight, panting happily from the game.

There was still no sign of Casey, Chris, and the rest of the crew from Stink's place, but Amanda knew she didn't have much time before they returned. She spotted Thaddeus, the fisherman who'd been helping Casey work on the boats earlier.

"Is there a spare boat I can rent for a few hours?"

The fisherman jerked upright, his eyes narrowing. "What for?"

"To go down the coast a bit, see if I can spot my friend. How far is Englee? Do you think Stink's boat could make it all the way?"

Thaddeus snorted. "She'd need a whole lot of prayer and luck for that trip. Twenty kilometres on open seas."

"Then if it's as bad as you say, my friend might be stranded just a few kilometres down the coast."

"There's fishing boats about. All he has to do is flag one down."

"I know, but … well, my friend might be running scared."

"Running scared." The fisherman scrutinized her. She could feel the doubt and disapproval in his gaze. "And what are you going to do if you find them?"

"Bring them back."

"Could be dangerous."

"He's my friend. He's not going to hurt me."

"You never know what a man's capable of."

"I know him. He's probably frightened. Desperate."

"All the more reason. If he killed Old Stink —"

"He didn't!" She broke off to recapture calm. Above all, she needed to appear rational. "But if he did, it would have been an accident. I know him, Thaddeus. He needs help. And he's got his son with him."

Thaddeus said nothing. Amanda looked around at the half-dozen small boats moored at wharves or pulled helter-skelter up on the shore. Most in varying stages of rust and rot. She pointed to the only one with a motor.

"What about that one?"

He shifted his gaze from her to the boat. A frown creased his brow. "Know anything about piloting a boat?"

"I've piloted plenty of them overseas. Much more decrepit than that." It was an exaggeration, but all for a good cause. Most of the boats she'd piloted had nothing but a paddle or scull. However, she had driven a speedboat across the lakes in Quebec, so that experience would have to do.

"Ocean?"

"Big lakes."

Thaddeus grunted. "Lakes is nudding. I'll get my boy to take you down the coast. He's just up at the garden helping my wife harvest the potatoes."

Amanda's heart sank. She'd dug her own hole on this one, persuading Thaddeus that Phil would never hurt her. In truth, who could ever be sure? In Africa she'd seen kind, gentle neighbours rendered savage in the swirl of bloodlust. Never, ever, would she put a child into the middle of that again.

"No, I won't take him away from his chores. Helping his mother is much more important."

Thaddeus's eyes twinkled. "He won't see it like that."

"All the same, I won't hear of it. I have a hundred dollars hanging around just waiting for a good cause. I've got a compass, maps, and some emergency gear. All I need is a boat that won't sink and a couple of life jackets, and I'll be fine. I promise to be back before nightfall."

He gave her a long look. A man of few words, but many reservations. A man honed to expect the worst over a lifetime of struggle and resistance. She pasted a look of determined cheer on her face.

"She can't handle the big waves," he said.

"Then I'll stick close to shore."

He shrugged. "Your funeral."

CHAPTER FOURTEEN

Amanda made it out of Conche Harbour and around the tip of the headland out of sight of the villagers before the engine sputtered and died. The wind ripped across the open sea, and the boat pitched and wallowed in the swell. With each slapping wave, water splashed over the gunwales and tossed the boat like flotsam toward the jagged shore. Kaylee cowered under the seat in the bottom of the boat, her ears flattened and her eyes wide with reproach.

Amanda spread her legs to brace herself as she bent over the engine and struggled to prime it. Her arm ached from pulling the cord, and the rocks were metres away before the engine finally coughed and rattled to life. Gasping with relief, she fell into the seat and spun the boat away from the rocks.

To the north and south, the coast wove in and out like a ragged seam, splintering and crumbling into bays, fjords and points. Phil could be in any of the hidden inlets. She had told Thaddeus she was going south toward Englee, but now that she was out on the ocean, she wondered whether Phil would choose to go north instead, toward St. Anthony.

She forced herself to think the unthinkable. If Phil had killed Stink, he'd be in full flight, and if he were thinking at all logically, he'd be trying to get as far away as fast as he could. St. Anthony had a small airport, allowing him to get off the island within hours.

And even if he were simply seeking oblivion, the land to the north was as wild and empty as he could ever hope for. So she pointed the nose of her boat north.

As the boat fought its way along the coastline, she tried to find an ideal distance from shore — far enough that a strong wave would not throw her on the rocks but close enough that the land provided some shelter from the open sea. Close enough that she could see into the nooks and crannies of the shoreline.

Her progress was slow. She had to keep one wary eye on each approaching wave while she scoured the cliffs and dark woods and barrens that formed the ever-changing shore. Noon sun washed the land in greens, silvers, and shadowy black. Her eyes ached from squinting against the glare and the constant bucking of the boat.

This could all be a fool's errand. Phil could be anywhere by now! Even across the peninsula, as Jason Maloney claimed. Through her worry and fatigue, fury began to take hold. The man might be desperate, he might even be suicidal, but damn it, he had a son to take care of! A son who was probably bewildered and frightened by now. He had friends who were moving heaven and earth for him. And yet he couldn't spare a single, fucking word? Not even "sorry"?

The boat growled and whined as it inched up the coast. Kaylee ventured out of hiding and finally took up a sentry's post at the bow. They wasted precious time exploring every inlet and cove along the way. After three hours the sun was beginning to slip toward the western hills, and Amanda knew she was running out of time. No one knew she was heading north, and if she failed to return as promised, Chris and the villagers would be worried. There might even be frantic searches launched for her, drawing precious resources away from Tyler and Phil.

But worry drove her on. Just into this one last cove, around this one rocky point. By tomorrow the police would have descended, with their much greater manpower and equipment. If they found Phil before she did, he would get no mercy or sympathy, only the harsh, by-the-book judgment of Sergeant Amis. In his desperate state, who knew what he'd do?

She finally set herself a limit. Ahead in the distance she could see spumes of spray breaking over a barren point of land that jutted into the ocean. She wondered how many unsuspecting sailors had been caught unaware and had cracked up on the rocks. If Phil had come upon it in darkness or fog, he and Tyler might well be stranded there.

She slowed and approached cautiously, watching the water ahead for rocks lurking just below the surface. The boat pitched and rolled. Her hand ached from gripping the tiller and she shivered in the cold spray. As the point drew nearer, she steered the boat farther out toward the safety of the open sea. Her eyes raked the slick stones for signs of a wreck. A person standing on the shore. A distress beacon.

Nothing. Just bleak, empty rock littered with ocean junk.

She was just preparing to turn back when her eyes caught a flash of light on the shore. She spun the boat around and hardly dared to breathe as she inched closer. Her heart pounded. It could be anything. But it was something! Sunlight was dancing off metal, and, as she drew close, she could make out colours. Red and white against the grey shale of the shore.

Closer still, she made out the shape of a small boat aground on the shore. Once white but patched with rust and faded red paint. Its motor glinted black in the glare of the sun. The tide was coming in, and the boat heaved and banged against the rocks. She ran her own boat up on a nearby beach, pulled up the motor, and leaped out into the shallow water. Kaylee bounded nimbly ahead, grateful to be on solid ground. After tying her boat to a stunted shrub, Amanda scrambled over the rocks to the other boat.

It lay empty, abandoned to the whim of the surf, with no tie rope or anchor to hold it in place. She wondered whether the incoming tide had washed it in. It looked as if it had seen better days, held together by little more than rust and crusted grime. An inch of water sloshed around in the bottom and its wooden seats were cracked and warped with age. The tiny black engine was antique, and there was a jagged hole in the hull through which the seawater swirled with each wave.

Had the hull been ripped open by the surf after the boat was pulled ashore? Or had the boat hit a rock and swamped, dumping its crew into the icy sea? Alarmed, she peered up and down the coast. There was no sign of anyone. The coastal land was barren, but inland she could see a wall of tuckamore, stunted, spiky, and impenetrable. If this was Phil's boat and he had wanted to set up camp, he would not choose this frigid, wind-scoured shore. Could there be protection and shelter farther inland beyond the trees?

She glanced at her watch. She really ought to be heading back in order to avoid being caught out on the ocean after dark. She hadn't packed any gear for camping in the wilderness, and had only an emergency supply of food and water. She could make do, of course, with the berries along the shore to supplement her food, but the wise course would be to return in the morning with the equipment for a proper ground search. But any delay would put Phil farther out of reach than he already was.

She pulled out her cellphone in the slim hope that she could alert Casey and perhaps Chris Tymko to her discovery, but wasn't surprised to see no signal. She was miles from anywhere, surrounded by mountains and empty ocean.

I can spare ten minutes, she told herself. *Time to reach the tuckamore to see whether there is any path leading inside.* She clambered up the rocks and headed through the shore grasses toward the twisted wall of trees. Kaylee had her nose to the ground and snuffled excitedly as she trotted ahead. Following her, Amanda detected some subtle signs of trampled grass and broken stems, and her hopes surged. Something large had passed this way. The gnarled spruce seemed to huddle together, entwining their canopies to shelter one another from the brutal sea, but as she drew close, she spotted a small hole in the branches.

By now Kaylee was far ahead, invisible in the underbrush. Amanda crawled through the hole into an alien world of grey trunks and twisted limbs, where the sunlight was muted and the thick mat of needles muffled all sound.

Barely twenty feet inside the forest, she caught a glimpse of orange. As vivid and out of place in the web of grey as a shout in a graveyard. In a rush of hope, she plunged forward, ignoring the sharp branches that scratched her arms and legs. The lifejackets lay at the base of a tree, discarded as a snake sheds its skin. No longer needed and a burden to the travellers. Amanda picked them up and searched them for clues. They were sodden, whether from rain, dew, or a dunk in the ocean, she couldn't tell. Both were adult male sizes, but one was a large and the other a small.

Her mind made the instant leap to Tyler and Phil. She supposed she could be wrong, but she was sure she wasn't. She checked the jackets and found a whistle, a flare, a metal canteen, a pack of waterproof matches, and a compass that was stuck on south. The compass was useless, but why had Phil left the other items? As an experienced orienteerer with emergency training, surely he would never have abandoned them.

Holding the larger jacket while she puzzled over the contradiction, she noticed the tear in its back. She pushed her finger through the hole and peered at the darker stain around it. Her breath grew short and her heart began to pound. She turned the jacket over to examine the inside, where the dark wine stain spread across the whole fabric.

She dropped the jacket in horror. She raised her head, and terror propelled her voice above the roaring of the sea.

"Phil! Phil!"

It was nearly dark by the time Chris and Corporal Willington finally finished with the murder scene. The medical examiner had done her examination, ruled the death suspicious, and ordered the body removed to St. John's for autopsy.

"There's going to be a lineup at the morgue," Chris had remarked. Dr. Iannucci's opinion had confirmed the obvious: Stink had died from massive blunt force trauma to the head, but she had also suspected, after studying his filthy clothing and his living quarters, that he was in the early stages of dementia.

"Yes, but he was still bashed on the back of the head," Willie had said. "Homicide, no matter what else is going on."

"Agreed," the doctor said. "But if Stink was charging at him with a gun, the killer may have had little choice."

Chris forced himself to lean close to the body to sniff the man's hands, but the overpowering stench of decay and urine blocked out all other scents. "We'll ask St. John's to run a GSR test for gunshot residue."

Dr. Iannucci nodded. As she was loading her gear back into Casey's boat for the trip back to Conche, she paused. "While you're waiting for the extraction team and the investigation team to arrive, you might want to search the house and grounds for other signs of peculiar habits. I noticed he put his dirty socks in the fridge, for example."

Chris nodded. His grandmother had Alzheimer's, and although the family cared for her on the farm, her bizarre behaviour was often a strain. He had already conducted a thorough search of the cabin and grounds, but looking for evidence related to Old Stink's death rather than his state of mind. Now he and Willie divided the task between them and began a second search.

"Document, mark, and photograph," said Willie, who was nominally in charge. "Let's solve this case before that fancy cop from Ontario even sets foot on the cape. You know more about Alzheimer's, so you take the cabin and shed. I'll take the grounds and wharf."

After watching Willie head back down the path toward the bay, Chris steeled himself to re-enter Stink's home. He looked at the nearly empty shelves through new eyes. Stink had three bags of salt and four jars of pickles, but no staples like flour and sugar. The propane tank that powered his fridge was empty, but there were two full tanks in the woodshed. Inside the privy, Chris found a box of partially burned cash — about two hundred dollars — and an unopened can of baked beans with the label burned off.

This second search also failed to turn up Stink's rifle, but this time Chris found two shell casings on the floor by his mattress. There were no visible bullet holes, but Chris did wonder whether the broken window had been caused by a bullet. A forensic expert might be able to determine more conclusively, but Chris felt a flutter of relief. If Phil had come looking for Stink with the hope of procuring a boat, and Stink in his dementia had mistaken him for a threat and shot at him, Phil might have been forced to use the axe in self-defence.

Chris revised his earlier conclusion that the killer had brought the axe into the house as part of a premeditated attack. In his paranoid state, Stink might have kept the axe by his bed all along.

The rumble of a boat drew him outside and down to the shore just in time to see the Coast Guard vessel pulling in. The captain conferred with Willie briefly before unloading a stretcher and body bag onto the wharf. Within fifteen minutes, Stink was gone, on the first leg of his journey to the morgue in St. John's.

By then, darkness was descending and the chance to find further evidence was fading fast. Willie grinned at Chris with relief and nodded to the spare boat Casey had towed over for them.

"I'm ready for a shower and a pint. You, b'y?"

Chris nodded. "More than ready! It'll take more than a shower to wash the smell of that cabin out of my clothes."

He cast off while Willie started the engine. Once they were out on the open water heading for the mouth of the bay, Willie gave him another grin and shouted over the noise of the boat. "Did you solve our murder for us?"

"No, but I have a theory. Not about who, but how." Chris told Willie about the shell casings and the possibility of self-defence.

Willie listened with a gleam in his eye. "That's good," he said. "Because I've got a pretty good idea of who, and your theory will be a big help to him."

"Well, I know you're thinking of Phil, but we have no proof —"

Willie took his camera out of his backpack and braced himself against the rocking of the boat as he thumbed through photos. He leaned forward to show one to Chris. At first, Chris could barely make it out but as his brain deciphered the shape, he felt his earlier relief drain away. It was a baseball cap, with the name EXPLOITS CATARACTS across the front.

"If I'm not mistaken," Willie said, "the Exploits is the river running through Grand Falls, and the Cataracts is their hockey team. Didn't you say your friend and his son were from Grand Falls?"

Chris nodded grimly. He could think of no excuse. No other explanation.

"The cap is pretty wet and muddy," Willie was saying, "but I'd say it's a boy's size. I marked it and protected it with a piece of tarp." He looked sympathetic. "They'll likely be able to get DNA off it."

Chris rode the rest of the way through the darkening seas in silence, wondering how he was going to break the news to Amanda. As they approached the brightly lit harbour in Conche, he scanned the shore for the familiar sight of a bouncy red dog and Amanda's red straw hat. There was no sign of either. Only Casey, pacing the length of his wharf anxiously as he watched their approach.

"Any sign of your girlfriend out there?" Casey asked as he seized hold of the painter and tied off the boat.

"Amanda? No, why? Did she go out to meet me?"

"Some fool thing. Looking for your friend. Worried about his boat, but the one she's in ain't no better!"

"Why didn't you stop —" Chris checked himself. Casey had already helped far more than anyone had a right to expect. He started to apologize when Casey held up his hand.

"You know her. You think anyone was going to stop her? Weren't me she talked to, anyway. But she promised Thaddeus she'd be back before dark, and here it is like pitch, with no sign of her. The look in her eye, Thaddeus said. He should have knowed better."

So should I, Chris thought. *Damn it, so should I.*

CHAPTER FIFTEEN

Amanda scrambled along the shore, hoping to catch a single bar's worth of reception on her cellphone. She even climbed up on the barrens above the point. No luck. *Damn useless technology*, she railed. *There are cellphone signals all over the deserts in developing countries, but none here.* Then she noticed with alarm that the battery was low. Each moment it wasted searching for a signal drained it further. Reluctantly she turned it off entirely and pocketed it. No choice but to go back to Conche before the sky was pitch black.

When she turned to descend the head, she realized Kaylee was not with her. An irrational jolt of fear shot through her. Hurriedly she retraced her steps down to the shore, shouting for the dog. She forced her fear under control as she picked a path over the uneven rock, for a broken leg or twisted ankle would not help Phil. She had just reached her boat when Kaylee raced out of the tuckamore, her tongue lolling and her ears flying. As soon as she saw Amanda, she barked and wheeled about to head back into the woods. Amanda followed and found her standing over the lifejackets, whining. *She's picked up the smell of blood*, Amanda thought. But the moment Amanda appeared, Kaylee pressed her nose to the ground and ran deeper into the tuckamore.

"Have you got a scent, girl?" Amanda shouted. The dog was much smaller and more nimble than she was, and she wove back and forth through the dense spruce and fir with ease. Amanda struggled to keep up, hunched low and twisting to dodge the sharp branches. She cursed herself for not having put Kaylee on a leash. She needed to go back to her boat for some emergency supplies. She had her small backpack with her, containing a first aid kit, water, power bars, and a compass, as well as the matches and canteen she had taken from the lifejackets, but she'd left her beacons, blankets, and dry clothes in the boat.

The path Kaylee was taking through the woods turned her all around within minutes. When she paused to catch her breath, she took stock of her surroundings. Nothing but grey spruce trees on all sides, so densely intertwined that she couldn't see more than twenty feet in front of her. She could barely see the path she had taken, let alone the path ahead. Just as panic was creeping in, Kaylee appeared as a flash of red motion through the grey, stopping some distance ahead to check on her. The dog's expression was intense and impatient.

It was impossible to know how far she had travelled, nor even where the shore was. Impossible to know where danger lurked. A bear, a bull moose, a coyote … or even a killer. She was tempted to call Kaylee to lead her back out of the woods, but the dog was clearly on a mission.

Fearful and cautious, Amanda groped her way forward. A steep hill loomed ahead and the tuckamore thinned. Tangles of deadfall littered the forest floor, rotting and covered with moss. Kaylee leaped easily over the logs, but Amanda slipped and slithered. She was breathless, soaked in sweat, and scratched by the spruce spikes by the time she almost literally collided with Kaylee. The dog had stopped on the other side of a large tree that had been uprooted by some long-ago storm. The root ball formed a shelter of sorts, and behind it, Kaylee stood whining and sniffing the ground.

Amanda rounded the barrier and found a tangle of alder, spruce, and fir branches piled high. A man-made shelter! Made so recently that the alder leaves had barely wilted.

Her hopes surged. Had she found their camp? She began to toss aside the branches. But then she saw a hiking boot protruding from under the brush. Horror seized her throat. She tore at the branches with abandon, uncovering rocks piled to weigh the branches down. She hurled these aside, revealing a leg, another boot, a torso in a red jacket. The body lay on its back with its legs outstretched, its arms folded, and its fingers laced together as if at peace.

"No," she murmured. "No no no." She clawed at the face, brushing debris away until she could make out the features. Bleached of blood, eyes opaque, the locks of rakish hair plastered against the pallid brow ...

Phil.

She stifled a wail of pain. Fought for breath and calm, rocking gently as the waves of memory crashed over her. Dead bodies littering the village square, dead eyes staring, flies swarming. The village dogs and the vultures circling. In the African heat, the carrion eaters rushed in quickly.

Here in the cold, remote northland, only the flies had begun.

She didn't know how long she sat at his side, overcome, before rational thought began to return. She bent over to study the body. What had happened here? She could see no sign of injury. How had he died?

Then she remembered the bloody tear in the back of the life-jacket. Swallowing bile, she forced herself to reach beneath him. Grunting and struggling against his stiff, unyielding weight, she finally rolled him over. This time she screamed aloud, putting all her horror and grief into a single, primal howl that was swallowed in seconds by the dense, empty woods.

The back of his red jacket was a mass of crusted blood. She forced herself to probe through it, feeling for the injury, and found a ragged hole in the jacket. Tears streamed freely now as she poked the hole with her finger and brushed cold, rigid flesh.

She jerked her hand back and recoiled, staring at her friend's ravaged body in disbelief. Shot or stabbed in the back. Who would do this? Why? And had that same killer then laid him to rest in a peaceful pose? Simply to hide the body or to make some small amends for what they had done?

Or had it been Tyler?

Tyler! She jerked upright, her eyes raking the grey, silent gloom. Where was Tyler? What had happened to the boy? Was he lying in another shallow grave nearby, or had he escaped and fled, terrified, into the wilderness?

"Tyler!" she screamed, cupping her hands and turning in a slow circle. Over and over until her voice was ragged and her throat ached. Straining her ears for the faintest whimper.

Dead quiet.

Amanda looked around desperately, trying to see through the increasing gloom. Kaylee was standing a few feet away, watching anxiously as if awaiting instructions. She showed no inclination to lead Amanda farther, and yet there had to be a trail. Even if it was only to another nearby grave.

She rolled Phil over onto his back again, piled the rocks and brush on top, and stood over him, smearing tears across her cheeks with her bloodied hands. She whispered a quiet, apologetic goodbye. Then she rose to face the dog and gestured to the woods. Kaylee was not a trained tracker but she had a good nose. Surely she could follow a recent scent if there is one.

"Go find Tyler, Kaylee. Find him."

———

167

The next morning Chris Tymko was up at first light, pacing the wharf. No Amanda. He felt like a coiled spring, his gut twisted with frustration, anger, and worry. Corporal Willington had left to return to his detachment the previous evening, but not before apologetically informing Chris he was off Stink's murder case.

"Sorry," he muttered, "Sergeant Amis's orders. Conflict of interest for you, or some damn thing."

When Chris opened his mouth to protest, Willington shook his head. "I'm pretty much off it too, just doing admin. Amis will be here by noon, and the district commander is sending in an incident commander to coordinate the whole thing. Local detachments on the roads, Integrated Border Enforcement Team on the water, helicopter in the air. The Emergency Response Team and K-9 are on alert. Meanwhile we're putting roadblocks on the highways, checkpoints at the ports … the works. 'Armed and dangerous,' they're calling him."

Chris nodded in grim acceptance. In Amis's place, given the facts, he would have done the same thing. A gut feeling about Phil's innocence, based on a few months' acquaintance with the man, was not enough to counter the evidence. How well did he really know the man? *How well do any of us know one another?*

Amanda was a different problem altogether. She couldn't conceive of Phil as a killer, and it was not in her nature to sit back while he struggled. She had gone off after him in a dubiously equipped boat, with limited expertise and gear for an ocean search.

Chris had slept on the daybed in Casey's kitchen and the man's wife had made him sweet tea and fried eggs before the first hint of dawn. Now a pale grey light bathed the mountain peaks in brooding green, and the harbour glistened like glass. Barely a whisper of wind came in off the ocean and the village hummed with early morning purpose, belying the brutal murder and the police manhunt about to begin.

He stared out toward the mouth of the bay, willing Amanda to appear. "By noon this place will be hopping," he grumbled to Casey. "Incident command trailer, RCMP and forensics vehicles all over the place, police Zodiacs coming in and out. I'm damned if I'm going to do nothing."

"No sign of your girlfriend yet, then?"

Chris was about to correct him, but checked himself. The details of their relationship didn't seem important. "Is there a boat I can borrow?"

Casey rolled his eyes. "I should be going into the boat-rental business. Pays better than fish. But I think with all the searchers heading out on the water after this Phil fella, they'll spot her soon enough."

"But it's going to take time to get that manpower and equipment mobilized. Meanwhile I can be out on the water in fifteen minutes."

Casey shook his head. "Might be there's fog coming in."

Chris looked at the flat grey sky. "Search conditions look ideal to me."

"Looks can trick you, my b'y. You don't want to be out on the ocean when the fog rolls in so thick you can't see the bow of your boat."

"Then Amanda shouldn't be out there, either. Let me do a quick search up the coast, just up around Stink's cape."

Casey frowned. "Thaddeus says she went the other way. She was thinking your friend might be making a run for Roddickton. It's at the top of Canada Bay, and the highway leads across the pen from there."

"How far is it to Roddickton?"

"By boat? Fifty-odd kilometres?"

Chris did a quick calculation. Even the slowest and most capricious motorboat could do the trip in a little more than half a day, but there might not have been time for the return trip before dark. If Amanda had landed in Roddickton, she might still be on the trail of Phil within the town. He felt his hopes rise.

"I'll try that route. With any luck I'll meet her coming back. But if she's broken down, I'll see her."

"Nobody will come looking for the two of you if you gets caught in a fog."

"That's why I'd better get going before it comes in."

In the end, with an exaggerated sigh, Casey lent him the same spare boat he had used the day before, a small, open skiff once used for old-fashioned cod trapping. Chris checked Amanda's supplies before packing his own gear for the trip. She had packed light, obviously not expecting to be far from civilization. Not prepared for an overnight in the wilderness, either.

He loaded up his boat with food, foul-weather gear, shelter, and first aid supplies, and then stored his hunting rifle under the seat.

Casey eyed the old .308 askance. "Budget cuts? That what they're equipping you fellas with these days?"

Chris rolled his eyes. "Don't get me started. Maybe this century we'll get the C8 Carbines everyone else has. This is my own personal rifle. Old but reliable."

The sea was still calm when he shoved off. Hands on his hips, Casey watched him from the wharf as he fumbled the engine alive and headed out to sea. Once he'd cleared the mouth of the bay, broad swells rocked the little skiff. He headed south, hugging the steep coastal cliffs that swept down to the sea. He chugged slowly, searching the water and the shoreline constantly with his binoculars. Few boats were about. The commercial fishing boats were farther out to sea, and the autumn recreational fishery had not yet begun. Tourists rarely ventured this far from the attractions and amenities around St. Anthony.

The coastline sliced deep and straight through the ocean toward the southwest. White spray crashed against the towering cliffs, and gannets and gulls swooped eagerly overhead in search of fish. A couple of hours later, the cliffs receded into a wide bay as if the ocean itself had taken a huge bite out of the land. Soon he spotted a jumbled village and harbour nestled in the protected nook of the bay. The village of Englee.

Grateful for the break, he piloted his small boat between the wharves in the narrow harbour and pulled up beside a man doing repairs to his boat. He introduced himself as Corporal Tymko, but before he could ask about Amanda, the man's eyes brightened.

"Oh, you're here about the murder. Fella who chopped Old Stink's head off and stole his boat."

Chris put on his solemn cop face. "I'm making inquiries, yes. Have you seen anyone fitting the description? A tall man in his mid-thirties with a young boy?"

"Not yet, no. But we're all keeping our eyes peeled."

"Who's we?"

"Oh, all up and down the coast, you know. Word gets around. A friend of mine says he spotted a boat ashore down toward Windy Point, a ways north of Cape Rouge."

Chris cursed inwardly. Had he been going in the wrong direction? "Stink's boat?"

The man shrugged. "Abandoned, anyway. Of course, nothing to say it's not been there for months. Nothing there but barrens."

"Did you report it?"

"Yeah. To you."

Chris pulled out his cellphone and turned it on. "You've got a signal!"

The man laughed and pointed to the tower at the top of the hill that loomed over the village. "Yes, b'y. We gots civilization down here in Englee."

Chris reached Willington back in the RCMP station in Roddickton and reported what the villager had said. He waited patiently while Willington consulted his map. Then a brief, awkward silence fell.

"What are you doing in Englee, Tymko?"

"Looking for Amanda. This piece of information just fell into my lap."

"Amanda's missing?"

Chris could hear the dismay his voice. "Well, not really missing. Just on her own cockamamie hunt."

"For Chrissakes, Tymko! He's a suspect. And now we've got a civilian bumbling around in the middle of the investigation, screwing up the search area and putting herself at risk."

"She doesn't think she's at risk." He paused. "Neither do I."

"Which is exactly why you're not on this case! If things get ugly, she could be right in the middle of the crossfire."

Chris was silent a moment, clamping down his temper. "I'm not anywhere near the case. I'm at least thirty kilometres away, on my way to your town. There's a chance Amanda went looking for Phil up your way."

There was a pause. "Let me know if you need a hand."

Chris relaxed. "You've got enough on your plate, but if you see her — she's got her dog with her, so she'll be easy to spot — tell her I'm on my way."

"Why does she think he's here in Roddickton?"

"I have no idea. She must have found out something."

"Which she didn't tell us." Willington swore under his breath. "Amis and his team have already been here and are on their way out to Conche along with the incident command trailer. They'll go ballistic when they find out. We've got roadblocks up now, and I'll tell my guys to keep a sharp eye out in town here for Amanda as well as Phil Cousins. They can't get far on foot, and there's not many places here to hide. Who knows, maybe by tonight you and I can have this whole case wrapped up before the incident commander even gets her gear unpacked. Then I'll treat you to the lumberjack's platter at our world-class Lumberjacks' Landing. Best restaurant on the eastern shore."

Chris laughed as he hung up. Likely the only restaurant on the east shore.

Amanda had no idea how far she'd walked, nor even in what direction. The gunmetal sky obscured all hint of the sun, and the rhythmic hiss of the surf had faded into the distance. Her stomach ached from hunger and her legs shook with fatigue. She'd spent most of the day doubling back and forth in search of Tyler, fighting her way around tuckamore and bog. She had clambered over boulders, waded through alder thickets, and climbed to the top of steep hills. She had called his name until she was hoarse.

Through the thumping of her heart and the panting of her breath, her ears strained to hear even the faintest sound of human presence. A cry for help. The growl of a motorboat coming up the coast. She had expected a search party from Conche or, at the very least, Chris Tymko to come looking her. A wave of affection welled up at the thought of him. She had only known him for a week, but sensed he was one of the truly good guys. When Phil had disappeared, he had understood her fear and her need, and had jumped in to help without a moment's hesitation. When she'd failed to return to Conche last night, surely he would have collected a posse and gone out looking.

Eventually he would come. Someone would come. Someone would find her boat, and the small boat Phil had been using, and they would begin to search from there. She wasn't worried for her own safety. She had survived on far less. Fresh water from the small streams tumbling down the hillsides, together with the red berries that blanketed the bogs and the forest floor, were enough for now.

Tyler was all she cared about. Kaylee had not found his body or grave near Phil's, so Amanda assumed he'd fled through the woods on an erratic path, grief-stricken and alone. God knows how long and how far he would run. He was a smart boy, often left to his own devices in the Cambodian village where she'd known him, but he was only eleven. He had just watched his father die. The father who made him laugh, taught him magic tricks, and organized village baseball games.

What would he do? Where would he run?

Kaylee had been unable to make sense of the trail. Not a trained tracking dog, she had bounded off in several directions, doubled back, and then milled at Amanda's feet, looking up at her as if for direction.

So they had trudged together. Amanda had kept a close eye on Kaylee's ears and nose. The dog would detect a scent or sound far earlier than Amanda and turn her ears and nose in that direction. But now, hours later, both she and the dog were flagging. Hunger and fatigue were taking their toll. Amanda had fashioned a sturdy walking stick, but, despite its support, she found herself slipping and stumbling on the uneven terrain.

Then her boot crashed through a patch of moss and she plunged knee-deep into swampy water. Thrown off balance, she fell hard against a rock. A sharp pain shot through her hip. Flailing and cursing, she dragged herself back onto solid ground, where she lay a moment to catch her breath. Kaylee, her paws black and her red coat matted with mud, whined and nuzzled close.

Amanda flexed her limbs and whispered a silent thank-you. Nothing was broken. She probed her sore hip through the slime and felt a soggy hole in her jeans. A small price to pay, she thought, until her fingers brushed something jagged and sharp. She pulled out her compass from her hip pocket. Stared at its smashed face and twisted needle.

Her breath quickened and a quiver of panic thrummed through her. It didn't matter that the sun and stars would chart a guiding course and the ocean would always be to the east. She was back in Nigeria, scurrying through smoke-choked darkness, not knowing whether she was running south toward safety or north into the machine guns of killers.

She looked up at the sky through the lace of trees. Everywhere she looked, nothing but trees. Scraggly, twisted, almost ghost-like. High ridges pressed in on both sides, plunging the valley into near darkness, and not even the distant hiss of ocean surf was audible.

She was lost. Exhausted. Hungry. And now finally, afraid.

She struggled to sit and leaned against a tree to collect herself. She heard her therapist's voice in her head. *Don't fight the fear, don't run from it. You're afraid. Ride with it, ride through it. Deep breaths. Let it float with you.*

Bit by bit, her pulse slowed and her terror receded. She took a long breath and refocused on the present. In her head, she conjured up her topographical map. She knew that she was between Conche and Grandois, and that Phil's boat was somewhere south of Windy Point, which was about midway. However, a large bay lay between Windy Point and Grandois, with the odd little French colonial village of Croque at the end of it.

She had not seen a trace of Croque on her wanderings, so she must still be south of the bay. But how far south? Had she backtracked so far that she was now far south of Windy Point? To her untrained eye, every little inlet and point on the shoreline looked like every other. Even if she could find the ocean again, she wouldn't know which direction to head.

Crushing fatigue weighed her down. She just wanted to sleep. Surely it was foolish, even dangerous, to continue the search without a rest. She risked plunging down a ravine or getting sucked into a bog. She should find a dry patch of land, build a shelter of spruce boughs, eat a little more of her energy bar, and rest until morning.

She was just closing her eyes when a low rumble bubbled in Kaylee's throat. Amanda's eyes flew open. In the distance, she heard crashing in the underbrush. Twigs snapped like gunshots. She pulled Kaylee to her and raised her walking stick, wishing she had something more formidable.

"Tyler!" she called.

A grunt. More thrashing. Thundering. Thankfully receding. Soon there was nothing but the creak of the trees in the wind. Kaylee and Amanda pressed together, trembling. Adrenaline coursed through her. *No*, she thought as she hauled herself to her feet, *I have to keep going. I have to find the goddamn ocean and figure out where my boat is. So I can go get the personnel and supplies to launch a proper search.*

A frightened little boy is out there, and every moment counts.

CHAPTER SIXTEEN

The trip up the bay to Roddickton took Chris a little over an hour at the leisurely pace the boat seemed to prefer. The grey clouds hung low, but there was no hint of the fog Casey had darkly predicted. *The crafty bugger must have been pulling my leg*, Chris decided, *as payback for me borrowing his boat.*

Canada Bay sliced a deep gash through spectacular rounded mountains on either side. To the southwest a hulking mountain range formed silhouettes of barren, inhospitable rock, like giants asleep in the sky. They would be impossible to traverse except where creeks tumbled through. On the north side, however, trees and grasslands blanketed the hills, offering some camouflage. He piloted the boat slowly so that he could peer into the crevices and shadowy shelter of the forest.

Nothing.

Closer to town, scattered houses and wharves began to crop up along the shore. As the settlement increased, he found what looked like the main wharf and pulled up. Unlike most communities on the Northern Peninsula, Roddickton did not make its living from fishing, and the absence of fishing boats, nets, and crab pots on the pier was striking. Chris knew it was founded as a lumber town and he assumed the sawmills and lumber wharves were farther up the channel.

The afternoon sun broke through as he climbed onto the wharf. He was hot, hungry, and sore. Every bone was rattled by the pounding of the boat and the throbbing of the engine. Peeling off his jacket, he put in a call to Willington.

"No sign of anyone, sad to say," Willington said, sounding more disappointed than sad. "But I do have a bit of intel. You're just in time for an afternoon beer. I'll be there in ten minutes."

Beer's an inspired idea, Chris thought, stretching his cramped legs. "Can you check with the guys in Conche first, to see if Amanda's shown up back there? And then can we do a pass around town here?"

"Sure thing. That will take us five minutes."

While he waited, Chris studied his map and took stock of the town. Willington was right; there weren't many places to hide. The population of roughly a thousand people was concentrated on half a dozen little streets and strung out along the main highway that continued on to Englee. A strange woman landing in town with her dog would have been noticed within seconds.

He crossed the street and knocked on the first house on the block. The elderly woman who answered said she'd seen no one — not a woman and her dog, nor a man and his son. The answer was the same at the next three houses.

"No strange boats moored up either," said a big, beefy man who was mowing his lawn.

Chris cursed in frustration. Had he wasted a whole day? It looked as if Amanda had not come up to Roddickton, and unless Phil had snuck in and out in the middle of the night, neither had he. For all Chris knew, Amanda was now safely back in Conche, wondering where the hell he was.

That hope was quickly dashed when Willington picked him up. There was still no word on Amanda. After a brief, unproductive search through the streets, Willington took him to his bachelor bungalow on the outskirts of town. He settled Chris on the deck out back, propped his feet on the deck rail, and popped two QVs before sitting back with a sigh.

"I've been thinking," he began. "I wouldn't be so quick to assume this fella Cousins didn't come through here. He's on the run so he's hardly going to pilot his boat into the middle of town in broad daylight. He knows a thousand pairs of eyes would pick him up in a second. Likely he ditched the boat past the town under cover of darkness and walked up to the highway. Moose-hunting season starts tomorrow and this is the heart of moose country, so there's lots of strangers coming and going. Guys are heading out to their hunting lodges and others coming in from Corner Brook or Deer Lake. Some even from the mainland. It'd be easy to hitch a ride or even stow away in the back for a bit."

"Moose-hunting season." Chris pondered the implications. "That means lots more trucks on the road, lots more eyes in the bush."

Willington downed the last of his beer. "ATVs too, driving all over the backcountry. We've got more moose around here than pretty near anywhere else in Canada."

"That means the danger of stray bullets and civilians getting in the way."

Willington laughed. "And an even greater danger of meeting an enraged bull. It's rutting season and they don't take kindly to outsiders getting too close. Seven, eight hundred pounds of charging moose is not a pretty sight."

"Did Amis set up roadblocks?"

"Not him, but the incident commander did, yeah. Both ends of the highway through town here, and at the turnoffs to Conche and Croque. All the major points of entry to the island, as well. But if Cousins hitched a ride out of here two days ago, it's a case of the horse and the barn door. But —" Willington sat forward with a flourish. His eyes danced. "— I do have a few pieces of news. Want another beer?"

"Willie! Spill it!"

Willington roared with delight as he fished two more beers from the cooler at his feet. Holding one out to Chris, he laid his finger alongside his nose. "This is on the QT. Back door report. Amis and the incident commander aren't telling me shit, but I have my sources. First off, a fisherman spotted Stink's boat a couple of days ago, going like a bat out of hell. He was too far away to see who was in it, but it's a good bet it was Phil."

"Where?"

"Along the coast north of Stink's place. Unfortunately the guy wasn't paying much attention, because it was before the murder was discovered, but he thinks it was going north. They're sending a party out at first light tomorrow to check on that boat you reported up near Windy Point."

Chris tried to think through the increasing fog of alcohol. "But if it was him, why would he go ashore in the middle of nowhere? Why not keep going all the way to St. Anthony?"

Willington shrugged. "Well, the one thing the fisherman did notice was that the boat was going pretty fast. Faster than Stink's boat likes, he said. Anyway, at least it's a lead. Right now they'll take any lead they can get. They have no idea what direction Cousins has gone or where he might be heading. It's hard to even know where to initiate the search. And it's a hell of a lot of territory to search, all rugged, mountainous terrain. You could hide in a cove and not be seen by a boat passing fifty feet offshore. Hell, you could hide in the tuckamore and not be seen from twenty feet!" He leaned forward, his expression sobering. "If he doesn't want to be found, we may never find him."

Chris's thoughts drifted to Amanda. She too was groping in the dark, without the communications and manpower of the

RCMP, and nothing but her own stubborn grit to drive her on. How long would it take before she gave up and came back?

"Which brings me to my second piece of intel," Willington was saying, his round face creasing in a grin. "What are the chances? You tie an anchor around a guy and you dump him overboard 250 kilometres from shore. What are the chances of that body ever being found?"

"Pure luck," Chris agreed.

"Shit luck for the guy who threw him overboard. That body the shrimpers towed ashore? Preliminary post-mortem results show he likely died of hypothermia, but he was also near starvation. Six feet tall, but weighed little more than a hundred pounds when he died."

Chris cast his mind back to that night on the wharf in St. Anthony. Had it really been only four days ago? The poor man had been dressed in a thin jacket and even thinner shoes, providing poor protection against the chilly winds of the North Atlantic. And now it appeared that not only had he been inadequately clothed on the ship, but also inadequately fed. A stranger far from home, frozen and starving.

"Okay, but someone tied an anchor to the man's body, so it's more than just natural death. What is the medical examiner thinking? Just a cover-up?"

Willington shrugged. "I don't think they're ruling out criminal negligence causing death."

"But someone's hiding something! They went to some lengths to prevent the body from being found, and at the very least, the victim wasn't provided the bare necessities of life by the captain of the ship." Sensing his patience and his temper fraying, Chris took a cautious sip of his beer. He'd had little to eat that day and a second beer wasn't really what he needed before dinner. Facts and theories tumbled through his mind, trying to connect.

A boat carrying fugitives, possibly foreign, had been spotted not far south of St. Anthony, and that boat had later been found by some village boys hidden onshore even farther south. The fugitives had vanished without a trace. Neither the coast guard nor the local villagers had seen any sign of them.

"Have Border Services or the RCMP got anywhere identifying the ship that the dead man was travelling on?" he asked.

"If he went into the water where he was found — a big if, given ocean currents — then he was inside Canadian waters. And if we connect him to the men in the lifeboat —"

"I think we should. Absolutely. At least as a working hypothesis. How many boats were carrying foreign nationals?"

"Well, that's the problem, there weren't any foreign vessels in that area in that time frame."

"That we know of."

Willington gave his loud, boisterous laugh. "What? You're suggesting there's something we don't know?"

"Foreign trawlers sneak in all the time, no matter what the official line is."

"I'm shocked. But anyway, it might not be a trawler at all. The Feds are looking at smuggling operations, possibly involving foreign ships heading for the St. Lawrence. Because there's one last piece of intel ..." Willington leaned forward, wiggling his eyebrows and clearly relishing the suspense. "The dead man had a piece of paper in his pocket. Forensics is still trying to decipher it all, but it appears to be a name and phone number with a 315 area code. That's Saint Lawrence County in upstate New York. Not much there except big empty spaces, but its main claim to fame? It borders the St. Lawrence River."

He watched as Chris drew his own conclusions. The St. Lawrence River formed a thousand kilometres of undefended, sparsely populated border between Canada and the United States.

With its many islands and hidden coves, it had a long, colourful history as a smuggling route between the two countries for everything from guns and bootleg liquor to illegal refugees, who often paid thousands of dollars to crooks and conmen in their search for a better life.

Northern Newfoundland was a long way off course, but if the boat had originated in northern Europe and had travelled through the North Sea, it's possible it was headed across to the Strait of Belle Isle and down to the St. Lawrence.

"So the hunt is now ramped up for those fugitives from the lifeboat," Willington was saying. "They might provide some information on the smuggling theory as well as the man's death."

"If they were desperate to escape detection, they might even have been involved in his death," Chris said, his thoughts turning dark. *There are a lot of desperate people on the run in the wilderness around here,* he thought. *I hope to hell Amanda is not smack in the middle of it all.*

Amanda stood on the side of the hill, looking around her. More grey, endless trees and ravines. Even the sky was a grim, gunmetal grey. The adrenaline of earlier had long since faded from her system, leaving her shaky and more tired than ever. Where was the goddamn sun? Would it hurt to give her a little glimpse, so she'd have a clue as to her direction.

She studied the pattern of moss and lichen on the trees — another basic orienteering technique — but it seemed to be everywhere, clinging to the trunks and branches like a grey shroud. Perhaps if she were a native Newfoundlander, she would be more adept at reading the land, but her knowledge of the lush jungles of Africa and Asia were no use to her here.

She listened for sounds of surf, and thought she detected a distant whisper, but it evaporated in the wind. For good measure, she shouted Tyler's name and cupped her ear for a response. No response. Only Kaylee, who bounded over to drop a stick at her feet.

In spite of herself, Amanda laughed. "Okay, princess, we need to get some food into our bodies, and then you're going to put that nose of yours to something more useful than finding sticks."

She struck out toward what looked like a clearing, pausing to pick berries and to turn over rocks and rotten logs along the way. Her years overseas had taught her not to be squeamish. Frogs, snakes, snails, and bugs were excellent sources of protein, the latter preferably deep fried to a nice crunch. In Asia they showed up on elegant restaurant menus as well as morning market stalls. Bugs would not be her first choice for breakfast, but when starvation loomed, they would do in a pinch.

The clearing turned out to be a small lake — Newfoundlanders would call it a pond, as if every body of water were measured against the enormity of the sea. She and Kaylee both drank from a small stream flowing into the pond, and Amanda ate more berries growing along the shore. She stuck to partridgeberries, which she recognized, and bright coral berries that seemed safe. But still her stomach roiled.

The dog watched her intently as she ate, and Amanda gave her a regretful smile. "Sorry, princess. I know I've fed you every day of your life, but this morning you'll have to harness your wolf DNA and try to catch us something."

Having seen refugees survive for days on the move without food, provided they had water, she knew she and Kaylee would manage. While she filled her water canteen, she took stock of her options. Tyler was her overwhelming concern. There was a terrified young boy on the loose in this wilderness, possibly injured or being hunted by the person who'd killed his father.

But she was surrounded by four or five hundred square miles of mountains, bogs, forests, and ponds. She had limited emergency supplies, no weapon, no navigational tools beyond her wits, and no idea where she was. In the twists and turns of her trek through the dense tuckamore, she could have been wandering in circles. She had heard no sounds of search helicopters or boats along the shore. If they were looking for her at all, they were nowhere near.

Common sense told her she should try to find the coast. From there, not only would she be more visible to searchers, but she might be able to find her boat and go for help. But it might take her a whole day to find the coast — twenty-four long hours in the life of a starving, frantic boy. Moreover, she didn't know which direction led to the coast. With no compass, no sun, and no sound of surf, she could flounder in the bogs and tuckamore for days.

I need a good vantage point, she thought, peering through the trees at the surrounding hills. She headed toward the tallest one and soon found herself scrambling up the steep incline on all fours. As the trees grew shorter and sparser, the barren rock of the summit came into view ahead. *I should be able to see for miles*, she thought, quickening her pace eagerly. Beside her, Kaylee grew rigid. The hair on her back rose, but she made no sound.

"What is it, princess?"

Kaylee backed up, belly flat to the ground, and circled to cower behind her. Her every muscle radiated danger. Her own fear spiking, Amanda stopped to take in her surroundings. She could see nothing. She crept forward cautiously, keeping low under cover of the bushes. She peered over the boulder and froze. The rocky summit offered no shelter, and in among the sedges and dwarf berry bushes was a large black bear.

The massive, shaggy creature was on all fours, staring back at her.

Amanda ducked back behind the boulder and waited for her pulse to slow before risking another peek. The bear appeared to be alone, probably foraging for berries, but Amanda searched the shadowy undergrowth for signs of a cub. Kaylee stayed safely behind her, and Amanda offered a silent thanks to her for not racing out to bark. She tried to remember what she'd been taught about bears. First rule; never run away. The bear will chase, at speeds of up to fifty kilometres an hour. Keeping a watchful eye on the animal, she groped behind her to secure Kaylee on her leash.

Second rule; talk to it in a deep, calm voice and make yourself as big as possible. Easier said than done. She slipped her backpack off and balanced it on top of her head. Then she tried for as calm a voice as she could muster. "We won't hurt you, Mr. Bear. We'll just leave the hilltop to you."

Third rule; back away slowly.

"Let's go, princess," she said, stepping backwards. One foot, another foot.

The bear huffed and swung its head back and forth. Kaylee yanked backwards, her nostrils flaring. The bear reared up.

Gripping the leash more tightly and struggling to keep the backpack raised, Amanda continued her careful retreat. Her foot slipped, sending rocks and gravel tumbling down in a rush of noise. She crouched, holding her breath as she listened for the bear's charge. Nothing. She lifted her head to look. The bear hadn't moved.

Amanda continued to talk in a quiet, level voice as she backed down the slope. Bit by bit she put distance between herself and the bear, until finally she reached the bottom of the ravine. Then she ran full tilt through the woods all the way back to the pond. Kaylee ran beside her, her tail tucked and eyes wide.

When they reached the shore, Amanda collapsed on a rock to catch her breath. She waited and watched until she was sure the bear had not followed, and only then did she allow herself a nervous laugh.

"Well, princess, that idea was a bust!" she said. "Here we are back where we started. Any other bright ideas?"

Kaylee was drinking from a trickle of water seeping into the pond. Amanda's hopes lifted. Streams flowed downhill toward the ocean. If she could find the flow of water leaving this pond, she could follow it, perhaps all the way to the ocean.

For what felt like hours, Amanda slogged around the perimeter of the pond, sometimes ankle deep in reeds and muck, following each trickle of water to its rocky end. Kaylee was bounding through the brush, tracking smells and chasing squirrels. Although Amanda paused often to eat berries, she was feeling light-headed by the time she came across a steady stream. She followed as it meandered through the berry bushes, wormed around boulders, and seeped through bright green moss. Afraid of losing it, she fought through brush and bog, tearing her clothes and flailing at blackflies. *Blackflies*, she thought with disgust. *In September!*

Finally she spotted a shimmer of water through a break in the trees ahead. Hallelujah! She quickened her pace, straining to hear the sound of surf and the cry of wheeling gulls. The water was too calm. Too silent. Maybe it was a protected inlet. Maybe the ocean lay just beyond the ridge ahead. Nature was so coy, hiding secret pathways through the faceless, lookalike land.

When she finally reached the edge of the water, she was gasping for breath and wet with sweat and swamp. She simply stood and stared.

Another pond. This one five times the size of the first. It would take hours to circle it in search of the exit stream. Useless, fucking waste of time! She roared her frustration aloud, her curses floating back to her across the rippling surface of the pond. She cupped her hands and shouted Tyler's name. Nothing. A cluster of ducks quacked their anxious surprise in the tall reeds nearby.

Kaylee was paying them no attention as she roamed with her nose to the ground. "You're a Duck Toller," Amanda grumbled. A duck could be dinner for both of them, as could a fish or two from the pond if she could figure out how to catch them.

"Kaylee!" she shouted, waving in the direction of the ducks. "Go get it!"

Kaylee jerked her head up, ears cocked. She had something clamped in her jaws. Had she managed to catch something? Urgently Amanda called her and the dog bounded forward, still clutching the object in her mouth. She leaped nimbly over deadfall and dodged around rocks. As she came closer, Amanda could see the object, about the size of a football, was caked and sodden with black mud.

Kaylee dropped it at her feet triumphantly and stood back, tail wagging. Amanda bent to peer at it. A shoe! She rushed to the water's edge to wash it off, revealing a black-and-khaki running shoe with a camouflage motif. With the mud washed off, it looked clean and new, as if it hadn't been in the mud too long. Amanda compared it to her own foot, which was a woman's size seven. This shoe was about the same size.

The size of a boy, not a man.

Her pulse quickened. Clutching the shoe, she began splashing along the path Kaylee had taken. The dog bounced beside her, clearly pleased with her trophy. Then she raced ahead to stand over a muddy hole.

Amanda studied the mud, which was criss-crossed with paw prints and gouges, but through it all she could clearly make out human footprints — three partial treads with the same deep ridges as the shoe in her hand. Water and rain had not yet washed the treads away.

She raised her head to scan the dark, silent forest. "Tyler!" she shouted over and over. No answer. But the find had galvanized her. She was on the right track! Tyler had been here and was perhaps less than half a kilometre away, scared to reveal himself.

"Tyler, it's Amanda!" she called. Then she turned to Kaylee, who was looking up at her as if awaiting instructions.

"Good girl!" she exclaimed, stroking the dog's head and gesturing ahead in the direction the footprints were leading. "Now go find it!"

With a flash of tail, the dog wheeled about and set off, as if she were playing her favourite game. Which she was.

Kaylee tracked more quickly than Amanda could, but from time to time Amanda called her back so that she could study the soil. Tyler — if indeed it was Tyler — had not chosen the least obstructed route along the water's edge, but had headed into deep cover instead, slogging through the slippery moss and ferns of the dense forest. Rocks and deadfall lay in ambush to twist an ankle or wrench a knee. Amanda could see bits of moss ripped loose by his fleeing feet, and the deep, sinking holes left by his running shoe.

For the first time she felt hope. Hunger and fatigue evaporated. Kaylee understood the task and showed no hesitation or confusion. Although she'd never had any formal training in tracking, Amanda had often played the game of hide and seek with her, and now that silly game, designed to entertain and tire her out, was going to pay off.

Amanda moved as fast as she could through the rugged terrain, clambering over ridges and down ravines, sometimes on all fours to steady herself. At times she stopped to call to Tyler, and in the ensuing silence heard nothing but her own heartbeat thundering in her ears.

Until a faint report cracked the air. Two. Three. Kaylee froze, head up and ears flicking. Amanda had heard enough deer hunts in the Quebec countryside to recognize a rifle shot. Distant and indistinct, but enough to chill her blood. Kaylee was staring off to the right, where a boulder-strewn ridge blocked her view. Amanda called Kaylee to heel, her heart hammering as she crouched down to see what would happen next.

The forest was serene. No shouts, no screams of pain, not even the warning chatter of squirrels and birds. Silence. Convinced it had been a gunshot, she leashed Kaylee again as they inched cautiously forward. The dog had lost her concentration. Sensing her master's fear and probably spooked by the shot herself, she moved forward aimlessly, her ears flattened and her shoulders hunched. Amanda rubbed her back and pointed to the ground.

"It's okay, girl. Find it. Go get it, Kaylee."

Kaylee's nose was up, sifting the air instead of the scent on the ground. A growl began to bubble in her throat.

"Shh-h!" Amanda clamped her hand over the dog's muzzle. Kaylee tore free and fought against Amanda's restraining hand, pulling her forward. Her ears swivelled forward now and her whole body quivered. She moved low to the ground and dragged Amanda through the ferns toward the roots of an upturned tree. Amanda couldn't see behind it and had no idea what dangers lay beyond. A bear? A coyote?

A killer aiming his rifle directly at her?

Kaylee was frantic with excitement. She tugged Amanda up over the rise, past a tangle of branches and around the huge root ball. Behind it, peeking out from the protection of his shivering arms, was Tyler.

CHAPTER SEVENTEEN

When Chris walked in the front door of the Mayflower Inn in Roddickton that evening, a short, toad-like man was arguing with the clerk at the desk. He had a frayed canvas travel bag slung over his shoulder, a rumpled leather jacket, and a fedora tilted back on his head. Perspiration ran down from his temples.

"What do you mean, you're fully booked? It's almost the middle of September!"

"Moose-hunting season, sir. It starts tomorrow. We get hunters here from all over the east coast."

Chris had walked by an entire row of heavy-duty pickup trucks parked outside and seen one small blue Ford Fiesta squeezed in the middle. Chris guessed it belonged to Mr. Fedora with the leather jacket.

"Moose-hunting. Jesus!" Mr. Fedora wiped the sweat from his face. "Is there any other place in town?"

The clerk smiled sympathetically. "There's Betty's, but she's all full up too."

"One small bed. It can be in a broom closet for all I care. I've had a long flight and then a long drive up from Deer Lake. I just need a place to crash and a good stiff drink. I'm heading to Conche in the morning, so I'll be out of the broom closet at first light."

Chris had been about to slip past, but the mention of Conche stopped him short. He sized the man up warily, noticing what looked like a camera bag and a laptop on the floor beside him. Press? And judging from the man's accent, not the local Newfoundland press either. Had the vultures descended already?

"Well, you won't find a place in Conche, either," the clerk was saying. "It's hardly larger than a broom closet itself."

"I'm meeting a friend there, and she has a tent." He shrugged ruefully and shifted his heavy bag to ease his shoulder. "I've slept in worse places."

Chris approached the desk. Was this man trying to cozy up to Amanda? "Excuse me, sir," he said, thinking fast. "But the police have sealed off Conche at the moment. There's a major search being conducted in the area."

"I know there is. My friend is right in the middle of it. Sealed off? Why?"

"Danger to the public, sir."

"Danger to the —" Fedora broke off, his eyes narrowing. He looked Chris up and down. "Wait a minute. You're a cop! You really think Phil Cousins is going to go around killing innocent bystanders, even if he did kill that old guy?"

Chris hid his surprise with an effort. Reporters intercepted police bulletins all the time, but the man's choice of words suggested a more intimate knowledge. "May I see your identification, sir?"

Mr. Fedora looked about to protest, but seemed to think better of it, as if he knew the wisdom of staying on the good side of the cops. He dumped his bag on the floor and, from a thick stack of cards, he pulled out his Canadian Association of Journalists card and his driver's licence, both of which Chris examined closely. Matthew Goderich, from a town in New Brunswick that Chris had never heard of. Likely little more than a crossroads and a few cows.

Then the name clicked into place.

"I'm a reporter," Goderich said, "but I'm also a friend of Amanda Doucette and Phil Cousins. We've shared several … adventures together."

"I know who you are, Mr. Goderich." Chris held out his hand. "I'm Chris Tymko, also a friend of Phil and Amanda's."

Goderich arched his eyebrows as he gave Chris a moist, pudgy hand. "Not a cop? My instincts aren't usually wrong."

Chris smiled. "They're not wrong. But I'm here off-duty, as a friend."

"Ah. Then we have something in common." Goderich sighed as he bent to pick up his bags. "Can we grab a drink somewhere? If I'm going to sleep in my car, I better be fortified."

Chris hesitated. He knew Matthew Goderich wanted to pump him for information. He'd already had more than enough drinks trying to keep up with Willington, and he wasn't confident of his ability to hold his tongue in the face of a seasoned reporter's questions. But he had to admit he was curious to find out the inside, unreported details of Phil and Amanda's ordeal in Africa, as well as the other shared adventures the man had hinted at. And who knows, he thought as he led the way to a corner table in the lounge attached to the inn. If he liked the man, maybe he'd take pity on him and offer him the spare bed in his own room for the night.

Matthew dropped into his chair and swung his bag down beside him with a groan. The hotel clerk popped the caps off two beers and plopped them down before sashaying away. Matthew rubbed his hand over his greying stubble as he watched her disappear.

"I don't suppose I can get some food here too. I haven't eaten since Deer Lake."

"Not at this hour," Chris said. "Count yourself lucky she opened up the bar to serve us."

"Oh, she did that for you, my friend. Not some pot-bellied, balding old hack like me." He lifted his hat briefly to reveal a polished bald dome.

Chris grinned. Despite his reservations, he liked Matthew Goderich. "The hat earns you points, though. There's nothing but baseball caps from here to St. John's."

Matthew took a long, grateful swig of his beer. He had a creviced, pock-marked face, and up close Chris could see the stress of years carved into it. He slouched in his chair and tipped his hat back to give Chris a friendly smile. "How do you know Phil and Amanda?"

And so the questions begin, Chris thought. But this one was harmless enough. "I met Phil at an ice-fishing derby last winter. We're both new to the island — well, everyone who doesn't have six generations of ancestors buried in the local cemetery is new to the island — and we hit it off. We like the same things. Angling, hiking, flying."

He figured that was close enough to the truth, but Matthew fixed him with a steady gaze. "Still. You dropped everything to come up here looking for him."

Chris shrugged. "You're here too. I guess there's something about the guy, and what he's been through. If anyone deserves a helping hand …"

Matthew twirled his bottle. "So what exactly happened? Do the police honestly think he killed that old hermit, or do they have other suspects?"

"I don't know, I'm not part of the investigation. Even if I was, I couldn't tell you, Matthew."

Matthew held up his hands. "I'm not here as a reporter, I'm here as a friend."

"Right."

To his credit, Matthew gave a sheepish, dimpled grin. "Can

you turn off being a cop, even when you're not on a case? It's who we are."

Chris couldn't argue that. "Right now there are too many wild cards at play for me to even hazard a guess about who's done what."

"You mean like Amanda wandering around in the wilderness looking for him."

Chris said nothing.

"Oh for Chrissakes, Tymko! Any fisherman south of St. Anthony can tell me that. And they can tell me a boat has been spotted on a deserted stretch of shore halfway up the coast. I learned that much making small talk with the girl at the gas station next door. Yeah, I'm a journalist. Smelling out information is in my blood. Making connections is in my blood. But I'm here because I care about those two people. I know what they've been through. Phil is one of the good guys. So is Amanda. Good guys are often the first casualties in our brutal, treacherous world, whether it's in the corporate boardroom or the international aid game. If I can also give them a voice, to make their efforts heard above the banal chatter that passes for daily news these days — some starlet's latest rehab or Will and Kate's new baby — then what's the harm in that?"

Chris saw his chance. "What exactly did happen to them in Africa? Beyond the obvious stuff in your articles. You hinted that they were betrayed by the Nigerian government. That the government forces knew in advance about the planned attack, but didn't warn them, and that their own private security force ran away."

Matthew had drained his beer and he sat for a while staring at the empty bottle. Finally he sighed. "I'm far too tired to try to explain all the intricacies of post-colonial, sub-Saharan West Africa. Suffice to say, these are some of the poorest countries in the world. Corruption and payoffs are rampant. Education, health, and other services are almost non-existent in many places, so anyone who comes along with an offer of a paycheque, the promise of a bigger piece of the pie, or the threat of violence is going to get followers. Doesn't matter whether it's a big corporation, a rival leader, or an Al Qaeda knockoff, it's the same principle — join our team and we'll take care of you. Don't join us, you better watch your back. No different than the street gangs in urban slums. It creates a balance of sorts until a turf war erupts."

Chris had been born in farm country and had had remote rural postings, so he had only a third-hand grasp of the urban gang culture. But power and poverty were a toxic mix in isolated communities as well. "Is that what happened?"

Matthew shrugged. "In essence. The turf being as much of that unstable, exploited part of Africa as the so-called rebels could capture. Some petty thug pumped up on half-baked jihadi rhetoric and supplied by the international arms market decides to take control of a remote corner of the country. It's not difficult. Kidnap or behead a few villagers, issue death threats to others, bribe some underpaid officials and give a bunch of kids an AK-47, a paycheque, and a cause. And suddenly you're the new Somebody. And don't forget the power of YouTube in spreading the news."

"So are there no good guys?"

Matthew bobbed his head ruefully. "Sorry, I've been on the ground too long. I don't mean to characterize all reformers as venal and self-serving, and or to make light of the situation. Not the struggles the locals endure nor the dangers these jihadist groups pose. Nor indeed of the suffering of aid workers like Amanda and Phil, who are just trying to help the people. Amanda and Phil were both working on the education side — setting up classrooms, designing curriculum the kids could actually relate to — stuff we take for granted over here. Education, health, and a sustainable economy will go a long way toward combatting the power and appeal of these groups. That's why the groups are so adamantly opposed to it."

Chris mulled this over. It seemed impossibly complex and far away, although he'd seen similar struggles on a smaller scale in the Native communities in the north and west. At least in those communities, jihadist extremism had not taken hold.

He leaned forward. "My friend Phil seemed to be tormented that he hadn't done more. That he hadn't seen the danger signs ahead of time and hadn't saved the kidnapped boys."

Matthew's eyes grew flat. "He couldn't have saved them. Their own security guards, some barely more than kids themselves, betrayed them and joined the attack. Got a better offer, no doubt, or one they couldn't refuse. But on top of that, one of the boys Phil did try to save — a kid almost the same age as his son, who had shown real promise as a student — was among those they killed, to show that no one should mess with them."

Chris felt sick. He pictured Phil as he'd last seen him, clowning and playing with the local kids at a winter fun day. Phil had organized a three-legged snowshoe race that had everyone collapsing in the snow in laughter. What did it cost him to keep that awful memory at bay?

"What about Amanda? Your newspaper article just touched on her ordeal superficially. Something about trying to smuggle a group of girls to safety in a neighbouring village."

"Right. At the time, they were afraid the girls were the kidnap target, not the boys, because of the Boko Haram kidnapping earlier. It turns out this time they wanted boys, to be child soldiers or suicide bombers. Not that it mattered. The girls would have been raped, sold, or killed either way. But ..." Matthew broke off, pressing his lips tight as if to stifle the words.

"I know she didn't succeed. What happened?"

Matthew shook his head. Thrust his empty beer bottle away and reached down to pick up his bags. "It's not my story to tell. If Amanda wants you to know, she'll tell you. Meanwhile I've got a car seat to squeeze into."

Chris noticed a faint red flush creeping up Matthew's neck. Over his years as a cop, he'd become adept at guessing the reasons for evasion, but the reporter stymied him. Matthew had been so free with his information about Phil, so why had he clammed up when it touched Amanda? Had the failure and the shame been all Amanda's, or had Matthew been complicit in some way? Or was there a more personal reason?

"Look," he said on impulse as Matthew hauled himself to his feet. "I'm staying at the inn here and there's a spare bed in my room. You're welcome to it. Beats a Ford Fiesta hands down."

CHAPTER EIGHTEEN

As he manoeuvred his boat back into Conche Harbour the next morning, Chris scanned the village in vain for signs of Amanda. The streets were awash in official vehicles and trailers as the full force of the investigation descended on the little place. The RCMP forensics van had arrived, and the mobile incident command was parked at the top of the hill, its roof bristling with antennae and satellites. Trailers and trucks crowded Harbour Drive, and as Chris was securing his boat to the wharf, a Zodiac from the Integrated Border Enforcement Team chugged into the harbour. At the front, a civilian in typical fisherman's garb was uncoiling a rope, and in the stern, he could see two Mounties conferring. When the civilian leaped ashore to secure the boat, Chris recognized him as Casey and hurried over to intercept him.

"Any news on Phil Cousins?"

Casey hesitated, glancing over his shoulder toward the officers.

"Here, let me give you a hand." Chris grabbed a tie rope and lowered his voice. "Did you see anything? Phil? Amanda?"

"We was up toward Croque, checking out that report you got of a boat washed up." He paused. "We found it. Two boats, in fact. The first one was that old boat we leaves in the back harbour to go across to the cape —"

"You mean the one we thought Phil had taken over to Stink's place. That we saw swamped with water?"

"Well now, we don't know that for sure. We saw some wreckage, das all."

"Okay, okay. What about the other boat?"

The two officers had jumped ashore and were coming their way. Casey gripped Chris's elbow to lead him up the road. "The other one was Thaddeus's boat that he lent Amanda."

Chris sucked in a sharp breath. "Any sign of Amanda?"

"None. Not Phil, not Amanda. Now the old boat had a hole in her side, but Amanda's was fine. Motor still working and everything."

"So she went ashore to search. Maybe she thought Phil was in the other boat."

Casey shrugged. "You knows a woman's mind. But these fellas here —" he jerked his head toward the officers behind them, one of whom Chris recognized as Constable Bradley "— they're after looking for Stink's boat, not that leaky old runabout. Stink's boat was spotted a couple of days ago, racing up the coast toward St. Anthony. The boys had a look around, but I told them there's nudding but mountains and ponds and tuckamore in there. No roads or trails to anywhere. Nowhere for Phil to escape if he went ashore there. Anyways, they think he was using Stink's boat, which is stronger and faster."

"What?" Chris spun around to intercept Constable Bradley as he came down the wharf. "But how did that little boat get there?"

"Well, sir ..." The constable looked sheepish. "Incident Command thinks maybe Cousins towed it up there and ditched it to throw us off."

Chris stared at him. Laughed in spite of himself. "That's ridiculous."

"Or else the little boat drifted there by itself."

Standing opposite, Casey rolled his eyes. "Some feat, that."

Bradley nodded in wry agreement. "Anyway, Stink's boat was spotted on the ocean a couple of days ago, so IC thinks he's probably in St. Anthony by now, if not gone to the mainland already. Not slogging through the bush."

Chris gave up arguing the point. "But what about Amanda Doucette? She's been missing for two days now."

Casey snorted. "They're some mad at her, Jesus b'y."

"Are they sending anyone back up there to look for her?"

The constable looked around as if hoping for an escape route. "We don't have the manpower, sir. Incident Command says the priority has to be apprehending the suspect, who poses a risk to the public."

"But she could be in serious trouble!"

"According to our information, she went into the wilderness voluntarily and Mr. Casey here says she's well equipped."

"Except most of her supplies are still in her boat," Casey interrupted.

"But she has access to them, and her boat is in working order. Her whereabouts and safety are not a concern at the moment." The constable flushed, as if even he could hear the cop bafflegab. He spread his hands in a conciliatory gesture. "Look, we're stretched as thin as a poor man's soup on this one. We've got air surveillance, officers on all the highways, Border Enforcement at all the ports ... I'm betting Miss Doucette steams back in here by this afternoon, but if she's still not here by nightfall, maybe Incident Command will call out the ERT team to search for her."

Chris's mind raced. Amanda had been adamant that Phil would never hurt her, indeed would never hurt anyone. But how could anyone be sure? He marched up the hill to the command truck, where he found the newly arrived critical incident commander, Sergeant Noseworthy, setting up maps and communications equipment. Noseworthy was a tall, cadaverous woman with cropped grey hair and a tight slash of a mouth, which pulled down in disapproval when he requested permission to help in the search.

"Sergeant Amis informed me of your involvement, Corporal, and also of your personal friendship with the suspect," she said in a deep, smoke-ravaged voice. "So you can't help."

"Would you authorize a civilian ground SAR operation to search for Amanda Doucette? I can coordinate that."

The woman turned back to continue sorting cables. "That seems premature," she said in a dismissive tone. "And I won't put civilians in harm's way with an armed suspect potentially loose in the area."

Chris sensed the dead end. "Then let me at least look for her myself. I'm concerned for her welfare. I have a boat and I'd like to go up the coast to check on her situation."

"No."

"But the suspect is probably in St. Anthony or beyond by now. You said so yourself."

The sergeant turned back to study him. Her blue eyes were unwavering. "The Emergency Response Team is on its way, and they'll take charge of the search. I don't want you in the way, Corporal."

"I'm dressed civilian. I'll look like a fisherman out in a skiff." He could see her calculating. "At least I can contribute some help, ma'am, until ERT is up to speed."

She scowled. "Strictly on your own reconnaissance. And get your ass back down here by noon."

Chris hid his smile. "Thank you, ma'am. But can I have a radio and a sat phone so I can communicate what I find?"

"I would insist on it."

As he fought his way up the coast, Chris kept a close eye on boat traffic, hoping to spot Amanda on her way back to port. The weather was picking up, and a fierce wind threatened to blow him onto the rocks. The sky was a swirl of blue and grey, and the ocean was an angry chop that tossed his boat around like a cork. He clutched the gunwales and the tiller with all his might, trying to steer into the waves to avoid being swamped. Despite his best efforts, spray drenched his rain suit and splashed into the bottom of the boat.

The salt stung his eyes, causing him to squint to make out the shore through the surf, which shot plumes of white spray into the air. Birds wheeled overhead, eager for fish.

After more than an hour battling the sea, he was passing a stretch of black rock when a flash of colour caught his eye. The waves curled back, gathering force for another assault, and in that brief lull, he saw the red-and-white hull of a boat. He steered toward shore cautiously, afraid that his boat would be dashed on the rocks. As he drew closer, he could make out not one but two boats lying side by side. Spotting a small sliver of inlet, he threaded his boat through it and leaped out into the shallow water to drag the vessel safely up on the sand. He was panting by the time he had wrestled it free of the undertow.

After tying his boat to a sturdy bush, he clambered along the slippery shore to inspect the two boats, one of which had a gaping hole in its splintered hull. Amanda's boat was intact and secured to a bush on the shore. Both lay beached at the high-water mark.

He knew the others had searched her boat that morning, but he did so again in the hope they had missed a crucial clue. She had left most of her supplies back in Conche, as if she had intended this to be a brief trip; yet that had been two days ago.

Under the front seat he found a dry sack containing locator beacons, an emergency blanket, and a change of clothes. A chill ran through him. Why would she have left all this in the boat? What had happened to her?

He scanned the shore and the grey forest, hoping to find a clue to her direction. The coast was nearly impassable, for the slippery crags and gullies would challenge the nimblest mountain goat. Inland, the tuckamore wove a twisted, nearly impenetrable wall. He approached, looking for even the tiniest tear in its weave. Finally he found a small, cave-like hole into a path of soft red needles.

He crouched in the opening and cupped his hands around his mouth to call her name. The wind snatched his words and scattered them. "Useless," he muttered, ducking into the ghostly labyrinth of spindly grey trees. As he fought his way forward, he studied the ground for signs of disturbance. He thought he detected swirls and scuffs in the needle floor, but it was some distance before he found a clear paw print in the damp sand. He examined it carefully. A coyote or fox? Was he on a fool's errand, following the well-worn path of local animals on their way to the rich tidal pools at the ocean's edge?

Then a very man-made flash of orange caught his eye. A moment later he was staring at the blood-stained lifejacket, his heart pounding. Horror slammed through him.

"Amanda!" he screamed. Over and over. Up ahead, a faint path twisted and wove through the dense trees. He stumbled on, thrashing, sweating, and terrified. "Please, please let her be safe," he whispered, pausing every few minutes to catch his breath and call her name.

It was then, as he sifted the silence of the forest, that he spotted the poorly fashioned hiding place. He tore away the spruce boughs and boulders and swept the dirt from the pallid face.

Fell back on his heels, tears welling.

CHAPTER NINETEEN

Amanda had almost given up by the time they finally caught a fish, a mid-sized brook trout that flashed silver and gold in the murky water of the pond. Even Tyler summoned the energy to cheer as he came down to join her on the water's edge. The expression of hope on his pinched face made all the frustrations of the day worthwhile.

When she'd found him the night before, Tyler had been subsisting on berries and roots for four days. He was almost beyond reacting. Pale, chilled, and traumatized, he had dug himself into a protective lair and prepared to die. He had not spoken a word or shed a tear when she enveloped him in her arms. She had spent the evening trying to coax him back to life with a roaring fire, hot berry tea with willow bark, some boiled roots, and the last of her power bar. When darkness came, she had drawn him and Kaylee close to her in the shelter of his lair and whispered words of hope in his ear.

"Tomorrow morning we'll catch some fish and have a real barbeque, and once we get our strength back, we're going to find the ocean."

He had not answered, but she felt his limp fingers tighten slightly in hers. The next morning he slept so late that she feared he was truly ill. She had time to build the fire back up to a good blaze, pick more berries and willow, and drink two mugs of hot tea before he finally opened his eyes. He stared at her a long time without speaking, but his gaze was clear. *He's not ill*, she thought with a rush of relief, just exhausted. After days of grief and terror, he had finally collapsed.

He was taller, thinner, and more angular than she remembered, and his blue eyes were bruised with defeat, but the rakish cowlick over his forehead reminded her of his devil-may-care father. As they shared berries and tea, she made no effort to ask about Phil, but instead tried to focus him on their plans for the day. He needed hope, not pain. She was met by silence and shrugs. Gone was the little boy who threw himself into each day, who asked a million questions and had an endless fascination with every jerry-rigged contraption in the village. He had not even asked her how they were going to catch a fish.

That morning for the first time, the sun was peeking through the canopy and the sky was a rich azure overhead. She knew now which direction led to the ocean, but she still had no idea of the distance. She could hear no murmur of surf or drone of motorboats. It might be a long trek through bogs and mountains. Without food, Tyler would grow too weak for the journey.

"Ever eaten bugs, Tyler?" she asked gaily as she began to pull together the filaments of a vine into a rudimentary net.

He made a face.

"In Asia they are a delicacy. Do you remember? They eat cockroaches twice the size of my thumb. I don't think there's a ready supply of cockroaches here, but crickets and grasshoppers fried up with some berries will do the trick. Butterflies and beetles too. You can use this net to catch them."

She counted herself lucky that he didn't reject her outright. Once she'd finished the small net, she handed it to him and looked around to get her bearings. She considered scaling the tall nearby ridge to get a better view, but wasn't sure Tyler had the strength.

"Okay," she said cheerfully. "Onward to the coast. You watch the sun. Wherever we go, whatever detours we have to make, try to keep it just to our right. And by noon, when it's almost overhead —"

"Our shadow will be pointing north," he answered.

"Right." She smiled. "Did your dad teach you that?"

His shoulders sagged. "Jason did. When we went camping last year."

"Ah. If he taught you any other useful stuff, you tell me, okay? Like which of these berries are edible and which will kill us. Because I know a lot about Asia and Africa, but not as much about these woods."

Tyler pointed to the scarlet berries she'd been eating. "Bunchberries. Jason called them the hiker's friend. And these violets are edible." He leaned over to pluck a plant and stuffed the leaves into his mouth. Kaylee had been ranging far into the woods, but she returned now to follow along. Amanda hoped she had found some mice or squirrels to keep starvation at bay.

As they walked, Tyler collected a small cache of insects and plants while she pondered the challenge of catching something more substantial. She had just decided it was time to cook up what he had, when they struggled over a rise to see a huge pond spread out below them. Amanda felt a thrill of excitement.

"Do you think that pond has fish in it?" she asked.

"Salmon and brook trout, maybe," he said. "Jason took us fishing once in a lake like this."

She was already salivating as she slithered down the slope to the water's edge. A large boulder a few yards offshore provided a perfect vantage point. She took off her boots, waded out to it, and climbed up to study the brown water. She tossed a few berries onto the water and watched the water come alive with silver flashes.

"Dozens of them!" she shouted. She sent Tyler to find a straight, sturdy willow branch while she set about designing a hook. During her time in Africa, she had seen simple hooks fashioned from wood and hemp. It took her a few tries to find a sliver of wood that retained its strength when whittled to a point. Together they scoured the shore for dried reeds or fibrous stalks that could be braided into cord. All over the world, she'd seen baskets and rope woven from grasses, so she knew it could be done. As he watched her struggle with grasses that broke and unravelled, Tyler fretted.

"Why don't we make a spear?" he asked. "Like the cavemen."

"Great idea! You're the Newfoundlander, go ahead. We'll have a race to see who catches the most fish."

He dragged branches out of the deadfall and whittled away at a few before throwing the broken sticks away and slumping down on a log wearily. Amanda's heart ached. The old Tyler would have loved the challenge of beating her, but this Tyler gave up with barely a fight. Was it just the hunger, or had the trauma of his father's death drained all the spirit from him?

Instead, she redoubled her efforts to catch some food. The sun was well past noon by the time she assembled a passable fishing rod and threaded an earthworm onto her hook. She climbed up on the rock, praying the hook would catch and the flimsy, twisted cord would hold.

It took three snapped lines, but she finally managed to wrestle a brook trout onto the shore. It was a glory to behold, a foot and a half of glistening silver. Tyler built a fire while she gutted it. She tossed the head to Kaylee and threaded the body onto a stick over the roaring flame.

Nothing had ever tasted so fabulous. By the time Amanda had licked her fingers clean and fed a portion to Kaylee, the sun was slipping toward the ridge to the west and the shadows were growing long. Tyler was slumped against a rock by the fire, drowsy from the heat and the food.

She had hoped to hear helicopters overhead, confirming that people were searching for them, but so far there had been nothing. If they were going to be found, they had to find the coast. *I'm sorry, Tyler*, she thought, *I know you need to sleep but we have to keep going just a little farther, while we still have daylight.*

The three police officers formed a silent, respectful ring around the body, which Chris had tried to protect with his jacket. He knew the scene was hopelessly contaminated, both by himself and by whomever had buried him there, but he'd covered the body more out of compassion than out of any desire to protect the scene. Phil looked so vulnerable splayed out on his back in the woods, prey to any beasts and insects attracted to an easy feast.

Above all, Phil hated to be vulnerable.

The two other officers, Sergeant Amis and the incident commander Sergeant Noseworthy, had made very good time up from Conche, thanks to the powerful Zodiac now pulled up on the shore. It was mid afternoon, leaving several hours of daylight despite the unnatural gloom of the forest. But even in the scant couple of hours since Chris made his urgent call, the flies had multiplied and the fragile flesh around Phil's eyes had begun to bloat.

Chris turned away, pretending to study the surrounding woods, while Amis prodded the body carefully. "Rigor's gone. Been dead a couple of days at least."

"How long before Dr. Iannucci and the crime scene team get here?" Chris asked.

"I had to ask HQ for extra personnel," Amis replied, wrinkling up his nose as if in distaste. He eased the body onto its front and bent close to inspect the bullet hole. "They're sending a team over from St. John's that can be on the ground in the morning. They don't want the body removed until they can have a look. But meanwhile we need to develop a working hypothesis. All hell seems to be breaking loose around here."

"I don't think he was killed here," Chris said. While he'd been waiting on shore for the officers to arrive, he'd taken a closer look at the damaged boat that Phil and Tyler had presumably used. Waves and spray had washed some of the blood away, making it difficult to detect at a casual glance, but he had found red smears and streaks on the seats as well as a small pool on the floor at the front of the boat. He had pointed it out to the officers as he led them up the shore, but Amis was more intent on getting to the body and hadn't given it a second glance.

Now he straightened and stared at Chris through narrowed eyes.

"I think he was shot either while he was in the boat, or just climbing into it," Chris said. "Probably back at Old Stink's place."

"For the love of God," Amis snapped. "The victim has a name. According to government records, Allister Parsons."

"Parsons?" Chris said in surprise. "Like the shrimp fisherman who hauled the body out of his net?"

Noseworthy, who was peering into the dense tuckamore, gave a dismissive grunt. "Half the Northern Pen are Parsons, or related to them."

As if Noseworthy weren't even there, Amis's eyes never left Chris. *Single-minded guy*, thought Chris uneasily.

"You know this man, Corporal," he said. "What's your theory?"

Chris paused to gather his thoughts. Waiting on the shore for their arrival and desperate to distract himself from worries about Amanda, he'd occupied his mind cobbling together scenarios. "Judging from the food and clothing missing from Stink — Parsons's — house, I think Phil Cousins took them —"

"Stole them."

"Probably," Chris said reluctantly. "He seemed hell-bent on going into the wilderness with his son."

"Hell-bent is right," Amis snorted. "Half crazed, according to the locals." He was standing ramrod straight over the body, vibrating suspicion.

This time Chris sidestepped the interruption. "I think Stink — Parsons — shot him as he was escaping in his boat."

"And then he got out of his boat with a bullet in his back, and took an axe to Parsons's head. Quite the superman."

"There was no blood on the wharf, sir. Parsons was attacked inside his own cabin. And I believe the rifle shots came from inside the cabin, as well. I found shell casings there."

Amis's gaze wavered. "That's what the crime scene team concluded, as well. So if Parsons and Cousins clashed, it took place in the cabin before Cousins went back to his boat. Perhaps Cousins surprised him in bed."

"But Cousins was already wearing his life jacket when he was shot."

"Perhaps he didn't bother to take it off!"

"Did the crime scene guys find any traces of blood on the wharf? This gunshot wound bled a lot."

Amis shook his head. "Possibly it hadn't soaked through the life jacket yet."

Or possibly Phil wasn't the killer, Chris thought. By now Noseworthy had stepped away from the scene and squatted to examine the spongy loam of the forest floor carefully, using a measuring tool from her pack.

"Forensics won't be here until tomorrow, but ERT should get started here right away." she said, still bent over the ground. "The boy Tyler is still out there. We need to rescue him ASAP. Air, ground, shore searches, and starting right here, K9."

Amis's mouth pinched in protest, but Noseworthy cut him short. "The missing child is our priority. Moreover, I think someone else has been here. Just eyeballing it, I found two possible prints here in the mud. And a mid-sized canine."

"Amanda!" Chris exclaimed, feeling the first stirrings of hope and relief. "I bet she found the body too! That's why she hasn't come back. She's gone off looking for Tyler."

Noseworthy's thin lips drew down in disapproval. "Without going for help? Meaning we now have two missing civilians to search for, and no clear idea what we're dealing with here." She unfolded her lanky body and headed back toward the shore. "Not a moment to lose, Amis."

Chris and Amis caught up with her at the water's edge, where she was consulting her satellite GPS as she fired off orders into her radio.

Amis nodded toward the Zodiac. "I brought a tent, evidence bins, and perimeter tape —" To his credit, a ghost of a smile crept across his face. "For all the good that will do. Constable Bradley will relieve you and guard the scene until the team from St. John's arrives tomorrow." He gazed out to sea as if he were addressing the waves. "You did a good job with the Parsons scene earlier, Corporal, and your insights into this scene so far has been duly noted, but this is too personal …"

His voice faded as Noseworthy signed off and stalked over to join them. "K9 is on their way, but possibly not until the morning, so ERT will establish a perimeter and start with a hasty search along the shore and the roads and ATV trails in the vicinity while there is still daylight. And —" She nodded toward Amis "— the medical examiner's officer in St. John's called for you with some information on the old man Parsons. They haven't conducted the post-mortem yet, but they thought you should know that the GSR on him was negative."

No gunshot residue. Which means that Stink didn't shoot Phil, Chris thought, his earlier relief vanishing. *There's another killer on the loose.*

CHAPTER TWENTY

By Amanda's estimation, she and Tyler had been following the stream for about an hour when an errant puff of wind brought with it the scent of smoke. Tyler shrank back, but Amanda's hopes soared. She turned in a slow circle, sniffing the air to pinpoint its direction, but the scent evaporated on the capricious breeze.

She picked a dry frond of moss from a tree and tossed it into the air in the hope the breeze would catch it. When it angled to the ground some distance away, she gave a cry of triumph and set off into the wind, shouting over her shoulder.

"Come on, it's this way!"

Tyler stood stock still, drawing into himself. "We don't know what it is."

"We know it's a fire. Could be a village, could be hikers."

He moved reluctantly, as if his feet were encased in chains, and dragged along behind her as she strode up a hill. On the other side, they came upon a broad circle of trampled ferns and strewn spruce boughs, hacked from their stumps by an inexpert hand. Amanda's excitement gave way briefly to disappointment, until she spotted the ashes of a fire at the centre of the camp. Lying beside it was a charred, empty can, which Kaylee began to lick. Amanda examined the fire, which was cold to the touch, but, when she buried her fingers deep into the middle, still gave off a hint of warmth.

The fire was recent! There were people nearby.

"Hello!" she shouted. "Help!"

"Don't!" Tyler whispered, hoarse and urgent. She turned in surprise to see him hunched on the ground, cradling his knees to his chest.

"Tyler, what's wrong?"

"It's the terrorists," he mumbled, his voice so soft she had to strain.

"Terrorists? What are you talking about?"

"They'll kill us!"

She knelt at his side and wrapped her arms around his trembling body. "What happened, Tyler?"

He said nothing. Merely held himself rigid in her embrace.

"Talk to me, honey. How do you know they're terrorists?"

Kaylee crawled up to press her warm body against them. Tyler's voice came from deep inside their embrace. "Dad thought they were refugees, but then … then … they killed him!"

Amanda caught her breath. Waited.

"And now they're after me."

She tightened her grip. "I won't let that happen. They're gone now. They left this camp hours ago. What happened to your dad, honey?"

"He only wanted to help them. He'd been trying to find them for days, ever since he heard they were stranded in a lifeboat. So he was going to buy one of this guy's boats to go look for them —"

"What guy?"

"This old hermit on the cape. We borrowed a little boat to get there, but when we did, we saw these four guys piling stuff into the guy's boat. They ran into the woods when they saw us coming, so Dad … Dad went looking. He made me wait in the boat." Tyler rocked. "I heard a shot, and when Dad came down the path, he was … he was …"

She held him. Rubbed his back. "Take your time, Ty."

"He told me to take our boat and go. Leave him. I said no. Is he dead?"

"Who? Your father?"

"I *buried* my father. The old hermit!"

Amanda hesitated. Truth was usually wiser in the long run, even with children. "Yes. So you got your dad back in the boat?"

"Dad couldn't drive it. He was so pale, and … gurgling …"

"I know, honey. So you drove it?"

"I was so scared. They took the other boat and I thought they were coming after us, so I drove as fast as the boat would go. Dad said to go straight to the Grenfell Hospital in St. Anthony. Straight up the coast. But I —" he gulped "— I crashed it. Didn't see the rocks. I got him ashore, I got him to the woods, but I couldn't … I couldn't … I couldn't save him."

A shudder began deep in his core and rose and rose. He howled. A raw, primal wail of pain. Again and again, until tears came and he sobbed as if he'd never stop.

A dozen questions clamoured in Amanda's mind. Who were the fugitives and what were they running from? Did it have to do with the angry Greek Phil had met at the Fisherman's Dory Café in Anchor Point? Did Phil know about the dead body found in the ocean, or the wrecked lifeboat near Grandois? All this, and possibly more questions she hadn't thought of yet. But she stifled them all. Now was not the time. Even when his tears stopped, Tyler lay quietly, too exhausted to speak.

A damp autumn wind was sweeping in from the east, chilling them both. She looked uneasily at the sky through the lace of overhead boughs. Tatters of deep blue still peeked through the afternoon sky, but the clouds looked bruised. Was it going to pour? She gave Tyler a reassuring squeeze and extricated herself.

"I'm afraid it's going to rain. We need to cover some ground before it gets dark," she said. "Get away from this camp and find some shelter. I want to try to reach the coast."

He didn't move. "I'm sorry I got you into so much trouble, Amanda."

"What on earth are you talking about?"

"If it wasn't for me, you wouldn't be lost in the middle of the forest."

"You think I'd leave you to fend for yourself with a horde of bad guys on your tail? We're in this together, Ty. Always have been, ever since those days in Cambodia when you used to ride on my handlebars down to market. Remember that?"

"That was to get me out of my mother's hair."

She looked at him in surprise. From the mouths of babes. Tyler had always been a chatterbox, and ever since he'd been able to string two words together, he'd craved someone to talk to. They had all taken turns. She hugged him. "I loved those rides, you made me see things through such fresh eyes. Everything was an adventure to you, even a hot, dusty, tedious trip into town." She extended her hand to haul him to his feet. "So come on. No more silliness about being a burden, okay? Together we're getting out of this."

He rose on unsteady legs and began to trudge after her. Head bowed and feet dragging. "But I know I wasn't supposed to come on this trip. This was for you and Dad, to help Dad get his head straight."

"Is that what your father said?"

"It was what Mum said. He was grumpy all the time, and sometimes he'd take off and come back hours later, drunk. They yelled at each other all the time." He paused. "Actually, she yelled and most of the time he didn't answer. That made her yell even more."

She laid a hand on his shoulder. "It's been a rough year for your dad, Tyler."

He shrugged her off. "He didn't want to be cheered up. Even on this trip. He promised we'd have fun, see whales and Vikings and stuff. That's why he said I should come! So we could have some fun together after all those grumpy months."

"You mean you, him, and me?"

"He said we'd meet you later. He wanted some time just with me first."

Amanda pondered this in silence. They were making slow progress through the forest, picking their way around rocks and over deadfall. She kept a close eye on the sun to ensure they kept going in a vaguely eastern direction.

Had Phil really intended to leave her dangling when she arrived in Newfoundland? Wondering where he was and where they were supposed to meet up? Or had he simply lost track of time? He was Mr. Unreliable, after all.

"Where were you supposed to meet me?" she asked casually.

"I don't know. I don't think Dad did, either. Maybe up at the Viking settlement. He said he was looking for a really great campsite. But every day he got grumpier and grumpier." Tyler fell silent and his pace slowed. He poked at a fern in his path. "I think I got on his nerves."

Amanda paused to wait for him. "Everything got on his nerves, Ty, but he was never happier than when he was with you."

"Then why did he go off looking for those stupid terrorists?" he burst out. "He forgot all about the Vikings and our boat tour and just kept chasing after them!"

"What do you mean?"

"Ever since he met that guy in the pub, he hardly paid any attention to me. Even in St. Anthony, we were supposed to be going on a boat tour, but all he wanted to do was talk to some shrimp-boat captain about the workers on his ship."

Tyler had stopped altogether now, and stood red-faced and

clench-fisted behind her. "He thought the terrorists were in danger, and look what happened. They fucking killed him!"

He hurled the curse into the air, shocking them both. They stared at each other, and in the silence, Amanda heard Kaylee's growl. She had been so caught up in the conversation that she had paid no attention to the dog.

The growl startled Amanda back to the present. The sun had disappeared and a strong, musty wind was blowing in from the north, rattling the spruce boughs. Kaylee was facing into the wind, her hackles raised and her nostrils flaring.

Amanda held up her hand to silence Tyler. Her eyes strained to see through the dense brush and her ears sifted the silence. She heard the cracking of twigs and the furtive swish of leaves coming from the side. Kaylee whirled around and took off, barking. Amanda bit back a shout and motioned to Tyler to get down. She pulled him behind a large boulder and crouched beside him.

A rifle shot rang out, followed by a howl of pain. *Kaylee! No!* She wanted to scream, perhaps she did. Guttural shouts erupted, and instantly the forest came alive with threat, with screams of pain, the sweet scent of blood and gunpowder, the eye-watering smoke of burning huts.

Not again! *Not now!*

She clutched Tyler to her in an iron grip. He squirmed, staring at her with wide eyes. Branches cracked as the killers raced forward, shouting over one another in a chaotic din.

Before she could think, she was on her feet and dragging Tyler with her. Ducking low, she bulldozed through the brush, weaving around trees and leaping over deadfall. Behind her she heard crashing, but she didn't dare look back. Didn't dare think. About the deadly hordes, the flashing knives, the bloodied dog left behind …

Barbara Fradkin

Tears streamed down her cheeks, blurring the forest ahead and blinding her to the branches that raked her skin. Her legs cramped in pain, but she forced them on. A sharp spruce bough slammed into her, spinning her around and hurling her to the ground. She lay stunned, gasping air into her paralyzed lungs. Her tears evaporated. *Must get up!* She groped through the moss and ferns for Tyler's hand, and closed, finally, on his warm, moist fingers. Still safe!

When she strained her ears for the sounds of their pursuers, she heard shouts that were too close for safety. "We have to keep moving!" she whispered, scrambling to her feet.

They raced blindly through the forest, panting up a ridge and windmilling down the ravine on the other side. At the bottom, a small creek carved a deep crevice through the valley. She splashed across it with Tyler right on her heels. He hadn't said a word, but she could hear him sobbing for breath. *He's exhausted, starving, and traumatized*, she thought. *We have to find a hiding place.*

Facing a steep embankment, she skidded to a stop to take her bearings. The creek tumbled through the ravine, and although she could hear nothing over the sibilant rush of water, she knew the killers couldn't be far behind.

Tyler was bent over, sucking huge gulps of air into his lungs. "You okay?" she asked.

He managed a slight shake of his head. Or maybe it was a nod.

"We'll follow the creek," she said. "It will be easier and it seems to be going somewhere."

She turned to forge ahead, ankle deep in water, but Tyler didn't move. She stepped back to take his arm. "Tyler, we can do this. As soon as we find a good place to hide, we'll rest. But we can do this!"

"Your dog!" His gasps turned to sobs. "I hate them! I hate them!"

"So do I. But don't let them fucking win!"

The curse shocked the boy into action. He began to move, slowly, his head hanging and his feet dragging through the water. Hugging the narrow bank, she picked up the pace, slipping and splashing through reeds and over rocks, but somehow staying on her feet. Up ahead, the roar of water grew louder as the creek rushed toward a drop. For safety, she scrambled farther up the muddy bank, clinging to roots and saplings while down below, the creek gathered force in its descent. Up ahead, she could see it disappearing over a steep, rocky drop.

Behind her, she heard a scream. She turned back just in time to see Tyler pitch down the bank, flailing and grabbing at branches before he fell into the water and swirled through the rocks.

She leaped down into the rapids. Although the water wasn't deep, the current tugged at her legs and she could feel her balance giving way. She seized an overhanging branch and pulled herself slowly back upstream toward him.

He was struggling to stand up, but each time he slipped and fell back into the relentless current. Finally he draped himself over a boulder in the middle of the brook and hung on in exhaustion, mere metres from the waterfall. He raised a ghost-white face to her.

"Hang on! Don't move!" she shouted over the din of the water. She inched her way up, from one branch to the next, all the while trying to think of the best way to get him safely to shore. She came alongside him and leaned out over the water. Her fingertips touched his, but she knew it wasn't enough. If he were pulled from her grasp by the current, he would be swept over the falls before he could even try to stop.

"Hold still," she said. "I'll get you, but I need …" Her gaze fell on two large rocks by the water's edge. She tugged and shoved and rolled them little by little into the brook until they formed a chain of obstacles leading from the shore to Tyler.

"Work your way around your boulder and behind these rocks. Don't try to stand. Hang onto the rocks. I'll get a branch to help you to shore."

He looked up at her, his whole face twisted with pain and panic. "I can't feel my right foot."

"It's probably just cold," she replied. "Crawl on your knees. The important thing is to keep these rocks downstream from you."

He crawled around the boulder and wedged himself between it and the next rock. Water sucked at his clothes and his lips were turning blue. He stretched a pale, trembling hand toward the next rock. "I ... I can't."

She broke off two branches of deadfall and splashed out into the water to brace them between the rocks, strengthening the bridge. Then she grabbed the top of his backpack and guided him to the bank. Tyler collapsed to his hands and knees. "I still can't feel my foot," he managed through clenched teeth. She bent down to examine his foot, but could see no signs of blood or injury around the shoe. When she touched it, however, he screamed in pain.

"Can you bend it?"

"Hurts too much."

"Wiggle your toes?"

He wrinkled his brow in concentration. "Yes," he said after a few seconds.

"That's good. I think at worst, it's sprained. I'll splint it and make you a crutch."

It took her fifteen minutes to fit him up with a splint and crutch fashioned from the branches she had torn loose. She tried not to think about their pursuers, and the gains they were making. When she hauled Tyler to his feet, he was able to hobble a few steps, but how they were going to manage the rugged terrain, she didn't know.

"I'm sorry," he said, "I can't walk."

"Let's see what's below these falls," she said. "If I have to, I'll carry you."

"You can't carry me. I'm almost as big as you!"

"You'd be surprised." He was probably right, of course, but she wasn't about to let him know. "And I know how to make a stretcher too."

"I'll sit here while you check out what's ahead." He started to ease himself down.

"No you won't! Come on, lean on me."

By bracing himself against her, he managed to hop forward. Their progress was excruciatingly slow, and all the while, she imagined she could hear crashing through the bush behind them. When they reached the bottom of the falls, the ravine opened up. Inky blue sky, a yawning drop, and beyond it the sparkling silver sea.

And down at the bottom of the hill, like a gap-toothed smile, a string of little houses clustered around a tiny bay.

CHAPTER TWENTY-ONE

As the police Zodiac steered back into Conche Harbour, Chris spotted the trademark fedora of Matthew Goderich. The journalist was pacing at the dockside, and he rushed forward before Chris or anyone else could disembark.

"The body — is it Amanda?"

"No comment!" Sergeant Amis snapped. "Let us get off the goddamn boat first."

"But it's a body, right?"

"I can confirm that human remains have been discovered, yes, but until we have more information —"

"Oh, for fuck's sake! Man or woman?"

Amis hesitated. He studied Matthew, and Chris could almost see him weighing his options. News travelled fast between the close-knit communities up and down the coast, and keeping secrets was nearly impossible. In the end, Amis fell back on standard prattle.

"We'll be issuing a statement at —" he glanced at his watch "— ten a.m. tomorrow, and until then I request that you keep this information confidential until we have a chance to speak to the parties affected."

Matthew wasted no further effort on him, but instead spun around to fall into step beside Chris. "Is it Amanda?" he whispered as they walked down the wharf.

Chris shot him an oblique glance. "No."

A spasm of relief passed over Matthew's face. "Phil, then?"

"Matthew, don't ask me! You know I can't say."

"Oh my lord, poor man." Matthew faltered and grabbed the side of a pickup truck for support. "How did he die? Suicide?"

"Goderich!"

Matthew held up a conciliatory hand. "I know. Ten a.m. But where's Amanda?"

"We don't know," Chris said. A wave of sorrow and fatigue crashed over him, tightening his chest. "Out there somewhere."

"Alone?"

Chris hesitated.

In the silence, Matthew sucked in his breath. "Or with the kid! She's with Phil's kid, isn't she? Oh Jesus, a nightmare for her all over again!"

"I didn't tell you anything."

"You think I'm an idiot? Goddamn it, Tymko! I'm on your side here. She's my friend. Phil's my friend. You think all I want to do is plaster some sensational story all over the headlines?" Matthew turned and stormed off toward the collection of trailers and tents that had sprouted up around the RCMP mobile command post on the hill above the village. He threw the last words over his shoulder. "Does his wife know? Someone will have to talk to her."

"Don't you dare!" Chris shouted, sprinting to catch up with him. "Matthew, I will do what I can to keep you in the loop, as soon as we know details. But don't go messing around in here. If you care about Amanda and Phil as you say you do, please don't make it all worse."

Matthew stopped. In the gathering twilight, his heavy-lidded eyes searched Chris's. "You'll keep me in the loop? Promise?"

Chris nodded. As he headed toward the police compound, he watched Matthew detour toward Casey's house and he wondered what the journalist's next move would be. And how much trouble he, Chris, would be in for it.

After a quick, hot shower to wash the blood, dirt, and fatigue away, Chris bundled up against the evening chill and headed up the slope to the command post. He walked out of the velvet dusk into a brightly lit world of computer screens, radios, and phones, all alive with the rapid-fire exchange of data. The Emergency Response Team had arrived — specially trained tactical officers mainly from the eastern part of the province who'd left their regular duties to conduct the search.

Their leader, Corporal Vu, stood beside Noseworthy studying the large, gridded map on the wall. She had four inches on him, but his lithe, wiry body radiated energy and his muscles rippled like a racehorse in the starting gate. As Noseworthy traced a long, bony finger along the highway toward St. Anthony, she seemed to sense Chris's presence without even shifting her gaze from the map.

"You're off duty until 0600 hours, Corporal."

"Someone needs to notify his wife, ma'am, before it's all over the news and Twitter."

Noseworthy turned from the map reluctantly. "Grand Falls-Windsor detachment has gone out to the house. The officer will call here with his report shortly."

Chris hovered just inside the doorway. He had no real excuse to linger, but was dying to know how Sheri would take the news and how much information she would share with the police, who were, after all, Jason Maloney's colleagues. Worse, perhaps it was Jason himself who had made the visit!

He strolled across the room to pour himself a coffee and to sneak a look at the map, which was divided into standard search quadrants and dotted with coloured pins. Noseworthy and Vu continued to argue logistics and assignments for the morning search, including helicopter coverage, roadblocks, and vehicle searches, as well as ERT search teams on the ground. It was a mammoth task. The air search was their best chance; the heat-sensing equipment could detect the presence and shape of live beings even through dense tree cover, down to the arms and legs, and could even pick up the residual heat of recent footprints. But the area to be covered was huge, and the weather and wind patterns unpredictable. Similarly, looking for a small boat bobbing on the endless seas would be like sifting through grains of sand.

Furthermore, having negotiated just a small section of the near impenetrable tuckamore to find Phil's body, Chris knew the ground search would be even more of a challenge.

On the boat trip back to Conche from Phil's body, Chris had argued again for the use of the local civilian ground SAR team, which was based in Roddickton and could be in place before nightfall. We need as many eyes on this as possible, he'd said. The nights are getting cold and Amanda has few supplies. The ground SAR team is experienced in wilderness searches and familiar with the local terrain.

Noseworthy had refused. There's a multiple killer on the loose and a firearm unaccounted for, she said. Civilians are not to be put at risk. We don't need a hundred people crawling all over the bush; we need professionals and an effective plan.

Chris had fumed in silence. *Effective plan, my ass*, he'd thought. *More like a by-the-book, "if we fail, we followed the most modern search protocols" plan. It would look good in a report, but it might not find Amanda and Tyler.* Although the ERT team was a crack unit, at full strength it was only twelve officers, and Vu had been able to round up only ten, the other two being off on training. None of the ten were local. None knew the terrain. Even the most effective plan had to cover at least five hundred square kilometres of ocean and forest.

Studying the map now, Chris saw that the search perimeter was even larger than he'd expected, stretching all the way from the shores of Canada Bay on the south to Grandois on the north and extending ten kilometres out to sea. Before he stopped to consider the wisdom of it, he blurted his thoughts aloud.

"Why is the perimeter so far out? There's no way she'd travel that far."

Vu had been consulting his second in command, and he swivelled around slowly, letting the silence lengthen as he sized Chris up. Apparently unimpressed, he signalled the other man to follow and he stalked out of the trailer.

Noseworthy kept her face dispassionate as she watched the door slam in their wake, but Chris sensed it was an effort. *Just what we need*, Chris thought. *A pissing match at the top.* Noseworthy's jaw was set as she turned to answer him. "Missing three days at a conservative ten kilometres a day, that's ERT's outer limit."

"But no one can cover ten kilometres a day in that terrain, and even if she could, she wouldn't. She'd be looking for a place to be found. The coast, or a road out."

"Vu thinks if she's running from the killer, she might be trying to get as far away as fast as she can. And she'd stay out of sight." Noseworthy paused. "I'm told this is a resourceful, savvy woman. We know from her history that she travelled four hundred kilometres through hostile territory to safety in Nigeria, much of it on foot under the cover of darkness."

Chris stared at her in surprise. "I'm former ERT myself," Noseworthy said. "First rule of search and rescue — know your subject. So I spoke to the journalist." She softened. "We know what we're doing, Corporal. We'll find her."

Chris drew in his breath and ventured farther out on his limb. "Maybe the civilian ground SAR coordinator could provide —"

Noseworthy's softness vanished. "For the last time, out of the question. This is a police operation."

On her hip, her satellite phone rang. She shot Chris a last warning glare. "Don't push your luck," she said, turning her back to answer. She spoke little, but jotted notes and when she signed off, she turned back to Chris.

"Grand Falls-Windsor has informed the wife."

"How did she take it?"

"Do you know her?"

"No, ma'am. Just of her, through her husband."

Noseworthy glanced at her notes. "She's holding up well, considering. She told the constable she has been concerned about her husband's mental health and had recently received a goodbye letter from him. She assumed it was suicide."

"Did she mention the reason for his ..." Chris searched for a neutral phrase, "troubles?"

"PTSD. Nigeria."

Chris nodded. So Jason Maloney's name hadn't been mentioned. "Did the constable tell her how he actually did die? Shot in the back? Definitely not suicide?"

"No, but he had to ask her about potential enemies and reasons why anyone might want him dead."

"And did she give him any?"

Noseworthy's eyes narrowed. "Why the intense interest, Tymko? I can tell you're an interfering son of a bitch, but is it just your nature, or do you know something?"

Chris felt a flush creeping up his neck. "He's a friend. Amanda and I have been tracking him and he's been acting more and more like a man on a mission."

"Well, I can't give you any more details. You'll have to talk to Sergeant Amis. The murder investigation is his responsibility." Noseworthy's lip curled and in that hint of distaste, Chris realized she didn't like Amis any more than he did.

"By the way," Noseworthy tossed off almost as an after-thought, "the wife really wants to talk to you. Maybe she'll tell you something she wouldn't tell the local officer. But you better clear that with Amis first if you want to keep your balls attached."

The sight of the little outport basking in the sunset gave Tyler hope. A smile lit his pinched face and he hobbled forward eagerly. Amanda propped him up as they both scrambled down the slope. They passed from the forest to open tundra, where there was no protection or place to take cover should their pursuers spot them, but Amanda barely gave it a thought. Civilization, and help, beckoned.

Beyond the houses lay a small, sheltered inlet in the cradle of jagged grey cliffs. As they drew closer, Amanda scoured the village for signs of life— laundry on the line, boats at the wharf, or smoke from the chimney.

Nothing.

Doubt began to creep in, and by the time they reached the first of the shacks, Amanda knew the place was deserted. Long ago.

Flecks of red still clung to the wood, but the clapboard was gap-toothed and weather-worn, the windows boarded and the doors broken in. The wharves sagged into the water, half ripped from their moorings.

Nonetheless she ran from house to house in the gathering gloom, looking for any remnants of habitation. A can of beans, a jar of pickled beets, a moth-eaten blanket. The houses smelled of fish and rot. Her boots echoed in the empty rooms, and the ocean wind whistled through the broken slats. The houses looked like decaying museums to a dead era, abandoned in the midst of daily life. Kitchens, tables, daybeds, rocking chairs, and dishes — all simply relinquished to nature.

She had left Tyler resting on the stoop of the first house, and she returned to find that he'd crawled inside to get out of the wind. His skin was blue and his teeth chattered. "There's no one here, is there?" he said.

She sat beside him and put her arm around him. "Must be one of those outport fishing villages that was relocated in the 1950s. But at least we have shelter, and I saw quite a few useful things. If we pick the best house, we can move a couple of chairs and beds into it."

He hung his head. "There's no food, either, is there."

"No, but there's still an hour or so of light. Once I get you settled, I'll see if I can catch some fish."

"I'm so cold." He was soaking wet, as was she, and she knew that unless he got into dry, warm clothes, he might not be able to go on in the morning. She had spotted an intact stove and a stack of firewood in the next house.

"Come on, tiger," she said cheerily. "Let's go next door and light a fire."

"But they'll smell the smoke! They'll know we're here."

"No they won't. Even if they can smell smoke, it will be too dark to see us. They'll just think people live here."

He gazed around in exasperated disbelief. "Here?"

"Why not? At first glance, it looks like a village. If they're on the run, they'll beat a hasty retreat." She spoke with more bravado than she felt, but she knew it was a risk she had to take. If Tyler didn't get warm, it wouldn't matter how many hordes of terrorists were on their tail.

It took a long time to coax a decent fire out of the old black stove and rotting wood. The fire smoked and hissed so much that she was afraid there was a nest in the chimney, but finally roaring orange flames filled the box and heat began to spread into the corners of the draughty little house. She hung all their clothes except their underwear from a beam above the stove, dragged some mouse-chewed bedding from the house next door, shook it off, and settled Tyler in front of the fire.

He fell asleep almost immediately, leaving her free to collect her thoughts. She stepped outside, shivering in her long-johns, and inhaled the fresh, salty air. In the last light of day, she scanned the hills behind, alert to any sign of movement. Hoping against all reason to see a flash of red bounding toward her.

Now, in this brief interlude of peace, her eyes filled with tears. Her decision to flee with Tyler had been instantaneous. There had never been any other option. Yet the image of Kaylee lying injured on the forest floor haunted her. As before, she had failed to protect someone she cared about. Her beloved, loyal dog. She made a silent vow that when this was all over, she would come back to find her and bring her home, dead or alive. But the time for regret would have to wait. Banishing her guilt to that already crowded corner of her mind, Amanda headed down to the waterfront.

She stepped into the gloom of the first stage cautiously, afraid the rotting floorboards would splinter and dump her into the sea below. As her eyes adjusted, she could make out a dusty array of fishing rods and nets hanging from the wall and larger piles of netting coiled on the floor.

Hallelujah! She hopped over the gaps in the floor to rummage through the equipment. Within ten minutes she was standing on the end of the wharf with a tin pail, a fishing rod, and a silver lure, casting out into the gentle waves. She knew nothing about ocean fishing, but her summers spent at her aunt's lakeside cottage in the Laurentians proved some help in assembling the rod and tackle. Whether there was anything to catch was another story.

In no time she had three decent-sized fish in her pail and had thrown back a couple that were too ugly and prickly to handle. Next she foraged on the heath behind the house in the semi-darkness for a supply of partridgeberries. Her mouth was watering by the time she noticed the little boat upturned in the long grass by the shore. She hurried over and inspected it for holes. It looked miraculously intact. She tugged, pried, and finally managed to flip it over. The seats were partially rotted away, but the hull looked sturdy. Her pulse quickened with hope. Could they use this to get out onto the open sea, where they might be spotted by searchers? Was it big enough to handle the waves?

She dragged the boat down into the water and watched with dismay as water began to seep through the seams of its floorboards. She tied it to the wharf and left it rocking in the gentle swell while she returned to the stage in search of a bailer. Hunting through the rusty cans lined up on the shelf, she came across a large can of whitewash that had never been opened. It sloshed when she shook it.

Better and better! She was so excited by the possibilities that she forgot the fish, Tyler, and her clothes drying inside, until a plaintive call stopped her short. She grabbed the fish pail and rushed back inside to find the fire almost dead and Tyler, partially clothed, wrestling with a fresh log. A couple of candles from the kitchen bathed the room in a golden glow.

He peered into the pail eagerly. "Connors!"

"Are they edible? I threw back these incredibly ugly things full of fins."

He grinned. "Yeah, sculpins. But these will be yummy!"

True to his promise, the fish was succulent and moist with its berry sauce. As they wolfed it down, she told him of her discoveries.

"In the morning, we'll use the whitewash to paint *help* on the slope behind here, big enough to be seen from the air. And if the boat doesn't sink, we'll take it out of the cove into the open ocean so we can be seen by fishermen and people searching."

"When?"

"As soon as it's light, so we can catch the early fishing boats."

That night she lay awake impatiently waiting for dawn, listening to the gentle rush of the waves and the rhythmic knocking of loose boards on the wharf. Soon it would be over! Soon she would be immersed in a hot, soapy tub, soaking every trace of dirt and pain from her body. Soon Tyler would be safe in the arms of his mother.

But by the time the first grey smudge of dawn lightened the sky and she went down to inspect the boat half-submerged in the shallows, dense cloud had blown in and a vicious wind had whipped the waters of the cove into an angry chop. She knew, with a sinking heart, that air surveillance would be treacherous. Even worse, the moment she and Tyler ventured out of the protected bay, their little boat would be smashed against the jagged cliffs.

CHAPTER TWENTY-TWO

His truck clock read 6:55. Chris Tymko had been at his post for less than an hour, but he'd worked himself into a state. Sergeant Amis had rejected outright his request to speak to Sheri Cousins, leaving him awash in speculation about what she wanted to tell him. Had she just suffered a belated attack of guilt that she needed to unload, or had she learned something important? He suspected she would never talk to the local police about the details of her personal life, particularly those involving Jason Maloney, but she might have been encouraged to open up to Chris himself. Who knows what insights he could have gleaned?

All stymied by Sergeant Poker-Ass.

Noseworthy was no better. ERT and the dog manager for the K9 unit had restricted all access to the search zone, leaving only highway surveillance and vehicle searches on the perimeter to the regular officers. Noseworthy had assigned Chris to man a roadblock in the middle of fucking nowhere, at the juncture of the main highway 432 and the gravel road to the seaside villages of Croque and Grandois. He was supposed to search every vehicle coming out and redirect every vehicle turning in. The whole area between the highway and the coast had been sealed off and the villagers evacuated as a precaution. Many had left grumbling, but others seemed to regard it as an adventure. So far he had stopped three moose hunters from turning into the area as well as one already coming out with a bloody carcass in the bed of his truck. Chris had checked long enough to verify that it was in fact a moose.

It was a job any rookie with a cruiser and a badge could do, but he'd had to fight for even that. You're too personally involved, Noseworthy had said. *Too nosy and demanding is more likely*, Chris thought as he sat in his truck with his police radio tuned to the chatter, clinging to the bits of information that leaked through.

It was a windy morning with dark clouds racing low across the sky. Rain threatened. Chris peered down the gravel road uneasily. Were the silhouettes of the distant mountains more blurred? The scraggly outlines of the spruce more smudged? Had the rain started on the coast? When the forecast had warned of the possibility of rain, even fog, the whole search team had cursed. Fog would cancel the air search entirely, and make the ground search a hundred times harder.

As he tried to judge the swirl of mist in the distance, he realized it was coming closer. A cloud with fading edges but a dense core. Not rain or fog at all, but a vehicle coming down the dusty road. Chris flicked on his roof lights and rested his hand on his pistol. The dot in the plume of dust became a pickup truck, not black but dirty red, driving at a steady, unhurried pace. As it slowed to a stop in front, Chris made out a red light affixed to its roof. He relaxed and climbed out of the cruiser.

He could see the tall, rangy RCMP officer talking on his radio, presumably reporting in. Chris knocked on his window and the man powered it down.

"Have you been searching down this way?" Chris asked.

The officer nodded. "Just calling it in. I checked the whole Croque-Grandois road, but no sign of them. No suspicious activity. You see anything?"

Chris masked his surprise. ERT had not wanted anyone

inside the search zone, not even other officers. "For my records, can I see your ID?"

"Sure thing." With an easy smile the officer unclipped his ID from his jacket. Chris stared at it in surprise.

"Jason Maloney! What the hell are you doing here?"

Jason stiffened and took a moment to find a retort. "Who the hell wants to know?"

"Sorry, I just didn't expect you. I'm Chris Tymko." He stuck his hand through the window.

It was Jason's turn to be surprised. He seemed to hesitate, as if unsure whether to shake the hand or smack it away, before enveloping Chris's hand in a strong, warm grip. "Phil was a good man, friend to both of us, and we both want the same thing. To find his killer."

He opened the door, climbed out, and stretched his long limbs with a groan. He wasn't as tall as Chris, but he moved with a fluid athlete's grace that Chris could only envy. No wonder Sheri had succumbed; the man radiated power.

"When did you get here?" Chris asked, his tone a little edgier than he'd intended.

"Late last night."

"Fast driving from Grand Falls."

Jason paused. "I was already on the peninsula looking for Phil." He rubbed the back of his neck and stared down the highway through slitted eyes. "Look, this is a mess. I mean, the stuff between me and Sheri, me telling Phil … man, I was afraid I'd pushed him over the edge."

"You pretty much did."

Jason flinched. "But that's in the past. Some bastard killed him in cold blood, and that's what's important now. Finding out who did that, for Phil's sake."

"And for Sheri's."

"That's over. It's not going to survive this."

Chris said nothing. Perhaps Jason believed that right now, but grieving widows turned to a comforting cop shoulder all the time. Jason seemed to read his mind.

"Believe it or not, I care about Phil. I felt like shit going behind his back, that's why I told him. And Tyler! Sweet Jesus, he's my son's best friend. A greater kid you'll never meet. You bet I want to be part of finding him and making things right."

Chris felt like punching the man's face in, but managed an indifferent shrug. "Whatever. Did you clear your search with Incident Command?"

"Do they know? About me and Sheri?"

The urge to punch grew stronger. "I don't know, but you might want to tell them yourself. The major crimes investigator is one hell of a prick, and you can bet he'll find out."

Jason looked grim. He poked his toe around in the gravel and Chris let him stew. Finally he nodded. "Okay. I appreciate you not spilling the beans."

"He hasn't asked me yet. I can't guarantee I won't. Just giving you a chance to get there first."

"I'm heading in now." Jason opened the door of his truck, then turned back. There was a tinge of shame in his gaze. "You good out here? Nothing I should pass on? Seems pretty quiet."

"It is pretty quiet. Just moose hunters who don't know the area is closed."

"Yeah, I passed one of those myself back down the road," Jason said. "I guess he got in ahead of the roadblock."

"Coming out this way in a beat-up old Sierra with a moose in the back?"

"No, he was driving in. He had an ATV in the back."

Chris grew alert. "No such vehicle came through. Did you stop him?"

"I told him to turn back, and he said he just had to pick up his buddy who was already in the bush with a moose. I told him to get his buddy, forget the moose, and get the hell out of the area."

It was a common enough scenario, Chris thought. It usually took an ATV and a couple of hunters to move a seven-hundred-pound moose carcass out of the bush. "Okay, they'll probably be along soon. Did you get a licence plate?"

"Yeah, hold on." Jason climbed back into his truck and reached for the logbook beside him. "Late-model silver F250, New Brunswick plates, ASCVE6."

Chris fetched his own logbook and jotted it down. "I'll keep my eyes peeled."

Jason gave a mock salute, started the truck, and revved off toward the highway in a spray of gravel, leaving Chris to the solitude of his cruiser and the police chatter. He listened for awhile. Nothing new in the search, but a misty rain was beginning to fall.

It was nearly an hour later, and the mist had long since smothered the mountaintops, when he thought of the moose hunters again. The truck had not come through. Unless the buddy was deep in the bush or they had stayed against Jason's orders to dress and haul the moose, they should have turned up by now.

As faint alarm bells began to ring, Chris reached for his radio to call in the plate.

"We'll hug the shore inland instead," Amanda announced, pointing down the forested shore opposite the scoured barrens of the point. They were both standing on the wharf in the rain, dressed in tattered rain gear and squinting out over the drenched landscape. Tyler had woken that morning with his ankle badly swollen, and every effort to move it or put weight on it elicited a cry of pain. If they were ever going to escape, they had no choice but to take the boat.

Tyler was staring at the half-sunken boat with dismay. "In that?"

"We'll bail it out and see how bad it is."

"But what about the searchers? No one will see us."

She picked up the two rusty cans she had found for bailing. She didn't want to tell him the searchers might not even be looking in this weather. "First things first. Let's see if the thing will float."

Miraculously, after fifteen minutes of bailing, the boat was bobbing high on the surface, with no water seeping through its seams. As she'd hoped, moisture had swollen and tightened the wood. She rummaged in the stage for a pair of oars and a paddle, and helped Tyler climb in. The boat rocked precariously, causing Tyler to clutch the gunwales with fear.

"Can't we just stay here until help comes?"

She shook her head. "We'd be sitting ducks, and if I remember the map correctly, I think this bay may lead inland to the village of Croque."

"Croque. Dad and I visited there. Some grumpy old man wouldn't sell us his boat." His face twisted at the memory. "Not much in Croque."

"But there's a road, and the search and rescue people will be patrolling the road."

Once she'd loaded all the supplies worth scavenging — fishing gear, a couple of cans they could use for cooking, a tarp, and a rusty old filleting knife that she planned to sharpen on a stone — she paused for one last look at the little village. She wondered again whether she should leave a message explaining where they were going, but she feared it would merely tip off their pursuers. The huge, whitewashed HELP sign she'd painted on the slope was bad enough. For a moment she dithered as she tried to think up a cryptic message that the searchers would understand, but their pursuers wouldn't.

A play on the word *Croque*? Or a reference to France? And then a brainwave hit.

"Just a minute," she told Tyler as she headed back into the stage for the can of whitewash. For an added measure of misdirection, she carried it to the opposite end of the village and painted a message on the flat rocks along the shore. *What did one frog say to the other?*

She was still laughing when she got into the boat. With any luck one of the police would have a brain and a sense of humour. As soon as they pushed off, the wind caught the boat, swung it broadside, and swept it out into the choppy water. Amanda's summers as a young girl at her aunt's cottage were a distant memory, but when she took the oars in her hands, the feel of the little rowboat she used to putter in came back to her in a rush.

With powerful tugs she seized control of the boat and fought the wind to get closer to shore. As they inched their way down the bay, Amanda watched the village recede into the distance. Once they rounded a rocky point out of sight of the forlorn shacks, another bay opened up before her. Forests pressed in, and more jagged points of rock. Amanda kept a respectful distance from them as she scanned the cliff tops.

"You're my eyes!" she shouted to Tyler over the angry slap of the waves. "Keep a watch for rocks ahead, and also for any sign of Croque."

As she rowed, she kept twisting around to assess sky. A dense mist swirled over the mountains farther inland in what she assumed — hoped— was the west. *Not fog*, she prayed. *We can't afford to get caught in the fog.*

Every foot of progress was hard fought against the wind, but she couldn't stop to rest without being blown backwards again.

After what felt like an eternity, her back ached, her arms shook like jelly, and the blisters on her palms from the rough oars had begun to bleed. As she rounded yet another point, she twisted around to look ahead at the new vista. More forest, more rock.

Where the fuck was Croque?

She ran the boat ashore on a small gravel beach, waking Tyler with a start. He had curled up in the bottom of the boat, dozing, and he bolted upright in alarm.

"What are we doing?"

She jumped ashore and stretched her stiff back. "I need to wrap my hands. Let's have a food break."

She handed him a little of the fish she had cooked that morning and poured some water into a jar. While he ate, she soaked her stinging hands in the cold salt water and rinsed out some rags to wrap them. Help would have to come soon, before infection set in. Exhaustion and pain robbed her of appetite, but she wandered a little along the shore to see whether she could detect any signs of habitation. As she walked, she thought she heard a crashing sound in the forest up the steep bank. She froze to listen. Another crack. The swish of leaves.

Her whole body quivered. Rescuers? Killers? She didn't dare call out. The crashing sound came nearer. She saw a flash of movement through the trees racing toward her. In panic, she glanced back at Tyler, who sat in the boat, completely exposed to danger. She turned to run back to him just as a moving blur burst through the underbrush and leaped on her.

Red fur, squirming, wagging, and yelping with joy as a wet tongue covered her face in kisses.

She burst into tears and hugged Kaylee to her. Her heart swelled with joy. For a moment she forgot all danger and pain as she turned around.

"Tyler, look!"

Something whizzed past her head. An instant later, a rifle shot cracked the air.

"Tyler!" she screamed. Ducking low, she raced along the shore with Kaylee at her heels, limping, Amanda noticed with alarm, from a blood-encrusted wound on her hip. Another shot. Amanda scrambled faster. A third whizzed by just as she reached the boat. Shielding Tyler with her body, she tried to tug him out of the boat. He was unharmed, but wide-eyed with fear as he struggled to get up. Another shot spat the bottom of the boat. Luckily the guys weren't crack shots. Bastards!

She searched frantically along the shore, but there was no place to hide. No way to escape. Out on the water, they would be easy targets, but with Tyler's injury they couldn't possibly outrun the killers on land.

A growl bubbled deep in Kaylee's throat. Slow, deliberate footsteps swished through the leaves, and Amanda peered up the embankment to see a trio of men moving toward them through the tangled woods. She saw their legs first, then their ragged jackets, and finally the rifle. Pointed straight at her head.

CHAPTER TWENTY-THREE

Matthew Goderich was on the phone, making yet another futile effort to reach Sheri Cousins in Grand Falls, when he glanced out Casey's window and spotted her driving past the house. He slammed the phone down and raced outside.

She was driving an ancient Cavalier that threatened to disintegrate as it rattled along toward the harbour. She must have seen him chasing her because she pulled over and climbed out.

He had only met Sheri Cousins once, when Phil had been home from Nigeria barely a month and Matthew had gone to Grand Falls for a follow-up interview. She'd struck him as a capable, no-nonsense woman, none too pleased with the public airing of her husband's struggles. Today she'd done her best with makeup and a styling brush, but she looked as if the past week had dragged her through the thickets of hell. Deep charcoal bruises circled her eyes, which searched his with the hope of the desperate.

"Do you know anything? They won't tell me anything!"

"Sheri, you know Phil is —"

"Dead. Yes, I know that. They just had me identify his body." She shook her head impatiently. "But what about Tyler? Where's Tyler?"

"Still missing." Rain was threatening, so he slipped an arm around her shoulder. "Let's go inside where we can talk."

"Fuck you, Goderich, I don't want a goddamn interview! I want my son. Goddamn it! How dare he?"

He eyed her warily. "Who?"

"Phil!" She checked herself. "I'm just so angry, I don't know at whom. God, maybe? Is this some goddamn big punishment He's decided to lay on me?"

He wanted to keep her talking. The woman was trembling like a volcano about to erupt, and it might do her some good to release the molten rage. Not to mention that he might get some excellent material for the piece he was writing. As the first national-calibre reporter on the scene, he'd persuaded the Canadian Press wire service to pick up not only his ongoing blog updates, but also a longer background feature.

But the Mounties were being their usual tight-assed, unco-operative selves, and so far he had few details on Phil's death itself, let alone the missing-persons search. He had managed to glean, from a disgruntled civilian ground SAR member who worked in the local convenience-store-cum-post-office, that the civilian team had been blocked from the search for Amanda and Tyler because of an ongoing threat from persons unknown. From which she, and Matthew, had deduced that there was still a killer at large.

Which meant that Phil had not died by accident or suicide. Someone had killed him.

As if Sheri could read his mind, she shook her arm free. "Don't print that, Matthew! Help me. I know you care about Phil. What do you know about Tyler?"

"They have a massive search out for him. Police combing the woods, eyes in the sky, police dogs tracking him from the site of Phil's body, although I gather that's proving difficult because dogs can only follow the freshest scent. So the police don't know whether they're tracking Tyler or Amanda."

"Amanda!" Sheri's rage bubbled up again. "This is her fucking fault in the first place. If she hadn't signed on for Nigeria —"

"That's a long way back, Sheri."

"Is it? It's a chain reaction, don't you see? If she hadn't gone, he wouldn't have gone, and they would never have met those fucking Islamic thugs, and Phil and Amanda wouldn't have made this blood pact to heal each other. Which ended here!" She flung her hand to encompass the ocean. "With Phil dead and my son in jeopardy."

"Amanda is taking care of him."

"Is she? Isn't that just peachy! How do you know that?"

"Because she hasn't come back. And if anyone can keep Tyler safe, it's her."

Sheri stared out toward the harbour, where a handful of locals worked on their boats and stages. Despite the ominous clouds, pickup trucks trundled up and down the harbour road as people went about their daily chores. Phil's body had been taken away, the ERT team was out in the field, and the village had returned to some semblance of normal. An alert and watchful normal. Sheri's jaw worked as she fought to bring her storm of emotions under control.

"You know she will," Matthew added quietly.

"Amanda told me to start a Facebook page for them, so I did. Now Tyler is all over the goddamn Internet, and someone started another one — Prayers for Tyler. That's my son, not some new fad!"

Matthew nodded his sympathy, deciding now might not be the best time to mention his own blog. "Every little bit helps, Sheri," was all he said. "That's what matters."

"He must be so scared," she whispered, tears crowding in. "I hope he didn't see his father die. I hope Phil shielded him at least from that."

Matthew didn't know how to counter that, so he didn't try. "Did they tell you how he died?"

She shook her head. "I only saw his face. He looked peaceful. No bullet hole to the temple, but I … I assume he killed himself."

"I don't think so."

She frowned. "Accident?"

Matthew feared he might have gone too far. He wanted to ask whether she had any theories about who would kill him, but he risked unleashing a further, futile wave of panic and terror once she realized Tyler was out there in the sights of a killer.

But Sheri wouldn't stand for half-truths. She grabbed him and shook him. "What? Fuck, Matthew! Don't leave me in the dark. I'm sick of being left in the dark! Phil did that for months! Was he involved in something that got him killed?"

He shrugged. "Can you think of anything? Do you know any reason someone would want to kill him?"

"This is Newfoundland! No one kills anybody in Newfoundland. Jesus fuck!" She clutched her head and spun in a circle as if trying to shake off the idea.

"Has he been doing anything that might …? I mean, mixing in anything that might get him in trouble?"

"You mean like drugs?" She lifted her shoulders in disbelief. "I don't know what he's been up to the past year. He could have joined a cult of hermits for all I know. He was seriously disillusioned with his fellow man."

Noticing that villagers were watching them curiously from their yards and shop stoops, Matthew placed his hand in the small of Sheri's back to guide her along the road out of earshot. "There's been some excitement in this area about a possible boatload of foreign nationals who crashed their boat and disappeared into the woods. And another whose body was found at sea. I can't get any confirmation, but the police may be operating on two theories. Either they were smugglers, maybe forced to ditch at sea —"

"Smugglers of what?"

"Well, most likely drugs destined for the U.S. market. Guns are another common item, but most of those come the other way, up from the states to cities in Quebec, Ontario, and B.C. Smuggling a bunch of guns into northern Newfoundland doesn't seem very likely."

She scoffed. "Smuggling anything into northern Newfoundland doesn't seem very likely. What's the other theory?"

"People smuggling."

This time she didn't scoff. She grew very quiet as she stopped to search his face. "Phil wouldn't care about drugs. He wouldn't like the guns, but I can't see him sticking his oar in. He'd just report it and carry on. But people smuggling …"

"He'd want to help."

She raised her hands in a helpless gesture. "The mood he's in, I don't honestly know. But old habits die hard. We saw a lot of poverty and oppression in the countries we worked in, and people trapped in countries they had no way of escaping. We saw them falling prey to the promise of a good job and better prospects somewhere else. Paying an international employment agency their life savings to get a job in a factory in Phnom Penh or a cotton farm in Vietnam or the oil fields of Nigeria, only to discover they were paid almost nothing, locked in by debt, and sold to another company across the border. Or worse. Slavery, in plain English. Human trafficking — both the sex trade and the forced labour trade — is a big problem in all those impoverished, little countries that broke off from the Soviet Union too. It infuriated Phil — well, it infuriated all of us — but it's rampant in the poor parts of the world. Look at all those desperate migrants drowning in the Mediterranean. That was tying Phil in knots!"

"What about the Middle East?"

She shot him a look. "You know something."

He shrugged. "Chris Tymko has some suspicions. Africans or Asians would stick out like sore thumbs on a Canadian fishing boat, but some lighter-skinned Arabs or Afghans might not."

"I've read the same headlines you have, Chris. Four million Syrian refugees alone. People are desperate to escape war and chaos, and they're paying smugglers thousands of dollars to sail on rickety boats to Greece. But most of them are seeking asylum in Europe." She paused. Her haggard blue eyes searched his with growing fear. "It's a long way from Greece to the North Atlantic, but wherever there is desperate need, there's shameless exploitation. If Phil encountered it here, in this sheltered little pocket of Canada … yeah, he'd go ballistic."

Chris drummed his fingers on the steering wheel and watched the approaching rain uneasily as he waited for the comm coordinator at Incident Command to run the plate number. A couple of pickups tried to turn off the highway onto the gravel road, but veered back when they spotted him.

"Vehicle is registered to a company, Acadia Seafood, based in New Brunswick," the coordinator said.

"Who are the listed drivers?"

"It's part of a fleet, sir. Employees probably sign it out."

"Can you dig a little deeper? Find out from the company who signed it out and for what purpose?"

The coordinator didn't answer, and Chris could almost hear her hesitation. "Is it busy there? Any new developments?"

"Very busy, sir. All the teams, including K9, are in place, but there have been no sightings yet."

"Any clues to narrow down the search area?"

"No, but with weather conditions worsening, both from the air and on the ground, we're in high gear, racing against time."

"This may mean nothing, but someone from Acadia Seafood has entered the search area, Helen. We need to know quickly who it is and what he's up to."

"Probably moose-hunting, sir."

Chris gritted his teeth. Newfoundlanders and their goddamn moose! "We need better than *probably*. Radio me the minute you find anything."

The coordinator muttered her grudging acceptance, tacked a reluctant "sir" after it, and signed off. Chris had been waiting less than five minutes when he remembered where he'd seen the name Acadia Seafood before — in St. Anthony, at the pier of the fish plant. Acadia Seafood was the owner of the freezer trawler Phil was interested in. Phil had planned to talk to the captain about taking a tour on it, but Chris hadn't been able to confirm that he had, because the captain was away, ostensibly down the coast looking for a mechanical part for the ship.

Had he taken the company truck to pick up this part? If so, what was he doing in the wilds of the east shore? Not many parts for a trawler, or even smaller boats, in these small villages.

Something felt wrong. Phil had been discussing the shrimp fishery with a bitter, foreign-sounding fisherman on the west side, and later he'd been asking the campground operator all sorts of questions about foreign trawlers and workers. At the same time, a boatload of possibly foreign illegals had gone ashore near Grandois, and the illegals had fled on foot toward the south.

Not so far from where an unidentified employee from the seafood company had supposedly gone to pick up his moose-hunting partner.

This time, figuring there was no need for the entire search team and the local press to listen in, Chris phoned the communications coordinator back on his satellite phone. Before he could even ask about her progress, the woman interrupted. "I have nothing to report yet, sir, and I can't talk now. Noseworthy and Vu have us all hopping."

"Look, whoever this guy is, I think we should apprehend him. At least question him and verify his story. I'm prepared to do it. Is Corporal Jason Maloney there?"

"Not yet. He radioed he was grabbing some breakfast in Roddickton."

"Radio him back, ASAP. Tell him I need him back here with me, and send someone to relieve me at this roadblock —"

"Noseworthy won't authorize that, sir."

Chris rolled his eyes. He flicked on his wipers to clear the rain misting his windshield, and peered down the empty road for the tenth time. Each moment, the visibility worsened and the fine rain washed away more tracks. "Can I talk to her?"

The coordinator's voice grew muffled as if she had turned away and covered the phone. It took her less than ten seconds to return. "Sergeant Noseworthy is tied up. I'll have her call you back the minute she's free."

"Tell her it's urgent. Please." Frustrated, Chris hung up and located the number of the Roddickton detachment. He was relieved when Willington himself answered the phone. "Willie, have you got an officer there who can take over the Croque Road roadblock?"

"Are you kidding? I haven't got anyone for anything! Everyone who's awake is out on the highways."

"Can you run your detachment from the junction of 432 and the Croque Road? I have to check out a potentially suspicious intruder in the search area —"

"You can't go in there! Radio ERT."

"The weather is worsening fast, and ERT is stretched thin

as it is. If I don't want to lose the man altogether, I have to go ASAP." He listened to Willington dither. "There's a whole case of QV Premium in it for you when it's over."

Silence descended on the line. Finally Willington grunted. "Make it two, you cheap bastard, and I'll be there in twenty."

True to his word, Willington turned off the highway in less than twenty minutes. His flashing roof lights made eerie haloes in the mist. Chris had just filled him in and given him the description and plate number of the suspicious truck when he spotted Jason's red truck trundling down the highway. The man had not turned on his roof cherry and his slow pace seemed almost insolent. *But maybe I'm imagining it*, Chris thought, *because I don't like the guy any more than he likes me.*

When Chris explained the situation, however, Jason was smart enough to recognize that he might have screwed up and to see a possible path to redemption.

"Yeah, I can remember where I saw him," he said, peering at the detailed forestry map Chris had unfolded across the dashboard of Jason's truck. "Not sure exactly where it is on this map, but I'll know it when I see it."

Chris snatched up the map and opened the door. "Lead the way. I'll follow."

"Lights?"

"No. If this is a bad guy, I don't want to tip him off."

With a final wave to Willington, the two vehicles set off in tandem down the Croque road. Jason drove slowly, dodging potholes and pausing at each curve and rise, presumably to match the terrain to his recollections. Once he slammed on his brakes to avoid a moose that ambled across the road out of the bush ahead.

Chris's heart was in his throat. He had nothing in the cab with him but the 9mm service pistol Noseworthy had provided and his old hunting rifle in the trunk. He didn't know what Jason had. Why the hell hadn't Noseworthy called him back?

About ten kilometres in, Jason pulled to the left side of the road and signalled to Chris to pull in behind him. Both men climbed out.

"This is where I stopped him," Jason said. "He was driving toward the coast."

Chris bent down to examine the gravel on the right side of the road. It was a faint hope, quickly dashed. Hundreds of indistinguishable treads had tracked through the dirt in the last few days, and all were blurring in the fine rain.

Chris straightened to study the road ahead. It was unremarkable. Just a road slicing a meandering path through the ubiquitous spruce and fir on either side. Every now and then, the boughs of a slender birch glistened white through the green.

"Did you watch him in your rear-view mirror?"

"Yeah, I did. He continued on and disappeared around that curve up ahead."

"All right then, let's go see what's around that curve."

Back in their vehicles, they resumed their hunt. This time Jason kept to the middle of the road. *Wise move*, Chris thought. *If the truck turned off the road or pulled over to the edge, there's a chance we'll spot the tire marks.*

Around the curve, more forest. More endless, potholed road winding toward the smudged silhouette of hills ahead. Rain streaked the windows. Chris leaned out his window to scrutinize the gravel shoulder as they drove past. Another hundred metres farther on, a thin, overgrown track led into the bush off the right side of the road. Jason stopped again and climbed out. When Chris reached his side, he was squatting at the edge of the road, peering at a pair of tire treads that were deeply carved into the wet gravel. Up ahead, the ferns, moss, and ground cover of the ATV trail had been flattened in twin parallel tracks.

"He drove the truck in here," Jason said. "A brave man."

Chris began to walk down the track, careful to stay clear of the tire marks. About a hundred feet in, the marks petered out, but when Chris scanned the dense brush on either side, a glint of metal caught his eye. He approached the overhanging boughs, pushed them aside, and stopped to stare.

"Oh fuck," said Jason from behind him.

CHAPTER TWENTY-FOUR

Instinctively, Amanda seized Tyler and stepped in front of the boy as a shield, all the while keeping her eyes fixed on the man with the gun. He was tall, but so thin that he looked as if he'd blow away in a brisk wind. His bony arms protruded from a ragged jacket that was two sizes too short for him, but hung on his skeletal frame. His feet were protected only by socks, and even through the caked mud, she could see the bloodstains. A toque was pulled down over his ears, but tufts of dark hair stuck out beneath it and a scraggly black beard obscured much of his face. His eyes, however, were extraordinary. Deep-set and emerald green, they stared at her with something akin to terror.

The rifle he pointed at her was almost antique. It looked like a lever-action hunting rifle that might just as easily blow up in his hands. Not that she was about to test that theory.

Huddled together behind him were two smaller men, one draped in an old quilt and the other in a thick, moth-eaten sweater that was too big for him. The one in the quilt looked glassy-eyed and unfocused, but the other stared at her fiercely as he tried to prop his companion up. He was shorter than the leader and his features were coarser, but his shoulders betrayed his strength. All three men were sodden from the rain.

These men are not evil, she thought, *they are desperate.* She had seen desperation many times in her career. "Who are you?" she asked as gently as she could through her own fear.

Behind her, Tyler grabbed her arm. "That's the terrorists!"

The leader shifted his rifle toward Tyler. "No talking. Give food and the boat!" His voice was hoarse, the accent thick and guttural.

She squeezed Tyler's hand and shot a warning glance over her shoulder at him. "Now's not the time," she muttered. She held out the pail with the rest of the berries. "There's not much, but we can pick more."

The leader snatched the pail, looked inside with disgust, and swung his rifle toward Kaylee. "I shoot the dog."

"No!" Amanda screeched, leaping to Kaylee's side without thinking. "This dog helps us. You will not shoot her!" Holding up her hands, she forced herself to calm down and lower her voice. "I know you are hungry. I will help you catch fish."

The leader looked incredulous. The other two stood as expressionless as pillars, probably not understanding a word. Amanda reached into the boat for the fishing rod. The man's gaze wavered briefly as he looked at the rod. She thought she glimpsed a spasm of pain. Of recognition.

"I won't hurt you," she said. "I can tell you are hungry and lost." Steeling herself, she took a risk. "I know you are running away from bad people."

The look of sorrow vanished, and the man stepped forward in alarm. "What you know?"

"I know your friend died on the ship and you escaped in a lifeboat that broke up on the rocks. You are running away, but you don't know where to go."

The man was frowning. She had spoken slowly, but she suspected that, even so, he was struggling to translate.

"Let me help you," she said. "We are lost too. We must find a way out of this forest and find help."

Behind her, Tyler muttered his outrage, but fortunately had the good sense not to object.

"Not police! Want your boat!"

"You're in Canada. The police will help. We have laws to protect you if you are running away from bad people." She cringed inwardly at her own lies, knowing the trio would more likely face detention or deportation, if not outright imprisonment for killing Phil. But one step at a time. First she had to gain the trust of the man with the gun. "I promise to help you. But first put down the rifle and help me catch some fish."

"We not want kill him."

Startled, she took a moment to collect her thoughts and consider the wisdom of opening up this discussion. She needed them to put aside the past — the difficulties they had been through and any loathsome acts they'd been forced to commit — and see her as an ally.

But Tyler couldn't resist. "Who?"

"Crazy old man. We want some food, he shooting us. Bullet hit Ghader on his arm." He gestured to the man draped in the quilt, whose glittering eyes suggested fever.

"So what did you do?" Amanda asked softly, unable to resist.

"We hit …" He swung the rifle butt to imitate a blow with an axe. "Too hard. Very much blood. We have lots trouble now."

She could hear the quaver in his voice. "I understand," she said. "All you wanted was a new life, not trouble. What's your name?"

"Mahmoud. And this Fazil." He jerked the rifle at the third man still standing at the sick man's side. Then he looked sharply at Tyler and his eyes flared with anger. He spat on the ground. "Not terrorist! *Kurde*."

Amanda absorbed this with surprise. "You're a long way from home."

"Our home is …" He shook his head. "Everybody is bombing. America bomb, Russia bomb, all from sky. DAESH bomb from streets. My mother and father killed in their house. Burn my city, burn my business. Shut the schools, the shops. So much suffer there, you cannot live there."

DAESH, Amanda knew, was an Arabic term for the Islamic State, one of the many brutal players in the chaos of the Middle East. "How did you end up here?"

"My brother and I … we go to Turkey. No papers, no visa. We pay very much money to Russian man to make papers for … going to America in a ship. But work all day with shrimp. Very cold. Shrimp, shrimp, always shrimp. I hate shrimp."

She wanted to ask more, but she could see Ghader about to topple over. His teeth were chattering. Only Fazil's strength kept him upright.

"What happened to you is terrible," she said. "Those people will be punished. But right now I can see your friend is sick and needs help. I also want to check my dog. Please, give me the rifle and help me make a fire."

Mahmoud stared at her a long minute, and she forced herself to hold his gaze and reach out her hand. Despite Fazil's hoarse protests in what Amanda assumed was Kurdish, Mahmoud finally lowered his gaze and held out the rifle to her. "It no work now. Bullets finished."

As her fingers closed over the cold steel barrel, waves of emotion almost knocked her off her feet. Relief that the threat was over and outrage that he had deceived her about the gun. She held the heavy, alien firearm with a shiver of repugnance and forced herself to check the chamber. Mahmoud was right. The rifle was empty.

She led the small ragtag group along the shore to a protected overhang where they could build a fire and wade out into the shallows to fish. She gestured to the injured man to sit down, and as Fazil helped to lower him, the quilt fell from his shoulders, revealing a primitive bandage caked with blood.

Tyler was hovering near her, his fists clenching and unclenching in silent rage. "Tyler, can you get me some water while I light a fire?" she asked softly.

"What about Dad!" he hissed. "That wasn't an accident. Ask them about that!"

"Not now I won't. I want us all to get out of this alive. Water."

Within a couple of hours, a measure of tense co-existence settled on the group. A healthy fire blazed, Ghader's wound had been cleaned and dressed to the best of Amanda's ability with the minimal supplies at her disposal. Some spruce gum and willow leaves had been mixed into a compress and held in place by strips of her thermal undershirt, which she'd decided was marginally cleaner than Old Stink's clothes. Kaylee had been lucky; a bullet had sliced her hip, but the bone had not broken. Amanda washed the wound, applied some spruce gum, and left it to nature.

Hot tea had been dispensed and both Kaylee and the injured man were now asleep by the fire. She knew the reprieve was temporary, for the man's wound looked infected and he might die within a week without proper help.

Fazil sat apart, staring sullenly into the fire as if he too realized this. Amanda moved closer to Mahmoud. "Are those two close friends?"

"Cousins." He sighed. "We were six who come from Turkey. Now maybe soon only two."

"Six? What happened to the others?"

"Ship captain promise we go down river to New York, but he lie. Working many weeks on ship at sea. Tired, cold, sick from the sea. At the morning I find my brother dead in his bed. They throw body in the sea, like rat in the night." He spoke haltingly, supplementing his broken English with vivid hand gestures. "That night we take a lifeboat. One man afraid, his wife drown on little boat, so he stay on the ship, but we go. Four days after, find land, but very big waves." More hand-waving. "Lifeboat break. Old man have more bigger boat with motor, but so much ocean! No cities! Boat sink, we have to swim to the land. But Fazil's friend not swim."

"I'm sorry," she said, rethinking Fazil's rigid stillness. "Then he must be doubly upset."

"Is okay. Fazil is strong."

She remembered the sad, desperate stories she and Phil had heard over the years. Stories of both incredible cruelty and resilience. "Tell him we won't let his cousin die. This boat can carry us all, and we will find our way to Croque. It's not a city, but it's a way out."

Chris Tymko stood in the middle of the logging trail, listening for the distant drone of an ATV. He and Jason Maloney had searched the mystery truck, which was unlocked with the keys left in the ignition, but the only useful clues they had found were a couple of local maps, a brochure of restaurants and accommodations on the northern peninsula, and a ferry schedule. Behind the seats in the cab was a stash of blankets and warm clothes.

If the man was up to something nefarious, there was no sign of it. Nor of him. The woods were silent, except for the crackling static of Jason's police radio as he searched in vain for a signal.

"Worthless piece of shit," Jason muttered eventually. "What happened to the fancy new system they bragged about, with coordinated coverage all across the island?"

Chris rolled his eyes. "Whoever designed it probably lives in Toronto. Why don't you stay here to keep the truck under surveillance while I go out to the road and see if I can raise a signal?"

Chris had to drive almost a kilometre up the Croque road toward the main highway before the signal was clear enough to call in. This time the comm coordinator must have sensed trouble because she switched to a private frequency and passed him directly to Noseworthy.

"Tymko, what the hell are you playing at?" Noseworthy snapped before Chris could get a word in.

Chris scrambled to regroup. "You mean checking out the unauthorized truck in the search area?"

"No, I mean blabbing confidential material about an active investigation to a reporter. Not just a local part-timer; a major news service! It's all over the goddamn Internet."

"What is, ma'am?"

"Matthew Goderich. He's leaked the fact Cousins was murdered, even though we haven't even told his widow yet. He's hinted at the fact Cousins was suspicious of a smuggling ring. Possibly people smuggling. Twitter is fucking eating it up!"

Chris was dumbfounded. *Goddamn you, Goderich!* "I … I don't know where he got all that, ma'am."

"He mentioned an anonymous police source."

"I never told him a thing!"

"But you talked to him? You two shared a room in Roddickton."

Chris held his tongue. He didn't even want to speculate how Noseworthy knew about his sleeping arrangements, and he suspected every protest he made merely dug him deeper into the hole. Because he needed the sergeant's co-operation for an even more crucial problem, he plunged ahead.

"He's just speculating, ma'am. But did Helen tell you about the unauthorized intrusion into the search area near Croque?"

Noseworthy was silent a moment. "This isn't over, Corporal."

"I understand, ma'am. But did she?"

"She did. And I know you also asked her to run a search on the vehicle, while we're juggling reports in and out of the field at a critical phase of the investigation."

"Well, we found that unauthorized truck hidden in the bush off a logging road. Driver and ATV missing."

"What do you mean, 'we'? What the hell are you doing away from your post?"

"Following up the lead, ma'am. Corporal Maloney and I."

"I didn't authorize you to leave the roadblock, Tymko! What do you think I'm doing here, playing tiddlywinks? We need the perimeter secured!"

"I got Corporal Willington to relieve me." Chris winced and held his breath. "I tried to clear it with you, but —"

"Corporal, get back to that roadblock!"

"Sergeant, just hear me out. The truck is registered to a seafood company and it's possible they're involved in this whole incident."

"You're talking about a pickup truck on a logging road with an ATV in back."

"Yes, which is now missing, along with the driver."

Noseworthy's voice dropped several octaves. She sounded dangerously calm. "You're not from here, Tymko, so you don't know this is exactly how hunters do things. We bring a truck in as close as we can and then we take the ATV into the bush to get the moose. That seafood company probably owns a hundred trucks, and any one of its employees could have signed it out for his own personal use. You know this is the biggest hunting weekend of the season, don't you?"

"But he was ordered to evacuate the area —"

"And if I'd just bagged an eight-hundred-pound bull, I'd have ignored that order too. This is Newfoundland."

Chris counted to three in his head and forced his shoulders to relax. He knew he was in deep trouble over Goderich and the roadblock, but he needed to find a way to rouse Noseworthy's police instincts. If the woman had any. "Ma'am, I believe it's a lead worth following. In St. Anthony, Phil Cousins was asking the trawler captain about working conditions and workers, but when I got there, the captain wasn't there. He'd apparently driven down to Corner Brook for a replacement part. In what? Maybe a company truck? Meanwhile a body is pulled from the sea and a lifeboat carrying foreigners wrecks on the shore just north of here. Maybe Matthew Goderich's speculations about people smuggling are not that far off the mark."

He braced himself for an explosion, but instead Noseworthy chuckled. A smoker's cough rumbled in her throat. "Quite the imagination, Tymko. Maybe you're more suited to writing thrillers than police work."

"But that lifeboat, and the body, are real! What theory is the RCMP working on?"

"All that stuff is being handled by security services in Ottawa, and they don't tell me jack shit. That's not my problem. I've got a civilian and a kid to find. End of story."

"But —"

"I don't give a fuck who killed Cousins, Tymko. Let Sergeant Amis try to pry some information out of the spooks and security freaks in Ottawa."

"I understand, ma'am, but it's possible someone from the seafood company is trying to find our missing persons too."

"Then our job is to find them first, Corporal. One lone guy on an ATV against our ERT team, our dogs, and our aircraft?

Our coordinated plan? Except you fucked up, opened up a chink in that plan. Vu needs to know that every single officer is fulfilling their part of the plan. So tell Maloney to get back to cover the roadblock, and you get your ass back in here, while I figure out what to do with you."

As frustrated as Chris was, he knew he was coming within a hair's breadth of being shipped back to his Deer Lake detachment, if not worse. He had no choice but to obey.

When he drove back to the logging road turnoff, however, Jason's truck was nowhere to be seen. Since it had not passed him on the way to the main highway, he concluded Jason must have headed toward Croque. Had he seen something?

Chris knew he was on very precarious ground with Noseworthy already and if he didn't show up as the woman had ordered, he might be kissing not just this case but his entire career goodbye. But what if Jason had seen something important? What if he was heading into danger, against orders, and without backup?

Cursing, Chris continued down the road toward Croque, searching the bush on either side. He had driven about a kilometre when Jason's truck appeared over the rise, racing down the middle of the road. He slewed to a stop in front of Chris.

"I thought I heard an ATV farther down this road," he called as soon as Chris pulled abreast. "But I lost it. Might have been the search helicopter out by the coast, flying really low to try to get below the clouds."

Chris squinted through his windshield at the swirling mist that was already obscuring the treetops on the higher slopes. Unless the weather lifted, before long the air search would have to be called off altogether.

"Is Noseworthy sending in an extra team?" Jason asked.

Chris shook his head. "She's seriously pissed off. Because we went against her plan, she's going to ignore everything we found. Might even take me off the case."

"You mean you didn't clear it with her?" Jason stiffened and revved his truck. "Fuck, Tymko! I know her; she's one tough bitch. If you've dragged me down with you ..." The rest of his threat was lost in the roar of tires on gravel as he accelerated down the road.

Fuck you too, Chris thought as he turned his cruiser around to head back to the command post. *You're no prince yourself.* He drove at a slow, thoughtful pace, reluctant to leave the mystery of the truck unsolved and even more reluctant to face Noseworthy. He wondered whether Jason would get to her first and put a spin on their adventure that would exonerate himself and place all the blame on Chris. He'd met men like Jason Maloney. Smooth, confident, and slippery as an eel, they always managed to make themselves look good at others' expense.

Chris had never mastered that skill. Whenever he tried, he felt grimy. Right and wrong were important to him. He'd signed on as a cop not just to follow orders and uphold the law, but also to do some good. In the remote rural communities where he'd worked, that meant being a social worker and youth mentor, an advisor on all things medical to legal, and a catcher of stray livestock. Why people acted as they did intrigued him, and the behaviour of the mystery truck driver nagged at him. Put together with all the other small mysteries, he knew in his gut it wasn't random. But now, his very job would be at stake it he tried to find out why.

He was still in a foul mood when he detoured briefly into Roddickton to check the latest Internet news. Sure enough, Matthew Goderich had managed to cobble together quite an imaginative tale based on supposition and hints, as well as an interview with Sheri Cousins. But tucked between the stories of smuggling and international intrigue was a poignant testament to Phil and to the tragedy of his death. On his blog, *Witness from the Frontline*, he recapped Phil's heroic but ultimately tragic efforts in Nigeria, his struggles with PTSD, and his final sacrifice, which had left a young son fatherless and lost in the wilderness.

As he read, Chris felt his anger dissipate. Noseworthy was an insensitive, tunnel-visioned tight-ass. No matter how much of Matthew's story turned out to be pure fantasy, at least he had put his finger on the human dimension. The spooks and the brass could freak out as much as they wanted; this was a story worth telling. Phil's epitaph.

When he crested the hill above the village of Conche and spotted the little blue Fiesta parked outside Casey's house, he had a flash of brilliance. He tucked his cruiser into a back lane and slipped through the backyards to Casey's kitchen door. Matthew looked up at him from his makeshift desk at the table. His expression was unapologetic, but uncertain.

"You saw my piece?"

Chris nodded, working hard to keep a stern scowl on his face.

"Your bosses are furious." Matthew grinned. "God, I love Canada. It feels great to be able to piss off the police and not get my head chopped off. I'm working on a follow-up, but I can't get a word out of your Sergeant Noseworthy, or the head honcho in St. John's. As for Ottawa — hah! But the public is eating it up! Someone has even started a Facebook page called Prayers for Tyler. Well, I can do without the praying bit, but the sentiment is nice. We have to keep the ball rolling. Have you got anything for me on the search?"

In spite of his vow, Chris couldn't suppress a grin in return. The segue was perfect. "I may have a tip for you, but I'm going to need you to sit on it for a while."

"Anonymous source, I promise."

"No. Noseworthy will see through that in an instant. Two people's lives are in jeopardy and I know you care about that. The risk has not been contained —" Chris broke off as he heard the cop-speak.

"You mean the bad guys are still out there."

Chris laughed. "Yeah, that's what I mean. But there is something you can do to help, and in the end it will give you more material for your reports." He paused to glance out the window. The command trailer and the police compound were out of sight up the hill, but as a precaution, he gestured to Matthew to come into the small front parlour, where the lace curtains and the rain obscured the window.

In brief strokes he related the story of the mystery truck belonging to Acadia Seafood and Phil's interest in the foreign workers in St. Anthony. "I want to know who was driving the truck and what it was doing in the area. And I want to know more about the trawler. Does it employ foreign workers? Is it still in port and has the captain returned?"

Matthew's pen raced across the page and he bobbed his head up and down so excitedly that Chris thought it would fly off. "Do the spooks — sorry, security — know about this?"

"I don't know, but as you say, they wouldn't tell us if they did. Whatever you can dig up, pass it on directly to me."

Matthew nodded. He was vibrating with excitement as he prepared for a quick escape. Chris grabbed his arm.

"But remember. This guy, whoever he is, is out there in the woods and so are Amanda and Tyler. I don't know what he's up to, but I don't want to panic him into damage control."

"Mum's the word," Matthew said.

"I mean it, Matthew!"

With a tip of his fedora, Matthew was out the door. Chris sat in the house a moment longer, trying to calm his nerves. He had just ventured way, way farther out onto his precarious limb, with nothing to cushion him should the limb come crashing down. He had not only gone behind Noseworthy's back and given confidential police information to a reporter, but he'd potentially endangered Amanda and Tyler's life if Matthew didn't keep his word.

His hands were still shaking when he parked his cruiser up beside Incident Command and strode resolutely inside, ready to face the firing squad. He was greeted by a buzz of excitement that raced through the entire room. Personnel were clustered around the wall map, consulting laptops and chattering at once.

Chris felt an overwhelming rush of hope. "Have they been found?"

Noseworthy swung around. The faint smile on her dour face vanished at the sight of him. "No. But the helicopter picked up a thermal spot and what looked like the word *help* drawn on the slope behind an abandoned outport. Weather conditions are risky, but ERT is sending a Zodiac up to verify it. It's early days, of course ..."

"But it's a lead," the coordinator burst out.

CHAPTER TWENTY-FIVE

Corporal Vu spent the next fifteen minutes trying to juggle assignments to move some of his teams from the more remote sections closer to this latest sighting. Chris sat quietly in the corner, keeping his ears open and his eyes on the screens. The helicopter camera showed very little but a big swirl of cloud, effectively blocking their eyes in the sky and providing no support to the ground searches. As Vu fretted over the assignments, Noseworthy worked on road patrols and pointedly ignored Chris until he could barely stand it.

"The Croque road is the only road access to the part of the peninsula near this sighting," Noseworthy said. "We'll need an extra unit at the entrance."

"There isn't one," Vu snapped. Noseworthy pursed her lips.

"I can do that," Chris said. "Ma'am."

Noseworthy didn't even favour him with a glance. "No you can't, Tymko. You're off the case."

"But —"

"Don't waste my time."

Chris held his tongue, recognizing from Noseworthy's steely tone that his next interruption might get him kicked out of the command post and ordered back to Deer Lake.

The whole staff was on tenterhooks waiting for the Zodiac to report in. As the afternoon wore on, the rain and wind eased up, but a thick fog rolled in, blanketing the hills and grounding the helicopter completely. Chris tried to fade into the woodwork, but with more pressing concerns on her mind, Noseworthy seemed to have decided to ignore his existence altogether, which suited him fine. She paced, fretting aloud about the visibility along the shore.

It was mid-afternoon before the Zodiac report came in. A hush fell over the trailer as everyone strained to decipher the broken garble emanating from the radio.

"Deserted village … subjects not here, but evidence recent visitors … ashes in stove, cooking pan, mattress on floor …"

Chris nearly shouted aloud, clapping his hand over his mouth at the last moment. He fought a lump in his throat. They were alive! Not only alive, but finding food and shelter. Brilliant, brilliant woman!

Vu traced his finger over the map. "Any indication where they went?"

"Negative, sir. But we can search the surrounding terrain on foot to see if we can spot a trail."

"Hold off on that. I don't want their scent disturbed. Do a shore search from the boat. It's a large bay, and they could have walked in either direction. I'll send K9 in."

"Copy that, sir."

The K9 team did not respond to its call sign, however, despite Vu's increasingly loud and frustrated efforts. "Keep trying," he ordered Helen as he headed outside. "I'll have their asses for this."

Noseworthy was frowning at Corporal Vu through the window. The ERT leader was like a spring wound too tight, quick to action but also quick to anger. *How much experience did he have with killers and victims on the loose?* Chris wondered. *Did Noseworthy have concerns?*

Chris was no longer able to keep quiet. "Ma'am, I've been in there. Radio reception in the interior is spotty. The woods are dense and the terrain is mountainous."

Noseworthy bristled at the interruption, but seemed to consider. "There are only four hours of daylight left and the weather is worsening. Heavy fog is forecast for tonight. Worst-case scenario for Vu's team. But we're not getting this close only to have our subjects vanish into the fog. I am going to round up another K9 team for him. I'll airlift them in from Moncton if I have to."

She swung around and was about to get on the phone when the radio came to life again. "Ma'am, we found another message down on the wharf. Not sure what it means, but it's fresh paint."

"What's the message?"

"'What did one frog say to the other?'"

Astonished silence descended on the room. A couple of titters rippled through, but Noseworthy just blinked at the radio. "What the fuck?"

"Croque," Chris said.

Frank laughter burst out. Noseworthy spun around, and stared first at Chris and then at the map.

"They've gone to Croque," he said.

"But … why the riddle? Why not just say that?"

A niggle of worry wormed in Chris's gut. Why indeed? Was Amanda becoming unhinged? Delirious? After all she'd been through — discovering Phil's body, slogging lost and disoriented through the bush, perhaps starving and dehydrated — was she losing touch?

All these possibilities raced through his mind, but he voiced none of them. Merely shrugged. "The important thing is she's looking for Croque."

Noseworthy was already at the map, tracing her finger down the long, narrowing inlet, at the end of which was tucked the village of Croque. She called in Vu and handed the Zodiac team over to him.

Vu looked calmer now as he studied the map. "The village of Croque is about five kilometres farther inland. Do a search along the shore inland from your location. Meanwhile I'll send a ground unit into Croque from this end."

After signing off, he examined the assignment roster. "Fuck, I need another unit."

Noseworthy's usually dour face was pink with excitement and her blue eyes glittered. "I'll call Moncton."

"Too long. I'll have to go myself."

"You can't," Noseworthy said. Her tone brooked no discussion. "Helen, get me Moncton HQ."

"Let me do it, ma'am," Chris said, unable to restrain himself. "ERT's stretched thin, you said so yourself, and there's no point me just sitting here like a bump on a log. I know that road, I know that village. I even talked to some of the local residents last week."

Vu was shaking his head vigorously, but Noseworthy stood very still, sizing up the map and the assignment roster. Chris held his breath, debating how to press his case.

"I know I've been a pain —"

Noseworthy silenced him with a slice of her hand. "You've been more than a pain, Tymko. You've shown a reckless disregard for orders and jeopardized the integrity of the search."

"Let me make it up. I can do this, ma'am. I had plenty of search-and-rescue experience up north. Including against active shooters."

"And just who the hell would you take as your partner? The journalist?"

"Jason Maloney?"

"Corporal Maloney is on the roadblock, doing what he's supposed to."

Chris sensed her weakening. "Corporal Willington, then. He and I have worked together before, and he's local. He knows the area better than anybody."

Vu finally erupted. "I can't have a bunch of untrained regulars running all through the zone!"

"Which would you prefer, Corporal?" Noseworthy said. "A pristine search, or two live subjects?"

"More likely two dead subjects!"

Ignoring him, Noseworthy walked over to the small window that overlooked the bay. Fog obscured the mountains and most of the village below. She shook her head slowly back and forth, as if she didn't believe what she was about to say.

"Go on," she said to Chris. "Corporal Vu will send in a team to replace you as soon as it arrives, but you and Willington can do the advance recon. Tymko?" she snapped as he moved to go. "Advance recon of the village only. Stay out of sight."

Chris stopped in Roddickton only long enough to pick up Willington and some supplies before the two of them rocketed down the highway to the Croque road. When they turned in, they passed Jason's roadblock. Parked next his truck was a rusty white Cavalier. Chris blasted his horn twice as they passed, while Willington craned his neck to see inside the truck.

"Can't wait to see them fit a moose on the roof of that Cavalier," Chris quipped.

"Looked like a woman in his truck," Willington said.

Chris grunted. How like Jason Maloney. Leave no woman behind. He pressed the accelerator closer to the floor and they continued on down toward Croque. Passing the logging road where the Acadia Seafood truck had been hidden, Chris tightened with worry. That truck was a loose thread, potentially a danger to the whole operation. But there was no time to check out whether it was still there.

Soon the familiar roadside gardens and stacks of firewood began to break the monotony of the forest, announcing the proximity of the village. Each time they rounded a curve, Chris kept hoping to see Amanda and Tyler walking up the road. Each time, there was no one.

Having been evacuated, the village itself was eerily quiet. Most of the vehicles were gone and the yards were empty. No washing hung on the lines and no smoke drifted from the chimneys. Nonetheless, Chris scanned the houses scattered through the rolling hills for any sign of Amanda.

Nothing. He parked the cruiser above the small harbour, and he and Willington climbed out to survey the area.

"Amanda!" he shouted. A faint echo drifted back from down the bay, but no other response. He cupped his hands. "Amanda!"

Willington gave two short blasts on the emergency whistle. Still nothing. "Keep doing that," Chris said, "in case they're nearby."

They descended the slope to the ramshackle wharf and peered down the bay. Mist shimmered on the water and blurred the trees, but he could detect no shadows moving along the shore. No sign of the police Zodiac either. *What the hell*, he thought. *The search boat should have been here by now, even in this weather.*

Unless they'd found something.

His gaze fell on the little fishing dory moored to the wharf. The motor was still on the back and its life jackets and gas tank were still in the bilge, as if the pilot had left it in a hurry. He nodded at it. "Should we borrow that and go meet the boat, in case they need help?"

Willington's brow wrinkled. "We're just supposed to recon the area."

"That is reconning the area."

"You know what I mean. She said the village."

In vain Chris listened for the whine of the Zodiac. "They can't be far."

"Noseworthy will have our balls."

"She's not here, is she? And look, there's no radio signal."

Willington took out his radio. With a quick hand, Chris batted it aside before he could check. "There's no signal." He climbed into the boat and checked the motor and fuel. The little 9-horsepower engine fired to life on the second pull. "You're right. You should stay here to meet the backup team."

"Chris …"

"Be back in a jiffy." Chris reversed the boat and pointed it down the narrow fjord, lifting his hand for a jaunty wave as he opened up the throttle.

The drone of the motor and the slap of waves against the hull drowned out all other sound as he chugged up the twisting, widening bay. Half-blinded by mist, he hugged the southern shore so that he could search the rocks and woodlands for the Zodiac. Or Amanda. At each curve, he hesitated, wondering whether the boat had followed the opposite shore or wandered into an inlet he could barely see through the fog.

After awhile, he began to worry in earnest. The fog had chilled and soaked him to the core. By his rough estimate he had travelled about three kilometres and was more than halfway to the abandoned outport where the HELP sign had been found. Where *was* everyone?

Up ahead, the murky silhouette of a point jutted into the wide bay. At first he could see nothing but the grey rock and the blurred greens and browns of the bordering woods. But then, tucked into the lee of the point, he thought he saw a smudge of black and some shadows of movement. He squinted through the mist. As he drew closer, the black took on the shape of a boat and the moving shadows became two people upon the shore.

Nearer still, he was able to make out a second, smaller boat half sunk in the shallow water. The two searchers turned in surprise to watch his approach. At the last second, he remembered to pull the propeller shaft up before running the dory up on the gravel beach. He jumped out, wiping the rainwater from his eyes.

"What have you guys found?"

The two people were covered head to toe in foul-weather tactical gear, but their eyes stared out at him in bristling unison. "Corporal Tymko," he added hastily. "I came out from Croque. No sign of our missing persons?"

One of them pulled off her hood, revealing a tousled head of blond hair, and extended her hand. "June Halliday. Did Vu send you?"

Chris made a vague gesture. "Until backup arrives."

A brief frown flickered across her face before she pointed to the sunken rowboat. "We found this. They may have been trying to come up the bay by boat, but this baby only got them half way. She's some old, this little gal."

Aren't they all, Chris thought irrelevantly. He glanced around at the forbidding forest. "Any trace of them?"

Halliday shook her head. "We radioed it in, they told us to sit tight. They're bringing K9 up to take it from here." She paused. "The poor buggers may not even have made it to shore anyway, in that thing."

With an effort, Chris fought off the ominous implication. If they had swamped out in the bay, hypothermia would have claimed them within minutes. He turned instead to study the shoreline. The tide was almost at the high-water mark, so that the steep bank made walking along the shore very difficult, but the lower tide of earlier in the day would have provided a swath of shoreline along which to walk. Why wouldn't Amanda and Tyler have followed the shore, which at least provided them with a direction. Slogging through the dense, hilly woods, they could get lost again in an instant.

Yet he had seen no trace of them along the shore.

"How do you know it's theirs?" he asked, clinging to faint hope.

"They left another message." She leaned over to point at a word raggedly scratched onto the side of the boat. "*Frogmarched*."

He stared at her. More riddles! He walked over for a closer look. The rain had covered the boat with mist, but he thought he detected some red smears on the gunwales and oars. A chill of dread crept up his spine. He squatted down, and through the water he saw two holes in the bottom of the boat. He sucked in his breath.

"Help me move it!" he cried, shoving at the boat. Water sloshed as it slid sideways on the gravel, revealing, as Chris feared, two bullets partially buried in the sand beneath.

"Fuck," he whispered as the remnants of hope drained from him.

CHAPTER TWENTY-SIX

Amanda had lost all sense of time and direction. She was so used to being hungry that she could no longer use it as a guide. *One foot in front of another*, she thought as she trudged through the woods with her head bowed and her shoulders leaning in. She hoped they were still heading west in the general direction of Croque, but in reality she had no idea. Wisps of fog had collected in the hollows and she hadn't caught a glimpse of sun in what felt like hours.

Mahmoud was carrying Tyler on his back. At first the boy had refused to go near the man or accept any help, but eventually the pain wore him down. He slept now with his head resting on Mahmoud's shoulder. The group plodded along in a straggling line that detoured, backtracked, and bunched to a stop as they clambered over fallen trees and around boulders. Amanda led the way and all she could hear was ragged breathing and twigs snapping in her wake.

At the top of a rise, she paused to check behind her and saw that Fazil and his cousin were no longer there. The two had been taking up the rear, so that they could follow at Ghader's hobbling pace. She called for a halt. Relieved, Mahmoud eased Tyler to the ground while Amanda headed back down the trail. She found Ghader collapsed in his tracks, deathly pale and unconscious. Fazil stood at his side, his head bowed. As Amanda checked the fallen man's pulse, which was thready and faint, she detected the rancid stink of infection emanating from his body. The smell filled her with dread, bringing back memories of weak and injured refugees who had collapsed during their long treks to safety.

Mahmoud came to kneel beside her. "We must leave him."

The pain of memory knifed her. "We can't."

"He is dying."

Shaking her head, she laid her hand on Ghader's cold, papery forehead. "Let's give him time to rest."

"He is dying." Mahmoud turned to speak to Fazil in a quiet murmur, and the other man shook his head. Mahmoud turned back to Amanda, his tone flat and resigned, his green eyes bleak with sorrow. "Fazil say his cousin is not continue. Very sick for his home."

"Homesick?"

Mahmoud nodded. "He have a wife and daughter in Kobani. He want better life in America and bring them."

"Kobani? That's in Northern Syria, isn't it? I've read about the terrible fighting there."

"Ghader is afraid his family gone. DAESH … take women. He has no news from them."

Every ounce of her wanted to fight against the man's death, but she sensed the futility of it. She eased him into a more comfortable position and took off her jacket to keep him warm. She could think of nothing more than to stroke his brow, feeling helpless and bereft as the life ebbed from him.

Tyler came limping back down the path to join the mournful circle around the fallen man. Amanda looked into Tyler's eyes, stricken and huge with tears, and realized that for him it was like watching his father die all over again.

"We will leave you two to stay with him until …" she murmured as she rose to draw Tyler away, grateful for the chance to escape the death vigil and the pain of her own memories. She sat on a nearby log and held Tyler's trembling body close.

"I'm sorry, Tyler," she murmured, pressing her lips to his tousled head. "I'm sorry you have to go through this."

"Why don't we just leave them?"

"Because they are lost and scared too."

"They are killers!"

She tightened her grip and rocked him. Kaylee lay at their feet quietly, as if she too sensed the sadness of the moment.

Time stretched. Fingers of fog slipped through the woods, obscuring the men huddled down the trail and muffling their soft murmurs. Amanda could hear the chanting of prayer, and her heart began to race. She felt trapped, unable to see her way out. *No one is going to find us*, she thought as she felt the hot wetness of tears upon her cheeks. *I will sit here, holding this child as Phil held Alaji all those months ago, and feel the pulse of his life slip through my fingers.*

"Why are you crying, Amanda?" Tyler whispered.

Straightening, she brushed an angry fist across her face. "I feel bad for Ghader," she said. "He left his home and came all this way to escape the cruelty of ISIS and Assad, only to meet more cruel people here."

When Tyler twisted his head so that he could look at her, she could see the doubt in his eyes. Twigs snapped in the underbrush, and Mahmoud's tall silhouette startled her as he loomed abruptly out of the fog. Without a word, he knelt at their side and bowed his head. Her fingers found his.

"I'm sorry about Ghader," she said. "Did you know him in Kobani?"

"Friends. We have a business together. I am a engineer, and Ghader make machines."

"What kind of machines?"

"Simple things. Electric, power tools. But our factory was destroyed by bomb. Syrian army think we make guns. No future for Kurds in Syria. Me, I have education, some money, cousin in Chicago, but no documents. In Turkey, can't get visa. So this ..." He shrugged eloquently as he gestured to the desolate scrubland around him.

"So you paid someone to get you out."

He nodded. "I pay many people. Turkey, Hungary, so many little countries. Walk, train, truck, then ship. All my money — ten thousand American dollars — to Russian man Fazil find on Internet. It look like good plan. We go fast, because the train leaving. No time for pack, tell friends, just run." His lips grew taut as a darker memory descended. "But Russian man lie. He cheat. Promise passport, but not give it. Give to captain on the ship."

"And he kept them," Amanda said grimly. It was an old trick smugglers used to ensure control.

Mahmoud's lips quivered. "I had a good life before the war. Happy. I never do bad things. Never hold a gun. Never kill man ..."

Tyler lifted his head to fix Mahmoud with a bitter glare. "What about my father?"

"I not see your father."

"You shot him!"

"I not —"

"Stop!" It was Fazil, emerging from the fog. Amanda was startled, having never heard him speak English before. He held himself rigidly straight, like a man struggling not to feel. "No fight. We go."

"Not in this fog," Amanda said. "We will lose each other."

Fazil held up a belt. "Tie together."

"Take the time to bury your cousin," Amanda said. "Maybe by then the fog will have lifted."

Fazil looked about to argue, but Mahmoud spoke to him in Kurdish. As they discussed back and forth, they glanced at Tyler a few times, and Amanda felt a small chill. How much English did Fazil understand, and were they using Kurdish as a code so they could make secret plans?

Matthew Goderich hung up his phone and stared out the window in frustration. Where was the man? He'd left two voicemail messages and three texts for him, without a single reply. Even in this godforsaken part of the world, surely one of the messages should have gotten through. It was a simple message. *Call me, important info!*

While he waited for Chris Tymko's reply, Matthew continued his research into the Acadia Seafood Company and its wandering trawler captain. As a journalist covering the world stage, he'd learned to be suspicious, and the pattern that was emerging rang all his alarm bells. He'd tracked them both on the Internet, placed some judicious phone calls and even managed to speak to a couple of the man's neighbours in Miramichi, New Brunswick.

The Fisheries and Oceans Canada officer up in St. Anthony was unwilling to make any comment on the trawler or its crew, but Matthew had uncovered enough to believe Chris was right. There was a bigger international picture here.

His fingers itched to file a news update on the information he'd gleaned, but he'd made a promise to Chris. Instead he updated his *Witness from the Frontline* blog on the dangers Amanda and Tyler faced from the worsening weather and fog. The social media response had been astonishing, and both the Prayers for Tyler Facebook page and Twitter hashtag #lostboy were flooded with expressions of concern and exhortations to keep them posted.

As the afternoon wore on, he watched with increasing alarm as the fog settled in. Searchers would be stumbling half-blind while the killer could slip through the cordon with ease. Perhaps the fog was also interfering with Chris's satellite phone reception. Perhaps he was inside his cruiser or a house. He might not check his phone until late that night, when the damage might already be done.

Finally he shut his laptop and left the Mayflower Inn to head over to talk to the local Roddickton RCMP. A friendly young woman behind the glass reception counter informed him that Corporal Willington was out, but could she help? No, she didn't know when he'd be back, there was a major incident in the region, and yes, all available officers were committed to that.

Matthew had never been able to rely on his sex appeal when talking to women, but he had found that the bumbling teddy bear approach sometimes worked. He tilted his fedora back to scratch his head, and furrowed his brow. "Oh, dear. I need to speak to one of the officers, Corporal Tymko," he said. "I have urgent information for him."

A lovely smile softened her face. "Oh, Corporal Tymko is down in Croque with Corporal Willington, in fact. But you should pass on all information to Sergeant Noseworthy down in Conche. She's the —"

"Yes, I know who she is, but I hate the thought of that long drive to the coast in the fog. Can you contact Tymko by radio and let me speak to him?"

The smile wavered. "Oh, no, sir. The radio channel has to be kept open for search information. But I can give you the sergeant's phone number."

Dutifully Matthew wrote Noseworthy's number down, thanked the nice woman, and left the station, thinking it would be a cold day in hell before he passed Chris's precious information on to that tight-ass. Shoving the card into his jeans pocket, he headed back to his car. Fog now obscured the white mountains across the bay and blurred the outlines of shops and homes along the highway. Street and car lights lit up the canvas like an impressionist painting.

Croque. The friendly young receptionist had let that slip. Did that mean the search was narrowing to the area around the village? The Croque road was more than half an hour north of town, but at least the main highway up to the turnoff was paved and relatively flat. It would be closer to the action, and maybe he'd have more luck with the officer manning the roadblock there.

To his disappointment, however, the junction was empty and there was no sign of a roadblock. Perhaps the officer had been reassigned as the search narrowed. He sat in his car for a few minutes, absorbing the muffled silence of the woods ahead as he pondered his next move. Not only did Chris need this information, but as a reporter Matthew could not move forward on his own story if he couldn't discuss it with him. That had been the deal.

Thousands of people around the world were reading his blog, more attention than he'd ever had, even for his reports from the Boko Haram war front last year. Thousands more followed his Twitter feed and the Facebook page created to support Amanda and Tyler. Astonishingly, people were offering not just prayers, but money to help the fatherless boy cope in the months and years ahead. So far, thousands of dollars had been donated.

In the end, Tyler and Amanda were what mattered, he decided. Not his own big exposé, not even Chris's personal tussle with Noseworthy over the scope of the case, but the safety and rescue of two lost and frightened people.

Grudgingly he turned his Fiesta around and drove slowly back south toward Conche through the fog that swirled in his headlights. The command post was relatively quiet, suggesting all available officers were either in the field or catching some much-needed rest after more than twenty-four hours of searching. In the corner, surrounded by computer maps and assignment sheets, the ERT leader was hunched over his radio, presumably monitoring calls.

Noseworthy looked more exhausted than annoyed when Matthew entered the trailer. Her lean frame stooped a little lower and her skin was grey.

"We have things in hand, Goderich," she said. "When I have something to report, I will issue a statement but at the moment the last thing I need is your cockamamie scare stories about people smuggling."

"I have obtained some information that —"

"Do you know where our MisPers are?"

"No, but the trawler captain —"

"Then I'm not interested."

"Hear me out! Unless you want your name in a headline about how the RCMP's secrecy and tunnel vision fucked up the search by discounting crucial information."

Noseworthy snapped to attention and flushed fuchsia. "If you want one iota of co-operation out of the RCMP — *ever* — you won't print that."

Matthew wanted to say "Just watch me," but checked his childish defiance, which he knew would not advance his cause. Instead he opened up with both barrels. "The captain of the trawler is the truck driver who's disappeared in the Croque area. He said he was going for ship parts, but instead he drove inside the search area and hid the truck. The trawler is jointly owned by Canadian and Finnish companies. Finland may be a nice, innocuous country, but it serves as a transit station for human trafficking from all the little former Soviet countries to the south."

"This isn't relevant."

"It is, when the trawler had some supposedly Finnish crew that, according to the Newfoundland crew, didn't know a damn thing about shrimp fishing and were paid a fraction of proper union rates. And according to his neighbours in Miramichi, the captain makes way more money than any shrimp boat captain they know. I think you have a much bigger problem on your hands than a lost woman and child. You've got a bunch of illegal aliens on the loose and a captain desperate to shut them up. And God knows who killed Phil Cousins."

Noseworthy stood very still. A silence had fallen over the handful of staff still in the trailer, and Vu's eyes were narrowed. Matthew paused to catch his breath.

"Now do you want to hear exactly what I know?" he said finally.

After glancing at Vu, Noseworthy nodded brusquely, grabbed her radio, and gestured toward the door. "I need a cigarette. Let's go outside."

Outside, she leaned against the side of the trailer and lit up. Matthew took five minutes to sketch out what he'd learned from talking to neighbours, disgruntled ship crew, and skeleton staff at Acadia Seafood. The ship's crew had been told that the Finnish crew was part of the ownership agreement, but they never mingled. The Finns worked in the trawler's processing plant and had their own sleeping and eating quarters. They were kept separate in order to minimize discord over their different working conditions, the Canadian crew had been told. More likely to keep both sides in the dark, Matthew said. Then one morning, only one Finnish crew member showed up for work."

As Noseworthy smoked, her scowl deepened. "Who told you to look into this?"

"I'm a reporter. It's what I do. I look for the story behind the shadows. I knew about the body in St. Anthony, the lifeboat spotted offshore, and the trawler stuck in port. I also knew Phil

Cousins became interested in foreign workers when he met one in a pub last week. That guy had been hitchhiking down from St. Anthony. Dollars to doughnuts he was the one worker who didn't go in the lifeboat. He's probably long faded into the underground immigrant community in Toronto or Ottawa, but you might want to let the spooks know."

"But who told you all this?"

"Around here, people notice things. They talk. They love to share in the drama."

Noseworthy blew out a long trickle of smoke and stared him down in silence as the seconds ticked by. Matthew knew the woman didn't believe him, and he was thinking up his next lie when her radio crackled to life. The caller's voice was broken and distorted, but Matthew could hear the urgency. Noseworthy obviously did as well, for she stomped out her cigarette and snatched up her radio.

"Tymko, it's Noseworthy. Where are you?"

"I'm with the search team that found the abandoned rowboat, ma'am. The radio signal is poor, so I may lose you."

Matthew saw Noseworthy try to interrupt, but Chris rushed on. "There's been a development, ma'am. Looks like someone shot at them. There are two bullet holes in the bottom of the boat, likely what sunk it, and we found bullets in the sand. They're badly damaged but they're big-game calibre, like Stin — Parsons. Over."

"Any sign of the shooter? Over."

"Negative, ma'am. We've been searching the bay and the shoreline by boat, but so far no sign of Amanda and the child, either."

"If they weren't wearing life jackets, in that water ..."

"But we did find another message, ma'am, etched into the boat. 'Frogmarched.'"

"Oh for fuck's sake!" Noseworthy caught Matthew's eye and scowled as if she'd only just remembered he was there. She pursed her lips and seemed to come to a decision. "Well, we do have some relevant intel at this end. That truck you reported yesterday was driven by the captain of the trawler in St. Anthony, and there may be an overseas connection to illegal immigrants." Noseworthy's nostrils flared, and Matthew suspected the admission was difficult for her. "Corporal Vu is sending in as much ERT backup as he can round up, but this damn fog is a serious impediment. Sit tight. We don't know what the captain is up to, or why he'd be hunting for Amanda and Tyler. We can't run an operation on wild guesses. A second K9 is on its way, and Vu is covering all the ATV exits, so sit tight with the ERT unit so that back-up can find you."

"Yes, ma'am, but —"

"And Tymko? For once, obey me."

With that, Noseworthy signed off. She flung open the door to the trailer, now fully recharged, and snapped her fingers at the comm clerk. "Get hold of Corporal Maloney. He's on the roadblock at the Croque road turnoff. Ask him for the GPS coordinates of that truck while I bring Corporal Vu up to speed."

While the comm clerk placed the radio call, Noseworthy filled the ERT leader in and then picked up her phone. She glanced at Matthew as if debating whether to send him away, but then shook her head. "Wait, in case Corporal Vu or Major Crimes has some questions."

Matthew tried to keep track of the two conversations. The coordinator, Helen, was trying to raise Jason, and Noseworthy was passing on to Sergeant Amis the latest information Matthew had uncovered. The discussion was brief, and when she hung up, Noseworthy made a face and began jotting notes on her computer. Matthew watched until he could stand it no longer.

"Was Sergeant Amis aware of the captain connection?"

"He is now. We'll take it from here, and I should warn you, if you publish any of this, you may jeopardize our investigation." She drew her mouth down. "I'm sure you don't want that any more than I do."

Matthew tipped his fedora slightly as he trotted out his favourite line of sap. "I only want to help. I have tremendous respect and admiration for Amanda and Phil."

"Sergeant?" Helen called from across the room. "Corporal Maloney isn't answering his radio."

"Then call back."

"I have, ma'am. Five times."

CHAPTER TWENTY-SEVEN

Out of respect, Amanda and Tyler sat some distance away while the two Kurds prepared and wrapped their countryman's body and laid spruce boughs over the grave. Moist fog cocooned the woods, reducing their conversation to a muffled murmur and blurring out all but their spooky silhouettes as they foraged for deadfall.

After a while, even their voices died away. In the silence, Mahmoud called out. Waited. Called again. Twigs cracked in the distance. A few moments later, Mahmoud materialized out of the fog, his shoulders drooping with fatigue and grief.

"Fazil here?"

Amanda shook her head. "Isn't he with you?"

"He looking for big stone for put on top. Go away, not come back."

"I heard branches breaking," Amanda said, rising to peer through the darkening cocoon. "I think it came from that direction."

Listening to the silence, she heard nothing but her own heartbeat. Kaylee lay at her side, supremely indifferent to the brooding woods. If Fazil was out there, he was already too far away to catch her attention.

"I wonder why he didn't call out," she said.

"I make a lot of noise, calling him."

"Call again. In this fog, it's hard to tell direction and he may panic."

Mahmoud cupped his hands and bellowed several times. No answer. Darkness was gathering fast. "What we do?"

"We stay here, light a fire, and hope he finds his way back. If we try to look for him, we may get even more lost and farther away. By morning the fog may have lifted."

She and Mahmoud gathered small bits of wood for a fire and she searched the clearing for berries and roots. It was a dismal harvest but she didn't dare venture farther afield. In the clammy darkness, they hunkered down around the fire, listening to it spit and hiss and drawing comfort from its flames.

Tyler looked wan and listless as he wrapped his jacket more tightly. "I'm so hungry," he whispered.

Amanda draped her own jacket around him and rubbed his back. "In the morning we will look for a pond or the ocean to catch some fish."

"I don't hear any waves."

"Then we will climb a hill."

"God willing, Fazil will find us," Mahmoud said. "He will see the fire."

Amanda kept her fears to herself. It was an unforgiving landscape. They were surrounded by cliffs and bogs that could swallow you up within minutes. It was a dreadful way to die, slowly drowning in the soupy mud that sucked you down.

As if he sensed her worry, Mahmoud nodded toward the woods. "Fazil say he was in Syrian army. He train this, learn how ... survive. He will find his way."

Amanda heard the doubt in his words. In the flickering orange firelight, his features were grim and worried.

"Did you know him back in Syria?"

Mahmoud shook his head. "Ghader talk about him sometimes. He drive a tank, but in Syrian army, everything — tanks,
guns, trucks — old from Russians. DAESH steal better from Iraq
army. And they are killing everybody with guns, knife, even the
children and soldiers … *bap, bap, bap!*" He mimicked the action
of machine-gun fire and his mouth drew down in disapproval.
"Fazil not fight back, he run away."

She flinched as if the pain of memory were physical.
Sometimes not fighting back is not a choice, but an instinct, she
thought. *A reaction driven by panic and self-preservation, which
steamrolls over conscious will.* How often she had wondered
whether her own reaction on that fateful night would have been
different, had the children been her own. "No one ever knows
what they will do when they face danger," Amanda said. "Soldiers
see terrible things. They have to do terrible things too."

Mahmoud shrugged. "Everybody see terrible things. Assad
bomb homes, gas children, and when DAESH come, they do …"
His voice faded as his English failed him. "You can't even imagine. I feel bad. I am here, my country is there, my sisters are
there. I run away, too."

"But dying on the street over there doesn't do any good,
either. From here, you can try to rescue your family." It was a
rationale she'd trotted out before, for her own behaviour on that
fateful night, and it rang just as hollow now.

He poked the fire angrily, sending sparks spitting into the dark.
"You can't understand. You never have war here on your own land."

A dozen retorts rose to her lips, but she stifled them. She was
too worn out and worried to debate the guilt and blessings of privi-
lege, or to tell him that she understood far more than he imagined.

Instead she laid a hand on his arm. "Let's be thankful for that
and save our strength for tomorrow. Tomorrow we're going to
get ourselves out of here."

———

Growling woke her with a start. She bolted upright to see Kaylee standing at the edge of the clearing, staring into the woods. Her hackles were raised and a soft whine bubbled up in her throat.

Amanda took rapid inventory. The fire was out, Tyler and Mahmoud were asleep, but a pale pre-dawn light washed the sky above. The fog was retreating, clinging in tendrils to the trees, but allowing glimpses of the wooded slope beyond. The forest sparkled with dew, promising a freshly washed day.

Kaylee uttered a single, sharp bark.

"Sh-h!" Amanda lunged for her collar, but her fingers slipped uselessly through fur as the dog bolted for the trees. Instinctively Amanda shouted, but Kaylee didn't even break her stride. *She'll come back*, Amanda told herself. *Let's hope she spotted a rabbit or a squirrel that will serve as her breakfast.*

The moments crawled by without sound or sight of Kaylee. Wakened by the commotion, the others began preparations for the day. Amanda built up the fire while Mahmoud went in search of water for the berry tea that had become their staple. Dawn had brought hope.

Amanda kept a worried eye on the woods, which had come alive with the twitter of birds and the scrabble of small animals. Suddenly the woods erupted in furious barking, thrashing, and crashing.

"There's someone out there," Tyler said as it grew louder.

Amanda stifled her own alarm. "Probably Kaylee freaked out by a moose."

"I think it's a person."

Amanda gripped the fish knife and scanned the woods. The barking had died as abruptly as it began, but leaves rustled and twigs snapped as the footsteps came closer. Too large and heavy to be Kaylee. She glimpsed a figure slipping through the trees, hunched low as if to hide.

"Fazil?" she called.

A flash of orange danced through the woods and for a moment Kaylee was visible through the leaves, her tail waving in delight as she barked at the figure. She was smiling as only a Toller can, proud of her prize.

"Fazil!" Mahmoud shouted something in Kurdish.

The figure glanced around, then straightened and headed toward them. Twigs and leaves clung to his clothes and hair. Amanda felt a flood of relief as she recognized their lost companion. He stepped into the clearing with a sheepish smile on his face and hurried to the warmth of the fire, ignoring Mahmoud's running tirade in Kurdish.

"What happened to you?" Amanda interjected.

Fazil reached over to ruffle Kaylee's fur. "I get lost. The dog find me. Cold night. Thank you, dog."

"We calling you," Mahmoud said. To Amanda's surprise, he was scowling, relief having quickly given way to accusation.

"I hear. But not know where."

"Well, at least you're here, and the fog seems to be lifting," Amanda said. "The search teams will be out looking again."

"Yes!" Fazil's eyes lit. "And I find a road. Not big —"

Amanda's hopes soared. "A *road* road? With cars?"

"Not cars." Fazil laughed. "Small, but maybe, God willing, it go …" With his English failing him, he gestured excitedly into the distance.

"Can you find it again?"

"Yes, yes! Over the hill."

Amanda started stomping out the fire. "Drink your tea and grab your stuff. We're on our way!"

This time when Chris opened his eyes, a faint blush of lavender lightened the sky. The fog had lifted! He unfolded his chilled, stiff limbs cautiously. Judging from his restless sleep and the crick in his neck, his life jacket had proved an inadequate pillow and the tarp, although it had kept out the dampness, had been no great success as a mattress.

The Zodiac team had spent a more comfortable, albeit cramped, night in their tent, and they still seemed fast asleep. Now that dawn was near, however, Chris was anxious to get on with the search. He'd lain awake half the night wondering and worrying about Amanda's cryptic notes, and, in the blackness, the answer had come to him. He smiled with relief. Amanda was not losing her mind or becoming delirious. She was trying to send a message that only certain people would understand. The key was in the idiom. Almost any native English speaker, especially one familiar with local geography, would probably guess the word Croque from the first riddle, whereas a non-English speaker probably wouldn't. She wanted to tip off the search-and-rescue teams to where she was without tipping off whoever was after her.

Which meant her pursuers were not English-speaking. Maybe not the trawler captain after all, but the fugitives!

The second riddle was less clear. Maybe she just wanted him to know they were still alive and travelling on foot to Croque, but later, in his pre-dawn sleeplessness, he thought of another, more sinister significance to her choice of words. Frogmarched. What if she meant forced? Compelled to move?

As in at gunpoint?

In an instant, his excitement turned to dread. What if she and Tyler were captives, forced to follow whatever erratic, desperate path the fugitives chose. Would she hold any sway over them? Could she persuade them to continue on to Croque, and toward the ERT officers who would soon be converging there?

He threw his supplies into his boat, woke the search team to explain his plans, and shoved out into the bay. The ocean was dead calm. Mist still curled off the water into the lacy hills beyond, but the thick fog had retreated to a sullen bank out on the open sea. *Finally*, Chris thought with a silent cheer.

As he aimed his boat inland, he searched the shadowy shore-line for signs of movement. A series of long finger bays slowed his progress and as he rounded a steep, rocky point, he was finally able to connect with Incident Command. To his surprise, Noseworthy herself answered. Grudging respect rose within him. Had the woman slept at all?

Probably as much as I did, he thought. For both of them, there would be time enough for sleep when Amanda and Tyler were safe and sound.

He explained his theory that the two were being held by the foreign fugitives. "I know it sounds farfetched, ma'am —"

"No worse than any other theory, Tymko," Noseworthy muttered, her voice even hoarser than usual. He wondered if she'd been subsisting entirely on cigarettes and coffee. "That boatload of illegals is still on the loose, that much the security guys have condescended to tell me."

"I'm heading down the bay toward Croque —"

"Fuck, Tymko! I told you to stay put!"

"But the ERT backup is not here yet, and Croque is Amanda's last known destination."

"Corporal Vu has two teams already en route to Croque. ETA one hour. So we'll be prepared for the bastards if they show up. I don't want you in the way." Papers rustled and he heard her cursing. "To keep you busy, I want you to check on Corporal Maloney's whereabouts. We need to verify if that trawler captain's truck is still there and to disable it if it is. You and Maloney are the only ones who know its location, but Maloney is not answering his radio. He's been out of touch since yesterday afternoon, and his shift replacement at the roadblock last night reported he wasn't there."

Chris frowned in surprise. Jason was a by-the-book cop with a watchful eye on his career, so it wasn't like him to disregard orders. "He was there yesterday afternoon when Corporal Willington and I passed through the roadblock. In fact he was talking to someone in his truck. Willington said it looked like a woman."

"Any description?"

"The vehicle was a white, old-model Chevy Cavalier. I didn't give it much thought." *Except to wonder whether Jason was putting the moves on her*, Chris thought, but he kept that to himself.

"Hmmm." Noseworthy broke off for a deep, rumbling cough. When she resumed, her voice sounded like chains dragged along the ground. "Mrs. Cousins, the victim's wife, drives a white Cavalier. She's been in and out of here every hour or so since she arrived, demanding updates on the search for her son. Do you know if she knows Maloney?"

Chris swallowed his astonishment as he cast about for a safe answer. "Well, they're both from Grand Falls, ma'am."

"That likely explains it. She probably figured she'd get more info out of him than I'm giving her." Noseworthy was being positively chatty, probably punch-drunk from not enough sleep and too much solitude, Chris suspected. Now she seemed to remember that he was a pain in the ass. "Anyway, Corporal, report in on Maloney one way or the other. And disable that damn truck."

Chris signed off with a nagging sense of unease. It made sense that Sheri would try to get inside information out of Jason, but Jason's subsequent disappearance and failure to report lent an ominous implication to the meeting. What the hell was the man up to?

Twenty minutes later, when Chris turned into yet one more narrow finger bay, he finally spotted the little red stages of Croque propped along the shore. Once he got ashore, however, he was disconcerted to find not a soul in the place. The ERT reinforcements had not yet arrived, Willington had presumably gone back to Roddickton, and there was no sign of Jason or his red truck. He retrieved his own truck, and as he drove back up through the scattered houses, he reassured himself that behind the scenes, the troops would soon be closing in. Some, led by the K9 unit, would be following the trail over land from the sunken boat, while others would be combing the bush and logging roads around Croque.

Driving up the Croque road, he found the ATV trail without difficulty. A hundred feet in, still hidden by the screen of trees, was the captain's truck, looking exactly as Chris and Jason had left it. The captain's cab door was still unlocked and the keys still in the ignition. At a quick glance, nothing appeared to be disturbed, as if the captain had not returned.

Chris took the keys, locked the truck, and then left his own truck at the entrance to the trail, facing out to facilitate a quick departure while at the same time blocking the exit of the other truck. After updating Noseworthy and giving her the coordinates of the truck, he stood on the trail to consider his next move. Restlessness and unease thrummed through him. As he weighed the wisdom of violating more orders, he noticed that the trail looked more trampled than before. A new set of fat, wide tire tracks had churned up the mud and crushed the small shrubs in two lines leading down the trail into the bush beyond the point of the Captain's truck.

Someone had driven a larger vehicle along this road after the ATV. Jason? If so, how far would he go? It was a challenging road for any vehicle, overhung with branches and littered with rocks and holes. Chris had no intention of subjecting his brand-new truck's undercarriage and suspension to such a punishing ride, but perhaps Jason had less attachment to his own older truck.

Or more at stake.

After retrieving his hunting rifle from his truck, he began to walk along the track, keeping to the side in order to preserve the tread marks. He had gone less than a kilometre when he rounded a curve and came face to face with Jason's truck, facing toward him, but half off the road and mired deep in a mud hole. It was abandoned. He felt the hood, which was cold. Dew lay heavy on the windshield, suggesting the truck hadn't been driven since at least the dead of night.

Looking down the track ahead, he noticed that the wide tire treads continued, trampling the grass and digging into the soft soil. It looked as if Jason had driven the truck even farther into the bush and was on his way out when he got stuck in the mud. If so, where was he? Why hadn't Chris come across him already?

His scalp prickled with unease. He listened to the woods, which were eerily silent for this time of year, when the distant clamour of chainsaws, axes, and ATVs usually filled the air. Where was Jason, and what was he doing? Playing Lone Ranger to the rescue, against an unknown and unseen enemy?

He debated the wisdom of shouting Jason's name, but he didn't know where Amanda and her captors were, or indeed where the captain was. He didn't want to give away his position or alert them to his presence. Instead, he crept forward along the logging road, trying to keep out of sight under cover of the shrubs along the edge.

Steep bluffs rose on either side, blocking out all radio and satellite signals. The logging road twisted and turned as it snaked deeper into the bush. *This is folly*, he thought as he panted his way up yet another steep rise. Cresting the top, he startled a magnificent cow moose and her calf, who were grazing on the tender shoots in the middle of the road. He froze, as did they, their heads raised and their eyes riveted on him. He edged carefully behind a tree to wait. The mother twitched, flattened her ears, and stared at him in challenge for a long moment. Neither moved, until abruptly she wheeled around and bolted into the trees on the other side. Her calf scrambled to follow.

Chris waited for his nerves to settle, for a cow moose protecting her young could be a formidable enemy. He wondered whether he should return to Croque to wait for ERT. As he was debating, he saw what had spooked the moose.

A dishevelled, mud-caked apparition was coming down the middle of the road toward him, staggering and weaving like a man long past the legal limit. Chris registered the bloody hair and face before he recognized the RCMP field jacket. He rushed forward.

"Jesus H! Jason!"

The man sagged into his arms and Chris eased him down against a tree trunk. "I'm all right," Jason muttered, struggling to rise. "I'm all right."

"Hold still, for Pete's sake! Let me look at you!" He bent over to probe Jason's body. Blood was thick and sticky from an open wound on his crown, and Jason jerked away with a curse when Chris touched it.

"Are you hurt anywhere else besides your head?"

"I don't think so."

"Do you know where you are? Who I am?"

"Don't play fucking doctor, Tymko. I'm all right. It's him you should be going after!"

"Who? What the hell happened?"

"I don't know. It was dark, and I couldn't see a thing in the fog. Whoever it was sneaked up on my truck. All I remember is the door opening. When I came to, my truck was gone and I was face down on the road, feeling like I'd gone ten rounds with Mohammed Ali."

"Did you get any description at all? Tall, short, skin colour?"

Jason was shaking his head. "Strong. In shape."

"He knew exactly where to hit you too. Did he say anything?"

Jason groaned. "Not a word. He appeared out of nowhere like a stealth bomber and dragged me out of the truck." He began to shiver.

"Here." Chris took off his jacket and draped it around the man's shoulders. He offered him water, which Jason drank eagerly. "It looks like he was trying to escape in your truck, but it got stuck. We'll need to go back to my truck."

Jason shook his head back and forth before yelping aloud in pain. "No! I'm all right! I can make it back on my own. You go after him. You have to stop him!"

"Stop him from what?"

"How the hell should I know? But the bastard took my radio and my 9mm, so I'm betting he's up to something bad."

Chris took out his own radio. "You need help and we need backup."

"You forget the fucking radios don't work around here. You got your sat phone? I'll phone once I get out to the main road. I'm good to go that far."

Chris sat back on his heels, trying to decide the best course. Jason looked as if he'd been through a wheat combine. Beneath the blood and dirt, his face was ghostly pale and he was shivering. The first rule of policing was to ensure the safety of yourself and your fellow officers before all else. On the other hand, at least one dangerous assailant, whose identity and motives were unknown, was wandering around the woods armed with a police radio as well as a service pistol. Jason was coherent and he had proved he could walk. Even superficial head wounds bled like a bitch.

"What the hell were you doing out here, Jason?"

"Same as you. Trying to find Tyler. And Amanda."

"But on your own? Leaving your post?"

Jason thrust out his chin stubbornly. "I had a lead. I followed it."

"Does this have anything to do with Sheri?"

Jason jerked away.

"I know you were talking to her yesterday. Noseworthy knows too."

"About what?"

Chris didn't answer.

"Fuck," Jason muttered. He glared at the ground. "This isn't just a missing-persons case for me, you know. So back off."

"I know," Chris said softly. "It isn't for me, either." He handed over his phone along with the keys to his truck. "Get yourself warm and don't try any heroics. Watch that head wound."

Afterward, he stood in the road worrying while Jason limped down the hill out of sight. He wondered why Jason had come out here all by himself. Feeling guilty for pushing Phil over the edge? Wanting to play hero in Sheri's eyes?

Or trying to cover his tracks.

CHAPTER TWENTY-EIGHT

They heard the sound of an engine long before the road was in sight. They were scrabbling up a steep slope strewn with boulders. Amanda's head was spinning. Fazil had made it sound so simple. Just over the hill, he'd said. In their eagerness, they had foregone breakfast and headed straight for what they hoped was imminent rescue.

To call it a hill was a cruel tease. More like a cliff, soaring out of the bog at an impossible angle. How Fazil had navigated it in the darkness and fog, she couldn't imagine.

They were all struggling, each within their own cocoon of pain, hunger, and fatigue, focusing only on the next rocky foothold and the next branch to hang on to. Amanda was listening to her own panting when a distant whine caught her ear. Kaylee too seemed to hear it, for she leaped nimbly over a boulder and bounded up the slope.

"Kaylee!" Amanda shouted. The dog glanced back and tilted her head to sniff the air before turning to continue her ascent. Within seconds, she had vanished. "If I ever get out of this alive," Amanda muttered to herself, "remind me to get that dog some obedience training."

The distant drone grew louder, rising and falling as the engine revved. It was too loud for a truck, even an old local jalopy, and too even in pitch for a chainsaw. An ATV! Her heart leaped. She glanced up the hill, which still loomed high above her. *We'll never make it in time*, she thought. *The search party will pass us by, never knowing that we are just on the other side of the ridge.*

She looked back at the others trailing behind. Mahmoud was carrying Tyler on his back, and he had to pause frequently to shift his weight and navigate the next step. Fazil brought up the rear, scanning the woods warily and making no offer to share the burden.

With a rush of adrenaline she shrugged off her backpack and began to race straight up the hill. Grabbing at branches, hauling herself over rocks, slipping and scrabbling on the mossy ground. "Don't you fucking drive on by!" she swore through gritted teeth.

The roar of the engine filled the air now. So close! "Help!" she screamed. "Help us!"

You're an idiot, she thought as the engine droned on. *No one can hear anything over that racket.* She remembered Kaylee. Perhaps the dog would alert them. Amanda hurled herself forward, up over the rise and across to the other side, where she skidded to a stop. Below her, the ground fell away again in another steep, impossible drop. *Fucking country*, she thought furiously.

At the bottom, nestled in a lush, overgrown valley between the hills, ran a thin, wavering track. On that track and crawling slowly out of sight, was an ATV.

"Help!" she shrieked, flailing her arms and plunging headlong down the ridge. As she ran, she picked up a rock and threw it into the abyss. Another and another. The ATV continued on. Amanda reached for another rock, lost her footing, and pitched forward. Tumbling and crashing, she grabbed for anything to break her fall. Pain shot through her as branches stabbed her and rocks scraped her limbs. All the while she screamed and screamed.

She jolted to a stop finally against a boulder near the bottom of the ridge, smacking her head so hard that stars burst in her eyes. She gasped, groped for balance, and staggered to her feet, ignoring the throbbing and the fire exploding in her head. Dragging a deep breath into her lungs, she summoned every shred of her remaining strength.

"Help!"

The ATV stopped. The driver turned. She stumbled into the middle of the track. Warm liquid poured into her eyes, blinding her. She blinked to clear them and wiped them with fingers that came away sticky and red.

What a sight, she thought irrationally as the ATV turned around and came toward her. Above her, she heard the others descending the hill. As the vehicle came close, she heard Mahmoud's strident, panicked voice.

"*Na! Na, na!*" He swung around to Fazil and the two shouted back and forth in Kurdish. Mahmoud set Tyler on the ground at the edge of the road and turned to flee back up the hill.

"Stop right there!"

Amanda looked around in surprise to see the man standing by his ATV with a rifle trained on them. He was an ugly toad of a man dressed head to toe in camouflage gear, with a week's growth of coarse black beard and a filthy ball cap pulled low over his eyes. "You are not going anywhere."

"What are you doing?" Amanda cried. "They are not criminals. We're lost!"

"This is not rescue people," Mahmoud said. "This is the captain of ship."

Amanda struggled to absorb this new twist. It felt as if reality had shifted into another dimension. "That captain? The one you paid to come to Canada?"

"Yes. The one who kill my brother."

"I didn't kill your brother, Mahmoud," said the captain. "He died of seasickness. I never wanted any of this to happen."

"And now you want kill us."

"No. I came to find you. To bring you to the next rendezvous."

Mahmoud gestured to the rifle. "With that?"

"I don't want trouble. I just want to complete the deal and get you across the border."

Amanda was trying to think through the fireworks in her head. They faced off in a frozen tableau — the three of them and a child against a single man with a gun. Kaylee, she noticed, was nowhere in sight. Could the dog provide the unexpected distraction that could tip the balance of power? Or would she get herself shot again in the process? Amanda opted to keep the man focused on talk.

"So you can collect your money and make sure no one squeals on you," she said.

The captain gave her a long, chilly stare. She stared back at him. After the brief standoff, he lowered the rifle to let it hang loosely by his side. "Look, it's win-win for the people over there. They want to get out of Europe, and we have the ship and the means, so why shouldn't we work together to help them get a better life?"

"I've seen your kind of help before," Amanda snapped. "You promised them papers and visas, but instead, you worked them like slaves, you starved them and froze them —"

"I'm not interested in debating my business practices with you," the captain said, turning to address Mahmoud. He patted his pocket. "I have the papers right here. If you want to avoid going to jail over here, I'm your only chance. So start walking."

Fazil took a few steps but Mahmoud stood his ground. "No. You kill a man."

"I told you, your brother died."

"Other man."

"What are you talking about?"

"Where the old man live, on island. You shoot the man in boat."

"I don't know what you're talking about. I never saw a boat, I was never on any island. I've been looking all up and down this fucking countryside!"

From behind her, Amanda heard a sudden rush of movement. Kaylee? But then Tyler roared past her, his eyes blazing with rage, and flung himself at the captain.

"You shot my father!"

The captain knocked Tyler aside with the rifle butt. Howling with pain and fury, the boy launched himself again.

The captain trained his rifle on him. "Stay out of this, boy!"

Amanda reached out to grab Tyler's arm and haul him to safety. He fought to wrench himself free but she hung on. She could feel him trembling beneath her grip. She stepped in front of him.

"Or what?" she demanded. "You'll shoot an eleven-year-old boy? Who's already lost his father?"

"I didn't kill his father."

"Bullshit!" Tyler snapped, renewing his struggles.

The man tightened his grip on his rifle ominously. Amanda's thoughts raced for a toehold of reason.

"Then don't make this worse," she said. "If you kill us, you will have crossed a line you can never come back from. Not just in the eyes of the law, but, more importantly, in your own soul. If you're a decent man, it will crush you."

The captain wavered. His eyes flickered and his grip on the gun loosened. Holding her breath, Amanda took a cautious step forward. "These people have been through more than we can imagine. You say you're not a bad man, just a businessman. Prove it. Give me the rifle."

He shook his head. "I didn't kill your father, son. I just want to get these men out of here undetected, for their sakes as well as mine."

Out of the corner of her eye, she saw Mahmoud glance at Fazil with a puzzled frown. He asked him a question in Kurdish, and Fazil issued a vehement denial. The two began to argue loudly, flinging words back and forth, until abruptly Mahmoud cursed and spat at Fazil's feet.

Fazil's nostrils flared. Before anyone could react, he reached under his jacket and pulled out a pistol.

Mahmoud's jaw dropped.

"You!" Amanda gasped. Her thoughts raced to make sense of this latest twist. Where had the pistol come from? He held it with the practiced ease of an expert. Had he kept it hidden all along, from his time in the army, or had he found it during his night foray?

The captain jerked his rifle back up and Mahmoud's shouts escalated. Fazil whipped his head back and forth. "Not go prison. Not go back Syria." He seized Tyler and dragged him toward the ATV. "You, Captain —" He spat out the word. "You give me the rifle and the car. And the boy is coming with me."

Chris paused to take a sip of water and listen again to his surroundings. The sun was rising, warming the valley floor and bringing the forest creatures, including the blackflies, out in force. Earlier he'd thought he detected the faint drone of an engine up ahead, but now as he swatted away the flies, he could hear only the sounds of the forest. A breeze rustled the branches and nearby, a stream gurgled down the hill. But the drone had dissipated in a puff of wind. *My imagination*, he thought. Or perhaps the direction had been deceptive and it was a rescue team coming up behind him from the main road.

For the tenth time he questioned the sanity of his mission. In this vast, empty wilderness, the chances of him finding the group of lost people, by himself, on foot, and armed with only a service pistol and a hunting rifle, were infinitesimal.

He was considering turning back to link up with reinforcements when another sound reached his ears. Distant, mere snatches on the wind, but the unique sound of human voices. He swung around, straining his ears as he tried to distill meaning and pinpoint direction, but the voices seemed to bounce and echo off the very cliffs. Sharp and desperate. Damn it! Down the road or over the hill?

The hilltop would at least give him a vantage point. Without hesitation he began to run up the hill, taking long, powerful strides to propel himself over rocks and fallen trees. Halfway up, he turned to get his bearings, but could see nothing but dense branches pressing in. Farther up, the trees became dwarfed, and he hauled himself up on a stony outcrop to take in the view.

Through the bush down below, his eye caught a flash of red, leaping and dancing as it approached. It disappeared behind outcrops and shrubs, only to burst into view again, all fur and wagging tail.

"Kaylee! Oh sweet Jesus!" he cried aloud, falling on his knees to envelop the dog in his arms. *I'm close, I'm close*, he thought, blinking back the unexpected tears that flooded his eyes.

The dog slobbered him with kisses before stepping back to look at him expectantly. She barked, ran a few steps, wheeled around, and barked again.

"Yes!" he cried, stumbling to follow. "Take me to her!"

For an instant, they all froze. The captain opened his mouth as if to make one final appeal to reason, but Fazil's rigid stare stopped him. The captain held out the rifle, forcing Fazil to walk forward for it. "All right, but you still need me to get you out of here."

"I have the little car. Need papers. And the boy." Fazil reached toward the rifle, yanking Tyler with him.

"No!" Amanda roared. She dived in front of Fazil and snatched the rifle from the captain's hand. Without a moment's hesitation she whirled around to point it at Fazil. "Let go of him!"

Fazil stared at her, tightening his grip on Tyler. Gradually the shock in his face twisted into contempt. "You not shoot. Not killing."

The rifle was heavy, and her arms shook with the effort of holding it level. Only rage sustained her. "Don't try me, you bastard. You killed Phil."

"He see us."

Tyler thrashed in his grip, tears streaming down his cheeks. "He was only trying to help you! To get you food and clothes."

"He see we kill the old man."

"*You* kill old man," Mahmoud corrected.

Fazil swung the pistol back and forth angrily. "Old man shoot my cousin." Beneath the contempt, confused emotions raced across his face. Pain, even fear, like a cornered animal lashing out. But before she could think how to use that, Tyler tore himself free and attacked, feet and fists flailing. In a flash Fazil's face hardened and he aimed the pistol.

Amanda had no time to think. No time for anything but blind instinct. The trigger pressed against her finger.

"Tyler, down!" she screamed. The boy dived, and in that split second, she squeezed. The explosion blew out her eardrums, and the kick knocked her backward onto the ground. She scrambled to sit up and groped beside her for the cold steel barrel of the gun. Her ears were ringing but she could make out snatches of screaming.

Fazil lay on the ground with blood pouring down his face. *My god, my god*, she thought, *I shot someone!* In the next instant she registered Tyler lying face down on the ground, his hands pressed to his ears. Fazil was struggling to reach his pistol, which lay on the ground just beyond his groping hand.

The stench of gunpowder, blood, and burning flesh filled her nostrils. Beside her in the dust, the two schoolgirls cowered, trying to shield their heads with their bare arms as the machetes were raised. She dragged the rifle around to aim it at him, but the steel against her finger was an alien thing, hard and cold. She couldn't move.

Not again!

Fazil's hand closed on the pistol and as he lifted it, a cold, deadly calm spread through her.

"No you don't! Not this time, you bastards." Her finger began to close.

"Amanda, don't!" The shout came faintly down the tunnel of her rage. A familiar voice. Not Phil. Not Africa.

Salvation.

CHAPTER TWENTY-NINE

"You're a fucking superwoman," Matthew Goderich said, draped over his beer and shaking his head.

"If it weren't for Chris, I'd probably be a dead woman. Or in jail."

"No, you wouldn't," Chris said. "You wouldn't have killed him. It's a lot harder than most people think."

Amanda sensed Matthew's eyes upon her, gentle and devoid of judgment, but she resolutely averted her own. "This time I would have, Matthew," she replied. "In a heartbeat."

Chris looked from her to Matthew and back again. He seemed to detect an inviolable secret in the silence between them, for he reached forward to touch her hand. "A heartbeat is sometimes all that stands between one outcome and another. The important thing is that you had him stopped, at least long enough for me to move in."

The threesome was grouped at a table in a private corner of the Plymouth Dining Room. This time the manager of the Mayflower Inn had not only opened up the dining room for them, but had personally gone to the local liquor store to buy the best Shiraz and Chardonnay Roddickton had to offer to accompany their perfectly grilled steaks. And, tossing all regulations out the window, he had placed a third steak on a plate at their feet for Kaylee.

Both wine bottles now sat empty on the table along with the remains of the T-bone steaks and three half-finished bottles of QV Premium. Amanda had been cautious with her food, aware that her stomach, after days of semi-starvation, would not cope with a full plate of rich Newfoundland food. But she had tossed back the wine as if it were the water of life itself, and she was well on her way to a coma.

"The media are all over this!" Matthew crowed. "Twitter is on fire and donations to the Facebook page are through the roof. The prime minister tried to call you, for fuck's sake!"

"Oh, joy," she muttered. She'd seen the storm of reporters and curiosity-seekers who had heralded their arrival in Roddickton and followed her from Dr. Iannucci's clinic to the RCMP detachment, hoping for a quote. With Matthew running interference, she'd managed to duck them all, but she knew the time would come, as it had last time, when she would have to face the clamour of recognition. But not tonight. Not tomorrow. She had too much else to wrap her head around first.

She rested her chin in her hand blearily. "What will happen to them?"

Chris gave the little-boy grin that crinkled his eyes. "I just arrest 'em, ma'am, and pass 'em up the line. No one tells me anything."

"The spooks will likely get their claws into them," Matthew said. "Ten years from now, once the cases have finally wended their way through all the appeals, the captain will probably be in prison and Fazil will be deported back to wherever."

"Or joining the captain in prison," Chris said. "To be deported once he's served his time. If we can't get him for the murder of Phil, we've got him dead to rights on the assault on Jason Maloney. His fingerprints on the truck and his possession of Jason's gun will nail that case shut."

She pictured the brooding, aloof man sneaking away through the fog that evening, and tried to makes sense of it through the blur of painkillers and booze. "He could have gotten away cleanly. I wonder why he came back to us?"

"Because he needed your help getting the truck free. Then you can bet he'd have left you all stranded there. Your friend Mahmoud doesn't have a single nice thing to say about him. Lazy even on the shrimp boat, he said."

"Poor Mahmoud. His only crime was wanting to escape the war, and trusting some unscrupulous people smugglers who took advantage. What will happen to him?"

Chris shrugged. "I hear he's applied for refugee status here. But he's unlikely to get it."

Amanda had heard that story of heartbreak many times. So many refugees had fled from war-ravaged and failed states with nothing but the clothes on their backs, without passports or proof of status. The process to qualify as a refugee through the United Nations was long and arduous, even with proper documents, but Canada had added layers of red tape and security that nearly strangled the process.

"So he'll be deported," she said.

Chris nodded. "I suppose he can apply for an American immigrant visa, but I don't know their rules."

Matthew snorted and took a deep swig of his beer before signalling for another round. He was freshly groomed and shaved, and glowed with good cheer over his prime-time appearances on national TV news. "Good luck with that, Mahmoud. The Yanks love illegals who try to gate-crash their country."

Amanda remembered how the tall, melancholy Kurd had slogged through the bush for hours with Tyler on his back. A wave of sympathy washed over her. "If he's willing to apply to Canada instead, I could sponsor him. That might help."

When the next round of beers arrived, Matthew chugged his with alacrity, but Amanda merely groaned and pushed hers away. "I'll talk to him in the morning."

"He and Fazil are in hospital in St. Anthony," Chris said. "As Tyler is, and you should be."

She lifted her head to grin at his disapproval. "Dr. Iannucci here fixed me up just fine. I wanted a hot bath, a drink, and the company of my friends, not some sterile round of hospital tests. And I couldn't leave my little hero here alone." She leaned down to scratch Kaylee's ears. The dog, still drowsy from her visit to the vet, managed a single tail wag. Amanda sobered. "Any word on Fazil?"

"Bullet just grazed his head. That big-game rifle had such a powerful kick it almost jerked right out of your hands. Spoiled your aim."

"Luckily, I have no aim." She twirled her empty wineglass. "Fazil is no prize, but the bottom line is they were six desperate, panicked fugitives caught in a nightmare they never imagined. Four of them died. What about the guys behind this? The smugglers and fraudsters who took their money and their documents, then threw them on the mercy of a trawler working weeks at sea? Six of them gave up their life's savings. That's tens of thousands of dollars! Not to mention the weeks of unpaid labour. Will anyone ever catch those guys? Bring them to justice?"

"Well, we have the captain —" Matthew began.

"But he's one small cog in the wheel. He's just a greedy little man who convinced himself that all the while he was lining his pockets, he was doing them a service too. Who's behind all this smuggling at the point of origin? The Russian mob?"

Matthew shrugged. "Among others. Asian, African, Middle Eastern — these international criminal cartels are all connected. The smuggling rings just switched their product from drugs and weapons to people, to cash in on the lucrative new market. Then there's the chain of intermediaries, all the little opportunists who take their bribes and do their little bit for the operation. Right now, there's huge money to be made in the smuggling and trafficking of desperate people, but many of the players are almost untouchable. You watch. The Canadian co-owner of the trawler will deny all knowledge and blame the Finnish co-owner, who will do likewise. Acadia Seafood has already gotten out in front of this by issuing a statement this evening expressing their shock, disappointment, and utter lack of knowledge. One step removed equals plausible deniability. All bullshit."

Amanda slumped sideways in her chair. "Too much bullshit for this fried brain, guys. I can't take on the world, at least not tonight. I can barely tackle the stairs to my room."

Chris caught her just before she slid to the floor. He hoisted her up and, with a firm arm around her waist, half carried her along the corridor and up the stairs to her room. She sank down onto the plush mattress with a groan of pleasure and reached to snuggle Kaylee, who had jumped up beside her. Through the descending haze, she was aware of Chris trying to unlace her boots.

"You're a good guy, Tymko," she mumbled. "Forget the boots and pull the blanket up. Wake me in a day or two, so I can go see Tyler."

Amanda clung fast to the railing and hunched her shoulders as she turned her face to the ocean wind. The little whale-watching tour boat pitched and wallowed in the chop as it chugged past the rugged cliffs north of St. Anthony. The sky was blue, and the whitecaps sparkled in the sunshine, but the wind sweeping across the open Atlantic had the bite of fall.

She was grateful for these few moments of solitude. The last two days had been a whirlwind of police and media interviews, responses to well-wishers, and awkward phone conversations with her parents, who had felt they should come, but sounded relieved when she told them there was no need. As always, she was on her own. The support, compassion, and even physical embrace that she needed were beyond their repertoire. The holiday season, with its stilted but comfortable rituals of family joy, would come soon enough.

The one person she longed to see, and yet had barely spoken to, was Tyler. Sheri had been fiercely protective throughout their stay in St. Anthony, hounding the hospital staff, controlling the police interviews, and putting off all visits from the media and Amanda alike. Amanda suspected she kept her own feelings at bay by fretting about Tyler's trauma and grief. Amanda had been limited to brief glimpses of him, mainly from a distance, hobbling around on his crutches, picking at his food, or staring out into nothingness.

By the third evening, unable to stand it any longer, Amanda had driven out from St. Anthony to nearby Burnt Cape, where Sheri had rented a little cabin getaway on the seaside. She found Tyler sitting motionless on a rock by the water, watching the sand pipers. When Kaylee trotted down to greet him, he wrapped his arms around her neck.

Amanda walked in the cabin door to find Sheri packing. "We have to talk," she said.

Sheri busied herself with folding. "We're going home in the morning. The doctor has cleared him, and she says it's important for him to get back to his regular routine. School, friends, hockey as soon as his ankle is ready."

"I agree. But I'd like to see him before he goes. He and I have some things to ... kind of ... work through."

Sheri straightened and crossed her arms. "I appreciate all you did, Amanda. Finding him, taking care of him, keeping him safe.

Don't get me wrong. But I think, being with you right now … you're a reminder of that whole awful experience."

"It's only been three days, Sheri!"

"I know. But he needs a rest from it. Maybe in a few months …"

Amanda looked out the window to gain some distance before she blurted out something ill-advised. Tyler was standing at the water's edge, gazing out toward the open sea. *Remembering?* she wondered. *Or wishing?*

"I have an idea," she said. "It's getting past the season, but I bet I can persuade the tour boat operator in St. Anthony to take us out. If nothing else, it's great publicity for him. Let's give Tyler a fun day before you go back. No sadness, no talking, no trying not to think. Just whales and icebergs and puffins, oh my!"

Sheri had even laughed, but only now, feeling the salt wind on her face, did Amanda realize what an inspiration the boat tour had been. Tyler had spent the first hour with her up on the crow's nest, peering through the binoculars and chattering excitedly about whales and icebergs. He had been crushed to learn there were no icebergs in September, but was soon enthralled by the antics of a flirtatious humpback whale flipping its tail almost within reach of his hand.

His eyes were watering and his cheeks were burnished red by the wind, but his smile lit his whole being. When he tired of the binoculars, he'd rushed down to the wheelhouse to help the skipper pilot the boat. Over the music of the waves, she heard him asking a thousand questions of the skipper as he tried out the controls.

She sensed movement behind her and turned to see Matthew, who had been clinging uncertainly to the edge of the boat downstairs. He came up behind to put his arm around her. "You're a genius, you know that? This is just what the poor kid needed."

"It's what so many poor kids need, Matthew. A chance for fun, for escape, for adventure. A break from the daily sadness of their lives."

He cocked his head and looked at her for a long moment. "I'm glad I came. I've never been on the ocean before and I was sure I'd be seasick. But it's given me an idea."

"It's given me an idea too."

He grinned. "You first."

She rested her chin on her hands and watched the waves below. "I don't know if I can face Africa again. Or even Cambodia. And I'm not ready for a desk job at headquarters in Ottawa or London, let alone a regular teaching job over here. But I am ready for this. If I could find a way to give young people a few hours or days of fun, an adventure to inspire them and give them hope ... that would be my dream." Embarrassed, she broke off to study him. He was a world-weary journalist as burned out as her, but his smile could swallow the Grand Canyon. "You've eaten the canary."

His grin broadened further. "You've raised $150,000 through the Prayers for Tyler campaign."

"You have."

"No, girl. You have. Through your story. Your inspiration. Sheri doesn't want that money. She says she doesn't want the notoriety or the media circus that comes with it."

"I can't use that money, Matthew. People gave it with the intention of helping Tyler."

"But —"

"Sheri may change her mind," Amanda said. "Or we can set up a scholarship for him, maybe for others in his name if there's enough. He's so smart, he should be given every opportunity."

Matthew sighed. "Okay. Fair enough. But you can raise money, girl. You're a genuine hero. Social media is an amazing tool. If you did a fundraising tour across Canada, say, to raise money for struggling or traumatized families ..."

"Like Clara Hughes's Big Ride?" Amanda smiled at the memory of the celebrated Olympic speed skater cycling across Canada for mental health. "Raise money and awareness by some kind of tour?"

"Through which you'd finance your family-adventure trips, and the rest could go to an overseas children's charity. For child soldiers, or for education in the refugee camps."

She fell silent. Took a deep, steadying breath. For the first time in a long while, she felt hope. A way forward. It needed work, but it was a thrilling idea. But could she manage all the minutiae — the planning, the promotion, and the fundraising?

As if reading her mind, he grinned. "I'd be your manager and fundraiser. I've got the connections, and my human issues blog is already up and running. Don't give an answer right away. Think about it; take the time to be sure. But man, this is the most exciting idea I've heard in a long, long time. Almost gives an old hack like me goosebumps."

She kept the secret dream to herself, cradled and sheltered from judgment. But that night, she shared a complimentary dinner and bottle of wine with Chris at the Lightkeeper's Restaurant on the tip of Fishing Point outside St. Anthony. The local community had thrown itself into the celebration of its heroes. Amanda had been given a haircut, massage, and manicure at a local beauty salon, as well as her pick of the latest fall fashions in a local women's shop. Her hair, freshly washed, fell soft and loose down her back. The long black skirt and silk top felt deliciously foreign and exotic against her skin. Chris too had been outfitted by a local seamstress who had managed to fit a grey shirt and navy sports jacket perfectly to his gangly frame.

They sat at the window table of the restaurant, like strangers newly met. She didn't know which felt more unreal, the past or the present. His long fingers rested on the table, and a boyish grin twitched at the corner of his lips. She sensed that he, like her, was searching for words.

She finally broke her gaze and settled for the mundane but safe. "You're going back tomorrow?"

He nodded. "Reporting back to duty at Deer Lake. Sergeant Noseworthy said there may be a commendation coming down, but I'm not holding my breath. It's enough she didn't haul my ass before the disciplinary board. Corporal Vu is furious."

"She's a smart woman. She knows the RCMP needs its heroes, and that all's well that ends well."

"Yes," he said. "I'm not so sure about Jason Maloney. But in the fog of the operation, his disobedience may get swept under the carpet too. He's got one hell of a headache and a badass new scar on his forehead, but he may be going to go back to life as usual."

Not as usual, Amanda thought. *Some things will never be the same. His sense of confidence — his belief in the power and invincibility of his badge — will be gone forever.* And Sheri had refused all contact with him, blaming him for setting the wheels in motion that had destroyed her husband and traumatized her son. Even though those wheels had been set in motion months before, on the arid killing fields of northern Nigeria.

The memory sobered her, and a silence settled between them. She knew it was time to say goodbye, but she found she couldn't find the words. Not this time.

He was watching her in the candlelight, unusually solemn now, as if he felt the same. "You'll be all right," he said finally.

Was that a question? Was she that transparent? Unnerved by his insight, she looked out the window at the soft, black sea. A thousand stars showered the night sky.

"Remember that night we sat on the seashore and looked up at the stars?"

He grinned. "I recall we were very drunk."

"Drunk enough to marvel at the power and meaning in those little pinpoints of light that have been guiding wanderers since the dawn of time." She slipped a finger around his. "To answer your question, I think I will."

ACKNOWLEDGEMENTS

The inspiration for *Fire in the Stars* owes much to my father, Professor Cecil Currie, who was born in Newfoundland during the early part of the twentieth century and whose tales of his childhood exploits and misadventures were the highlight of our bedtime routine when my brother, sister, and I were growing up. Through them, not only did I learn some of my earliest lessons in storytelling, but I also developed a deep affection for the rugged spirit, irreverent humour, and precarious life of those who live on The Rock.

Although my father died some time ago, I invoked his spirit often in the writing of this book. I am also indebted to my Newfoundland cousins, Lloyd and Maxime Currie and Liz Waye; Newfoundland friends, Sheila Gallant-Halloran, Jason Stuckless, and Tom Curran, who all cheerfully answered questions on everything from boats to fish to flowers, and fellow writer Susan Forrest and her husband Don, motorcycle aficionados. My friend and neighbour Rudy Broers volunteered an insider's glimpse into aid work in Africa, and fellow author Don Easton provided helpful details on RCMP search procedures.

During my research trip to the Great Northern Peninsula, many Newfoundlanders provided insight and information along the way, among them shrimp fishers, Fisheries and Oceans Canada staff, Search and Rescue volunteers, fish plant workers, and others in tourism and national parks. I'd especially like to thank Bettina Lori of Norris Point, the Civilian Ground Search and Rescue coordinator for the Bonne Bay team, who volunteered a wealth of details about dog tracking and search and rescue on the peninsula. Any inaccuracies, whether intentional for the purposes of the story, or made out of ignorance, are mine alone.

A manuscript passes before many critical eyes on its way to print. As always, I'm indebted to the members of the Ladies' Killing Circle — Joan Bosell, Mary Jane Maffini, Sue Pike, and Linda Wiken — all cherished friends who dropped everything to read the manuscript on a mere week's notice and provided thoughtful critiques. I'd also like to thank everyone at Dundurn Press for their continued support of me and of Canadian stories in general, especially Kirk Howard, Beth Bruder, my publicist Jim Hatch, my astute and enthusiastic editor Shannon Whibbs, and the cover designer Laura Boyle.

And last but not least, a huge thank-you to booksellers and readers, whose support makes it possible for me to continue doing what I love.

BY THE SAME AUTHOR

NONE SO BLIND
An Inspector Green Mystery

Did Inspector Green put the wrong man behind bars?

Twenty years ago, a raw and impressionable Detective Michael Green helped convict a young professor for the murder of an attractive co-ed. From behind bars, the man continued to hound Green with letters protesting his innocence. Shortly after being paroled, he is found dead. Is it suicide? Revenge? Or had Green made the biggest mistake of his career — a mistake which cost an innocent man his liberty and ultimately his life? To determine the truth, Green is forced to re-examine old evidence and open up old wounds to stare down a far greater evil hiding in plain sight.

NOMINATED FOR THE
2015 ARTHUR ELLIS AWARD FOR BEST NOVEL

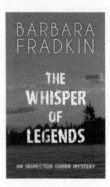

THE WHISPER OF LEGENDS
An Inspector Green Mystery

**An empty canoe washes up on the shore of the Nahanni River —
has the river claimed four more lives?**

When his teenage daughter goes missing on a summer wilderness canoe trip to the Nahanni River, Inspector Michael Green is forced into unfamiliar territory. Unable to mobilize the local RCMP, he enlists the help of his long-time friend, Staff Sergeant Brian Sullivan, to accompany him to the Northwest Territories to look for themselves.

Green is terrified. The park has 30,000 square kilometres of wilderness and 600 grizzlies. Even worse, Green soon discovers his daughter lied to him. The trip was organized not by a reputable tour company but by her new boyfriend, Scott, a graduate geology student. When clues about Scott's past begin to drift in, Green, Sullivan, and two guides head into the wilderness. After the body of one of the group turns up at the bottom of a cliff, they begin to realize just what is at stake.

 DUNDURN

Visit us at

Dundurn.com
@dundurnpress
Facebook.com/dundurnpress
Pinterest.com/dundurnpress